The Buccaneer Coast

Blood, Steel, and Empire: Book I

James L. Nelson

Fore Topsail Press
64 Ash Point Road
Harpswell, Maine, 04079

ISBN-978-0-578-98110-9

To the buccaneer crew: Elizabeth, Nathaniel, Jonathan and Abigail.
And to Lisa, Admiral of my Ocean Blue.

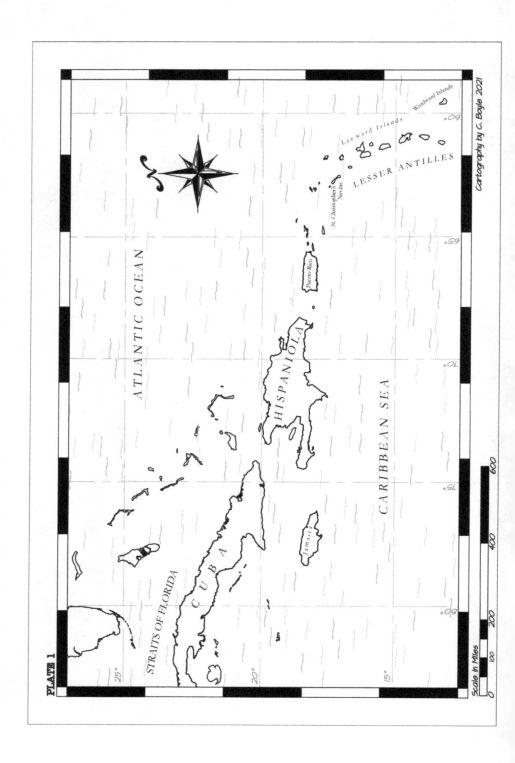

PLATE 1

ATLANTIC OCEAN

STRAITS OF FLORIDA

C U B A

HISPANIOLA

Puerto Rico

LESSER ANTILLES

Leeward Islands

Windward Islands

St. Christopher's
Nevins

CARIBBEAN SEA

Jamaica

25°

20°

15°

80°

75°

70°

65°

60°

Scale in Miles

0   100   200   400   600

Cartography by C. Boyle 2021

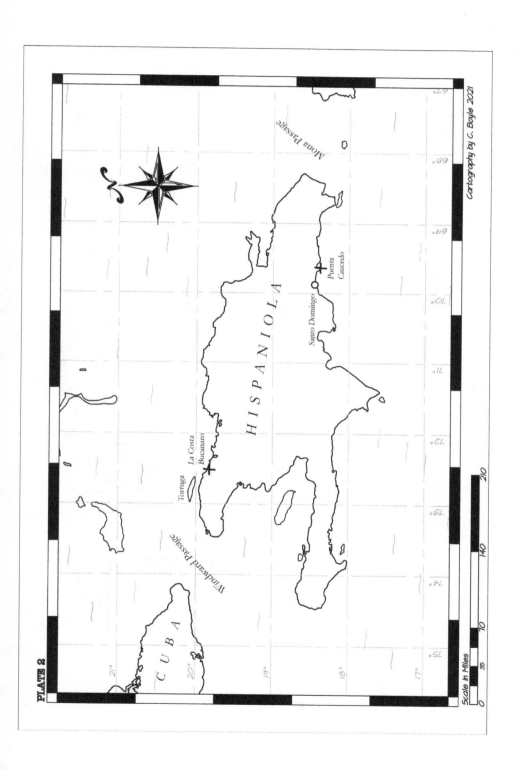

PLATE 2

Cartography by C. Boyle 2021

CUBA

HISPANIOLA

Tortuga
La Costa
Bucanaro

Santo Domingo
Puerta
Caucedo

Mona Passage

Windward Passage

Scale in Miles
0   35   70   140   210

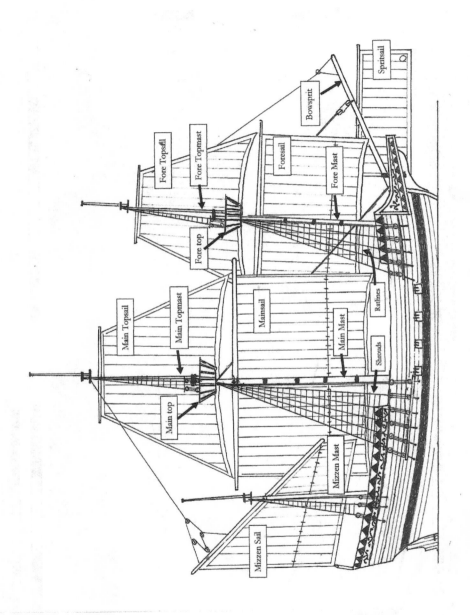

Spritsail

Bowsprit

Fore Topsail

Fore Topmast

Foresail

Fore Mast

Fore top

Main Topsail

Main Topmast

Mainsail

Main Mast

Rathnes

Main top

Shrouds

Mizzen Mast

Mizzen Sail

For terminology, see Glossary, page 337

Chapter One

A soft blanket of sound settled over the open, hilly country, woven from the buzz of the insects hidden in the fields, the birds lost in the distant canopy, the palm fronds and mango leaves rustling in the light breeze. And that was good. As quiet as the hunters were — and they were very quiet — they welcomed anything that helped cover their approach.

They were well out of the trees now, having emerged from the cool, green forest into an open country of tall, dry grass and stunted, straggling brush. The land rolled away in a long series of hills like the swells of the sea. There was no relief from the sun now as it beat down on the fields and on all of Hispaniola, on all of the Spanish Main, without respite or mercy. But the hunters were used to that. There was not much in that part of the world that showed any respite or mercy.

There were two men hunting that patch of island. They were nominally equals, though in practice they were nothing of the sort. The foremost of them was on the move, advancing forward at a crouch, his musket in his left hand, the ramrod in his right. He knelt and jammed the ramrod into the ground beside him like a small flagpole. He held the musket in both hands now, and with the long barrel parted the grass that blocked his view.

The heat seemed to engulf him, to wrap itself around him. He felt a line of sweat creep out from under the thin canvas cap he wore on his head. His right hand was resting on the musket, thumb on the hammer of the flintlock, finger just brushing the trigger, but he let go of the gun and wiped his arm across his forehead. It was futile and he knew it, but he needed to keep the perspiration out of his eyes, at least for the next few moments.

Putain de chaud... he thought, but he was pretty much resigned to the heat. He figured he would live out his life on the Spanish Main and then certainly be cast into eternal flames after that, so there was really no getting away from it.

He was a big man, six feet tall and then some, weighting eighteen stone. His hair was long and tied in a queue that hung down his back. It had once been chestnut brown but now was bleached nearly yellow by sun and salt water. His face was half-covered in a beard like the impenetrable undergrowth of some ancient forest which made him look considerably older than his twenty-six year. A powerful man, he spoke little, and his reactions, physical and otherwise, seemed slow, sometimes nonexistent. Brawny and oversized, quiet, unflappable: that was as much of an impression as anyone seemed able to form of him. An enigma, hard to fathom and not worth trying. Most men reckoned him stupid. He was known simply as LeBoeuf. The Ox.

LeBoeuf heard, behind him and on either side, the sound of soft panting and he turned his head to the right. His chief hunting dog was crouched at his side, coiled and ready. He was a big, sinewy beast which LeBoeuf had raised from a pup and trained well for his work. He had named the dog *Gros Chien*. Big Dog.

Big Dog met his eye as he turned, and LeBoeuf could see the animal was trembling in its eagerness to be at the game.

"Patience," LeBoeuf whispered. He turned his head and looked over his left shoulder, to where his other dog, a bitch he called Other Dog, was also crouched and ready. Behind him he knew there were three more of the creatures, each of which he called simply "Dog", and they were all in similar states of eagerness.

"Patience," he said again.

There was rustling in the brush ahead, grunting, the crunch of dried vegetation. LeBoeuf looked down the barrel of his musket where it was parting the tall grass in front of him. This was an ambuscade, a trap carefully set. LeBoeuf knew that his quarry would come, because he knew their habits and he knew the trails and the fields and the forests of that part of the island, the north west coast of Hispaniola.

The first of the pigs emerged from the brush fifty yards away across the open ground, a boar leading its drove. It moved with confidence, its bristled back arched high, its tusks visible even from that distance. He was wily and dangerous and he seemed to know it. But he did not know that LeBoeuf was there, down wind and hidden by the grass, watching. Waiting.

This is good, the breeze, LeBoeuf thought. He had no delusions about the way he smelled. His raw hide breeches and canvas shirt were caked with dirt and dried blood, and now both were nearly soaked through with sweat. He could smell the stink rising off of him, and he knew the boar would smell it as well, if the light air had not been in LeBoeuf's favor.

He looked over to his right. The other man was there, one hundred feet away: LeBoeuf's partner in matelotage, the means by which the hunters on Hispaniola lived and did their work. The men in the matelotage were partners. They hunted together, lived together, shared in all things. To some the partnership was more like that of man and wife.

LeBoeuf was not bothered by that sort of thing — he had seen enough of it in his travels — but it was not an arrangement he would embrace. In truth, the entire concept of matelotage was not the sort of thing he would embrace, and he did not in any real way.

His partner was called simply Le Rongeur. LeBoeuf did not know if that was his real name and he did not care. Le Rongeur was a filthy, thieving, vile bit of humanity, but he was wiry and quick, an expert at sneaking around, which seemed to be his natural state, and an extraordinarily good shot, all of which made him an excellent hunter. He greatly admired LeBoeuf, and he was also jealous and terrified of him, and those conflicting forces seemed to keep him where LeBoeuf wanted him. He had learned to never ask personal questions of any sort, and though he was naturally talkative, he knew to speak to LeBoeuf only when speech was necessary, which was not often.

This was the sort of partnership LeBoeuf was looking for. One that was not really any sort of partnership at all.

Le Rongeur sensed LeBoeuf's eyes on him and turned his head so they were looking at one another across the open ground. Le Rongeur was also crouching, also holding his long musket so that it peered through the tall grass at the drove of wild pigs slowly stepping out into the open, following behind the boar. Four dogs lay crouched behind Le Rongeur as LeBoeuf's five were crouched behind him.

LeBoeuf glanced back at the pigs and then back at Le Rongeur. He held up one finger, then pointed to himself, then held up three and pointed them at Le Rongeur. Le Rongeur nodded and turned back to peer down the barrel of his gun.

The sweat was running freely down LeBoeuf's face now and he gave his eyes one last wipe then settled his hand on the flintlock. His thumb found the hammer and he eased it back, pulling gently on the trigger as he did, then eased the trigger forward so that the weapon was cocked without even the slightest click of the lock. He lifted the barrel of the gun with his left hand, his left elbow resting on his knee. He sighted down the long, dark steel shaft, then moved it a fraction of an inch until the sight was just a bit above and to the left of the big boar in the lead.

He knew exactly how his gun would behave, in the same way that he knew how his hands and arms would behave. Like them, the gun was a part of him. He knew that at this distance the ball would drop and tend to the right, just slightly, but enough to require an adjustment of aim if he wanted to put his ball through the beast's head. Which he did.

One hundred feet away, Le Rongeur was taking aim at the third pig in line, another boar, smaller than the first but potentially just as dangerous. They were the only two boars visible. Between them they seemed to be sharing the half-dozen sows that moved in company with them.

Pigs... LeBoeuf thought, and pulled the trigger. The big musket slammed back against his shoulder with enough force to half twist him around, which took considerable force indeed. The gun was still in its recoil, and LeBoeuf was leaping to his feet, when he heard Le Rongeur's musket go off as well.

He stood at his full height and looked out over the cloud of smoke that had jetted from the muzzle of his gun. The big boar was down and motionless, which meant the lead ball had hit him in the skull and made a hash of what brains he had, killing him standing. The other boar was also down, also motionless. Le Rongeur, too, had put his bullet in the beast's skull.

The sows were frozen where they stood, too surprised and confused to move. But that would not last for more than a few seconds, and then they would bolt, running in terror in half a dozen directions.

"*Allez! Allez!*" LeBoeuf shouted, the two words for which Big Dog, Other Dog and the Dogs had been trembling in anticipation of hearing. The last syllable had not left LeBoeuf's lips before the animals were up and crashing through the tall grass, baying as they raced forward.

LeBoeuf watched them as he hefted the musket and pulled the hammer back to half-cock, snapping the frizzen shut. He dropped the wide butt of the gun to the ground as he reached behind him and pulled a paper cartridge from the leather box on his belt. He had never used paper cartridges before arriving in Hispaniola, where he had learned of them from the hunters there, but he had quickly seen the advantage they offered and embraced the idea.

He lifted the cartridge to his mouth and bit off the end, holding the lead ball between his tongue and teeth as he spilled the powder down the barrel. He spit the bullet down after it and then wadded up the paper and shoved that down as well. He snatched up the ramrod and drove it down the barrel, driving wadding and bullet down on the powder. He jammed the ramrod back into the ground and at the same time thumped the butt of the gun against the earth to drive power out of the touchhole and into the pan, priming the weapon to fire.

All this he did with his eyes fixed on the leaderless drove of pigs. He lifted the gun again as his dogs and Le Rongeur's reached the panicked animals, circling around them as they had been trained to do, coming in behind the pigs. Their barking and snarling sent the sows running in terror, running right toward the hunters' guns.

LeBoeuf put the sight of his gun on the foremost pig, swiveling at the waist to follow the animal's flight. He pulled the trigger again, and again the gun slammed against his shoulder as the first and second pig went down. For an instant LeBoeuf though he had killed them both with a single shot, then realized that Le Rongeur had fired at the same instant, the sound of his gun lost in the deafening blast of LeBoeuf's own.

Once again LeBoeuf's hands went through the motion of loading the long gun, his eyes on the dogs circling the sows, corralling them as best they could, trying to keep them penned in the killing field. LeBoeuf was spitting the ball into the muzzle when he saw a sow, more terror-stricken than the rest, charge at one of Le Rongeur's dogs and knock it high in the air as it raced for the shelter of the grass.

The dog came down whimpering on its side and the sow was gone. LeBoeuf thumped the butt of his gun down, lifted it, cocked it, found another of the sows and fired. He saw the animal knocked sideways, kicking and thrashing as it went down. Then Le Rongeur fired his third shot and another dropped and the last of the drove of pigs charged off into the grass, Big Dog, Other Dog and the rest at their heels.

LeBoeuf put two fingers in his mouth and blew three short, sharp whistles and the dogs stopped their chase and came trotting back, moving more slowly and reluctantly than they had on the attack.

"Good dogs," LeBoeuf said. "Good dogs." That was all the praise they would get, but that and a couple of haunches from one of the feral pigs would be reward enough.

LeBoeuf snatched up the ramrod that was still standing upright in the dirt, wiped the end on his breeches and slid it back into its housing under the barrel of his musket. He pushed forward through the tall grass and out into the open ground where the dead pigs lay scattered about. The dogs were trotting and circling around him with a new found eagerness, as if they had all just remembered what came next after the quarry was dead.

One hundred feet away Le Rongeur also pushed through the grass, the two men converging on their kill. They stopped next to the boar and looked down at his ugly face, his massive, muscular body, the tusks that gleamed in the brilliant sun.

"Big bastard," Le Rongeur observed. LeBoeuf nodded.

"Don't much want to carry this son of a whore back," Le Rongeur said next. LeBoeuf grunted, a noncommittal sound that Le Rongeur would correctly interpret to mean that he, LeBoeuf, did not give a single damn what Le Rongeur did or did not want.

He looked away from the boar and surveyed the other pigs. Nearby lay one of the sows, the top of its head taken clean off by the heavy bullet from LeBoeuf's gun. The smallest of the lot.

LeBoeuf pulled a long knife from the scabbard on his belt and pointed toward the sow. "That one we give to the dogs," he said. He stepped around the dead boar to where the sow lay. Le Rongeur followed dutifully behind, with the dogs leaping and panting and twirling in circles in their growing excitement. LeBoeuf knelt and laid his musket carefully on the grass. He lifted the pig's hind leg and reached in with his knife to cut the haunch free. Le Rongeur did the same with the fore-leg.

Le Rongeur's knife had just pierced the animal's flesh when he paused and looked up, his expression one of concern, a touch of fear.

"Oh, *merde*..." he said, cocking his head to one side.

"What is it?" LeBoeuf said. Le Rongeur had extraordinary hearing, which was pretty much what LeBoeuf would expect from Le Rongeur's sort. LeBoeuf's own ears functioned well enough, though his hearing had not been improved by years of close proximity to heavy cannon fire.

"Horses," Le Rongeur said standing and looking off toward the east. LeBoeuf wiped his knife on his breeches and slid it back into its sheath as he, too, stood and looked off to the east.

Horses. That meant Spanish *lanceros* most likely, sent out from Santo Domingo. Mounted soldiers armed with swords and long, deadly lances, dispatched in companies to kill the wild pigs and cattle and deprive the hunters of their prey. Or, if the lanceros got lucky, to kill the hunters themselves. Spain would suffer no interlopers on her New World colonies, as insignificant as their impact might be.

LeBoeuf still could not hear the horses, but the dogs could, and their enthusiastic barking in anticipation of fresh-killed pig had turned to low growls as they moved slowly away from the hunters and toward the sound.

"Down," LeBoeuf said and his dogs dropped to the ground. Le Rongeur gave the same order to his own dogs.

"The Spanish whores' sons, they heard the guns," Le Rongeur said, and LeBoeuf could sense the rising panic in his voice. "We better go. Run."

"Too late," LeBoeuf said, nodding to the far hill as the first of the lanceros came up over the crest. He was a couple hundred yards away and riding hard, and more soldiers were on his heels. Their steel helmets flashed in the sun, their lances were held straight up, the wicked points high over their heads. Their gear, helmet and leather armor, sword, lance, possibly a carbine, was nothing fancy, nothing compared to the finest of Spanish soldiers, but it was serviceable, and their horses were nimble and well-trained.

LeBoeuf knew perfectly well how far he and Le Rongeur were from the tree line, and he could see how quickly the riders were approaching. He was well used to calculations of speed, time, and distance, and he knew that he and Le Rongeur had no chance of fleeing now. The lanceros would ride them down and kill them if they tried.

He reached down and snatched his musket up from where it lay in the grass. "Load," he said as he pulled back the hammer, his hands going through the familiar moves once more, fast but unhurried. He heard Le Rongeur curse as he fumbled with his own weapon.

There was no question that the lanceros had seen them. They charged down the hill and straight for the hunters, their horses parting the tall grass like ships through the sea until they broke out onto the more open fields.

One hundred yards away and they lowered their lances, leaning forward in their saddles.

A dozen of the bastards…not so bad… LeBoeuf thought as he thumped the butt of his gun on the ground. Sometimes the horse soldiers would come out in patrols of fifty or more, but this column was considerably smaller. Small enough that they might just be able to fight them off if they were lucky, though LeBoeuf had to admit he had not felt very lucky as of late.

He raised the musket to his shoulder, thumbing back the hammer as he did. The dogs were snarling louder now and squirming in place. "Patience," LeBoeuf said, loud this time since the need for stealth was long past. The snarling and the squirming withered, but it did not die.

LeBoeuf swung the gun until the sight was just ahead of the lead rider. The man was close enough now that LeBoeuf could see the dark slash of a moustache under his nose, the black hair spilling out from under his helmet. He was leading the others, likely the officer in command, and thus the one to put down first.

"I have the first, you take the second," LeBoeuf barked at Le Rongeur. "Take care, aim well, or you're a dead man!" As he spoke, he kept his eye trained over the barrel of his gun and as the last word left his lips he pulled the trigger. The gun banged into his shoulder and the world was lost in a glut of gray smoke. Then the breeze whipped the smoke away and LeBoeuf could see the riderless horse pulling up short in confusion, could see the lancero twisting and kicking on the ground behind it.

Le Rongeur, standing a little behind LeBoeuf, fired in that instant, the muzzle just a few feet from LeBoeuf's ear, the sound so deafening that LeBoeuf could not even hear himself curse. Through the smoke from Le Rongeur's muzzle he could see the second rider knocked back in his saddle, his arms flying up in the air, his lance sailing off into the grass. He tumbled off the side of the horse but his foot remained in the stirrup as his body hit the ground, his arms flailing as the panicked horse twisted to the side, dragging the lancero around in a wide circle.

All this LeBoeuf watched as once again his hands went through the motion of loading his musket. The ten riders who were left seemed less eager now to be at the hunters, their pace slowing as they came on.

Stupid bastards… LeBoeuf thought. Now was the time for them to charge, while the two men were reloading. But happily it seemed not to have occurred to them, or perhaps the sight of the lead riders shot out of their saddles had made them gun shy. Either way, their slower speed just might give him and Le Rongeur time to get off another shot.

LeBoeuf thumped the butt of the gun on the ground to prime the pan and lifted it to his shoulder, sweeping the barrel across the line of approaching riders. "I have the one center left!" he called to Le Rongeur. "You take the one center right! Don't miss the bastard!"

Before Le Rongeur could reply, LeBoeuf pulled the trigger. He saw the man he was aiming for, center left, twist around and drop his lance and clap a hand over his shoulder as he slumped in the saddle. Not dead, not dismounted, but out of the fight and that was good enough.

He grit his teeth, watching the rest of the riders come on, waiting for Le Rongeur to fire. He did not bother reloading now — the lanceros would be on them long before he was halfway done. Le Rongeur had to take his man down and then they would somehow deal with the remaining eight.

"Le Rongeur, shoot! Now!" LeBoeuf shouted. He could not imagine what the man was waiting for. He turned to see what the problem might be, and the answer was immediately obvious: Le Rongeur was not there.

Chapter Two

"Son of a bitch!"

LeBoeuf turned in time to see Le Rongeur race over the crest of a small rise in his headlong flight for the trees, his dogs bounding around him. Had LeBoeuf run as well, the lanceros would surely have charged forward and rode them down, skewering them as they fled. But with LeBoeuf left behind, gun in hand, to distract them, it gave Le Rongeur a decent chance of escape. That, certainly, was Le Rongeur's only concern.

No matter, LeBoeuf thought as he turned back toward the lanceros. Nine riders, nine long lances held low in front of their mounts, converging on him alone. They were moving faster now, spurring their horses forward, reassured that they were up against only one man, that they would have to face only one more bullet, if that.

Big Dog and Other Dog were growling, their guttural sounds rising toward a bark. "Patience!" LeBoeuf called and the sound of the dogs stopped as if it had been snuffed out.

The lanceros were no more than a couple hundred feet away, the pounding of their horses' hooves on the warm ground drowning out all the other sounds of the jungle and the fields. LeBoeuf could see the horses' wide eyes, the foam at their mouths, and the fixed, grim, moustached faces of the riders.

"Allez! Allez!" LeBoeuf shouted and the dogs were up and gone as if they had been fired from a cannon. They sprang from their crouch and flung themselves forward, barking and howling until the frantic sounds of their attack filled the air, louder even than the pounding of the horses.

They spread out like grapeshot as they ran, each dog making for a separate horse and rider, barking and leaping like demons released from hell. The horses stopped their headlong charge, some shying off one way or another, some rearing back, their riders tossing lances aside, clinging with arms and legs in their desperate struggle to remain mounted.

LeBoeuf was spitting the bullet into the muzzle of his gun before he even realized he had begun reloading, so fascinated was he by the wild drama playing out in the field beyond. Big Dog, as was his prerogative, had gone for the foremost rider. Now he was dancing and leaping around the horse's legs, snapping at its knees and fetlocks as the horse wheeled and kicked and stamped at its tormentor.

On the horse's back the lancero was trying to skewer the dog with his long lance, but mostly he was trying to keep in the saddle. He would be eager to stay mounted, because if he fell it would be right into the jaws of the vicious beast below.

Off to the right Other Dog was engaged in a similar dance, leaping with perfect timing and clamping her teeth into the lancero's leg. She held fast as the horse whirled around, lifting Other Dog off the ground and spinning her through the air as the lancero batted at her with his gloved hand. Other Dog released her bite and the momentum of the turn sent her flying ten feet through the air. She hit the ground and tumbled and came back up on her feet. The fresh blood on the lancero's leg glinted through the rent fabric of his stockings.

Oh, you have trouble now, my friend LeBoeuf thought. When Other Dog got the taste of blood in her mouth things could turn ugly fast.

Off to the left, toward the edge of the fight, LeBoeuf heard the sound of barking cut short, the howl of an angry dog suddenly shifting to a yelp and whine of pain. A lancero pulled his lance from the writhing body of one of the dogs, then lifted the weapon and stabbed it down again.

Bastard, LeBoeuf thought.

He brought the musket up to his shoulder and swung the muzzle around until it was pointed right at the Spaniard's chest. The lancero looked up and LeBoeuf saw that odd expression of confusion and fear, an expression he had seen before, many times. It came in that heartbeat between knowing death was about to come and truly understanding what that meant. LeBoeuf had worn that expression himself often enough, though in the end death had not come. Yet.

He pulled the trigger.

The world directly in front of him was lost in a familiar blast of flame and smoke but LeBoeuf did not need to see to know what had happened. He was too close, his hand too steady, his mind too calm for his bullet to miss. He lowered the musket and the smoke blew away and there, as he knew it would be, was a riderless horse, cantering off, and a man and a dog dead in the grass.

He moved his eyes over the field ahead of him. Horses turning and rearing, riders clinging to their saddles, dogs leaping at their feet. The cantering horse was half-way up the distant hill and two more horses were charging after it, their riders still mounted, though LeBoeuf could not tell if the lanceros were giving up the fight or if their horses had simply bolted in panic.

He remembered the gun in his hand. He lifted it and thumbed back the hammer. He saw one of the lancero's horses rear, front legs kicking, but the man on its back did not fall, he did not seem to have lost control of the animal. The horse came down again on all four feet, ignoring the dog that barked and leapt at its legs. LeBoeuf saw the lancero dig in his spurs, saw the horse bolt forward, not for the distant hills, like the others, but right at him.

One hundred feet away. There was no chance of LeBoeuf getting his gun loaded before the horse had closed the distance. So he just held the weapon in his hands and watched, fascinated, as horse and rider charged.

The animal's gait built to a gallop as the rider leaned forward and held the lance down and straight ahead. LeBoeuf looked at the weapon's long, shining tip. It seemed to fly at him like a bird of prey, as swift and direct and remorseless as a hawk, its single talon coming right for his heart.

Do it, you coward, do it... LeBoeuf said to himself. *Take the lance, right in the heart, take it and be damned with it all...*

The point did not waver as the horse halved the distance between them. LeBoeuf could hear nothing but the pounding of the hooves, could see nothing but the massive head of the horse and the thin, elegant tip of the lance, airborne, coming at him, implacable as death itself.

Do it, coward, stand fast, take the lance right in your miserable heart...

There was thirty feet between them now, a distance the horse would cover in a few seconds at most. LeBoeuf braced himself, clenched his teeth, pressed his lips together, watched the silver point as it came at him, unwavering despite the jarring motion of the horse.

He sighed.

Coward, damn you, you coward! he swore at himself as he flipped the musket over in his hands, holding it like a club wielded by some savage. The point of the lance was barely an arm's length away when LeBoeuf swung the butt of the gun around and knocked it aside. He twisted and lifted the butt up and to his right as he looked into the startled face of the lancero, who, just a second before, had thought he was coming in for an easy and satisfying kill.

Instead, the Spaniard met the butt of LeBoeuf's musket with all the force of someone riding at full gallop. Had the musket been wielded by any other man, both lancero and hunter would have been knocked to the ground, but hitting a musket held by LeBoeuf was more like hitting the outstretched arm of a massive marble statue. The blunt end of the musket hit the rider in the stomach and lifted him right off the saddle as the horse charged out from under him. For an instant he hung in the air, folded around LeBoeuf's gun, and then he dropped, hitting the ground splayed out like the hide of an animal on a stretch. His helmet came off with the impact and rolled away as if he had been decapitated..

The lancero thrashed and kicked as he fought to regain the breath that had been knocked out of him. LeBoeuf rested the musket on his shoulder and stepped closer, standing over the man, waiting for him to swallow enough air so that he would stop writhing. The Spaniard's mouth was open wide and LeBoeuf heard him suck in a big breath, and when he did he stopped thrashing and his arms and legs fell limp to the ground.

He lay there for a moment, then propped himself up on one elbow, still gasping. Then, as the gasping subsided, he looked up at LeBoeuf, looming over him.

LeBoeuf lifted the musket off his shoulder and held it up like an ax at the top of its stroke, ready to come down and shatter the man's head. The lancero's eyes went wide and he held up a hand, more in supplication than in defense, because there was nothing he could do to prevent LeBoeuf's heavy weapon from smashing his bones like reeds.

For a second they remained like that, motionless, LeBoeuf holding his musket poised, the lancero waiting for what might come: mercy or death or something in between.

Then LeBoeuf, who did not actually know what he would do until that instant, made a decision. He straightened and rested the musket on his shoulder once again. At his feet, the lancero's entire body seemed to unwind.

LeBoeuf looked up at the field and the hill beyond as the last of the mounted riders reached the crest and disappeared over it, the pack of dogs on his heels. LeBoeuf put his fingers in his mouth and whistled, three times. The sharp note carried over the fields, cut through the sound of the hoof beats, and one by one the dogs broke off the chase and came trotting back. A few riderless horses were milling about but the dogs, sensing it was pointless to harass a horse with no human attached, ignored them.

The lancero was struggling to get to his feet. LeBoeuf shifted his musket to his left hand. He reached down and grabbed the man by the collar of his leather jerkin, lifting him effortlessly. He looked out over the field once more and the Spaniard half turned and looked as well.

"Good friends you have there," LeBoeuf said, nodding toward the open ground, abandoned by the other lanceros. "Faithful comrades in arms." He looked at the lancero and the lancero looked back at him with a confused look on his face.

"You speak French?" LeBoeuf asked, and the lancero shook his head, not in answer to LeBoeuf's question but to indicate he did not understand.

LeBoeuf nodded. He poked the lancero in the chest with his finger, then pointed toward the distant hill. The lancero looked where LeBoeuf was pointing, looked back at LeBoeuf, a cautious relief on his face, and nodded vigorously. He turned his head toward the horse which he had been riding before LeBoeuf knocked him to the ground. It was fifty feet away, quietly grazing.

He looked back at LeBoeuf and LeBoeuf shook his head. He grabbed the lancero by the arm and spun him half-way around, then lifted his leg, set his foot on the lancero's posterior, and gave him a terrific shove. The lancero stumbled and flailed and just managed to keep his feet as the force of LeBoeuf's kick propelled him toward the hill. With that, the dogs, who had been watching closely, set in to barking and snapping and leaping back and forth, happy that the fun might not be over.

The lancero stumbled on, regained his footing, and using the momentum provided by LeBoeuf's foot began to run in manic and undisciplined flight.

Bad idea, LeBoeuf thought, but he could do no more than form those words in his head before Big Dog and Other Dog were off with a speed a rabbit could envy, the rest of the pack right behind. By the time LeBoeuf could shout "Down!" they had caught up with the Spaniard, knocked him to the ground and were starting in on him.

On hearing LeBoeuf's command the pack broke off the assault and couched in the grass, growling and complaining. The lancero was on his feet again, clothes torn, bleeding from several places. He started running once more, now with a pronounced limp, the dogs poised but motionless as they watched him stumble off.

LeBoeuf once again gave three short, sharp whistles and the dogs stood and trotted back to him as if nothing at all had happened. He sighed and looked around. There was still much to do, but at least he had horses now, a total of three that had not run off.

He rounded them up one at a time, leading each to a small sapling and tying their reins to the trunk. He stripped the beasts of saddles and blankets. He considered keeping them — saddles were valuable things, particularly in that part of the world, where they had to be imported from Spain — but he had no use for them and he did not care enough about the money to bother with selling them.

He tossed the saddles and blankets aside and returned to the open ground where the dead pigs still lay scattered around. Overhead, vultures were wheeling in broad circles, hungry but unwilling to land with all the shouting and barking and gunfire on the ground. But they were patient creatures, and they and LeBoeuf both knew their patience would be rewarded.

He pulled his long knife from its sheath and returned to the work he had been doing before the lanceros disturbed his morning, cutting the front and back haunches off one side of the small sow. As each came free he tossed it to the panting, salivating dogs, the half-wild and eager pack. LeBoeuf watched the animals at work. He had seen schools of sharks behave much the same way, had once seen them rip a man apart before the first shriek could clear his throat.

He thought about the lancero whom his dogs had just run to ground. Another half a minute and he would have been no better off than the sow's severed legs.

Lucky bastard, LeBoeuf thought. Lucky, perhaps, that he had caught LeBoeuf in such an oddly forgiving mood. And why was he thus inclined? Was it the disgust LeBoeuf felt with himself? His cowardice in the face of the lance, the fear that prevented him from standing fast and letting the lancero run him through?

He grunted. Maybe. But that was enough introspection for one day. He rolled the small sow over and cut the other two haunches away, tossing those to the dogs as well. They had earned extra rations that morning.

With the dogs cared for, LeBoeuf started in on the other pigs, beginning with the big boar he had dropped first. It was hard work in any circumstance, but now the day was getting on and the sun was hammering down on him and the mosquitos swarmed in a cloud around his head. His shirt, breeches and rawhide shoes, already stiff with dried blood, dirt and soot, were soon awash again in the fresh blood that ran freely from the bodies of the pigs as he stripped one after the other of all the meat worth taking.

He was starting in on the third carcass by the time the dogs reached the limits of what they could consume and trotted off to find some bits of shade in the tall grass. But LeBoeuf labored on, building a pile of severed haunches and bellies and the meat cut from the loins. The mosquitoes kept up their maddening swarm and LeBoeuf swiped at them on occasion, but in truth he did not care over much about them.

At last he stood and arched his back. He looked around and then up at the sky overhead. In the hours he had been looking down, concentrating on his bloody task, a ragged blanket of gray had brushed the soft clouds aside and covered the blue sky. He had not even noticed.

The sun was somewhere behind the clouds now and well past its zenith, but LeBoeuf still had hours of daylight left. Happily, the overcast brought some relief from the grinding heat, and the breeze that had been building all day brought even more.

LeBoeuf grunted. There was a strange feeling in the air, an odd quality that he could not quite name. It made him strangely uneasy, but the heat was bearable and the work was mostly done and LeBoeuf reckoned that was as good as it was going to get. He untied the horses from the saplings and led them over to the pile of meat, then retrieved the haversacks that and Le Rongeur had left on the ground fifty feet away.

He dropped Le Rongeur's pack by the pile of meat and opened his own. He reached in and fished out various lengths of line and began tying the hunks of feral pig together in pairs and draping them over the horses' backs. The smell of the blood made the animals shift nervously and paw at the ground, but LeBoeuf spoke to them in a soft voice, running his hand down their necks, and that seemed to calm them.

Once he had used all of his own line, he opened Le Rongeur's haversack and pulled out a tangle of small rope. Beneath the cordage, near the bottom of the canvas bag, he could see something glinting. He reached in and pulled out a fine dagger, its ivory grip entwined with gold wire, diamonds set in the ends of the crossguard.

LeBoeuf turned the weapon over in his hand, appreciating the weight and balance. He recalled the time he had cut this dagger off the belt of a Spanish naval officer. He recalled putting it in his sea chest, but that was all he remembered about it. He had forgotten that he even owned it. But apparently Le Rongeur had not.

"Little whore's son," LeBoeuf muttered, but he did not really care about the dagger any more than he cared about the mosquitoes or the lanceros or much of anything else. He put it back in Le Rongeur's haversack and set to work on the last of the meat.

It took another hour or so before LeBoeuf had slung all the meat he had butchered over the horses' backs, leaving only the dismantled carcasses on the ground. He looked up at the vultures overhead. There were more now, and as he watched, two of them broke off from the swirl and came circling down to the ground a hundred feet away. They landed where the dead lanceros were hidden from view by the tall grass.

"*Bon appétit,*" he muttered. He picked up his musket and loaded it one more time, making ready for any chance encounter in which a loaded weapon might be handy. With his last length of rope he tied the horses in a line, whistled to the dogs, then headed off down the trail that had been beaten into the earth by thousands of wild pigs, wild cattle, wild horses, and the hunters who had come after them.

He walked through fields of chest-high grass and open country marked here and there by stands of trees. He came at last to the place where the trail left the meadows and plunged into the jungle of mango trees and fruit trees and sundry types of palms. He led the horses into the cover of the canopy and it was as if they had stepped from one world to another. The air was cooler and pungent with the smell of growth and decay. The sounds of the birds and insects and animals, which before had been a distant sound, now engulfed them. LeBoeuf's footfalls and even the horses' hooves were silent on the soft earth of the trail.

LeBoeuf knew this trail well. He knew they would cover about three miles through the thick forest before they broke out onto a high hill that looked over the sea and the distant, green mountains of Hispaniola. They would continue along the crest of the hill for another half a mile before winding their way down through the jungle once more, to the bay where the hunters made their home, such that it was.

They walked steadily on; LeBoeuf, the horses, the dogs. They startled unseen creatures that scurried away in the undergrowth. They stepped over fallen trees, half-rotted, slowly turning back into the rich soil of the forest floor. As LeBoeuf felt the first signs of weariness in his legs and back he stopped and fished a thick, green bottle out of his haversack.

He shook the bottle and determined it was more than half-empty, but that would be enough to see him through. He pulled the cork free and took a deep drink, feeling the soft, burning sensation of strong liquor in his mouth. He drank brandy, mostly, but this was something different, a drink they were making on the plantations, conjured up by the slaves who labored there. It was a distillation of molasses, a magical concoction called kill-devil or rumbullian and it was spreading like a weed through that part of the world. And with good reason.

LeBoeuf heard a panting sound and looked down to see Big Dog resting on his haunches, looking up at him, tongue hanging from the side of his mouth.

"What? It's not enough that you ate an entire pig? Now you want my kill-devil?" LeBoeuf said. "Forget it. You're getting fat and lazy."

It was not as if LeBoeuf was unsympathetic — he certainly understood the clawing need for liquor — but he also knew well enough that dogs did not take to it the way men did. Once he had thought perhaps these half-wild mastiffs of Hispaniola might be made of sterner stuff, so he had given one of his dogs a healthy swig from his bottle. It had not gone well. Certainly not for the dog, which had staggered about for an hour or so until it fell over and died.

"Not for you," LeBoeuf said as he corked the bottle and slipped it back into his haversack, ignoring Big Dog's plaintive whining.

They walked on, and soon LeBoeuf became aware of a low, pervasive sound, like a harsh and continuous whisper. It must have been building for some time, but had only just reached the threshold of his notice. He looked up. Through the trunks of the trees he could see the canopy above swaying, the palm fronds and the highest branches waving as if calling for help.

Wind's getting up, he thought, but gave it no more consideration.

Soon the land began to tend up hill and LeBoeuf knew they were close to where they would break out of the jungle and onto the high ridge. Another hundred yards or so and the trees began to thin out and the light penetrated deeper into the woods, and then they stepped out of the tree line and into the open. A meadow of tall grass spread out before him, leading to the far edge of the hill that sloped away toward the sea.

"Damn my eyes," LeBoeuf muttered. In the shelter of the forest he had not realized how hard the wind was blowing. Now he could see it was whipping the tall grass and making the trees in the distance bend and dance. The breeze had been building since he and Le Rongeur had set their ambuscade, but it had doubled and tripled in strength while he and the animals had been trudging along the wooded trail.

He continued on down the beaten path, to a place where he knew the vista would open up and give him a grand view of the island to the south and the sea to the north. He stopped, as he always did, and turned slowly in a circle. He knew he would once have taken great pleasure in such a thing and that was why he did it still, as if this ritual was something he owed to his former self.

To the south he could see great mountains marching along in ragged line. They made up much of the interior of Hispaniola, or so he had been told. He personally did not know if it was true or not, but certainly from that vantage point it seemed true enough.

He turned slowly to the west. He could see various headlands jutting out from the northern shore of the island and the occasional bone-white strip of sandy beach. A little north of the coastline, separated by a channel just a few miles wide, was the green hump of an island called Tortuga, the Turtle, where more and more people seemed to be finding refuge from the Spanish. LeBoeuf had heard that tobacco plantations were flourishing there, but he did not know that either. He had never been to Tortuga.

LeBoeuf continued his long turn to the north, his eyes now looking out over the sea, a place where he had most certainly been, and the smattering of islands off the coast. Then he paused, looking northeast. There was nothing there but open ocean, but still it held his eyes — nothing but salt-water between the edge of Hispaniola and the coast of France, many months' voyage away.

The seas of the West Indies were like nothing he had ever seen before. They were generally a stunning blue, an ethereal blue, a color that had seemed unreal to him when he first came to that part of the world. It was like something painted by an artist who had never actually seen the ocean and had based his pallet on some romantic image of what it must be.

But there was nothing inviting in what he saw of the ocean now. The water was an ugly gray color under the ugly gray sky, with flashes of whitecaps heaving in long, serrated lines as far as he could see. On the horizon the clouds were piling up, tall and threatening, as if any moment they would come rolling down on Hispaniola like an avalanche.

The wind tugged at his beard and made his long hair whip and twist. He shook his head. He thought about the bottle of kill-devil in his haversack and considered fishing it out again. A drink would be good, because whatever was coming in from the east would be bad, he could see that. A powerful and malevolent thing, it alone would decide what would remain standing and what would be swept away.

Chapter Three

The *Nostra Sennora de Regla*, a galleon of some five hundred tons burthen, was starting to labor in the rising sea and wind. This was obvious to Don Alonso Menéndez de Aviles, Knight of the Order of Santiago. It was obvious despite his being down below in a cabin completely enclosed and lit only by the swaying lanterns, and despite his not being a mariner of any description.

He had been aware for some time that the sounds and motion of the ship were changing. He kept silent track of the deeper rolling, the more noticeable pitching, the louder groans of wood on wood as the vessel worked. He wondered how long it would take for his wife Francisca, who tended to be oblivious to such things, to notice the change. In the end it was longer than he would have guessed.

They had breakfasted that morning with the master of the ship, a gruff old mariner named Ignacio in his great cabin aft. Through the fine glass windows that stretched across the stern of the ship, Don Alonso had looked out over a notably calm blue sea that moved in long, lazy swells, and a blue sky above filled with the most kindly-looking white clouds.

To the north, and two leagues astern, there was a green hump of an island which the master informed them was Puerto Rico. They were well into the West Indies now, with nothing but open water between them and Hispaniola.

The seas had been so calm then, and the motion of the ship so easy, that even Francisca had been able to eat a respectable breakfast. That had certainly not been the case for most of their nine weeks at sea, since they had left the Canary Islands astern.

Nostra Sennora de Regla was part of the second plate fleet, the Panamanian *galeones*, the ponderous and stately collection of galleons and Spanish men-of-war that brought goods from Spain to the New World and returned with holds stuffed full of gold and silver from the Spanish Main.

The ships had departed Seville for their southerly route across the Atlantic. Now, as they neared Hispaniola, *Regla* broke off from the fleet, making for Santo Domingo while the others laid a course for Cartagena and

eventually Portobelo. There they would overwinter befc
Spain in the spring.

Regla, like the other ships, carried aboard her a mixed cargo: c.
ironwork, olive oil, wine, flour, shoes, sundry fine furnishings. Ana
carried Don Alonso Menéndez de Aviles as well, newly appointec
lieutenant governor of Hispaniola, and his wife, Francisca, and their fairly
extensive retinue.

Following breakfast Don Alonso and Francisca had taken a turn on the
quarterdeck, strolling the forty feet or so from the break of the poop deck
aft, past the row of cannons squatting behind their gun ports, to the ornate
rail at the forward end. From there they could look down on the ship's
boats resting on the main hatch below, more cannons lining the sides, and
the sailors working at various mysterious but no doubt essential tasks.

"There, husband," Francisca said, pointing to a man sitting on the hatch
and working at a length of rope with an odd pointed tool, like a spike of
some sort. "What is that fellow doing?" She was nineteen years old and
curious about this sea-going world when she was not too busy praying or
vomiting.

"He's repairing that rope," Don Alonso said. "It's hard to explain, really,
but that is the very rope that controls that highest sail on the front mast."
Alonso had no idea what the man was doing, or what purpose was served
by the rope he held, but he was not about to admit as much to his wife or
anyone else.

They watched the activity on the deck below for a few moments, then
turned and walked back to the poop deck, then turned again and walked
forward to the rail. And then they retraced their steps. Alonso glanced
down. He wondered if they were wearing a path in the deck.

Don Alonso was a vigorous, active man of thirty-one years, and the
confines of the ship grated on him. He was desperate to ride or to hunt or
to fence or do anything at a pace quicker than a stroll. But there was no
chance for that aboard the lumbering galleon. Francisca did not care to be
left alone in her cabin, and it would hardly be proper for her to appear
alone on deck, so Don Alonso was obliged to accompany her on these
monotonous walks.

Happily, if the ship was rolling or pitching in any way that frightened her
— and it took little to frighten her — Francisca refused to leave her cabin,
so Don Alonso was generally spared the monotony of the quarterdeck
stroll. But not so that morning.

Once Francisca decided they'd had exercise enough she insisted they
return to their cabin, which was situated just below the quarterdeck,
forward of the master's great cabin. There were thirty-three passengers
aboard *Nostra Sennora de Regla*, each relegated to quarters commensurate
with their status. A half dozen Dominican friars were crammed into a

meager closet set up on the gundeck below. Eight men destined to fill minor government posts in Santo Domingo or Portobelo or Nombre de Dios were housed in tiny cabins on the same deck as Don Alonso, but farther forward.

Also on that same deck were a handful of military officers bound for the West Indies to take the place of others who had died fighting the French or the Dutch or the savages or, more likely, had succumbed to some fever or other. One of the larger cabins, which was about the size of two horse stalls, housed a bishop, sent across the sea to help bring the Word of God to the native people in Spain's more far-flung outposts. Don Alonso wondered who that worthy had so offended that he had been given such an unenviable mission. It might as well have been a sentence of death. The bishop seemed to regard it as such. There were many ways a man could die in the West Indies.

Four of the passengers were Don Alonso's people, since a man such as Don Alonso Menéndez de Aviles, Knight of the Order of Santiago and now Lieutenant Governor of Hispaniola, did not travel unaccompanied. Don Alonso's personal secretary, Juan Cardero, was in a cabin nearby, and his three servants were...somewhere on the ship. Don Alonso did not actually know where they were holed up, and he did not much care, as long as one of them at the very least was on hand at any hour to attend to him.

Francisca's people made up the rest of their company. Foremost in Francisca's mind was Father Pedro, a young Benedictine from Cadiz who, following ordination, had served in the household of Francisca's father, Don Cristóbal de Seville. Francisca had favored Father Pedro from the first, and on hearing of her husband's appointment to Santo Domingo, she had prevailed on him to join them, that he might pray with her and Don Alonso and hear her daily confession. To this Father Pedro had agreed.

Also housed nearby were Francisca's two maidservants, Maria and Gabriella. There was a dressmaker and a cook and an assistant cook as well. Don Alonso did not know their names, nor did he know where they were to be found on that voluminous ship. Fornicating with the sailors, he would imagine.

They returned to the cabin following their morning stroll, the space remarkably dim after the brilliant sunlight of the upper deck, and it was still dim even after their eyes had adjusted somewhat. Don Alonso and Francisca sat on chairs lashed in place and read by the light of two tin lanterns that hung from the deck beams overhead: Francisca her Bible and Alonso from a stack of correspondence to which he had needed to attend for some time.

Alonso had made his way through four letters when he heard a sharp banging noise forward, something falling on the gundeck. He looked up and realized that the roll of the ship had grown deeper and more pronounced after the relative calm of the morning. He frowned and listened. He could hear the hull creaking in a way it had not been before. He could hear the slap of water on the sides of the ship and the sound of feet running back and forth on the deck above.

He looked over at Francisca. She was still concentrating on her Bible and had not noticed any change, so Don Alonso went back to his letters. He made it through another two before looking up again. The groaning of the hull was louder and more insistent, the ship heeling farther with each roll.

They had encountered one storm during their largely uneventful passage from Seville, and that one had come on while Don Alonso was sleeping. The captain had warned him there might be dirty weather, but the words had made little impression on him. He went to sleep and did not wake until a wild roller sent him flying out of his bed and tumbled him across the deck.

The pounding of the seas and the working of the ship were nearly drowned out by Francisca's screams and sobbing prayers as she, too, had woken to this new, storm-tossed world. She summoned Father Pedro and Maria and Gabriella to join her in her crying and praying.

For ten hours Don Alonso stayed by her side while they prayed their rosaries and the women wept. It was the longest ten hours of Don Alonso's life. He hoped Francisca did not expect him to endure the same again, because he had no intention of doing so.

He returned to his letters but now his mind was entirely on the gathering storm. The ship seemed to stagger every now and again and Don Alonso imagined her bow slamming into the mounting waves. The fabric of the ship was making a wonderful array of sounds, from a sharp cracking and snapping to a deep, soft groan as the rigging transmitted the strain on the masts down to the hull. He wanted desperately to be on deck, to witness what was going on. He glanced over at Francisca and, incredibly, she still had not noticed the change.

*Now...I must go now...*he thought. He opened his mouth, ready to blurt out some nonsense about needing a breath of fresh air, when the ship took its hardest roll yet, tipping far off to the larboard side. A chamber pot, thankfully empty, flew off the shelf where it was stored and shattered on the deck.

Francisca dropped her Bible and grabbed at the chair and her eyes went wide.

Too late, damn it all... Don Alonso thought.

"Husband!" Francisca gasped. "What's happening? Are we in another storm?" She looked frantically around the cabin as if the answer might be hiding behind one of her many trunks.

"No, nothing of the sort, my sweet," Alonso said. "The wind's a bit stronger, I think, but that's all. It only means we reach Santo Domingo all the quicker."

Francisca's eyes remained wide and she shook her head and Don Alonso could see she was not mollified. "No, Alonso, methinks you're wrong," she said. "I fear this is some great storm, some great peril."

"Oh, no, I'm certain…" Alonso began but Francisca cut him off.

"We must pray, husband. We must pray for God's mercy. You recall how our prayers were answered in the last storm. We must do the like again."

Before Alonso could say another word Francisca picked up the small bell she kept nearby and rang it with great urgency. A moment later Gabriella stuck her head through the door.

"Gabriella!" Francisca said. "My husband thinks there's a great storm outside that will require our prayers, and I agree. Please fetch Maria and Father Pedro. We must pray as we did in the last great tempest."

"Of course, my lady," Gabriella said. "The Lord delivered us then and I'm sure He will again." With that she was gone, and Alonso had just time enough to store his papers away, moving carefully from hand hold to hand hold over the heaving deck, before she was back, Maria and the young priest following behind her. Moments later they were on their knees, rosaries hanging from their fingers. They braced themselves against the furniture secured to the deck and Father Pedro led them in their prayers.

Don Alonso alone was not kneeling, pleading a pain in his knees that bothered him whenever it was convenient. He remained in his seat, holding a rosary which was serving no purpose other than to provide something with which he could fidget irritably. He had been mouthing the prayers along with his wife and the others, the Ave Marias and the Pater Nosters, but he stopped when he realized that their eyes were closed and there was no need for him to make even that much effort.

He considered the people kneeling on his cabin floor. He had never seen Father Pedro without his baggy clerical robe, but his general proportions and the way he moved suggested he had a naturally athletic build. He was handsome despite the tonsure. It made Alonso wonder sometimes about his wife's insistence that the young priest accompany them to Hispaniola. He wondered at how she seemed so devoted to him.

He shook his head. That was absurd and he knew it. Francisca could no more commit adultery and fornication than she could take wing and fly. She went to daily Mass and Confession. What she found to confess every day Alonso could not imagine, but he was certain it was not adultery and fornication.

He shifted his gaze to Maria, whose face and body reminded Alonso of raw dough. Francisca had engaged her soon after their wedding, and Alonso had wondered at the time if she had purposely chosen a maidservant who would present no temptation to her new husband. Francisca herself was a lovely woman, lauded for her beauty, the object of numerous lustful thoughts, Alonso suspected, but even the most beautiful women did not welcome competition.

In the end he concluded that Maria had not been chosen just for her unfortunate looks: she was an excellent servant. What's more, it would never occur to Francisca that her husband might commit adultery, any more than she could imagine herself doing so. This Alonso had not understood at first, but as he came to know his wife better he saw it was true.

And then, as final proof, Francisca had taken on Gabriella.

Don Alonso's eyes moved on and came to rest on Gabriella, kneeling on Francisca's right side. Gabriella was a genuine beauty. Seventeen or eighteen years of age, with thick black hair that fell in waves down her back when it was cast loose. Her skin was as white as Francisca's, but her eyes were a startling blue to Francisca's brown. And while Francisca's lips were fine and delicate, a dainty slash across her face, Gabriella's were full and impudent and brimming with promise. How often Alonso had lost himself in the sight of those lips. Often enough that Gabriella had caught him at it, and had given him a long and thoughtful gaze before turning away.

Alonso had toyed with the idea of Gabriella. He longed to lie with the girl, to experience those lips in a dozen ways. He was not wanting for carnal satisfaction — he bedded Francisca often enough — but she seemed to approach it all as an obligation to be endured. Gabriella seemed like the sort who would be a more active and vigorous companion.

Still, he resisted. He feared that any dalliance with Gabriella would lead to complications, more than the pleasure would be worth.

On the other hand…

Back in Spain he had enjoyed the company of many women at court, before and after his marriage, who could satisfy his needs in ways Francisca could not. Women who knew how to be discreet, who would take what they wanted from a man like Don Alonso and ask no more. But in his new post, in Hispaniola, he would have access to no such women. Perhaps cultivating young Gabriella was worth further consideration.

The *Nostra Sennora de Regla* took a hard roll to starboard. The four kneeling supplicants were facing aft, where a small painting of the enthroned Madonna and Child was mounted on the bulkhead, and as the ship rolled they reached desperately for the edge of the bed, the nearest fixed structure, to stop themselves from being splayed out on the deck. Don Alonso just managed to grab the seat of his chair before he was flung sideways across the cabin, and as he did he remembered two things.

Nostra Sennora de Santiago …Trois Frères…

The ship began its slow roll back upright and Alonso stood, hand gripping the chair back. "Forgive me, Francisca...Father," he said. "I'm loath to leave off prayers but I fear my station requires that I go on deck and see if I can be of any assistance in this moment of peril." He already knew the answer of course. At best he would be useless, at worst he would be in the way, but there was something that he needed to see, and he knew he could not stand another moment below, mumbling prayers with the women and the priest.

Francisca looked alarmed. "Must you, my dear Alonso? It will be dangerous on deck!"

"I know, my sweet, but I am the lieutenant governor of Hispaniola now, and I must set an example for the men."

Before anyone could protest further, Don Alonso lunged for the cabin door, timing his move with the roll of the ship. He got hold of the latch and lifted it, then staggered out into the narrow space between the cabins larboard and starboard.

Twenty feet forward of his cabin door, a ladder ran up to a scuttle that opened onto the quarterdeck, a crude affair but one reserved for the better sort who lived aft. He made his way to the ladder, pushing himself off the bulkheads as he was tossed against them, got hold of the rungs and began to climb.

As loud and chaotic as it had been below, Don Alonso was still surprised by the world that greeted him topside. The blue sky of the morning was smothered under a solid blanket of gray, with darker, roiling clouds swirling low in counterpoint. The sea, too, had given up its benign blue color and now reflected the ugly gray of the sky. The easy rollers were gone, and in their place were steep cresting waves, marked by sharp lines of white foam where they curled over on themselves.

The wind was making a high-pitched, whistling sound in the rigging; the ropes twisted and whipped around and bowed out to leeward. Alonso looked up toward the top of the masts. The upper sails with their bold red crosses were gone, stowed away. Likewise, the triangular sail generally set on the mizzen mast, and the smaller one, the bonaventure, all the way aft, were also lashed to their respective spars, as was the square sail that hung under the bowsprit. The bottom sections of the lower sails — bonnets, he had heard them called — had been removed, the yards lowered down, and the *Sennora de Regla* drove on with only a fraction of her canvas showing.

At the forward edge of the quarterdeck a knot of sailors were working at something, though Alonso could not tell what. Then one of them waved an arm, the men at the rail began hauling away, and a massive wooden cross rose up from the deck, swaying and twisting with the wind and the rolling of the ship. Two men tended to a line made fast to the bottom of the cross, guiding it through the rigging as it was hauled up to the masthead, a sign of devotion to the God who had once stilled waters as angry as these.

The master was at the windward side, his outstretched hand clinging to the aftermost shroud of the mizzenmast. His hat was lashed down around his chin and the long gray hair that tumbled out from under it, and the mass of gray beard on his jaw, were whipping around in the same manner as the ship's rigging. Don Alonso, clinging to the rail at the top of the scuttle, waited as the ship rolled to leeward, and then as it came upright he stumbled across the deck to the master's side, grabbing hold of the mizzen shrouds aft of where he stood.

"Master Ignacio!" Alonso said. The wind was not such that he had to shout, but neither could he speak at his regular volume. "The wind is getting up, it seems!" He tried to sound like a man who was accustomed to such things, a man who was in no way concerned.

"Yes it is, Don Alonso!" Ignacio replied.

"Will it get worse?"

"I would not know," Ignacio said. "I am only the master of this ship, I am not God!"

Alonso did not care for the tone of the master's voice. It seemed to suggest that Alonso's question was a stupid one, and that he, Ignacio, did not have time for such idiots. In a drawing room Alonso would have cut the man down with a few words, fast and sharp as a rapier, but he could not do it on Ignacio's quarterdeck, shouting over the wind. For all Don Alonso's wealth and influence at court, his connections by marriage and by family, he had no authority here. The ship was a state unto itself, and Ignacio its king. It was a fact that Alonso accepted, even if he despised it.

Rather than reply, Alonso turned away and looked forward. The seas were coming from nearly astern, dropping the aft end of the ship into the troughs and sending its bow high in the air, like a horse rearing up in fright. And then the stern would rise on the next wave and the bow come down and the ship would seem to slide downhill until it slammed into the sea ahead with a great shudder and a burst of spray.

Alonso might have found it exhilarating if Ignacio's manner gave him confidence that this was all a great lark, that there was no danger, but that was not the sense he got from the old man, not from his words nor from the look on his face, nor from the conditions he could observe. Not at all.

He waited some moments for his annoyance to subside before he spoke again. "That ship that was in company with us, the *Nostra Sennora de Santiago*, is she still astern?"

Master Ignacio was looking aloft, studying something intently; what, Alonso did not know. For a moment he thought the master would give no answer, but finally he said, "No, the damned fool. He ran off toward the northward two glasses past." He continued looking aloft for a moment more, then looked over at Alonso. "Why do you care?"

Alonso shrugged. "I don't," he said. "But I am not a man of no consequence. If there's something that is the business of His Most Catholic Majesty, then it is certainly my business as well."

"Huh," the master said, and then, turning his back on Alonso, shouted, "Boatswain! We'll have the foresail off her now!"

Don Alonso turned and looked out to sea, running his eyes along the wide arc of the ocean, from the bow of the ship to the stern. He could see a long succession of waves moving toward the gray and indistinct horizon. He could see nothing else.

He waited until a wave passed under the ship, lifting its bow, then let go of the shroud and hurried across the wide deck, timing it so he would be running up hill, not careening down. He reached the starboard side and clapped on to a shroud as the bow began to rise again. He pressed himself against the bulwark and once more swept his eyes along the horizon.

He saw her then, a mile or so away, easy to miss in the big seas with her sails much reduced. She was *Nostra Sennora de Santiago*, a brigantine of only about one hundred and fifty tons burthen. She had joined them in the Canaries, her master begging the admiral of the plate fleet to be allowed to accompany them on her voyage to the New World and thus enjoy the protection of the heavily armed ships. Gold had likely changed hands, and the admiral had allowed the smaller vessel to join them, with the understanding that she would be left astern if she could not keep up.

But the brigantine proved quick and more than able to match the speed of the ponderous galleons, and she had taken her place in the center of the fleet, always within sight of the *Nostra Sennora de Regla*. Only now had she parted company with the larger ship, running off to the northward. Few aboard *Regla* had noticed, and none cared. None, save for Don Alonso.

He watched her rising and falling on the seas, her masts waving wildly as she rolled. *Nostra Sennora de Santiago*. She was, in truth, the *Trois Frères*, lately out of La Rochelle. Her master was a Frenchman names Pierre LeBlanc, though he had introduced himself to the admiral as Diego de Saucedo.

Trois Frères... In the same way that a great tree could spring from a tiny seed, so a great dynasty could spring from that small, storm-tossed ship. An empire. The empire of Don Alonso Menéndez de Aviles, Knight of the Order of Santiago. Marquess Don Alonso? Duke Don Alonso, with the dignity of Grandee? It was within reach now, with Santo Domingo just a hundred leagues to leeward.

Alonso heard a sharp crack, like a pistol shot behind him, and a sudden blast of shouting. He turned quickly, looking for the source of the sound. The mariners and Master Ignacio were staring aloft and Alonso followed their gaze.

The upper sail on the foremast, lashed in place, had worked free of its ropes. The crack Alonso heard was the sound of the canvas blowing to rags; now streamers of gray cloth were whipping out to leeward as the sailors pulled themselves up into the shrouds and began climbing aloft.

The galleon took a deep, sickening roll. Don Alonso staggered and held tighter to the shroud until he could feel his fingers pressing into the tar that coated the rigging. The ropes that held the cannons in place groaned as the ship rolled and they took the weight of the guns. And suddenly he did not feel so sanguine about the mission of the *Trois Frères*. Or about his future empire. Or even about the possibility of living through the night.

Chapter Four

LeBoeuf made his way off the high ridge and back down into the trees. There was shelter from the wind there, but overhead the palm fronds and branches continued their wild dance. He could feel the weariness now as he continued leading the horses along the trail. Even Big Dog and the others were not moving with the same alacrity that they had shown earlier.

The heady smells of the forest had surrounded him since leaving the open country behind: the vegetation and the decay, the perfume of wild flowers and the warm odor that lifted off the forest floor where the sun managed to work its way down through the foliage. But he was aware of other scents now. He could smell smoke and roasting meat, the occasional suggestion of unwashed men. The tang of salt water. He did not have much farther to go.

Once again the trees began to thin and the country ahead opened up, and LeBoeuf found himself on another low hill. From there the ground sloped down to a long, curved white beach that stretched away until its eastern end stopped at a headland like a small island. Just inland from the beach, marked by a line of palm trees where the sand met the edge of the grass was a great expanse of open ground. On that ground was a scattering of small shelters, like a crude mockup of a town.

The shelters consisted of tents mostly, though nothing like the neat, uniform tents of an army in the field, laid out in straight ranks and columns. There were maybe thirty of them, made of whatever came to hand, mostly bits of old sails, worn-out canvas acquired from the ships that called there. They were stretched over frames fashioned from limbs hacked off in the forest, or from long bits of driftwood that had been thrown up on the beach and lashed together with practiced skill.

As insubstantial as the shelters might have been, they did not look temporary or transient. Rather they looked as if they had been there for ages, as if the tents had sprung from the ground on which they stood, as if they were part of the island, outcroppings of the land. Some had been augmented with semi-permanent structures built alongside: lean-tos made out of small logs, or more permanent-looking outbuildings cobbled together from the bones of ships that had come to grief on the tricky sandbars in the roadstead just off shore.

A constellation of old barrels and crates, broken bottles, raw hides, stacks of lumber and bundles of dried meat surrounded each of the tents. Near each was a round, black fire pit with a few logs for seats rolled up beside them and stacks of split wood nearby.

The tents were not bunched close together but rather spread out over an acre or so of trampled, grassy field. The men who lived in those shelters, even in the partnership of a matelotage, were not a particularly sociable lot. They had come to that place to escape debtors' prison, or having fled from military service of some sort, or from an apprenticeship, or slavery, or the hangman. They were there because the hunting was good and the money they made from selling the meat was tolerable and no one asked any questions and no one much cared about anyone else.

The tents and their attendant outbuildings were not alone on the open ground. There were also a half-dozen framework structures consisting of rough posts driven into the earth and supporting a wood rack above. Beneath each rack was a fire-pit in which low, smoldering flames were kept burning with cordwood and the bones of the pigs that were hunted inland.

The meat of the pigs was arranged on the racks above the fire pits, where it bathed in the smoke that dried it and flavored it. In that way it was rendered it into something quite valuable: a foodstuff that would last for months on shipboard, or in a plantation's storehouse, without turning rancid, even in the brutal heat of the West Indies.

The hunters had learned this technique for smoking meat from the natives of that island, the Arawaks, who were now mostly gone. The natives called the structure a *buccan*; the French called it a *boucan*. The hunters who came to Hispaniola, who hunted and dried and sold the meat, took their name from this lash-up as well. They were the *boucaniers*.

LeBoeuf shambled along the last hundred yards down the hill and past a line of tents to the closest of the boucans. Four men were sitting on logs near the low fire, bottles at their feet, clay pipes in their hands or mouths. A fifth man was standing, turning the sides of meat spread out above. A screen had been set up on the windward side of the boucan to keep the gale from whisking the heat clean away.

The five men looked up as LeBoeuf approached, but they did not move or speak.

Big Dog and the rest of the pack peeled off and headed for the tent that LeBoeuf called home. The horses, unused to carrying a load heavier than a lancero, were too tired now to do anything but stand motionless, so LeBoeuf let them do just that as he unloaded the cuts of meat and stacked them near the boucan.

"You're alive," one of the men said at last. He was a Dutchman named Van Lauwersoog, a name which one of the Englishmen there had deemed too hard to pronounce and so dubbed him Van Loudersong. All of the others boucaniers — mostly French but also English, Dutch, African, or a mix of any of those — agreed that the new name was an improvement, and so Van Loudersong he remained.

"I'm alive," LeBoeuf agreed.

Van Loudersong and the others nodded.

"Not what Le Rongeur seemed to think," said a Frenchman who called himself Pierre le Chasseur. French was the common language among them, and it was what they all spoke with greater or lesser fluency.

"Huh," LeBoeuf said as he continued to unload his kill. "Le Rongeur...he came back?"

"He did," Van Loudersong said. "Said the lanceros did for you. Said he killed half a dozen of them, but there were too many. Said he saw you die."

LeBoeuf nodded. Le Rongeur must have been pretty certain that he, LeBoeuf, could not have survived the lanceros. It was not likely he would have returned to the camp after running off if he thought there was a chance LeBoeuf might follow after.

"Nice horses," Le Chasseur said.

LeBoeuf grunted. "Too skinny. Been rode too hard," he said.

"They look Spanish," Van Loudersong said and LeBoeuf nodded again.

"What do you mean to do with them?" Le Chasseur asked.

LeBoeuf shrugged. He hadn't really thought about it, beyond using them to haul his kill back to the camp. "Butcher them and smoke them, I suppose," he said. "Sell the meat to some damned Dutchman. They'd never know the difference."

This was met with more nods. A blast of wind rocked the framework of the boucan and the man turning the meat grabbed the screen before it became airborne. LeBoeuf looked out to the east, though most of the horizon was blocked from view by a high point of land that formed the eastern end of the big half-moon bay. "This is a bad one," he said.

"A proper gale," Van Loudersong said.

LeBoeuf shook his head. "No," he said. "Worse. Much worse than that."

From the high ridge he had seen the storm building. He had seen storms like this before, though not often. But beyond just seeing it, he could feel it. Deep in his guts, in his bones, he could feel a change in the pressure of the air and knew this thing would roll down on them like a vengeful god.

LeBoeuf pulled the last of the meat off the horse he was unloading, pushed the animal aside and pulled the next one closer. "We can't stay here," he added.

The other men exchanged glances, and LeBoeuf might have smiled if smiling was a thing that he did. He knew what they were thinking: they were wondering if they should heed his warning. They were thinking that LeBoeuf sounded quite certain of what he was saying. But they were also thinking that LeBoeuf was a dimwitted beast of a man, and not the sort to be listened to.

On the other hand, they would be wondering if perhaps LeBoeuf actually knew things about such storms that they did not. They knew very little about him and nothing of his history or what knowledge he might or might not have.

Van Loudersong opened his mouth to speak, perhaps to ask a question, but before he could say a word the screaming cut him off.

It was a high-pitched, feminine shriek and it tore like a skinning knife through the howling wind. It carried tones of fear and outrage and anger. It came from a tent about two hundred feet to the west. It came from LeBoeuf's tent.

The six men at the boucan turned to look but there was nothing happening that they could see. Five of them turned back and looked up at LeBoeuf. Van Loudersong drew a lungful of smoke from the clay pipe he held to his mouth. He blew the smoke out and it was whipped away by the wind. Once again the woman screamed and it was followed by a crashing sound.

LeBoeuf sighed.

He tossed the bloody haunch he was holding onto the pile, set his musket and cartridge box down, then headed off toward his tent. The canvas was flogging and the frame was swaying in the wind, but he could still hear the scuffling inside, the shouted words he could not make out, the crash of objects being thrown or knocked aside.

He ducked through the canvas door and into the gloom of the tent's interior. Most nights they would light small fires inside to create smoke that would keep the mosquitoes at bay, and now the tent reeked of that stale odor. The smell of their blood-caked, unwashed bodies and clothes also filled the tent, as did that of old food, of brandy and rumbullian and tobacco smoke and, oddly, perfume.

Henriette was at the far end of the tent, pressed up against a great bundle of old sailcloth. The kercher she wore over her shoulders and around her neck had been pulled half-off and was hanging by one corner. Her smock was torn ten inches from the neck down and her overbody was askew, as if it had been tugged hard. She had a look in her eyes that suggested madness, and a large iron skillet in her hand. She was shrieking curses, eyes fixed, and she did not notice LeBoeuf as he came through the door.

Le Rongeur was standing in front of her, his long hunting knife in his hand, keeping just out of striking distance from the skillet. He, too, was screaming curses and his voice, if not quite so high as Henriette's, was high enough. His back was to LeBoeuf so LeBoeuf could not see what condition he was in, but he guessed it was not good.

None of this was terribly surprising. If Le Rongeur genuinely thought LeBoeuf was dead, which he must have, then his first impulse would be to take Henriette the way he had yearned to since he first saw her. So far the result was about what LeBoeuf would have predicted.

Henriette's eyes darted toward LeBoeuf, and seeing him there she abruptly stopped screaming and adjusted her stance so she was more or less facing him and Le Rongeur at the same time, skillet held like a broadsword in front of her.

The move, and the sudden quiet, told Le Rongeur that something had changed. He took a step back, farther from the skillet's reach, and half-turned toward LeBoeuf. The man's face was bleeding from a single cut and one eye sported a massive bruise that was already tending toward purple. On seeing LeBoeuf his expression went through a wild array of contortions, one emotion tumbling over the next, and for the second time that day LeBoeuf nearly smiled.

"LeBoeuf!" Le Rongeur cried, having decided, apparently, to feign joy at seeing his partner. "You're alive! God be praised! I stood with you to fight the lanceros, you know that, but there were too many for us!"

LeBoeuf slowly approached Le Rongeur across the packed dirt floor. There were embers glowing in the hearth fire and piles of bedding and furs in three of the tent's four corners, a table and stools crudely built from jetsam scavenged from the beach. Two of the stools had been knocked over and the trenchers and cups and bottles generally left on the table had been swept to the ground.

"Prithee, how did you get away?" Le Rongeur asked. "Are you hurt?" He took a step back and kept the knife raised as LeBoeuf continued his silent approach.

"LeBoeuf, we're partners now, you know," he said, the confidence draining from his voice. "Matelotage…"

Now it was Henriette's turn to chime in. "Don't you touch him, LeBoeuf, you stupid ox!" she screamed. "I'm going to cut his throat, you leave him alone!"

LeBoeuf was three feet from his erstwhile partner and well within the arc of the skillet when, at the same instant, both Henriette and Le Rongeur attacked. From the corner of his eye LeBoeuf saw the skillet coming toward him, Henriette swinging it at an upward angle, backhand at his face, an awkward line of attack for her. LeBoeuf did not dare take his eyes from Le Rongeur, but happily he did not have to. With his left hand he grabbed the edge of the skillet as it closed with his face and using the force Henriette had put behind the blow, plucked the pan from her fingers.

Le Rongeur seemed to have decided that charm would not work on LeBoeuf, and the time had come for lethal force. He lunged with the long knife, putting all his arm and body into the move. Thin as he was, Le Rongeur was a strong man and there was considerable power and speed behind his thrust. The blade was just inches away when LeBoeuf got the skillet between its point and his chest. The blade rang as it struck the iron bottom and Le Rongeur's hand made a crunching sound, followed by his scream of pain a heartbeat later.

Henriette launched herself off the sailcloth and LeBoeuf was not sure at first who she was going for, but she fell on Le Rongeur with fingers crooked and nails brandished like talons. She managed to get one good swipe across Le Rongeur's face, opening up four fresh parallel bleeding gashes before LeBoeuf grabbed her by the arm and sent her sprawling back into the pile of canvas.

Le Rongeur was still screaming and dancing around, holding his right hand gingerly in his left when LeBoeuf took another step forward and grabbed him by the collar of his filthy shirt. Le Rongeur's eyes went wide as terror eclipsed the pain. He shook his head and gasped, "No! LeBoeuf, no!"

LeBoeuf turned and half-dragged Le Rongeur across the tent and out through the canvas door, into the fresh and powerful wind. He spun the man around and grabbed the back of his neck; with his left hand he reached down and grabbed the seat of Le Rongeur's breeches. With a grunt of effort he lifted Le Rongeur up over his head, then walked off toward the beach, where the wind was kicking up a considerable surf.

"LeBoeuf! LeBoeuf! What are you doing? Damn you, LeBoeuf!" Le Rongeur shouted up at the sky, kicking and punching, but in that position he was unable to land a fist or a foot. He twisted like a fish on a hook, but being held aloft by LeBoeuf was akin to being held in the branches of a massive tree, and for all his twisting and flailing he did not cause LeBoeuf's arms to falter in the least.

LeBoeuf continued on past a dozen tents, their occupants gathered to see what the screaming was about. He could see the amused looks on their faces but did not acknowledge them as he marched on. He reached the edge of the water and kept on going. The seas were up to his calves at first, and then another wave rolled in and soaked him to the waist, but he did not hesitate in his advance. The sea pulled back and he marched on and then the next wave came in and wetted LeBoeuf to the middle of his chest.

Le Rongeur was still screaming, but the pitch was higher, the note of panic more clear and true. "LeBoeuf! No! Son of a bitch, LeBoeuf, I can't swim, you know that! No! Son of a bitch!"

LeBoeuf stopped as the next wave came in and washed over him, half-way up his chest. Then as the water drew back he cocked his arms and flung Le Rongeur as far out to sea as he was able, which was fairly far, though not nearly as far as he would have liked. Le Rongeur hit the water in a great spray of expletives and flailing limbs, and then the water closed over him and only his hands were visible above the surface.

For a moment LeBoeuf just stood there and enjoyed the rush of sensations. The water was warm and clean and he could feel it soaking away the dried blood and the sweat and the grime that a week of hunting had layered on. The wind was blowing hard, but it too was warm, and like the salt water it seemed cleansing and pure, sweeping the putrefaction away.

Then Le Rongeur was up again, flailing, beating at the surface. He tried to scream but got a mouthful of salt water for his efforts. He made a coughing sound, eyes bulging, arms reaching out to LeBoeuf, and then he went down again.

Once more LeBoeuf paused to savor the moment. He pulled the fresh air deep into his lungs, he let the warm water surge over him. The cresting waves made him stagger, but he braced against them and took pleasure in the way they seemed to wash him clean. He was in need of being washed clean.

Le Rongeur came up a second time, still beating at the water as if it was on fire and he was trying to put out the flames. He was near exhaustion now. He had swallowed quite a bit of water, and his movements were slower and more awkward. He was going down for the third time when he twisted in an odd way and suddenly stopped slapping at the water, stopped his terror-driven frenzy, and LeBoeuf guessed he had discovered that the water was shallow enough for him to stand.

Reluctantly LeBoeuf turned and headed back to shore. Behind him, between ugly fits of coughing, Le Rongeur hurled guttural curses at his back. LeBoeuf would have like to stay there in the surf, with the warm water and the strong tropical wind washing over him; he would have liked to remain there as the coming storm rolled down on him, to plant himself with outstretched arms and meet the hurricano in a contest of strength.

He knew who would win, of course. There were certain things even he could not fight. But he would have liked to see how much he could endure before the hurricano crushed him at last.

But he didn't, and he cursed himself, just as he had cursed himself for not standing fast when the lancero was riding down on him.

Henriette... he thought. God alone knew what would become of her if he allowed himself to be killed. He wondered if that was really why he seemed so oddly determined to preserve his own life. He somehow did not think so.

The waves smacked the back of his legs, as if trying to knock him down, as he made his way to shore. Henriette was standing at the edge of the surf, arms folded, her smock and kercher straightened out. She was unarmed as far as LeBoeuf could tell, though he suspected she had a knife in the waistband of her petticoat, tucked in the small of her back.

"He's still alive," she said, scowling, nodding out toward where Le Rongeur was waving his arms and shouting obscenities at LeBoeuf.

"Seems so," LeBoeuf said.

"Aren't you going to drown him? Hold his head under the water like the rabid cur he is? Isn't it the least he deserves?"

"Probably," LeBoeuf said.

Henriette frowned. "Probably you'll drown him, or probably he deserves it?"

"Both," LeBoeuf said as he brushed past her and headed for the tent. The wind felt cool now on his soaked clothing, but the sensation was not unpleasant. It was good, in fact.

"If you don't kill that little bastard, I will!" Henriette yelled at his back.

"Whatever you wish," LeBoeuf said without turning. He wondered if she meant to drive the knife right between his shoulder blades. He did not think so.

When he reached the door of the tent he stopped at last and looked back. Henriette had followed him from the beach, her face still set in its scowl. He had not heard her footfalls in the sand over the low rumble of the wind, the cacophony of flogging canvas and shaking palm fronds. She stopped beside him and she looked as if she wanted to speak but for once had nothing to say.

"This storm that's coming, we call this a hurricano," LeBoeuf said. "Very bad. If you have anything you want in there — ," he nodded toward the canvas door of the tent —, "get it now. There won't be a damned thing left when this is over."

Henriette frowned again as if she did not understand, but LeBoeuf figured that was all the explanation she needed, certainly all that he intended to give, so he turned and ducked through the door. Inside he straightened, the canvas roof just brushing the top of his head, then crossed the dimly lit space, nearly tripping on the skillet that was still lying on the ground.

He had no need to gather his belongings. He had very little that he wanted to keep, and what he needed he had already packed, because he saw to it that he was always prepared to make a hasty exit. From behind his bedding, half-hidden underneath, he pulled out a canvas haversack. He unbuckled the straps and angled the opening of the sack toward the muted light coming in through the door. He was just able to make out its contents: a shirt and breeches, a knife, a small pistol with powder and balls, shoes, some cordage, a bottle of brandy.

He reached deep into the bag until his fingers fell on the hidden compartment sewn into the bottom. He could feel the gold coins in there, two dozen eight reale pieces with the crest of Philip the Third of Spain stamped into one side. LeBoeuf did not have time to count the coins, but he imagined they were all there. If Le Rongeur had rifled the bag he would not have thought to leave any behind to cover his tracks.

He set the haversack aside and reached behind his bedding once again and withdrew a sword, wrapped in a sleeve of oiled canvas and bound with marline. This sword, he had told Le Rongeur, had been taken from the corpse of a Spanish naval officer. He assured Le Rongeur, with profound sincerity, that if it ever went missing, he, Le Rongeur, would die an immediate and notably unpleasant death, even before any inquiries had been made. LeBoeuf was therefore not surprised to find that the sword was still there.

"What's that?" Henriette asked. Under the thick blanket of noise from the approaching hurricano LeBoeuf had not heard her come in. He found it slightly unnerving how she could just appear like that under cover of the wind.

"Sword," LeBoeuf said as he draped the strap of his haversack over his shoulder. Henriette was looking around the interior of the tent as if searching for something. She still looked angry, as she usually did, but confused as well. And worried.

"This…hurricano…" she began.

"Get what you need," LeBoeuf said. "Only what you can carry. Easily carry."

Henriette hesitated a second more, and then began to move. She grabbed up an old bread bag and began to stuff her few bits of clothing into it: a second smock, petticoats, a cape. She stuffed in a small wooden box, containing what, LeBoeuf did not know. She looked around again, as if searching for whatever else she should take, but LeBoeuf knew she had nothing else beyond that pathetic collection. Defiantly, she picked up the skillet and shoved that in the bread bag too and said, "Very well, I'm ready."

LeBoeuf nodded. Haversack over his shoulder, sword in hand, he ducked out of the tent once more.

Big Dog was standing there, Other Dog beside him and the rest of the pack gathered behind. "Come on," he said and the dogs fell in step with him as he marched across the camp, Henriette taking up the rear.

The five men were still at the boucan when LeBoeuf arrived, but they had put the fire out and seemed to be in discussion as to what they should do next.

"LeBoeuf," Van Loudersong said as they approached. "This storm…"

"It's a hurricano," LeBoeuf said, retrieving his musket and cartridge box. "Most likely it'll kill us all. That cave, Van Loudersong, where you hide your things, we must go there."

Van Loudersong's mouth opened but no words came out. That was not like the man, but he could not hide his surprise. The Dutchman had been certain that no one, most especially the dim-witted LeBoeuf, knew about the cave. Or so LeBoeuf imagined.

In truth, LeBoeuf was an observant fellow and knew a good deal about Van Loudersong, and had guessed at considerably more. He felt sure that Van Loudersong was the most clever of all the boucaniers, a man who knew how to care for his own interests, to look out for himself. But not like Le Rongeur. Van Loudersong was not the type to stab everyone else in the back. And anyone he did stab in the back likely would not see it coming.

"There's room for all of us there in the cave, yes? Everyone in the camp?" LeBoeuf asked, though he already knew the answer. As for the others, this was the first they had heard of Van Loudersong's cave, and they were staring at the man with odd expressions of wonder and suspicion.

"Yes, yes," the Dutchman said, still recovering from the surprise of finding his secret was no secret to LeBoeuf.

"Good. Me and Henriette, we'll join you there," LeBoeuf said, not waiting for an invitation. "The rest of you," he said to the others, "Grab what you can grab immediately…your muskets, food, brandy or rumbullian, whatever, and gather here. Tell the others. And be quick."

As LeBoeuf finished speaking a gust of wind like a rogue wave slammed into them, making those standing stagger on their feet. It lifted the wooden rack off the boucan, tore it clean off the posts and sent it whirling away down wind, as if God himself was suggesting that there was little time to waste.

Chapter Five

Don Alonso could still hear the shouts of the sailors and the boatswain and Ignacio, even over the groaning of the ship and the increasingly furious sound of the wind. He was clinging tightly to the ladder that led below, his head just at the level of the deck. The ship rolled off to larboard and Alonso waited, holding tight, timing his next move with the motion.

He thought of the sailors climbing up into the rigging to do something, he did not know what, with the blown-out sail. Here he was, clinging to a ladder and barely able to hang on, and they were making their way sixty feet up the foremast. He could scarcely imagine how they would manage, but then there were many things that the lower sort did that Don Alonso could scarcely imagine, and he wasted little time in trying.

Nostra Sennora de Regla continued her roll to larboard, and just as Alonso was thinking she would never recover, that she would just remain there on her beam ends, the ship began her slow roll back. He braced as his world shifted again, then climbed down the last few rungs to the deck below. That part of the lower deck was lit by a single lantern which was swinging wildly and casting shadows like mad whirling spirits around the cabin fronts and the rows of big guns lashed along the sides of the ship.

Alonso let go of the ladder and stepped carefully down the passageway to his own cabin aft. He was certain the ship was rolling harder now than it had been even a short while before, when he had first gone on deck. The sound of the hull working in the seaway was deeper and more labored, and the vessel shuddered more frequently as her bow slammed into the cresting waves.

Stout ship, well-built ship, Don Alonso thought. *Far from the first storm she's weathered.*

He took comfort from Master Ignacio. The man had been insufferably rude, and while in most situations that would have been intolerable, in this case it served to show the man's mettle. The master was not afraid of the power and authority that Don Alonso Menéndez de Aviles wielded. And if Don Alonso had to put his life in the hands of another man, he wanted him to be a man of courage.

The *Regla* took a sudden, unexpected roll, as if the ship had tripped over its own feet. Don Alonso was thrown across the open space and slammed hard against the cabin occupied by the minor government officials. He clenched his teeth against the pain. Through the thin wall he could hear men cursing and one, he thought, weeping. From farther aft, from his own cabin, came a sharp burst of shrieking: Francisca or Maria or Gabriella or, most likely, all three.

Alonso shook his head. He would have vastly preferred to remain on deck, but he felt duty-bound to comfort his wife for at least as long as he could bear it. He staggered on, pressing himself against the cabin fronts in an effort to remain upright. If the rolling grew much worse he knew he would have to crawl, and that was something he did not care to do.

He came at last to his own cabin and paused outside the door. The shrieking had stopped and he thought he could hear the muttered sound of prayers. He paused for a moment, getting his footing, letting the ship roll, then grabbed onto the latch of the door and pushed it open.

Don Alonso was not prepared for the tableau of anguish and misery that greeted him inside. The four of them, the three women and Father Pedro in his brown robe, seemed little more than moving shadows in the light of the whirling lantern. At the sound of the door opening their four ghost-white faces turned to look, eyes and mouths wide. The light from the lantern glistened off vomit that ran down the front of their clothes and across the deck. The stench filled the small space and made Alonso gag.

They were on their knees, pushed up into one corner of the cabin, wedged against the bed built into the side of the ship. They were each gripping the frame of the bed with one hand to keep from being flung across the cabin, and in their other hands they held their rosaries which were swinging wildly.

"Oh, husband," Francisca cried, her voice hoarse and weak from the fear and the vomiting. With her free hand she made the Sign of the Cross. "Praise to God and the Virgin Mary that you're here...come and join us. We make our last plea for God's mercy..."

"Praise God," Alonso said, speaking loud to be heard over the terrible noise that filled the storm-battered ship. He clung to the doorframe with his right hand and used his left to make the Sign of the Cross.

"What news, Don Alonso?" Father Pedro said, his voice stronger than Francisca's, but not by much. "Do we sink or break apart? Is the ship lost?"

"No, no, never fear," Don Alonso said. "Stout ship, well-built ship. And the master has things well in hand!" In his mind he heard the crack of the topsail blowing out, saw the shredded canvas flogging away downwind.

The ship rolled hard again and the women gasped and held tighter to the bed, and wrapping their free arms around one another. Don Alonso held tight to the doorframe with both hands, hugging it like a lover as the vessel made its ponderous dip. He waited until it began to right itself again, then leapt from the door frame to the chair lashed to the deck. Standing or sitting was out of the question, so he knelt beside the chair and put his arms around it.

"What will the good master do?" Gabriella cried. "How can he save the ship in such a storm?" Her voice was strong, stronger than Father Pedro's. She was kneeling in the vomit that was running across the deck, but Alonso could see that she had none down the front of her gown.

"The ship will save us!" Alonso shouted back. "Stout ship! The master will take in the sails and the ship will just float like a duck, just float up and down on the waves! It seems like she's in great danger, but in truth she'll just ride the seas! Like a duck!"

As with most things nautical, Alonso had no notion if that was true or not, but he said it with surety, and Francisca and the others would not think to question him. They nodded, but they did not look terribly comforted. Maria's head just lolled with the rolling of the ship. She seemed too spent to even hear or understand the words.

"We must keep to our prayers!" Father Pedro called. "The Lord alone will save us now! Please, Don Alonso, join with us! Your prayers are powerful, I know!"

Don Alonso nodded, though he was not so certain about the worth of his prayers. Francisca and Father Pedro might be blind to his impiety, but he doubted that God was. Confession and absolution on his deathbed, that had always been his plan for attaining Heaven.

He wondered if he should take that precaution now. Father Pedro would certainly be willing to hear his confession. But if his final reconciliation was to serve any purpose it would have to be genuine and comprehensive. Doing it now meant doing it in front of his wife, and if he spoke loud enough for Father Pedro to hear then the rest would hear as well. That was not a risk worth taking. There was always a chance that they would live through this, and then what?

He wrapped his arms around the back of the chair and clasped his fingers together and closed his eyes, assuming the appearance of one who was deep in prayer. He thought about how he might condense his many sins into a few short sentences that he could shout out to Father Pedro as the ship was breaking up and all hope lost. It would not be easy, but he thought he could manage.

The ship dipped hard to larboard and Alonso felt the warm vomit soaking through the knees of his stockings and breeches and he felt his own stomach twist. Then the ship rolled back, swinging them all through a sickening arc as it went starboard side down. Alonso clutched the chair tighter and hoped that the lashing would hold.

Someone started gagging and Alonso opened his eyes. Francisca was bent over, mouth wide, coughing and hacking and trying to vomit but there was nothing left in her guts to throw up. Alonso closed his eyes again.

I cannot bear much more of this...

He tried to form coherent thought but his mind seemed to be twisting and rolling and pitching as wildly as *Nostra Sennora de Regla*. The sounds of the retching and the smell of vomit threatened to make Don Alonso vomit as well, something he had never done before despite having spent considerable time at sea.

But worse than his growing revulsion was finding himself down below in a cabin with the women and a priest while things of great importance were happening topside. Men were engaged in a struggle for life itself — for Don Alonso and Francisca's lives — while he was on his knees, hugging a chair. Don Alonso Menéndez de Aviles had fought in Spain's bloody wars. He was many things, but he was not a coward, nor was he a man to step aside when the real work needed doing.

"I must go," he announced before his whirling thoughts had even coalesced into an actual decision. He stood as best he could, still gripping the chair which groaned and flexed and threatened to break into its component parts.

The others looked up at him, save for Maria, who might have fainted or died for all Don Alonso could tell. Francisca looked at him, wide-eyed, the unspoken question on her face: *Why must you go?*

"Forgive me, my sweet," he said, nearly shouting to be heard over the storm. "Every man must be on deck now, to help where he can! A man of my station cannot shirk such duty!"

He did not wait for an answer, nor did he think one was coming. He turned and lunged for the door. The ship rolled under him and threw him forward. He hit the doorframe with terrific force and hung on tight. He felt blood running down his cheek.

He paused again. He was growing accustomed to the rhythm: holding firm, waiting, moving in the brief moment that the ship was more or less upright. He went through the sequence again, letting go of the doorframe and staggering down the passageway, careening off the cabin doors larboard and starboard. Water was spewing from the deck planks overhead and coming in torrents down the few open scuttles. It ran inches deep along the lower deck, crashing in miniature surf against the cabin fronts and the various things stowed and lashed in place.

Don Alonso felt the ship dipping under him. He ran with a staggering gate the last few feet and managed to grab the quarterdeck ladder seconds before he would have been flung aside like a doll in the hands of an angry child. He held tight as the ship laid down on her side, as if maliciously trying to wrench him free.

With each wave it seemed less likely to Don Alonso that the *Regla* would right herself. But once again she began her labored, ponderous recovery and Alonso raced the few rungs up the ladder to the quarterdeck above.

He was not prepared for what he found topside. The wind slammed into him with breathtaking force and sent him reeling. The seas that swept over the deck were a foot, two feet deep as they piled up around his legs. The air was filled with driving rain and spray from the seas crashing over the weather rail. He sucked in water with every breath and gagged with each briny mouthful.

Alonso was just able to grab the rail around the scuttle to keep from being washed across the deck and into the bulwark to leeward. Or over the side. He knew that the sun was not due to set for several hours yet, but still it was nearly as dark as full night, and what light there was seemed to have a strange greenish-gray tint.

For a moment he just clung to the rail, braced against the wind and the rolling of the ship and the surging water on the deck, just trying to make sense of this insane world. Five rungs up a ladder from the lower deck and it seemed as if he had traveled to a new world, to some mythological place where land and sea were all churned together. The close, fetid atmosphere of the cabin was blown away by shrieking wind, the warm vomit that had run free across the cabin's deck supplanted by a pounding surf, pouring over the high side of the ship and cascading around the quarterdeck.

Don Alonso looked around as the shock and disorientation subsided. Master Ignacio was still where he had been when Alonso left, halfway across the deck on the windward side, pressed against the bulwark, one hand on the mizzen shrouds. But Alonso could see he had passed a rope around his waist and tied himself off to the rail. His hat was gone and his gray beard and long gray hair, soaked through, looked black in the failing light. His eyes were everywhere, up aloft, looking down the length of the deck, looking out to sea, but his face showed no expression at all that Alonso could make out.

He looked aloft. There were no sails at all set, but the wind on the bare spars alone seemed to be driving the ship. The upper part of the mainmast — what the sailors called the topmast, Alonso believed — had been lowered down and lashed against the lower mast. The fore topmast had snapped near its base and hung like a broken wing against the lower rigging, tendrils of the blown-out sail still whipping around like ragged banners. Incredibly, there were sailors up there, struggling it seemed to lash the broken spar in place before it did any more damage.

Don Alonso shook his head in wonder. He considered himself a man of courage, but he was not sure he could ever gather enough courage to climb up there on such a night.

He remained where he was, clinging to the rail, because there was nothing else for him to do. His desire to help was sincere, even if it had more to do with self-preservation than anything- but he did not know how to help, and in those conditions he certainly could not ask.

Forward, a gang of five mariners stood in a rough line, hauling away on a rope, stumbling and heaving, mouths open, shouting words that were whisked away by the wind.

There... Don Alonso thought. He did not know why they were hauling the rope, but it seemed important, and they seemed to be struggling, and it was certainly a place where he could lend a hand.

He waited as the ship came upright and began its roll to larboard and he used the momentum of the roll to make his way to that side. He stumbled and fell to his hands and knees, the water piling up around him, the wind tearing at his hair and clothing, but he pushed himself up and stumbled on, the most difficult twenty feet he had ever walked.

The tail end of the rope was swirling around in the foot-deep water on the deck and Alonso fished it out and wrapped his fingers around it. Ahead of him the mariner who had, a minute before, been the last in line turned and looked at him. He had a dark slash of a moustache and a short beard and a face the color of the oiled wood of the ship's rails. He looked at Don Alonso with a curious expression, gave a quick nod of approval, and turned to face forward again.

Alonso took up the slack and the men forward gave a shout and jerked on the line and Alonso jerked it as well. He could feel the rough, wet rope abrading his skin, but he could not tell if their hauling had moved whatever they were trying to move. Then the men shouted and hauled the rope again, and Alonso hauled with them once more.

For some time they remained there, stumbling, holding onto the rail as the seas came over the side and tried to sweep them away, hauling the thick rope in the quick moments they were able to haul. The sky was completely black now, any vestige of daylight gone. The wind was screaming in a way that was simply terrifying and the ship was laboring harder as it rose and plunged in the massive seas. The waves rolled in out of the dark, unseen until they were pushing *Regla* down on her beam ends and breaking like surf over the weather rail, rushing in torrents now several feet deep down the length of the deck.

Whatever the sailors had been trying to do in hauling the rope they apparently accomplished it, or gave up, because suddenly all the men forward of Don Alonso dropped the rope to the deck and staggered off in various directions. Alonso dropped the rope as well and lunged for the bulwark.

He grabbed onto the top of the rail as another boarding sea came crashing over the side, a massive breaking wave, far bigger than any they had yet felt. The water covered Alonso completely, pummeling him, trying to tear his hands free of the rail and send him whirling away across the deck. He squeezed the thick oak plank, his hands aching with the effort. He felt his feet come off the deck as the ship heeled far over and the seas lifted him up. He caught a mouthful of water, and he spit and coughed and felt his grip on the bulwark begin to slip.

Then *Regla* rolled back again and the water drained off and Alonso's feet came down on the deck. He spit and breathed as deeply as he could in that admixture of air and spray. He turned and looked aft, wondering what Master Ignacio might do now, what sailor's trick he might employ to save the ship on such a night. But it was dark, and Don Alonso's eyes were filled with water, and he could not see the master in his usual place, standing like a tree by the bulwark, hand on the shroud: a comforting, stolid presence.

Alonso frowned. He blinked and wiped his eyes. He looked again and he saw the rope that had been tied around Master Ignacio's waist whipping in the wind, the frayed end of the broken cord just visible. He looked around the quarterdeck but the master was nowhere to be seen.

He didn't go overboard...I've no reason to think he went overboard, Alonso thought, but he did not believe for a minute that that was true. And for the first time since they had set sail many weeks before, Don Alonso was afraid.

Chapter Six

They reached Van Loudersong's cave just as the real fury of the storm rolled down on them.

About forty of the boucaniers had heeded LeBoeuf's warning. They assembled with their women — those who had women — and their few things worth saving: muskets, powder and knives foremost.

Le Rongeur was among them, with his haversack and musket. He kept as far from LeBoeuf as he could, kept a minimum of three people between them. He could not know if LeBoeuf intended to kill him or not, because LeBoeuf himself had not decided. Nor had he put much thought into it. If he did kill Le Rongeur then he would do it on impulse.

As LeBoeuf watched the boucaniers assemble he thought, *I'm not sure that damned cave is big enough.* He had counted on at least half the men being too drunk or too stupid to listen to him, but it seemed most had decided to come along.

Nothing for it, I suppose.

He looked down at Big Dog who was sitting on his haunches at LeBoeuf's feet. He meant to take the dogs with him, or at least Big Dog and Other Dog. But if he did that, the other hunters would want to take their dogs as well, and the cave was certainly not big enough for all those creatures. He knelt down so he and Big Dog were face to face.

"Now, see here, Big Dog," he said. "There's a bad storm coming. You know it as well as I do. So you go off into the jungle now, where I got you. Take the others. We'll meet back here when it's over."

He stood again. Big Dog did not move. "You're a dumb cur," LeBoeuf said, and then there was nothing more to say on that subject.

He turned to Van Loudersong. He jerked his head in the direction of the trail that led off into the jungle. "We better go," he said.

"Of course," Van Loudersong said. "Do you care to lead the way?"

"Me?" LeBoeuf said. "I don't know where your cave is."

"Indeed? You seem to know everything else about it."

LeBoeuf shrugged, which was as much clarification as he was wont to give.

Van Loudersong looked around with a sour expression, still not at all pleased by this development. The Dutchman, LeBoeuf knew, would spend all of their time in the cave keeping a watchful eye over the goods and specie he had hidden there. Then when the storm was passed he would have to find another hiding spot and move it all in secret.

LeBoeuf liked Van Loudersong, after a fashion, though he did not particularly trust him and he did not care in the least about the man's troubles. Nor did he think Van Loudersong had much to fear from his fellow boucaniers. Le Rongeur would certainly steal anything he could, as would a few of the others, but mostly they would leave the Dutchman's hoard alone. Honor among thieves and all that.

Van Loudersong rested his musket on his shoulder and led the ragged line of beach dwellers into the forest. The wind had picked up noticeably by then. The palms that lined the shore were whipping and bending madly, and it seemed impossible that they had not already snapped like twigs. Any loose bit of canvas was beating and flailing in the mounting gale, and one tent had already been torn from its framework and blown across the camp.

LeBoeuf could hear the faintest sound of singing coming from one of the tents, the boucaniers drinking and mocking the approach of death. He heard the barking of dogs, creatures not as sanguine as their owners about facing the hurricano on open ground.

The rain came next: big drops at first, and just a few, not falling from the sky but rather carried on the wind so they struck almost horizontally. LeBoeuf felt them first on his hands and on his neck, the only skin not covered in linen or canvas or hair. But soon the rain began to build in force and volume, striking them from behind, soaking them as quickly as if they had fallen into the sea, and turning the firm earth soft underfoot.

LeBoeuf did not mind. It was a warm rain and he was already wet and the fresh water would rinse the salt from his clothes.

Soon they got into the trees and the wind and the rain were not so bad, though the upper branches were whipping around and the forest was filled with a whooshing sound that rose to a full-throated roar in the bigger gusts. But there they could walk without being knocked sideways or having to lean into the gale to keep from tumbling to leeward.

LeBoeuf was following right behind Van Loudersong and keeping an eye on the treetops as they walked. He could almost see the force of the wind increasing as the trees bent farther and farther over. He could hear audible snapping all around them as limbs were torn from trunks and dropped down through the branches of other trees.

He knew they had about another mile to go before they reached the cave. He figured it might be a near thing. He wondered how deep the roots of those trees ran, if they could stand up to the hurricano or if they would start dropping around them.

The answer came soon after, and it came crashing down in a most dramatic fashion. They were stumbling in the wind and nearly blinded by the rain, crossing over a high spot that was more exposed than the path through the jungle. They were moving through a stand of pines that swayed with ominous and exaggerated motion, bending over and then flinging themselves upright again. They reminded LeBoeuf of the trebuchets of an earlier age.

He thought the great cracking sound was thunder at first, which surprised him because he knew thunder and lightning did not usually come with hurricanos. Then a tree just ahead of them and off to the right began to lean over, farther and farther, moving faster as it fell, tearing up the branches of the neighboring trees and crashing to the ground. It looked for all the world to LeBoeuf like a ship's mast coming down in the fury of a sea battle.

The tree hit the ground forty feet ahead of them, dropping right onto the path. It bounced a little then came to rest on a bed of the wreckage it had taken down with it. The boucaniers stopped short, staring with amazement, bracing for the next tree to drop, and then the next. Bracing for the one that would drop right on top of them.

A moment passed and no more trees came down, and it looked like none would, at least not immediately. LeBoeuf yelled, "Best move a bit quicker!"

"I agree," Van Loudersong said and he headed off at a fast march, his reluctance to lead these people to his cave now eclipsed by his desire to get there himself. He scrambled over the fallen pine and LeBoeuf followed, turning to help Henriette, who was right behind him.

Her arms were over the trunk and she was trying to get her leg up, but she was not a tall woman and she was having some difficulty. LeBoeuf leaned his musket against the trunk, reached out and grabbed her under the arms and lifted her up and over like he would a child, then set her down again. He could just see the curses and invectives forming on her lips, and before they broke like a wave he snatched up his musket, turned and hurried to catch up with Van Loudersong, who was waiting for no one.

They reached the cave soon after, unmolested by any other falling timber. It was situated in a rocky outcropping, a long wall of granite forming the base of a ridge that rose incongruously from the floor of the jungle. It looked like a dyke from Van Loudersong's native Low Country, the trees and vegetation above like the water threatening to crest over the top. Van Loudersong had placed a few saplings against the entrance, which did an effective job of hiding it. Now he tossed them aside to reveal the tall, narrow crack that was the mouth of the cave, so narrow that LeBoeuf knew he would have to turn sideways to get through.

The Dutchman went in first, but LeBoeuf, behind him, stepped aside to let the others go ahead. One by one they filed past, first Henriette and then Pierre le Chasseur and his woman and a small fellow named Levesque, and on and on. Le Rongeur was near the back of the line, clearly hoping LeBoeuf would go in ahead of him, but LeBoeuf had no intention of doing so. Rather he waited as Le Rongeur came closer, step by step, growing visibly more wary as he did.

Then at last it was just him and Le Rongeur, standing in the driving rain, looking one another in the eye. LeBoeuf wondered what Le Rongeur's move would be. Talk? Run? Pull a knife?

He did not wait long for the answer. With a rabbit-like burst Le Rongeur ducked and charged for the entrance to the cave and the relative safety of the crowd. He was quick and nimble and would have made it past LeBoeuf if LeBoeuf had not guessed he would do this and prepared to grab him low.

Le Rongeur's arm was straight out, reaching for the entrance to the cave as he ran. LeBoeuf snatched it and yanked it hard. Le Rongeur spun nearly all the way around and LeBoeuf could feel the arm twisting in an odd way. He wondered if he had pulled it clean out of joint, but Le Rongeur was not screaming in pain so he guessed not.

They were silent for a moment, Le Rongeur looking up at LeBoeuf with wide-eyed terror. LeBoeuf leaned close, until their faces were inches apart. He wondered if the impulse to kill Le Rongeur would strike him now. Le Rongeur clearly thought it would.

"Van Loudersong, he has things in there that are worth quite a lot," LeBoeuf said. "He has gold and silver, I think."

Le Rongeur nodded.

"When we leave here I will search every inch of you and your clothes and your haversack. If I find so much as a single real I'll spill your guts all over the ground. Do you hear me?"

Le Rongeur nodded.

"Do you believe me?" LeBoeuf asked.

Le Rongeur nodded again, more vigorously this time.

"Good," LeBoeuf said. He spun Le Rongeur around again and shoved him toward the cave. Le Rongeur bounced off the wet granite, recovered, then disappeared through the narrow open.

LeBoeuf followed behind. He turned sideways and pushed himself through the gap, despite his discomfort at doing so. There was sweat on his forehead mingling with the rainwater.

The light from the narrow crack in the granite reached a few feet into the space, and two paces beyond that the cave was completely dark, as if the light had been sucked right out of it. The extraordinary roaring of the wind and the pelting of the rain sounded muted and far off. He could hear muttered conversation from deeper inside, people talking even if they could not see one another.

"Van Loudersong, what say we build a fire?" LeBoeuf called out.

"No chance of that, I've nothing dry," Van Loudersong's voice came out of the dark. LeBoeuf did not reply. Instead he reached into his haversack and felt around until his hand fell on a leather tinderbox he kept there. He pulled it out and fumbled with the buckles and opened the top. He found some lint and his flint and striker and a few bits of dried twigs. He knelt down and put the lint on the ground and with practiced strokes, working blind, he struck the flint with the steel and watched as the sparks dropped onto the flammable stuff.

No reason for us to wait here in the dark, he thought to himself. *Son of a bitch Dutchman thinks if no one can see then no one can rob him.*

But that was not entirely the reason LeBoeuf wanted to make a fire, not the reason his palms were sweating or why he could feel slight tremors running through his arms and legs. He was a big man and he did not like tight, confined spaces. He did not like them at all. Add complete darkness to the mix and LeBoeuf was less happy still.

The click click of steel on flint was the only thing LeBoeuf could hear above the terrible rumble of wind outside, and the only thing he could see were the bright orange sparks falling onto the tuft of lint. Then one spark landed and caught. The lint around the bright ember turned black and a small thread of smoke rose up from that spot. LeBoeuf blew gently and the spark turned to flame and LeBoeuf added a few of the dry twigs to it.

The firelight was not strong but it was enough to see a dozen feet or so in any direction. LeBoeuf felt the tension ease a bit. He held the sticks in his hand and stood and walked a bit farther in. The cave was just a few feet wide near its entrance, but it opened up as it went deeper into the ridge until it stretched nearly ten feet across. The men and women lined either side and they pushed back to make room for LeBoeuf as he passed.

"Here, Van Loudersong, here's some wood. Methinks it's dry enough!" he called. He was standing over a small pile of branches and cordwood split thin. "I'll make a fire, yes?"

"Yes, yes, fine," Van Loudersong called back. He was deep in the cave, back where his bounty was hidden, LeBoeuf guessed, keeping careful watch in the pitch blackness.

A man named D'Anton, one of the pig hunters, a black man, an escaped slave or so they guessed — like most he was not too forthcoming about his past — was standing beside the pile of wood. On hearing Van Loudersong's agreement he knelt down and quickly assembled the dry sticks into a pyramid. LeBoeuf squatted down and touched the flame to the kindling D'Anton had spread around and a moment later a foot-tall fire was reaching up from the floor of the cave.

LeBoeuf stood and looked around. The light from the flames lit the people gathered there with an orange light and threw bold shadows against the sides of the cave. He could hear the muted roar of the wind, constant and threatening, a deluge of noise, as the hurricano tore up the land outside. The sound filled the cave like it was a physical thing, and even the granite walls seemed to tremble with the force of the storm.

There was nothing more to do, nothing more that could be done, and LeBoeuf was profoundly exhausted. He sat down on the floor of the cave which was covered in fine sand, and leaned his back against the granite wall. He sat close to the fire where the light was greatest, and told himself he was choosing that spot so he could add wood to the flames as needed.

The others in the cave began to settle in as well. Henriette pushed her way through the crowd and sat down next to LeBoeuf. It was not out of any fondness for him, LeBoeuf understood. Henriette despised him. He flattered himself, however, that she despised him a bit less than she despised the rest of the boucaniers.

She sought him out because she felt safe by his side. Or safer at least than she would otherwise. Like her hatred, it was a matter of degrees.

In the three weeks they had been together, the three weeks in which she had ostensibly been LeBoeuf's woman, LeBoeuf had not molested her in any way. He had hardly even spoken to her. Lifting her over the fallen tree was one of the few times he had touched her at all.

At the same time, LeBoeuf knew she had noticed the deference that the others gave him, due to his size if nothing else. What the boucaniers might lack in respect for his intelligence they made up for in fear of his strength. It was only when LeBoeuf was thought dead that the trouble started for Henriette.

The two of them sat in silence for some time, the quite talk of the others punctuating the storm's constant roar. LeBoeuf leaned over and put another stick on the fire and watched the flame climb up the dry wood.

Then, over the sound of the voices, the fury of the wind, came a thunderous crash. LeBoeuf felt the cave wall tremble, heard people gasp and cry out in surprise. Henriette was staring up at the cave roof, her eyes wide.

"What was that?" she said. She spoke quietly, as if afraid to disturb whatever god had made the granite shake.

"Tree falling, I reckon," LeBoeuf said. "Might have fallen right on top of us." For that matter it might have fallen across the entrance to the cave, trapping them all, but he did not say as much. "We're safe here," he added.

Soon the excitement died down and those in the cave returned to doing what they were doing before, which was waiting, because there was nothing else to do. LeBoeuf closed his eyes and leaned his head back.

"LeBoeuf?"

He opened his eyes again. "Yes?"

Henriette was leaning a little closer to him, as if she wanted to talk. He suspected that she did not wish to be left alone with her thoughts. He understood that impulse.

"What..." she began, then paused, then began again. "How did you end up here?"

"I walked. From the camp. You were right behind me, remember?"

"No, stupid," she said. "Here. This place. What is this wretched place?"

"Hispaniola. The northwest coast of Hispaniola. About fifty leagues from Santo Domingo."

"Yes, Hispaniola. How did you end up here, hunting pigs?"

LeBoeuf shrugged. He wondered if she expected a real answer. Probably not. She was just talking.

"I've done a lot of things," he said. "Sailor, fisherman. I did some farming for a while. Gunner on a privateer. Drifted around, ended up here. Seemed as good a place as any."

Henriette nodded. It was a vague answer, devoid of any real information, but she seemed satisfied enough. That was good. He liked that. He waited for her to demand he be more specific, but she did not, and he liked that, too.

"What's your full name?" she asked instead.

"LeBoeuf," he said.

"Your mother did not call you LeBoeuf," she said.

He looked into her eyes and she looked into his and her eyes were steady and probing. Bluish-gray. He debated whether or not to answer, and if so, what answer to give.

"Jean-Baptiste," he said at last.

"Jean-Baptiste..." She seemed give the name a try.

"And you?" he asked. He saw her expression shift, like a fighter putting up his fists.

"Me what?"

"What's your full name?" He knew her only as Henriette.

She seemed to consider how to answer, just as he had done. "Henriette de Labonté," she said at last.

LeBoeuf nodded. It seemed odd, these questions, given that they had been living together for weeks now.

"Henriette de Labonté..." he said. It was quite the name for a woman such as her. "And how did you end up here?"

He saw the anger flare up, the eyebrows come together, the lips press tight. "You know how I ended up here, on this dung heap of an island."

She was right, of course. He did know. The latter half of the story, anyway. But they had time, and he was curious to hear the rest of the tale that Henriette de Labonté would tell. He doubted it would be any truer than what he had told her, but it would pass the time.

Chapter Seven

Hand over hand, Don Alonso made his way along the bulwark aft, still looking for the master, still unable to see him and more and more certain he would never see him again. He reached the mizzen shrouds and threaded an arm around the thick, tarred rope, and, with one hand on the bulwark, held himself in place. He was alone. Master Ignacio was gone.

The waves were breaking over the side almost continuously now, a constant deluge threatening to send Don Alonso off in the wake of the master, so he turned his back to the seas and held tight. He was a young man, strong and fit, and he knew he could stand up to the pounding, but he did not know for how long.

Back to the cabin, go back to the cabin, Alonso thought, and dismissed the idea immediately. It would be far worse to be trapped below in that nightmare space, blind to what was happening on deck. Nor did he relish the thought of trying to get across the open deck and down below. Better to be topside, even with the seas breaking over them. Better to stay where he was, clinging to the shroud, shouldering the seas and waiting for what would happen next.

And for some time that was just what he did, huddling in what shelter he could find behind the bulwark, measuring the passing minutes in the huge seas that broke with terrifying regularity over the side. He could feel his arms growing weaker, his grip becoming less sure. He was numb to the soaking, numb to the howling of the wind and the rolling of the ship.

It's worse, it's getting worse, he thought. *Regla* was rolling more heavily, recovering more slowly, a warrior worn down by battle. He imagined that much of the water running over her deck was finding its way down below, that her hold was filling and the ship was settling lower and lower.

The stern lifted again, the masts began their wild dip toward the black seas, and the water came roaring over the side, but Alonso held fast. The deck canted at its steep angle and Alonso's shoes began to slip on the wet wood until he was half standing, half hanging from the bulwark and the shrouds. He pressed his lips together and willed himself to hold on and waited for the ship to begin her slow recovery. But there was no recovery this time. *Nostra Sennora de Regla* was on her beam ends.

Alonso's foot slipped out from under him and he kicked at the deck, trying desperately to get traction, but the hard leather soles of his shoes could find no grip. His hold on the shroud began to falter and he could feel the panic rising. He kicked his shoes off and found that his wet stockings were less apt to slip as he pressed his feet hard against the deck.

Come back, come back... he urged the ship, but rather than starting the slow roll upright *Regla* remained where she was at that terrible angle, her deck nearly vertical, the seas pounding against her hull and crashing over her like surf at the foot of a cliff.

He could see a handful of sailors scrambling desperately around, working their way along the deck on hands and knees, or pulling themselves up on fixtures which were normally horizontal. Four cannons were arranged along the quarterdeck bulwark, hanging from the lashings that held them in place, and Alonso's eyes fixed on one just ten feet in front of him. He could feel the grip of his stocking feet begin to slip.

There, there... he thought. If he could climb onto the gun's carriage he would have a solid perch and be in no danger of sliding down the deck. He began to work his way forward, hand over hand, bracing his feet against the deck as he moved. Five feet were separating him from the gun when he felt something shift deep in the *Regla*'s hull, down in the guts of the ship. The vessel shuddered and seemed to roll farther still and the ropes that held the cannon groaned.

Alonso moved another foot closer, and as he did two of the cannon's ropes parted with a cracking sound he could hear over the wind and the gun slewed sideways. Alonso pulled himself back as the muzzle swung past, nearly sweeping him away. One of the ringbolts to which the gun was tied tore free in a burst of splintered wood, and then the gun was gone, sliding and falling down the near-vertical deck. It slammed into one of the mariners clinging to a hatch and carried him away as it dropped. It struck the opposite gun on the starboard side with a clang like a broken church bell and then the two guns and the sailor crushed between them smashed through the bulwark and disappeared into the sea.

"God help me! Jesus, Mary, help us all!" Alonso cried, the most sincere prayer he had uttered in many years. He would have made the Sign of the Cross but he did not dare take one hand off the bulwark from which he was all but hanging.

He opened his mouth to begin an act of contrition when he saw a figure moving in front of him, a dark shadow of a man working his way along the deck, and he recognized the sailor with whom he had been hauling on the rope. The sailor stopped in the space where the cannon had been. He set a foot on a ringbolt in the deck and shouted to Alonso and gestured to something above his head. Alonso could see the man's lips moving, his eyes opened wide in controlled terror. He could not hear a word the man was saying and he had no idea what he meant, but he nodded his agreement anyway because he did not want this man to leave him.

When the sailor was done yelling he jerked his head up toward the bulwark, which was above them now, a gesture that suggested he wanted Alonso to follow. Then he reached up and grabbed one of the main shrouds and hoisted himself up, squeezing between the ropes until he was on the outboard side of the bulwark, standing above Alonso, gripping the shrouds to keep from being knocked off by the wind and seas.

Alonso nodded again and reached up and wrapped his fingers around the shroud, then hoisted himself up the way the sailor had. He squirmed between two of the shrouds, up and out, then he and the sailor were both kneeling on the near-horizontal side of the ship, gripping the shrouds, clinging on as if trying to ride a wild horse.

Safer here…that's it…safer standing here, Alonso thought. That must have been the man's intent. Rather than hanging from the underside of the bulwark they could kneel on top of it.

He felt a slap on his shoulder and he looked up. The sailor had an axe in his hand and he was offering it to Alonso and Alonso took it, though he had no idea why. Forward he saw three other men make their way through the shrouds until they, too, were kneeling on the ship's side. Then the sailor beside him drew another axe from his belt, raised it above his head and chopped down on the smaller rope that secured the shroud to the side of the ship.

Alonso watched in amazement. The man was cutting the line that held the shroud in place, and the shrouds in turn held the mainmast up, and cutting that line did not seem like a wise idea. But forward the other sailors had axes as well, and they too were hacking at the lines. Alonso imagined there was some good reason for doing so, a reason that was foreign to him but made sense to those who knew better. He adjusted his position, raised the axe, and swung the blade down on the black ropes that he could most easily reach.

The axe bit into the rope, but the sensation was more like chopping wood, so great was the strain that the cordage was under. Alonso could see the fibers parting under the edge of the blade and he struck at the same spot again and again.

Then suddenly the rope seemed to blow apart, bursting into its component fibers. Its cut ends whipped through the strange, three-holed blocks of wood the sailors called deadeyes, and the shroud fell free. The ship seemed to jerk under Alonso's feet and he could feel it shudder.

He looked up. Most of the shrouds had been cut away now and the great bulk of the mainmast was shifting, its support suddenly gone. It was leaning to one side and making a deep cracking sound that could be heard even over the wind as the ship starting to roll back up on its keel.

The mast seemed to hang there for an instant, as if trying to decide what to do, and then the huge wooden shaft splintered and cracked ten feet above the deck. The ship continued to roll upright as the whole assembly came down around it: masts, yards, top, topmast, all of it collapsing in a great shattered heap over the starboard side.

And then Alonso understood: cutting the mast away, relieving the ship of all that weight high up, had allowed it to come up off its beam ends and stand upright again.

As the ship righted itself Alonso and the other sailors climbed back aboard, holding tight to the bulwark. The seas swept over them and flooded the deck and then poured back over the sides as *Nostra Sennora de Regla* shook off the tons of water that had threatened to drown her. Alonso could feel the change in motion now that the mainmast was gone. The ship was rolling quicker, her motion more lively, more sickening, with all that top-hamper gone. But she was upright again, the way she was supposed to be, and Alonso felt a bit of hope creeping in where before there had been only despair and resignation.

Thanks be to God I did not give my confession to Father Pedro, he thought.

The deck was strewn with a great tangle of wreckage. The shattered end of the mainmast was laying just ten feet from where Alonso stood, and the rest of the mast had fallen over the quarterdeck and the waist of the ship. The main yard had come down on the ship's boats and crushed them like eggshells and the maintop had flattened the starboard bulwarks.

There was more to be done, apparently. The sailors moved cautiously toward the wreckage, cutting away the ropes that still held it to the ship, letting it slip foot by foot toward the sea. But Alonso did not join them. He had no idea what to cut and what not to cut, and with the ship back up the greatest danger seemed past, despite the way she was still wildly rolling.

Instead, Don Alonso crouched down behind the bulwark, seeking what shelter he could from the boarding seas. He found a bit of rope swirling around in the water and wrapped it around his waist and tied it off to the pinrail behind him. He hoped it would do him more good than it had Master Ignacio.

He remained where he was for quite a while, squatting behind the bulwark, letting sea after sea wash over him. Time itself seemed strange and alien in that nightmare of water and sound and motion. He watched as the remnants of the mainmast slipped away over the side until there was nothing left but ten feet of broken stump jutting up from the deck and a great, black void where he had become accustomed to seeing the thick trunk of the mast and its yards reaching far out over the sides of the ship.

As the sailors finished their work they hunkered down in what shelter they could find and Alonso guessed there was nothing more they could do. *Nostra Sennora de Regla,* for all her wild rolling, seemed to be enduring the seas. She did not seem to be sinking. The storm, certainly, could not last forever. If things remained as they were then they should be able to ride this out, wait for dawn, wait for the gale to dissipate, then see where they were, and where they had to go. Master Ignacio might be lost, but surely one of the other officers still lived. And if not, surely there were men among the sailors who could bring the ship safe into harbor.

That fellow with the moustache, he seemed capable enough, Alonso thought.

At some point Alonso fell asleep, or passed out, he did not know which. He just knew that he had been unconscious and then he was conscious again, still tied to the rail, still enduring the beating from the waves and the rolling of the ship that slammed him against the bulwark again and again. He looked around. Nothing had changed that he could tell. It was still black night and howling storm.

Where are we? he wondered.

The wind and seas had been driving them for hours, and driving them quickly, he had to imagine. He tried to picture a map of the West Indies, tried to recall where they had been the last time Master Ignacio informed him of their position, but he could not summon either memory.

We were not so far from Hispaniola, Alonso thought. *That was what the master said. How far?* He could not remember. But close enough that it would not take them long to reach Santo Domingo, even with the mainmast gone, once the storm blew itself out.

Alonso was wrapping himself in that comforting thought when he heard a cry from the far side of the ship, a loud and panicked cry that cut through the screaming wind. One word.

"Breakers!"

Breakers? Alonso thought. His mind did not seem to be working as it should. It was one word, a word he knew well, but he could not make sense of it, or recall why it was important.

And then the entire ship, which had been in constant motion for months, slammed to a sudden stop. A tremendous vibration rippled through the hull as if *Nostra Sennora de Regla* was shaking herself to pieces, and for just an instant the ship's motion ceased. He heard more cries, men shouting all around him. Then the ship lifted again, waterborne as she was meant to be, but only for the space of a few heartbeats, no more. She came down again on something solid and unyielding and once again every splinter of wood in her shook as if in a death rattle.

Don Alonso Menéndez de Aviles made the sign of the Cross. He could hear, thirty feet down, the deep groan of *Nostra Sennora de Regla's* keel breaking like a twig. The seas lifted her and slammed her down again and again, and the heavy-built ship of some five hundred tons burthen began coming apart.

Chapter Eight

It was no simple tale that young Henriette de Labonté told LeBoeuf, concerning how she came to be sitting there in a cave on Hispaniola, hiding from the fury of a hurricano. Beyond the mere facts of her life there were layers and layers of complexity spanning oceans and continents, geopolitical forces of which Henriette was not even aware and did not understand.

LeBoeuf understood them, or at least he understood more than she did, newcomer that she was to the Caribbean. He knew that the once incontestable power of Spain in the New World was now very much contested indeed. The French and the English and the Dutch, who for a century and more had been nibbling at the edges of the West Indies, were now helping themselves to bigger and bigger bites. And the boucaniers, unwittingly, quite ignorant of the great game of empire, were playing a role that was out of proportion to the actual threat they posed.

They were growing in numbers, these half-wild men: Frenchmen, Englishmen, Dutchmen, Africans. *Les boucaniers*. The freebooters. *Flibustiers*. The buccaneers. They were spreading over the north coast of Hispaniola, battling for possession of the nearby island of Tortuga. They were a wound in the side of Spain. A small wound, but one that was starting to fester, and one that Spain's enemies hoped would rot the empire from the inside out until it collapsed. And then they would sweep in and take what was left.

But for that to happen, the buccaneers had to prosper. They had to remain where they were, tormenting Spain, making the feeble giant expend its strength lashing out at them. There was no controlling those savage men, however, no enlisting their aid or making them care about or even understand the great struggle between nations. So the ministry in France had come up with another way to tame them and keep them content, one that had worked well since the Garden of Eden. It was brilliant, and it addressed two problems at once: the power of Spain and the whores of Paris.

Courtesans, tarts, *filles des joie, cocottes*. The streets of Paris teemed with such women, and the ministers could no more eradicate them than they could rid the city of rats. But they could round up as many as they were able and offer them a choice: the known hell of a Parisian prison or an unknown hell of life in the New World, wife to a buccaneer.

LeBoeuf had often wondered what the whores of Paris, or anyone in Paris for that matter, knew of the lives of the hunters on Hispaniola. Not much, he imagined. He did not think any of the whores would chose this over prison, not if they knew what it was truly like.

But they did not know. They did not know about the mosquitoes and the heat and the fever and the half-savage men they were bound to wed, men caked in dried blood and sweat and tallow, hard-drinking, violent men who largely disdained any mark of civilization. And because they did not know, some chose the New World and were bundled aboard ships with whatever pathetic possessions they had and were carried off to the western sea.

That was how the other women had arrived there, at least. It was a story that was none too complex. But Henriette, whore that she might be, was not like them, and her tale had to be considerably more involved. That had been clear to LeBoeuf on first sight.

It was three weeks to the day since the ship that brought her and the other women had dropped anchor in the roadstead just off the beach and the camp of the buccaneers. A boat was put over the side and in it went the ship's master and the boat's crew and a dozen women. The hunters gathered on the beach to see this, a novel and welcome sight. The master beckoned them around, explained how the women had come to be there, their convictions for prostitution, their choice to make a new life in the West Indies. He auctioned them off like slaves brought in from the Ivory Coast.

LeBoeuf guessed that the man was engaging in a little side business here. The women were not his to sell. They were no one's to sell. But the master had probably bought them from whoever had been paid to transport them to the West Indies in the first place. These ignorant women in this alien land, handed from merchant to merchant, likely had no understanding of what was taking place.

No matter... LeBoeuf thought at the time. They would end up wife to a buccaneer, and that was what they had signed on for back in some fetid prison in Paris. And they would make lives for themselves, if they did not soon die of fever. He knew these sorts of women. If there was one strength they had, it was the ability to accept their lot in life and to go on living.

It was curiosity alone that brought LeBoeuf to the beach: he had no intention of buying a wife. He stood back from the throng of men, arms folded, watching as they examined the wares. He intended to do no more than that. And then he saw her. Henriette. Henriette de Labonté, apparently.

She stood apart from the rest, but it was not just distance that separated them. The women huddled on the shore, exchanging ribald shouts with the buccaneers, were the sort of women LeBoeuf would expect to be taken from the streets of Paris: pocked and misshapen, hair like oakum, hands as raw and tough as any sailor's. The sort of women who, if offered the chance to be shipped to the New World and married to a buccaneer, would actually accept.

But not Henriette. She stood straight and proud and kept her mouth shut, a bit of a scowl on her lips. She wasn't beautiful, but she was something very close to it. Her hair was dark brown with hints of red that were visible in the brilliant Caribbean sun. Her skin was pale and smooth with no sign of the pox. She was thin but not scrawny. Nicely shaped. She had all her teeth, as far as LeBoeuf could see.

Like LeBoeuf, she was standing back away from the rest. Why, he did not know. He doubted she had the luxury of deciding for herself what she would or would not do. It was only later, thinking about it, that he guessed the master meant to keep her for himself, or to sell her to someone who could pay what she was worth. The bastard probably brought her to the beach because he did not dare leave her with the rest of the crew while he did his trading.

The other women did not seem particularly horrified by what they found on that wild coast: they were ready to endure, if not embrace, this next bit of their short lives. Henriette, however, looked as if she would submit to nothing, as if she would gladly die before she allowed herself to be broken. But for all her boldness, LeBoeuf could see the fear in her eyes.

I cannot let this happen, he thought. *I cannot let this beautiful thing be crushed.* And before he thought another thing he was pushing his way through the ring of men. One of the sailors held a long pike, ready to keep the buccaneers at bay, and he lowered it toward LeBoeuf's chest as he approached. The master stopped in the middle of his pitch and turned toward the big man.

"Her," LeBoeuf said, nodding at the girl. "I want her."

"Of course you do," the master said. "But she's not for you. We have your women here." He nodded toward the cluster of more willing brides.

"No," LeBoeuf said. "Her."

The master furrowed his brow and frowned but LeBoeuf could see the hint of doubt on his face. He was accustomed to having his word obeyed. He was accustomed to dealing with dull-witted, drunken men who respected the dozen armed sailors he had with him. He was not used to such a man as LeBoeuf talking back in a tone of calm authority.

"I said she ain't for the likes of you," the master said, and to reinforce the point the sailor jabbed LeBoeuf with his pike. The tip pierced cloth, pierced skin, might have drawn a trickle of blood, but that was as far as it went.

LeBoeuf grabbed the shaft of the pole arm just behind the head and yanked it up and out, jerking it halfway out of the surprised sailor's hands. The sailor was strong, with a powerful grip, and he clamped onto the wooden pole before LeBoeuf could pull it free, but that was fine. LeBoeuf drove the shaft back toward the sailor, striking him in the chest with the butt end and sending him sprawling to the sand. He turned to his left and slammed the dull end of the shaft into the next sailor coming for him, sending him down and gasping as well, then flipped the pike around and held the tip to the master's throat.

"How much?" LeBoeuf asked.

The master leaned back as far from the point of the pike as he could get. "Ten escudos," he said.

Greedy bastard, LeBoeuf thought, but he was impressed. Even with a dagger-sharp pike aimed at his throat the dog still had the *couilles* to ask such an absurd price.

"Very well," LeBoeuf said. He looked up at the girl, who was watching and scowling. She had her arms crossed over her chest. "Come with me," he said.

"Go to hell, you filthy beast," she said.

LeBoeuf nodded. He could see how this was going to go. He turned around. "Le Rongeur, Chasseur, go fetch her."

The two men pushed past the master and advanced on the girl, arms out. Le Rongeur was eager to obey because he feared LeBoeuf and because he wished to lay his hands on that lovely creature. Chasseur was willing because he found the whole thing terribly amusing. The girl backed away, shouting curses, flinging language so vile that LeBoeuf found he was impressed with her as well.

The two men grabbed her by the arms and half dragged her toward the camp. She kicked at them with her soft shoes. Her screaming and cursing did not falter in the least.

LeBoeuf led the way back to his tent and the two men pulled the girl after him. He ducked inside and found the ten escudos in a leather pouch with his other belongings. A steep price, but he could have paid much more than that and would have done so. He was pleased that the master had not guessed as much.

"Stay here," LeBoeuf said to Le Rongeur and Chasseur. "And don't touch her." LeBoeuf returned to the beach and paid the man, then headed back to the tent to relieve the guards.

He found them and the girl inside. The girl had pushed herself up against the pile of old sails as if she was trying to bury herself in them. Le

Rongeur and Chasseur were standing close, but not too close. Not within range of her feet or nails.

"Go," LeBoeuf said. The two men left without a word. LeBoeuf could see the disappointment on Le Rongeur's face: he doubtless expected that he would have a turn with the girl once LeBoeuf was done, and LeBoeuf knew he would have to disabuse him of such notions.

He looked at the girl and wondered if she had managed to get her hands on a knife. He thought it likely. She seemed the type who could do such a thing. Then, when he came to rape her, which she clearly expected him to do, she could plunge the knife into his back. Even if she then had to plunge it into her own heart at least she would have sent him to Hell ahead of her. He could give the Devil fair warning of her arrival.

But rape was not what LeBoeuf had in mind. Instead, he picked up his musket and a wooden box that held various tools and oils and spare parts. He sat down on a stool and began to clean his gun, which he had been using for target practice that morning, before the arrival of the ship. He could feel the girl's eyes burning into him. He could practically feel the air vibrating with tension.

He took a screwdriver from the box and loosened the screws that held the lock in place and pulled the mechanism free. He wiped down the barrel and the touchhole that were now exposed. He heard the girl shift a bit, heard her make a small clearing sound in her throat.

"What's your name?" LeBoeuf asked without looking up.

"Don't you worry about my name, you filthy pig," she spat back. LeBoeuf nodded. He picked up the lock and loosened the jaw screw and pulled the flint free. He had cleaned the lock thoroughly and screwed a new flint in place by the time she said, "Henriette."

LeBoeuf nodded again but did not look up. He turned his attention to the barrel. He was using his ramrod to push a cloth down the tube when she asked, "And what's your name?" It was more of a demand than a question.

"LeBoeuf," he said.

"LeBoeuf..." she said. Her tone was all doubt and ridicule. LeBoeuf began to reattach the lock to the side of his musket.

"Well, what you mean to do with me?" she asked.

At that LeBoeuf finally looked up. He half expected to see her holding a knife in front of her, but if she had one she was still keeping it hidden. He shrugged. He had not really thought about it.

"Nothing. Do what you want," he said and returned to his work.

It took several days for Henriette to understand that LeBoeuf really meant it, that he had no intentions, honorable or otherwise, and that she could do as she wished. He certainly did not make any demands or dictates. He rarely spoke to her, since he rarely spoke to anyone, though he did make sure to tell Le Rongeur privately that if he wished to keep his hands attached to his arms then he would make certain they did not touch her in any way.

As to the others in the camp, he was certain they would keep their distance.

At last Henriette seemed to grow tired of doing nothing but glowering at everyone and waiting to be abused in some fashion. LeBoeuf woke one morning to find she had made porridge in the iron pot over the fire outside. Decent porridge, better than he could make, and he grunted his thanks as he ate. He came back from the day's hunting to find she had washed his cassock and spread it out to dry on the roof of the tent and had sewed a patch over a tear that a boar's tusk had left in his second shirt. He grunted his thanks again. And so it went, until the hurricano rolled in and tossed it all, literally, metaphorically, up in the air.

That was the end of the story of how Henriette de Labonté had come to be there, in that cave, with a great cyclical storm roaring outside. But how she had come to be on the whore ship in the first place LeBoeuf did not know, and he was curious. Not achingly curious, but he needed something to pass the time, and despite his exhaustion sleep would not come.

"Prithee, tell," LeBoeuf said. "How did you end up with those whores in the first place?" He nearly said *those other whores* but he thought better of it.

Henriette sighed. She closed her eyes and was silent for a moment and LeBoeuf wondered if she was debating whether or not to answer. Then she opened her eyes again.

"I wasn't some whore on the streets, you know," she said.

"If you say so," LeBoeuf replied.

"I was…to say it out loud it sounds like nonsense now, even to me. I was at the Tuileries…"

"The Tuileries? In Paris? The palace of Louis the king?"

"Yes, that Tuileries," Henriette said.

LeBoeuf nodded. "Were you a kitchen maid, or some such? Dress-maker?"

"No, you idiot," Henriette said. "I was not a kitchen maid. I was a *femme de chambres* to the queen. Queen Anne d'Autriche."

LeBoeuf frowned. "Femme de chambres?"

"A personal attendant. Not a common sort. My father was a *chevalier*. But he's dead now."

"Hmm…" LeBoeuf said. "You were in the court? Did you meet the king, ever?"

"Yes," Henriette said. "I knew the king. Maybe too well, I knew the king."

"He took a fancy to you?"

"He did," Henriette said.

"And did you…make yourself agreeable?"

"I did."

"What manner of thing was that?"

Henriette sighed. "It was not pleasant. Louis is not a pleasant man. Not to look at or be with. But he was…is…the king. Not to be denied."

"I've heard tell he has little use for his wife."

"Few kings have much use for their wives, save for them to give birth to a living heir. As for Anne, she's quite failed at that."

LeBoeuf nodded. He was getting even more entertainment than he dared hope for. "The Tuileries…it's a long way down from there to a cave in Hispaniola. I don't think you made a good bargain."

Henriette gave him a wry smile. "I made a good bargain. Or it seemed so at the time. Queen Anne might not care much for her husband, but she cares even less for women who keep company with him. She would have had my head but for Richelieu."

"Cardinal Richelieu?"

"The same."

"A good man," LeBoeuf said. "A man of God."

Henriette frowned. "Are you jesting?"

"Isn't he?" LeBoeuf asked. "He's a churchman. A cardinal, no less."

"He's a pig. A power-hungry swine. He plays his games and he weaves his webs."

"But you said he saved you from Queen Anne and her vengeance."

Henriette nodded. "He did, but not out of any sort of Christian kindness. Cardinal Richelieu is open to the same sort of…persuasion as any man is. And he promised I would go free, said he would see me placed in another noble household. But instead he bundled me off to this…shit pile."

"Why would he do such a thing?" LeBoeuf asked. "Just to be cruel?"

"No," Henriette said. "I don't think so. Richelieu, he's too calculating to do something just for cruelty's sake. I think he was afraid it would go hard on him if the queen learned I was still in France. Not to mention the tales I might have told about him and what he demanded of me. He could have had me killed, to be sure, but I think that was too much, even for that miserable pig. So here I am."

LeBoeuf was silent for a moment, thinking about that. "It's quite a story," he said.

"You don't believe me?" Henriette asked, and LeBoeuf saw the temper flair.

"No, I believe you. But still, it's quite a story. Tell me, what are the Tuileries like?"

"Have you seen them? I mean from the river? Or from the street?" Henriette asked, and LeBoeuf shook his head.

"Oh, they are magical!" Henriette said and LeBoeuf could hear the longing in her voice, the mourning for a life lost. "There are many parts to the palace, of course, but my favorite is the gardens. They are just grand! Laid out for a half a mile before you even get to the palace. There are flowers of every sort, and hedges trimmed to look like animals. And then, inside the palace, the floor is gold. Not all gold, of course, but inlaid with gold and silver, so that the inlay makes these magnificent pictures. When you enter, you step into a room that could hold twenty cottages, and at the end of it there's a staircase, one hundred feet wide and covered in rich carpet, that leads up to the floor above. But all of that is like a fisherman's hovel compared to the throne room."

LeBoeuf closed his eyes and let Henriette's voice flow though his head, a lovely, lilting voice, for once devoid of the usual bitterness and fury. It was the most beautiful thing he had heard in a very long time. More beautiful even than the sweetest song of the birds in the jungle. Her descriptions of the majesty of the king's palace warmed him like the morning sun. The wind roared outside the cave and the trees shook the earth as they fell and Jean-Baptiste LeBoeuf was carried off on the soft cloud of Henriette's words.

He fell asleep to her lyrical descriptions. He woke up some time later, but how much later he had no idea. He opened his eyes and looked into a darkness that was nearly complete. He looked down at the fire. A few coals were still glowing and he considered coxing them into flames, but Henriette had fallen asleep as well, slumped over, her head on his chest, and he did not want to disturb her by moving.

From deeper in the cave he could hear the sounds of the others sleeping: soft, rhythmic breathing and bestial snores. But beyond that, nothing. The roar of the wind had stopped, the sound of snapping limbs and falling trees was gone. The storm had passed.

Maybe.

LeBoeuf knew that storms such as these, hurricanos, had a calm spot in their middle. The wind would die away, the sun might even shine down with rays of false hope. And just when it seemed the worst had passed the winds would come up again, this time from the other direction, tearing down whatever the first assault had failed to destroy.

"Henriette..." LeBoeuf gave the girl a gentle shake. "Henriette..."

She shook her head as if in protest and then lifted it and opened her eyes. She looked around, and LeBoeuf could sense her confusion. "What's happening?" she asked.

"I don't know," LeBoeuf said. "Methinks the hurricano's passed, but I don't know."

Henriette sat up the rest of the way, pushing herself off LeBoeuf's chest, and LeBoeuf stood. His muscles and joints ached and protested and it took a moment before he could straighten out. When at last he was able to stand upright and walk he felt his way toward the entrance of the cave.

There was no light coming through the narrow mouth. That could mean several things. It could mean that the sun had set. Or it could mean that trees or even earth or stone had fallen over the entrance and sealed them in, perhaps turning their shelter into their crypt. He wondered which it was.

He reached out and felt the rough granite of the cave wall and trailed his fingertips along it as he moved slowly toward the mouth. He could feel the cave growing narrower and his panic starting to rise. He moved a little quicker and then he felt the other wall brush against his back and knew he was near the entrance.

He paused and thrust his arm straight out. His hand touched something that was not stone, something unexpected, and he gasped in surprise and jerked his hand back. He felt himself flush, embarrassed by the silly reaction, but the confines of the cave were making him tense. He reached out again, more carefully, and realized that his hand had brushed against leaves of some sort and small branches. A tree, apparently, fallen against the mouth of the cave.

Well, that's a fine thing... he thought. If they were trapped he wondered whom they would elect to eat first. But that was not a question that would need answering for some time, so he set it aside and took a step farther toward the mouth of the cave. He reached out again and felt around for the biggest branches, took a firm grip and pushed.

He did not have to push hard. To his surprise, the whole mass that was blocking the cave just tumbled away; the blinding light of day hit him in the face and made his eyes tear up as if he was weeping with joy at having been spared.

He blinked and turned sideways and squeezed out of the cave, into the warm, sunlit morning. He stepped over the tangle of branches he had just pushed aside and scanned the country beyond. It was a foreign place now, unrecognizable. If someone had told him just then that the hurricano had blown them all to the moon he would not have doubted it.

The forest through which they had hiked the day before was gone. The towering pines and the palms and the mango trees were now so much rubbish strewn on the ground, great heaps of twisted branches jutting up in every direction, broken trunks and massive clusters of roots with the wet earth still clinging to them. It was a land of epic destruction, a land of sinners swept clean by the hand of an angry God.

He heard movement behind him, feet stepping over the branches on the ground. Henriette came blinking from the cave and then D'Anton and Levesque and Pierre le Chasseur. One by one they squeezed from the mouth of the cave and spread out across the ground, taking in the devastation surrounding them. No one spoke.

LeBoeuf looked off toward the horizon but there was no sign of the storm. The blue sky came right down to the sharp line where it met the ocean, which he could see now with the tree line gone. They were not in the eye of the hurricano. The storm had passed, and it had left the ruins of the island in its wake.

"Dear God..." It was Van Loudersong, last out of the cave, who was the first to speak.

"Never seen the like," said another, an Englishman who called himself Billy Solent, and his words were met with muttered agreement.

They stood for a few moments more, taking in the extraordinary sight, then LeBoeuf turned and took a deep breath and squeezed back into the cave. He collected up his musket and his sword and his haversack and the few other things he had brought with him. One by one the others followed to gather their belongings as well.

LeBoeuf was the first back out into the sunlight. He waited outside the cave for Henriette, and once she appeared he marched off north, heading back to the camp on the beach.

He did not look back, but he could hear the others following, which they were welcome to do. LeBoeuf did not care, nor did he feel any need to lead them. The path they had followed the day before, from the beach to the cave, winding through the thick jungle in some places and over high ground in others, had required some knowledge of the way. But now there was no path, there was no jungle, there were only acres and acres of destruction. Navigating was not the problem — they had a nearly unobstructed view in every direction — the difficulty was in getting around or over or under the sea of fallen timber.

The country became more familiar to LeBoeuf as they walked, the contours of the land recognizable despite being all but denuded. He could see off to his right the ridge from which he had watched the hurricano rolling in from the east just the day before. Ahead of him a low hill obstructed his view, but he knew once they reached the top of that rise they would be looking down on the beach and whatever was left of their camp.

He ducked around the uprooted trunk of a big mango tree and climbed over a fallen palm and found a way through the rest of the debris, a clear path to the top of the hill. The earth was warm and soft and wet underfoot as he climbed the last hundred feet. He stepped up over the crest and looked out at the shore below.

The beach, the bend in the coastline, the stretch of sand and the open ground were all perfectly familiar, but nothing else was. The line of palms that had stood sentry-like between sand and shore were standing no longer. Some were lying on the ground, some were simply gone. The beach and the open ground where the camp once stood were all but scoured of anything put there by man or God.

Some shredded bits of canvas were tangled up in the fallen trees, but for the most part the tents and the boucans were gone, swept clean away. And with them, the riotous buccaneers who had decided they would not leave their camp, that they would laugh and drink and wait for the Devil to come for them. And he had.

All this LeBoeuf took in with a sweeping glance, but the destruction at his feet was not the thing that drew his eyes. The thing that drew his attention was a few hundred feet off the beach, fetched up on a sandbar that lurked just under the water. It was a ship, leaning hard to one side, oddly intact, or so it seemed. Her topmasts were snapped off like the palms on the beach, but her lower masts were still in place. She was partially smothered in torn sails and rigging and sundry debris, but still she seemed mostly whole. Wounded, but not dead.

LeBoeuf sucked in a breath. The sight of it stirred something deep in his gut.

Chapter Nine

Don Alonso woke to a multitude of horrors, each of them only vaguely defined, a cliff's edge of nightmares, and he, at the precipice, ready to tumble down.

Of those horrors, the agony was foremost. Alonso was sitting upright and his body, right at his midriff, was being squeezed so tight he felt certain he would be torn in two. Or perhaps he was being crushed by something lying across his middle. He did not know which. He opened his eyes and saw only blackness.

I'm blind...I'm blinded... he thought and the panic began to rise in his throat, enough that for a moment he forgot the searing pain in his guts. He turned his head side to side. Nothing at first. And then, finally, looking down, he saw it. A sliver of gray, a hint of daylight. He was not blind after all. He was in someplace dark, and over there, in the indeterminate distance, was light.

He tried to push off, to move toward the sliver of light like a supplicant crawling to the throne of God, but he could not move. The pain in his middle surged and pulsed through him and he cried out loud. Something was lying across his legs and his abdomen and he thought it might be his bowels, torn from his body and strewn out around him. He made himself look down but he could see nothing, save for the distant gleam, and that was not enough to illuminate whatever was on him.

He pressed his lips together against the pain and the horror and reached down slowly, thinking perhaps that he could tell by touch what this thing was. His hand brushed against something wet and smooth and pliant and he shouted in terror. He did not know what his spilled guts would feel like, but he imagined they would feel much like this.

Slowly he moved his hand and the texture under his fingertips changed. He paused, tried to conjure up what it might be. It was familiar, but he could not place it.

Hair... he realized. *Wet hair...* It was a person lying across him, someone still unconscious, someone who had yet to wake up to the nightmare. But that did not explain the vicious, burning pain across his middle. He slid his hand off the body and over the soaked cloth of his tunic to the place from which the pain radiated. His fingertips brushed against something unexpected — something hard and course, something he could not identify — and he gasped in pain.

The rope...

He remembered now. They had cut the mainmast free, and once that was done, once there was naught for him to do but crouch and pray, he had found a bit of rope and lashed himself to the rail. Now the rope had come bar taut around him. Twisted perhaps, or caught on something, it had drawn so tight it threatened to tear him apart.

He reached behind him, following the rope with his fingers. His breathing was quick and shallow. If he did not get himself free in the next few minutes he would surely die, the life squeezed out of him. He twisted as far as he could, trying to find where the rope was caught, but twisting was agony and he abandoned the attempt.

He turned back and gasped and fought the rising tide of panic.

No, no, think, think, think... he admonished himself. He was a soldier, he had faced such dangers before.

This fellow... He thought of the man strewn across him. *If I can wake him he can help me.* Alonso reached out again and pressed a palm against the man and jostled him as much as the pain would allow.

"You...you...wake up," he commanded but the man made no sign of waking up: no sound, no movement, no sign at all. "Wake up!" He pushed him harder and was rewarded with a dagger-thrust of pain in his guts.

Knife... Don Alonso thought next. If this whore's son was one of the mariners then he would have a knife on his belt, if he had not lost it.

He reached out and his palm came down on the wet fabric of the man's shirt. He slid his hand down and to the right, feeling the contours of the man's back under his clothing, and then his fingers touched what had to be a leather belt. He felt along the belt until his fingers bumped into the blessed shape of a leather sheath, and protruding from its end, the handle of a knife.

Alonso almost wept with relief as he pulled the knife free with his right hand and felt for the rope around his waist with his left, searching for the easiest place to slash it in two. The movement sparked an all but unbearable pain, but he was frantic now so he ground his teeth together and continued on. He brought the blade of the knife down on the rope and slid it back and forth in a sawing motion. The rope seemed as solid as the oak from which the ship was built, and Don Alonso was just wondering if perhaps he would not be able to cut through it at all when the fibers parted with a snapping sound.

The relief that spilled over Don Alonso was the most delicious he had ever felt. He sucked in a deep, luxurious breath, held it, and then expelled it slowly. His side still burned with pain and he was sure he had a wicked laceration in the wake of the rope, but with the pressure gone he felt light and free, almost giddy.

"Thank you, my friend," he said to the still motionless sailor across his legs. "Wake up now, and we'll get free of this place." He shook the man again, harder now that he was free of the rope, but still he received no reply, no reaction.

"Are you dead?" Don Alonso asked him. He ran his hand over the man's back and toward his head. He could feel the skin of the sailor's face, cold and wet, the skin he had mistaken for his own bowels. It felt like the skin of a dead man, a drowned man, but that was no proof that he was.

"Either way, you must get off me," Alonso said. He pushed harder and moved his legs to get them out from under the weight. He felt the sailor roll away from him, felt the weight coming off his legs. He could see nothing in the blackness, save for the slash of light, but he heard the sailor's body make a soft thumping sound as it came to rest.

Slowly, Don Alonso rose to his knees. The pain flared with every motion so he moved slowly, letting it settle as he straightened. He put a foot down and pushed himself up, but before he could get halfway to his feet his head connected with something hard and he dropped to his knees again.

What by all that is holy? he thought, once the pain had subsided. He had no idea where he could possibly be. He had no idea if it was night or day. In truth, he did not even know if he was alive or dead, though, if he had to bet, he would have wagered on his being alive. And that meant it was worth trying to extract himself from that place.

He went down on his hands and knees. He could feel wet gravel under his palms. He started to crawl toward the sliver of light, the only landmark in his black world. His hands came down on what he guessed to be a tangle of rope and broken spars and he crawled with care over them, at one point struggling to free his leg from some bit of stray rigging. He felt the agony in his side flair up again and he paused to let the pain fade a bit, then crawled on.

The closer he came to the sliver of light the wider and brighter it appeared, and soon he was close enough that he could make out details: the gravel earth and more broken debris, detritus of a shipwreck. He was under something, he realized, part of the ship, he assumed. Beyond the gap through which the light was spilling he could see more ground, more debris.

He reached the light at last, after what seemed an extraordinary effort. He sat, propped up on his arms, and let his breathing settle. He was certain now that he was still aboard the ship somehow. The light coming in was enough for him to see the rail and the tangle of rigging draping from it like seaweed off a rock. But still there was something wrong with what he was seeing. It was familiar, but it was wrong.

When his breath returned he pushed himself back onto hands and knees and crawled the last few feet to the bright-lit space. He could see that the gap, thankfully, would be big enough for him to crawl through with little effort. He squatted down a bit and worked his way forward. He could feel the wood rail against his back, feel the sunlit gravel warm against his palms.

He emerged from the dark place, stood up on his knees and looked around. He had crawled through his nightmare dream world and back into reality, but what lay stretched out before him was unlike anything he had ever seen, or ever imagined.

The trees were the first thing that caught his notice. He had not seen trees in many weeks. They stood a couple hundred feet away: three or four palm trees, tall and elegant and swaying a bit in the breeze, emerging from a jumble of greenery. Alonso stared stupidly in their direction. The greenery, he realized, were mostly lesser trees, mangos and such, but also dozens of other palms that had been knocked flat by the wind.

He craned his head back. Above him the sky was benign, blue and cloudless. It seemed impossible to believe that such a sky could produce the violence and destruction of the hurricano.

To Don Alonso's left and right, a wide swath of white sand beach, half covered in wreckage, stretched away in either direction. Masts and yards and sails and heaps of cordage lay strewn around, along with barrels and trunks and upended cannons and all the vast array of things that made up *Nostra Sennora de Regla*'s hull and top-hamper, or had been secured to her deck or had been stowed down below. All of it had been disgorged onto the shore, scattered around like feed tossed to chickens.

Nor was it only cargo and gear. Don Alonso could see bodies tangled up in rigging and lying sprawled out on the warm sand. And there were people still alive as well, sitting in small clusters or moving about, sifting through wreckage, wandering here and there. No one spoke or seemed to make any noise: no wails of anguish, no voice of command. He wondered what they were doing.

Nothing, he concluded. *They are doing nothing.* They were staggering around to no purpose, as disoriented and confused as he was. Moving aimlessly because they were alive and able to walk and there was nothing else to be done.

Don Alonso stood slowly, letting each stab of pain subside as he did, until at last he was standing upright. He turned slowly to see what was behind him, and he gasped and his mouth fell open. He had thought that the wreckage on the beach, the half-dead survivors, the incongruous line of trees in the breeze, and blue sky above, were as strange as anything he might see. But he was wrong.

Behind him, rising up like a cliff side, the massive *Nostra Sennora de Regla* lay stranded on the warm sand, flung completely clear of the ocean. But even that was not the most extraordinary thing. More incredible still, the ship was upside down.

He recalled the massive seas breaking over the rails and tossing the ship around as if it were a toy. He recalled her hitting bottom, driving onto some unseen shore. This beach, presumably. He could well imagine those same seas lifting the ship up and tossing her over the way a man in a fury might overturn a table, spilling whatever was set on it across the floor.

Mouth still hanging open, Alonso lifted his eyes so he could take in the awesome sight. The poop deck had been mostly crushed under the weight of the hull. The gallery that ran around the outside of Master Ignacio's cabin was torn free and hanging down like a broken wing. The elegant table where Alonso and the master had shared their last meal — in Ignacio's case his last meal on earth — had come free of its lashings and now hung halfway out of the cabin's shattered windows. The shrouds that once held the bonaventure mast, the mizzen mast and the main mast upright were still fast to the ship at their lower ends, and the rest lay twisted and jumbled on the beach like massive black serpents.

Don Alonso stepped away from the hull so he could see more of the grounded ship. It all made sense to him now: the dark place in which he had found himself, the sliver of light. The ship had rolled right on top of him and trapped him underneath, but by the will of God the poop deck had held the hull up off the beach so that it had not crushed him. He stared up at the side of the ship, black with its highlights of red and gold and green, and above it the ship's bottom, dull white and streaming with tendrils of seaweed, and he slowly made the Sign of the Cross.

He ran his eyes forward and was greeted by the next shock — the ship had been torn in two. The forward end, from the middle of the waist to the very bow, had been twisted off and cast aside, and now fifty feet of beach separated it from the after end. Unlike the stern, the bow section was still upright, its bottom resting in the sand, the stump of the foremast and the bowsprit reaching up like some poor damned soul pleading with God for mercy.

Don Alonso turned again and considered the debris strewn over the beach. *It's no wonder there's so much here*, he thought. Once the ship had been torn apart it would have spewed its contents out on the sand as the seas rolled the sections ashore.

He stepped away from the ship, working his way around the heaps of wreckage, the rigging and spars, the barrels, the guns and gun carriages, the shattered bits of cabin furnishings and sundry parts of the ship he did not recognize. He saw the body of a man flung face down on the beach, arms spread wide, and he guessed from the man's clothing that he was one of the minor government officials who had been aboard.

Now they'll have to find another, Don Alonso thought. *Or perhaps not.* Whatever office that man had been sent to fill would be of little consequence. There were more functionaries in the government of Spain than any nation could ever need or want. It was one of the few careers left in a country whose economy was based almost entirely on extracting precious metals from its colonial territories.

Men such as Don Alonso Menéndez de Aviles, men who were born to lead the lesser sort, would always be needed, of course. But the petty officials who formed the wide base of colonial rule were of considerably less importance. If a handful of them were left dead on the beach it would not matter much.

There was another body just beyond the government man, laying half on its back, and the sight of it triggered something in Alonso's head, but he was still too confused to know exactly what it was. He took a step closer, and then it struck him.

It's a woman... He looked at her face, white with a bluish tint and still glistening with sea water, eyes open in surprise, mouth open as well.

Maria... It was his wife's maidservant. The homely one. Alonso stared at her for a moment, then turned and looked back toward the ship. He wondered if Gabriella had managed to live through the wreck. Or Francisca, his wife. If she hadn't, what would that mean? Most of the wealth she had brought into the marriage was already under his control, but her death might bring additional holdings, something her father had kept in her name.

I'll have to write to Don Cristóbal, Alonso thought. *Express the depth of my sorrow. See if there was anything else that belonged to her. See what the stingy bastard was keeping back.* He would have to write to his people in Seville and Madrid as well. They would know if the old man was trying to cheat him.

She could be alive, of course... Alonso thought next. *So it could be that none of this matters.*

He stared at the upside-down section of the ship as if it might reveal something, as if it might open up and the dead within its confines would come walking out like Lazarus from the tomb. He considered going back there and seeing what he could find out, but it seemed an awful effort, more than he could summon just then.

Behind him, from the tree line, he heard voices, many voices, shouts of surprise, men barking orders. It was strange and incongruous in the grave-like quiet that was hanging over the beach. He turned slowly, thoughts of Francisca and the wrecked ship forgotten.

There were men moving out of the trees. They were wearing yellow jerkins and silver helmets and some were carrying pikes. Farther back, half-hidden by the thick jungle growth, he could see horses, some with riders mounted, some without.

Soldiers… Alonso frowned, not sure if he should be concerned by this new development. One of the soldiers, stepping out ahead of the rest, was carrying a sword rather than a pike, and he was pointing with it and shouting.

"There's like to be gold or silver in some of those chests, find it, stand guard over it. We won't tolerate any theft here! Gonzales, get your company aboard the ship, see what's there!"

Spanish… Alonso thought. *The fellow is speaking Spanish…good…that's good.*

But of course he would be speaking Spanish. Spain still controlled all of the bigger islands in the West Indies and nearly all of the Main. They would have to be very unlucky indeed to find themselves wrecked on an island controlled by the English or the French, or the native Caribs who would doubtless have eaten them by that point.

He watched the soldiers spread out over the beach, poking through the wreckage, looking for anything of value that had spilled from the *Regla*'s guts. They paid no attention to the living survivors as they turned over bits of wreckage or poked into shattered barrels and chests. Alonso watched a soldier cut the purse off a dead man's belt and tuck it into his jerkin.

"Don Alonso?"

Alonso pulled his gaze from the soldiers, turned in the direction of the voice. A man stood forty feet away, staring right at him. "Don Alonso Menéndez de Aviles?"

Alonso just stared back at the man. He did not know how to react. He had heard the man speak his name but it sounded so very odd.

The man moved closer. "Don Alonso Menéndez de Aviles?" he said again, and now there was a bit of confusion, a bit of doubt in his voice and on his face. But Alonso nodded and the man smiled. He turned back toward the trees and shouted, "Here! Sir, here!" He pointed toward Don Alonso.

More men came out of the trees, men on horseback who did not dismount but rather walked the horses over the sand, moving carefully around the wreckage. They wore helmets and carried swords at their waists but they were not soldiers, not simple men-at-arms. These were men of stature. The brilliant scarlet and gold of their clothing, the silk stockings, the quality of their mounts and the bright leather saddles with their silver buckles all said as much.

The horses stopped ten feet away and the men swung themselves out of their saddles. The man foremost among them, closest to Alonso, whipped his helmet off, handed it to the one who had called Alonso's name, and advanced a few steps. He was an older man with a great sweep of gray hair, a gray moustache and goatee, and a stout frame that spoke of many years of comfort and indulgence. His eyes were on Don Alonso as he approached.

"Don Alonso Menéndez…" he said, part statement of fact, part statement of wonder. He made the Sign of the Cross and then flung out his arms and wrapped them around Don Alonso and hugged him. Don Alonso's arms remained at his side.

The man pushed Don Alonso away and looked him up and down. "I am Don Gabriel de Chávez y Osorio!" he proclaimed, and when Don Alonso did not appear much enlightened added, "Governor…captain general of Hispaniola!"

At that Don Alonso nodded, recognizing the name, if not the man, whom he had never met. "Don Gabriel, thank the Lord," he said softly and crossed himself as well.

"Oh, Alonso! We were worried half to death!" Don Gabriel's enthusiasm seemed entirely genuine. "Some of the local people, they brought word a galleon had been wrecked, and of course we were waiting on *Nostra Sennora de Regla*, and feared it might have been her. And it was!" Don Gabriel took another step back and shook his head again in renewed wonder. "But you've survived, my boy! Your father will be so pleased to hear it. We are friends, you know, me and Don Hernando."

Of course I know that, you old fool. That was the first thought to float through Don Alonso's head, though in the confusion of the moment it came only half-formed, and Don Alonso did not give it voice. He was practiced and skilled enough in self-preservation that he would never utter such a thing even in the worst circumstance.

"Don Gabriel…" Alonso said as his thoughts began to coalesce. "So…" He looked up and down the beach. "So, we're on Hispaniola?"

"Ha!" the governor gave a short laugh and the men behind him dutifully laughed as well. "Of course we are, my boy! But sure, you wouldn't know that, would you? Might be on the shores of the River Styx for all you know. But yes, we are on Hispaniola. You wrecked on Puenta Caucedo, about ten leagues from Santo Domingo. We had to ride like the devil to get here so quick, I can assure you."

Don Alonso nodded.

"Dear Lord, look at you," Don Gabriel continued. "Manuel, give the Lieutenant Governor your cape."

Manuel, still holding Don Gabriel's helmet, whipped the cape off his back and draped it over Don Alonso's shoulders. Don Alonso looked down at the fine wool cloth and silk lining, a marked contrast to his own filthy, shredded clothes.

A voice called out from somewhere behind Don Alonso, and with it came the sound of shattering glass. Alonso turned back toward the ship. There was a soldier half outside the master's cabin, twenty feet above the beach. He had apparently smashed out what was left of the windows and now he stood with one foot on the underside of the broken gallery, waving an arm.

"They might have found some still alive there," Don Gabriel said.

"My wife," Don Alonso said. "My wife...our cabin was back there. I haven't seen her." Alonso felt a flush of guilt and recrimination. Don Gabriel would certainly know Francisca's father, Don Cristóbal de Seville. It would not go well if word got back to the old man that his son-in-law appeared indifferent to his wife's fate.

"I...I must have hit my head..." Alonso added by way of explanation.

"Well, come along," Don Gabriel said. He turned back toward the beach and shouted, "Get some men over there to help, come along you fools, go lend a hand!"

The words of the Governor spurred the soldiers like nothing else. They abandoned whatever they were doing and rushed toward the inverted stern of *Nostra Sennora de Regla*, with the governor and his entourage and Alonso following behind. Don Gabriel stopped fifty feet from the wreck and the rest gathered behind him as the soldiers hurried past to help those aboard.

More soldiers appeared in the windows of the great cabin and Don Alonso realized they must be walking on the overhead, which now served as a floor. There were a few sailors among them as well, and they had located a ladder made of rope and wooden slats. This they dropped from the window so it hung down the side of the ship.

Father Pedro was the first one out and down. Don Alonso did not recognize him immediately, his brown robe soaked through and sagging around him, his face pale, the hair on his tonsured head in disarray. He eased himself onto the ladder and came carefully down, one rung at a time, then stepped onto the wet sand.

Alonso's eyes moved up to the cabin once more. The next one through the window was a woman, her clothing wet and torn, a rag tied around her head.

"Is this your wife?" Don Gabriel asked. "Is this Francisca?"

"No," Don Alonso said. "This is one of my wife's lady's maids. Her name is Gabriella."

"Well, damn them, why do they not get Francisca out of that cursed wreck?" Don Gabriel fumed.

Alonso watched Gabriella negotiate the ladder with surprising ease, holding her skirts up, providing a view of her legs nearly up to her knees. She had survived, and Alonso was glad of it.

As Gabriella reached the sand there came a renewed bustle in the master's cabin above. "What the devil are these damned fools doing now?" Don Gabriel asked.

A moment later it became obvious. The next person out of the cabin came bundled in a blanket with ropes tied to either end, forming a sort of sling. The sailors helped ease their cargo out through the broken window and over the side. They slacked the ropes away gently to lower the blanket and its passenger down to the beach, where a handful of soldiers stood ready to catch.

"Francisca..." Alonso said. He could not see who was in the blanket, but still he knew it was her. But the question remained, was she alive or dead?

"Come along," Don Gabriel said and hurried off over the beach, Alonso at his side, the rest trailing behind. Two of the soldiers were holding the blanket-wrapped figure while two others were untying the ropes by which she had been lowered down.

Alonso pushed past them, looked down at the blanket. Francisca looked back at him. Her hair was soaked and her skin was whiter than Alonso had ever seen. There was a cut across her cheek but any blood had been washed away. She looked up at Alonso and a faint smile played on her lips, as if she could not summon the strength for any more than that.

"Husband..." she said, her voice just a whisper. "I feared the worst for you...but God has preserved us..."

"Yes, my sweet, yes, he has," Alonso said. He reached out and gently squeezed her hand. In his mind he saw Gabriella's shapely, naked calves as she made her way down the ladder.

Chapter Ten

Not everything in the camp had been swept away. Nearly everything. But not everything.

They walked slowly down the rise, down to the open ground where the tents and boucans had stood: the last of the hunters on that stretch of coast, the boucaniers and their women who had survived the storm, carrying what possessions they had left. The ground looked familiar enough in some ways, the few acres of cleared land, the berm where the grass ended and the long sweep of the beach began. It seemed more open now with the line of palms that had stood at the edge of the sand gone, blown away like the first rank of soldiers to face the cannons' blast.

As they reached the level ground they spread out, each wandering off to where their particular shelters had stood. From the crest of the hill the site looked scoured clean, but now they could see there were still remnants of the camp left. Stakes jutted from the ground with the tattered ends of ropes still made fast to them. In some places the bottom edges of tents, shredded and half-buried in mud, or the first row of logs, marked the spot of their former dwellings.

Here and there the bodies of the hunters who stayed behind lay tangled in rope and canvas and branches ripped from trees. Some were nearly naked, their clothing stripped away by the wind. In normal times a dead man's possessions would have become property of his matelotage, who would keep what he wanted and auction off the rest. But these were not normal times, and there was virtually nothing left to keep or auction.

"Say, LeBoeuf, will you look at this?" Le Rongeur shouted. He spoke with a forced bonhomie that suggested he was eager to get back in LeBoeuf's good graces. Or, if not his good graces, at least back to where LeBoeuf was willing to tolerate him, which was as close as the two men had ever been.

LeBoeuf stopped and turned. Le Rongeur was standing where their shared tent had been. The branch of a mango tree had fallen across LeBoeuf's bedding and the pile of old sails that had been heaped in a corner of the tent. The weight of the branch had apparently kept those things from blowing off into the hinterland. That was all that remained.

"Least you got a bed," Le Rongeur said. "And we got canvas for a new tent."

LeBoeuf nodded and gave a noncommittal grunt. He looked off toward the tree line, or what had once been the tree line. It was now mostly a tangled heap of trunks and branches and leaves. He thought of Big Dog and the others, wondered if they had lived through the hurricano. He was a smart one, Big Dog. Other Dog, too. If the rest had stuck with them there was a good chance they might have made it.

For a long moment he stared at the shattered forest, half expecting his pack to come running out from the undergrowth, tongues lolling, the way they had so often done before. He wondered if they would return to the camp at all. If they did not, he would have to assume they were dead or on their way to going feral.

LeBoeuf turned and continued on toward the beach. He walked past clusters of men and women sifting through wreckage, unearthing a few things of value, pulling the bodies of their former comrades out from wherever they were entwined. There would be funerals later, LeBoeuf imagined. These men would not want to leave the dead to be torn apart by gulls and wild pigs.

He stepped over the trunk of a fallen palm and then over the hump of grassy berm that bordered the beach and then down onto the sand. He walked to the water's edge and stopped and rested the butt of his musket on the ground. He looked out toward the submerged sandbar and the ship that lay stranded there, leaning hard on its larboard side.

She was stern toward him, a couple hundred feet from where LeBoeuf stood. Not a big ship, not a galleon or a man-of-war or a large merchantman. A brigantine, one hundred tons or there abouts. Her two topmasts were snapped off and hanging down like spindly arms reaching out to test the water. He could see the torn rigging draped over the rails and the masts, and the yards hanging at odd angles, the remnants of sails still clinging to them.

He felt a stirring in his gut. He could feel that his heart was beating faster, but he could make no sense of that reaction. It was not as if the sight of a ship was some sort of novelty. Ships came and went from the roadstead all the time, calling there to buy smoked meat or to trade bullets and powder and brandy and rumbullian for it.

But something about this ship was different. It was not the property of some merchant somewhere, not a vessel with a full complement of officers and men aboard, bound off for some predetermined destination, a spot on a chart, a harbor to offload cargo. This ship was just lying there, abandoned as far as LeBoeuf could see. Like a gift offered up on a silver platter.

He heard the sound of feet stepping on the downed branches behind him, but he did not turn. Henriette stepped up on one side of him and Van

Loudersong on the other, and Pierre le Chasseur and D'Anton and some of the others as well. No one spoke, they just joined LeBoeuf in looking out over the water at the stranded ship.

Levesque was the first to speak. "Something worth having in the guts of that bastard, I'll warrant." The others made guttural sounds of agreement.

"And plenty of good oak boards in that hull, methinks. We can build a new camp here, a proper place," Billy Solent said.

"No," LeBoeuf said. He said it quickly and without thought and his reaction surprised even himself. "I think we're best off not breaking it up," he added.

"You think there's anything worth saving?" Van Loudersong asked. "I would think she's stove in proper. Her back broken. Never float again."

"I don't think so," LeBoeuf said. He had seen plenty of ships with their bottoms crushed, half filled with sand and water, sitting ponderously in the shallows. This ship did not look like that, at least not to LeBoeuf. There was damage, certainly, maybe irreparable damage, but the way she was leaning on her side, as if she was not dead but resting, suggested a shifted cargo to him, but not a stove-in hull.

"Only one way to know," Van Loudersong said, and that was true, and it was a problem.

They would have to go out to her, climb aboard, go down below and see what there was to see. But they had no way of doing that. The buccaneers had boats aplenty, canoes made from hollowed-out logs and the more substantial *periaguas*, made from hollowed logs as well, but from two logs rather than one, and joined down the centerline, their sides sometimes built up with boards. They carried sailing rigs and they were stable and fast under sail or oar. The day before there had been a half a dozen of each such boats on the shore. Now there was not one to be seen.

But, happily, they were not all gone. A hundred yards down the beach they found one of the periaguas upended and jammed into a heap of shattered palms. One of the sides had been crushed in, but not entirely, and when the boat was dragged free and set in the water she floated perfectly well, with not a leak to be seen.

An oar and a couple of paddles were also dug out of the wreckage, as well as some shattered planks that could be used for paddling. LeBoeuf picked up his musket which he had leaned against the stump of a broken palm, grabbed the bow of the boat and shoved it off the sand. He set the musket down on the bottom of the boat and climbed over the side and sat in the stern. He was grateful that it was a periagua they had found, and not a canoe. For a man his size, negotiating a canoe was never an easy business.

A dozen of the rest climbed in after him, including Henriette who seemed less eager than ever to be left alone among the buccaneers. LeBoeuf held a broken board in his hands; he dipped it in the water and back paddled and the periagua made sternway off the beach. Then all the boards and paddles and oars came down together and the boat swung around in a wide arc until its bow was pointed at the sorry ship stranded on the bar.

They approached slowly, swinging around to the starboard side to avoid the fallen masts and the chance of running aground on the sandbar. The looked warily at the ship as they came closer, searching for some sign of her crew, someone able enough and motivated enough to put up some sort of defense. Two hundred feet off, LeBoeuf put down the board he was using as a paddle and picked up his musket. He thumbed the hammer back and set the stock to his shoulder and aimed the long gun at the stranded ship, ready to drop anyone who showed himself with the intent of firing on them. But no one did.

LeBoeuf looked at the name painted across the ship's transom: *Nostra Sennora de Santiago*. At least that was what it looked like. Much of the paint had been peeled away by the pounding seas and the hurricano's merciless wind. She was lying hard over, a wide strip of her bottom exposed, long strands of seaweed like tangled hair streaming down the side. But still LeBoeuf did not think she was stove in.

"Holloa!" LeBoeuf hailed as they drew alongside. "Holloa!" His cry was met with the soft slapping sound of the incoming waves against the motionless hull, and nothing more.

The periagua came gliding in alongside and bumped up against the ship's bottom. LeBoeuf stood and reached a hand up and grabbed the lowest rung of the boarding steps mounted on the ship's side. He handed his musket to Henriette and with a grunt hefted himself up. He secured his foot on the step and reached out and Henriette handed his gun back to him.

The side of the ship, which would have been vertical with the vessel floating on its waterline, was canted at a forty-five degree angle. LeBoeuf half climbed, half walked up the side and peeked over the rail at the deck. It looked as he had imagined it would, the rigging torn up and scattered around, pinrails and fife rails ripped clean away, remnants of the ship's boat which had been lashed down amidships still clinging to the lashings or flung up against the larboard rail. She mounted eight cannon, about what one might expect for a merchantman of that size sailing in dangerous water. They had been lashed in place before the storm, and the lashings had held. Even those on the high side seemed in no danger of tearing free.

A skylight aft, probably illuminating the master's cabin, had been torn away, leaving a square hole through which a considerable amount of water must have come pouring in. Just astern of that, what remained of the binnacle was still lashed to ringbolts in the deck. The corpses of two of the ship's crew lay twisted up in the rigging, their broken limbs sticking out at various unnatural angles, their skin white, their bodies starting to bloat. He could see no one else.

He turned and looked down at the periagua. "Just dead ones here, that I can see," he said, then swung his leg over the rail and stepped down onto the canted deck. The wood was dry and the grip of his wet rawhide shoes was good and he moved away from the rail and toward the main hatch, still mostly covered with a tarpaulin and battened down.

He rested his musket against the rail and considered the hatch. The after, larboard corner had been smashed in, the grating crushed by something that had fallen from aloft, and the tarpaulin was hanging down through the hole. He looked through the gap but could see nothing but blackness below. He grunted and pulled his big hunting knife from its sheath on his belt, and with the butt of the handle pounded out one of the wedges holding the larboard batten in place.

He moved onto the next one as Van Loudersong came over the rail and D'Anton behind him, then Joost Steen, a big fellow named Lessard, and the rest. They took a moment to look around then joined LeBoeuf in knocking the wedges free and lifting the battens from their brackets. When all the battens were out they grabbed the edge of the tarpaulin and pulled it back, revealing a series of gratings, all still intact save for the broken one aft.

They pulled the gratings up and tossed them aside and let the sunlight spill unimpeded down into the 'tween decks. They knelt by the hatch combing as if they were at an altar rail and peered down below. There they saw what LeBoeuf had expected to see, which was not much.

The 'tween decks was mostly empty, except for a few sundry crates and barrels lashed to either side of the hull. A makeshift galley had been set up forward, though there was not much left of that: the brick fireplace had been beat into its component parts and the various iron pots and pans and utensils were scattered all over the deck.

Most of the deck below was taken up by another hatch, the same size as the one they had just opened, and covered over by a row of heavy hatch boards. This hatch would lead to the hold at the very bottom of the ship, where the bulk of her cargo would be found.

LeBoeuf swung his legs over the edge and dropped carefully to the 'tween decks, a drop of no more than five feet, and one after another the rest followed. They grabbed up the hatch boards and tossed them aside and the sunlight streamed down through both hatches and illuminated the hold below.

Once again LeBoeuf felt his heart rate tick up, felt the odd and inexplicable twist in his stomach as one by one the hatch boards were pulled away. A few moments more and they would know if *Nostra Sennora de Santiago* was a broken wreck or a ship that might live again.

"Cargo shifted," Van Loudersong said as they all peered down into the brigantine's guts.

"It did," Le Chasseur agreed, and the others grunted and nodded.

It was clear what had happened. Dozens and dozens of barrels, their contents unknown, had been stored down below. At some point as the ship did battle with the massive seas and wind the barrels had broken free, and when the ship rolled to larboard the barrels rolled as well, their weight pinning the ship on her side. For *Nostra Sennora de Santiago* it was the end of the line. Indeed, it was something of a miracle that she had not rolled completely over, though simply staying afloat had not been enough to save her crew.

LeBoeuf once again swung his legs over the combing and lowered himself down into the hold. It was a farther drop than it had been from the main deck, but he reached out with his foot for the nearest barrel and was able to ease his weight onto it. He stepped carefully, one barrel to the next, pausing on each to see if the barrels would shift under him, but the cargo seemed frozen in its chaotic jumble.

No water, he thought. If the ship's bottom had been crushed in, egg-like, he would have expected to see water half filling the hold, the barrels floating and bumping against one another as the sea surged in and out. But that was not what was revealed by the sunlight falling down through the open hatch.

LeBoeuf worked his way down the pile of barrels toward the keelson as the rest swung themselves down into the hold and over the cargo, speculating as to what might be in the barrels. Numbers were burned into the heads of each, which likely corresponded to numbers on a manifest somewhere, but without the manifest there was no way to know their contents. Even with the manifest, LeBoeuf guessed, they would still be in the dark, since he doubted there was a man among them who could read. And if any of them could — Loudersong, perhaps — he doubted they could read Spanish.

Still, it was not too hard to guess what was in *Nostra Sennora de Santiago*'s hold. Many of the barrels would be filled with water for the voyage. Others would be wine or brandy. Olive oil. Dried fish. Salt pork. Flour. Cheese. Any of the hundreds of things borne about the ocean by small merchantmen such as this.

Or perhaps luck would be with them. Perhaps the ship was carrying more valuable goods, like shoes, or clothing, or gunpowder, or shot, or muskets, or musket parts or other necessities hard to come by in that part of the world. If that was the case then the cargo would be most valuable indeed.

Spain did not welcome trade with her colonies in the West Indies. English, French and Dutch merchants were forbidden from carrying goods to Spanish cities there. Yet Spain herself was unable, utterly unable, to provide for all the colonies' needs. Demand was sky-high, and any trade goods that made their way to the West Indies were worth many times what they would have been worth in Europe.

It was no surprise then that despite the efforts of Spain, those other nations maintained an active and profitable, if illicit, trade in the Caribbean. As far as building wealth in the New World, only mining silver and gold was more lucrative than smuggling.

But LeBoeuf cared for none of that. Instead, he worked his way down to the very bottom of the ship, as close as he could get, and peered down through the jumble of barrels. He could see water now, many feet of water filling the low part of the hull. But that was neither surprising nor discouraging. It was not possible for a ship to live through a hurricano, and sustain the damage that this one had, without shipping tons of water down below.

As he looked at the glint of sunlight on the surface he pictured in his mind those last moments in the lives of the crew of *Nostra Sennora de Santiago*. He could see the men standing at the pumps, furiously working the handles up and down as the seas ran waist-deep across the deck. They would have known it was pointless, but they would have pumped anyway, because they had to do something until their arms gave out or the seas swept them away.

When had the captain gone overboard? Early in the storm? Or had he lashed himself in place and clung on until the sea had unleashed fury enough to carry him off? Had the helmsman gone with him, and would it have mattered in the least if one or both had been washed away? Had the crew seen the breakers on the sandbar before they struck, or were they all overboard or dead by the time the ship came to its shuddering rest?

LeBoeuf shook his head. No way to know. Nor was it his problem, or theirs either. Not anymore.

Van Loudersong was talking. "Whatever the hell is in these barrels, it will be worth something. Anything worth putting in a barrel is worth something in this godforsaken end of the world."

LeBoeuf stood and stepped two barrels closer to the men clustered under the hatch. Even standing near the bottom of the hold he was taller than most of them, his shape suggestive of the barrels on which they stood.

"Good chance there's specie aft as well," he said. "In the master's cabin. Reals. Doubloons. If he was trading, he's have gold and silver."

The others nodded. LeBoeuf could see by the renewed delight on their faces that the possibility of gold and silver had not occurred to most of them.

"There's about forty of us left from the camp," LeBoeuf went on. "Ship washed up on our beach, so I reckon we each get an equal share. And, prithee, I have an idea each share is going to be worth a damned sight of money, even split among forty." The others continued to nod.

"Now, split it among thirty-nine and it's even more," LeBoeuf continued. "So here's what I say. I'll give up my share, every bit of it, if I can have the ship instead."

The others were quiet, and LeBoeuf watched their expressions as each weighed the benefit to himself.

"You want the ship?" Levesque asked. "It's a wreck. Worthless."

LeBoeuf shrugged. "I'm stupid, mayhaps."

A few nodded in agreement. LeBoeuf waited. It was silent in the hold. Most of the men were looking down at the barrels. Some exchanged glances.

"The devil take it," Van Loudersong said. "I sure as damnation don't want this rotten tub. I'd rather have my share of LeBoeuf's take."

The others muttered their agreement. It was as LeBoeuf had thought it would be. Most had no interest in the ship, and those who might had no interest in arguing with the big man who spoke so little. So it was settled. LeBoeuf had bought himself a ship.

Chapter Eleven

Maja leveled his pistol and pulled the trigger. The bullet, a lead sphere weighing just a bit over an ounce, punched a hole in the mate's forehead and blew out the back of his skull. The two men who were holding the mate up by his arms let go and his body tumbled to the deck.

And there was nothing that Benjamin Graves could do but watch.

There were things he wanted to do. He wanted to scream in fury and in terror. He wanted to puke. In the light of the lanterns held aloft he could see bits of the mate's brain and skull clinging to the rigging and dripping off onto the ship's rail in shining globs.

But he neither screamed nor puked. Instead he just pressed his lips together and locked his knees so his legs did not buckle.

Maja looked down at the dead man by his feet. The blood was pooling around his head. It looked black in the lantern light that glinted off its wet surface. He nudged the corpse with his shoe.

"Son of a whore, why'd you do that?" Benjamin Graves demanded, finally trusting himself to speak. It was a stupid question. He knew why Maja had done it. But he had to say something, if only to prove to himself and the others that he still had voice and balls enough to form words.

Maja looked up at him, his dark face unreadable, nearly devoid of expression. As it always was. He looked down at the still-smoking pistol in his hand as if he was surprised to see it there. He looked down at the dead man on the deck and then at the bits of the man's head dripping off the ropes. He looked back at Graves.

"When I shoot *you* in the head, you won't see it," Maja explained. "I'm taking care that you'll know what it looks like."

"Son of a bitch. I've seen bastards shot in the head," Graves said.

"I know," Maja said. His voice was unnerving. He spoke softly, and his accent was an odd mix of Spanish and French and Arawak and English, all of which the man could speak more or less fluently, and it was impossible to tell which was the dominant strain.

There was nothing about Maja's appearance to suggest he was in command. He was barefoot and wore canvas slop trousers and a well-worn linen shirt with a leather jerkin cinched over it. His head was bound in a red cloth. He looked like any of a thousand sailors in that part of the world, save for the elaborate necklace made up of multiple strands of beads and small shells and sharp animal teeth he wore around his neck.

But he was very much in command. He radiated command, just as he radiated danger.

Maja was the West Indies made manifest, five generations after Cristoforo Colombo had stumbled onto the New World. His hair was black and straight and hung down his back, plaited in a long braid and wrapped tight in a snake skin. His nose was thin and arched like a hawk's beak, his skin brown, but more mahogany than dark oak. He was slight of build, but that did not diminish his aura of strength and ferocity. In Maja the blood of Spaniards and Frenchmen and English and Dutch and Kalinago, the Carib people, all swirled together like the warm ocean water and the steady easterly winds of that country.

"And mayhaps I won't shoot you," Maja continued. He pushed the pistol into his belt, reached around behind and drew out a dagger, ten inches of double-edged steel. It glinted in the lantern light like the mate's blood.

"Mayhaps I'll take you apart, bit by bit. We'll see how much I need remove before you tell me about Señor Corregidor's cargo."

"Son of a bitch!" It was all Graves could think to say.

Benjamin Graves had crossed paths with Maja often enough during his time in the Caribbean. They tended to sail in the same professional waters which ranged from quasi-official to semi-lawless. Sometimes they found themselves working in something akin to alliance; sometimes, such as now, very much not. But for all that, Graves could never get a firm sense for what sort of man Maja was. It made him uneasy, and he guessed that was the point.

Maja took a step closer. "It's gone, do you hear?" Graves said, as emphatically as he could. "The cargo's gone, every damnable thing is gone! There was a hurricano, in case you didn't notice."

Maja's face took on a puzzled expression. He turned and looked out over the larboard rail, over the dark ocean. The sun was just on the rise. They could not see it from the ship's deck, but the light to the east was starting to illuminate the far side of the mountains that dominated the island of St. Christopher so their high peaks stood out against the night's sky.

"Gone?" Maja was toying with him.

"Yes, gone! It was all in the damned storehouse, all safe, like. Well, there ain't no storehouse anymore. There ain't nothing. Hurricano took it all, and if Señor Corregidor cares to blame anyone, he can blame God. Take it up with God."

Maja nodded. "Thing is, I'll warrant you'll be speaking with God before Señor Corregidor will. You'll be meeting God soon, I'd wager." He waited for Graves to respond but Graves had concluded he would do best to keep his mouth shut, so he did.

"The question," Maja continued, "Is why are you *here*?" He pointed with the knife toward the hulking black shape of St. Christopher. "Señor Corregidor's cargo, it was bound for the Main. And yet you've gone to windward with it. Why is that?"

Graves shook his head. "No market to be found on the Main, everyone knows that. The Dutch are there, swarming like maggots. Bunch of chiseling thieves. It'd do no good to go to the Main. But with them just bringing in the tobacco here on these islands, there's silver to be had."

"There is," Maja agreed. "So, on your own, you decided to come here and sell Señor Corregidor's cargo? For silver?"

"That's right," Graves said. "And there was no time to be writing bloody notes back and forth."

Maja nodded. "But when you got that silver, did you mean to put it back into Señor Corregidor's purse? Methinks not."

Graves did not reply. There was no reply to be made. Because Maja was right, and they both knew it.

"You're not a lucky man, Benjamin Graves," Maja said. "Man born with the name Graves, he's born cursed."

Again Graves did not reply, though this statement was more of an open question. In his thirty-six years of life Graves had indeed been very unlucky. But he had also been very lucky as well.

He had shipped out from Penzance at age twelve, lucky to find himself under a captain who was as kind as that sort was wont to be, which was not terribly kind, but kind enough. Thrown in with a decent bunch before the mast, all Penzance men and all related in some manner to one another, they gave young Benjamin a rudimentary education in the ways of ships and the sea.

Two years of that and then luck changed for both Graves and the captain when a main brace pennant carried away aloft, dropping the five-pound brace block on the captain's head and crushing his skull as if it was made of porcelain.

For Graves there followed a period of mixed fortunes, bouncing from one ship to another, advancing bit by bit — landsman to ordinary seaman to able-bodied seaman to mate — through hard work and native cunning and a bit of treachery when it suited. Graves had the good luck to wind up aboard a privateer with gold in his pocket. He had the not-so-good luck to end up a prisoner of war in Portugal until yet another change in luck allowed him to escape back to his native England.

He'd drifted at last to the West Indies, a place that drew men of his talent and inclinations with its siren song of opportunity. Honest trade, less-honest smuggling, some privateering, some piracy, the West Indies offered a cornucopia of legal, quasi-legal, and genuinely illegal enterprises — pursuits that were profitable, all. And for Benjamin Graves it had worked out well, on the whole.

Making off with Señor Corregidor's cargo might have been his most remunerative stroke yet, and he meant to disappear with the proceeds in his pocket, but his luck seemed to have shifted once again. The hurricano, which he could not have foreseen, swept away all the lading he had moved ashore, before he had earned a single real from its sale. The storm damage to his ship had kept him anchored at St. Christopher longer than he intended.

Graves certainly knew that Señor Corregidor had eyes all over the Caribbean, but he figured it would take longer than it had for the old man to learn that his cargo had not gone to the Main. He had also underestimated how determined Señor Corregidor would be to have his property back, and how clever Maja would be in sussing out where he, Graves, had gone with it. That was the worst of all, because it was his own fault.

Stupid, stupid...

There was a bustling from forward, the sound of bare feet on a ladder. One of Maja's men came up from below, lantern in hand, and behind him, five Black men wearing bits of worn, patched clothing, shuffling with heads down. They came aft, stopped a few feet from Maja. The Black men kept their eyes on the deck. They had been in bondage long enough to learn that boldness was not rewarded.

"Graves weren't lying," the man with the lantern said. "No cargo below. These was all that was there."

Maja nodded. He stepped closer to the men, looked them over, one by one. He turned to the man who had brought them on deck. "Did you unchain them?"

"Weren't chained," the man said.

Maja frowned. He turned to Graves. "Why didn't these blackbirds go ashore with the rest of the cargo?"

"Weren't going to sell them," Graves said. "Been training them up as foremast sailors. Worth more to me as crew." And that was the truth, but only part of it. Graves had done one voyage aboard a slaver and it had been enough to make him loathe the whole wretched business. But he was not going to admit such weakness to the likes of Maja.

Maja stared at him, and Graves was not sure how to read his expression — what little expression there was. Curiosity? Skepticism? Maja turned to one of the Black men.

"This man," he asked, indicating Graves with a jerk of his head, "he teaching you the working of a ship?" He spoke in English. The Black men looked up at him, but they did not answer, and they did not seem to understand. Maja asked again in Spanish, and that was met with a tentative nodding of their heads.

"Good," Maja said. "You're with me, now."

"Oh, taking these blackbirds for your own?" Graves said. "Now, prithee, who's stealing Señor Corregidor's cargo, hey?" He regretted the words even as the last syllable was leaving his lips.

Maja turned to face him again. "Trice him up," he said, but his voice did not carry the anger at such impudence that Graves had expected.

The men who were holding Graves's arms dragged him across the deck until his back fetched up with the starboard bulwark. They forced his arms straight up and another of Maja's men lashed his wrists to the shrouds.

Maja stepped close. He had his dagger in his right hand and he was tapping the blade against the palm of his left. He looked over Graves the way a sculptor might consider a block of marble as he decided where to make the first cut. He took his time with it, a thoughtful exercise he clearly enjoyed. Then he stepped away.

"Mayhaps we'll sail," he said. He looked down at the body of the mate, still sprawled out on the deck. "Throw that over."

Four of his men lifted the corpse and tossed it over the larboard side. Graves heard the sound of the body hit the water and he could not help but envision his own bloody corpse making such a splash.

Maja stepped up to the spot where the mate had gone over and put his hands on the rail. "Hold those lanterns over the side," he said and the men with the lanterns held them straight out over the water. Maja looked down for a long moment, down to where the mate's body was floating alongside. Then he straightened and turned back to Graves.

"Tide's still flooding," he said. "When that dead bastard comes floating back we'll sail. And then I'll decide if I kill you or take you back to Señor Corregidor."

Graves, wisely, said nothing.

You whore's son...toy with me... he thought. Maja had already decided what he was going to do. He probably knew even before he and his men had come rowing up to Graves's ship an hour before, oars muffled, and swarmed silently up over the bow, catching the deck watch passed out drunk and Graves in his cabin halfway there himself.

Still, there was some comfort to be found in Maja's feigned indecision. If Maja meant to kill him, then various parts of his body would already be laying on the deck. The fact that he had not yet started in with his knife suggested to Graves that Maja planned to bring him back to Señor

Corregidor. Which made sense. Señor Corregidor would want to witness Graves's death. He would want to enjoy it.

Mayhaps it would go easier for me if Maja just killed me now, Graves thought. *I'd be best off killing myself before Señor Corregidor does.*

But he knew he would not kill himself, nor did he genuinely wish that Maja would do it for him. As long as he was alive, as long as he could talk, he had a chance. He had been in any number of situations as dire as this, and had so far managed to wriggle out of them, one way or another. It was possible he could do so again. It was possible that this was not his time.

As if confirming that notion, Maja slipped his knife back into its sheath and turned away, like he had forgotten that Graves was even there.

"Sánchez," he said, and one of his men who had been leaning on the bulwark straightened. "Take two of these blackbirds and three men and go back to the ship. Tell Ortiz to make ready to sail on the turning of the tide."

Sánchez nodded, gestured to a few of the others, and they and two of the freed slaves disappeared over the bow and down into the boat alongside.

Benjamin watched them go.

Turning of the tide... he thought.

It had been just a few hours past slack water when Maja came aboard, and that meant it would be some hours still before the ebb. Graves could feel the cords cutting into his wrists, could feel his fingers going cold and numb from the tightness of the bonds. He pushed himself up a little taller and that took some of the pressure off, but he knew he could not stand so straight forever. He wondered how long Maja would keep him lashed to the shrouds. He wondered how long it would take before the damage to his hands was irreparable.

There were eight cannons on the weather deck, four-pounders, silly little things, but the sum total of the ship's defense. They were run out of the ports in the bulwarks and lashed in place. Maja sat down on the gun opposite where Graves was triced up, arms folded, staring aft, a signal to the others that they could take their ease. Some sat on the deck, leaning back against the bulwark, some stretched out flat, arms behind their heads.

Graves's own men whom Maja had taken prisoner were already sitting on the deck, hands bound behind their backs. Three others were still ashore and had thus avoided capture and two more — the dogs — had eagerly thrown in with Maja, had helped bind their shipmates and had brought the lanterns up from below.

Graves pressed his teeth together. It was going to be a long and miserable dawn. But he was a sailor and well used to prolonged misery, and since there was nothing to be done he resolved to endure it. His only other option was to complain to Maja about his discomfort and ask that he might be untied, but he did not reckon Maja would be terribly sympathetic. Indeed, such a request might make matters worse.

Somewhere behind the hulking mountains to the east the sun continued to rise, revealing more and more of the island, and overhead the sky appeared as bands of white and yellow and pale blue. The light spilled over the peaks and down over Old Road Bay, revealing the scattering of ships anchored there. Half a dozen others had been driven ashore by the hurricano and were lying awkwardly on their sides, like sea creatures hauled up onto the beach, unable to move outside their natural element.

Graves looked to the north. A ship was riding at anchor there, two cable lengths distant, a ship that had not been there when the sun went down the night before. Graves recognized it. She was called *Santa Rosa* and she was the property of Señor Corregidor, though there were no documents that would connect the two. She was a fine ship, a bit larger than Graves's, though she did not sail as well. Graves had commanded her himself on a few occasions, in Señor Corregidor's employ.

Maja must have sailed in and dropped anchor well after dark, which was better seamanship that Graves would have guessed the man capable of. He was surprised that Señor Corregidor had given Maja the use of the ship at all. Señor Corregidor was inordinately fond of *Santa Rosa*.

Guess he was pretty eager to get me back, Graves thought. He did not consider it a compliment.

There was no wind, no wind at all, but the air was thick with the pungent smell of earth and vegetation along with the tang of salt-water. In the stillness Graves could hear the call of gulls and the sharp sounds of the birds hidden in the foliage ashore.

And something else as well.

The sound hardly registered at first, a dull, innocuous sound, just another of many — a hatch board dropped on the deck of one of those other ships at anchor, or one of the wrecks groaning as it settled under its own weight.

But something about the sound rang an alarm bell in Graves's head. He frowned and looked in the direction from which it came, and Maja stood suddenly and stared off in the same direction. And there it was again: a flat, dull report, so far off as to be barely audible. One of Maja's men, pushed up against the side of the bulwark, began to snore; ugly, gravely and loud. Maja crossed the deck in three strides and kicked the man in the gut.

"Shut up," Maja said and the man, awake now, wide-eyed, doubled over, did not say a word.

Again they heard the dull booming sound off to the south. It sounded like heavy surf on a beach, but Graves knew it was not that.

Gunfire, he thought. Heavy guns, guns from a land battery. Maja was looking south as well, and Graves had no doubt he also recognized the sound. And he had no doubt that Maja was wondering the same thing that he was: *Who the devil is firing great guns, and who are they firing at?*

"I'd reckon yon gunfire's down at Nevis," Graves said and his voice sounded strange in the morning quiet. Maja turned and looked at him and Graves was certain he would tell him to shut his mouth, but he did not: he glared for a moment and then turned and looked south once more.

Nevis. The island was thirty miles from Old Road Harbor, separated from the southern end of St. Christopher by a stretch of water two leagues wide. The English had been there for just a few years, the settlers mostly men looking for more land and autonomy than St. Christopher could offer. The island boasted a number of tobacco plantations scattered around and for defense a single great gun on a spit of land called Pelican Point. And it was that single gun, Graves imagined, firing at some unseen enemy, that they were hearing now.

"Holloa, Maja, I'll warrant those are your friends there, the Spaniards," Graves offered next. It was a guess, but likely correct, and the look that Maja gave him suggested that he, too, thought that Graves had guessed right. The Spanish had come at last.

Chapter Twelve

LeBoeuf's world — literally, figuratively — was torn apart by the hurricano. Uprooted.

The tents and all their contents, the boucans, the meat that had been smoked and readied for market, the hides, the boats, the dogs, all of it had been shredded, swept away, strewn out over several miles of Hispaniola's north coast. But that destruction, complete as it was, barely registered in LeBoeuf's mind. It was like some odd bit of trivia, vaguely interesting but of no real personal relevance.

It was the ship that upended his thoughts, far more profoundly than wind or seas ever could. That providential ship, laid down on the sand like an offering to appease an angry god.

Jean-Baptiste LeBoeuf was a man come suddenly awake, a slumberer back from his dream state. This brigantine, insignificant in its finest day, now half-wrecked and near worthless, seemed to work on his spirit like a deep draught of rumbullian, or like the plant the natives called *yupa* on which they would become insensibly drunk just by inhaling its crushed seeds.

Why this bit of sea wrack had such an effect on him, he had no idea.

He could not sail the ship by himself. He could not repair it by himself, or even get it off the sandbar by himself, but he did not care. The others, the hunters, had little interest in lending a hand. Like LeBoeuf, they had lost everything to the hurricano. Unlike LeBoeuf, their chief concern now was how to get it back, how to return to the place they had been before the big wind had come.

But for LeBoeuf, that life — hunting pigs, smoking meat, bartering with passing ships — was done. It seemed as foreign to him as if it had been someone else's life, a life he had heard described once, like Henriette's days in the Tuileries. It did not matter to LeBoeuf if none of the others wished to help him. He would manage. He would find some way. When a gift such as *Nostra Sennora de Santiago* was laid at your feet, you found a way.

"Well then," Van Loudersong said, looking around the dark, musty hold. The ship was rocking a bit with each incoming wave, making the water in the bilges slosh back and forth. "Reckon we'd best see to getting this cargo off-loaded. For all we know this wreck will come off the sandbar and sink under us."

The others nodded and grunted agreement. They might have lost everything in the camp, but now they had gained the *Santiago*'s cargo, potentially a very valuable cargo. Even better, they had convinced LeBoeuf, the dumb ox, to trade away his share in exchange for the worthless hulk. And, LeBoeuf was sure, they were still figuring the ship would break up soon and they would build new huts out of its timbers.

"Yes, we best do so," LeBoeuf agreed. "Get these casks out, row 'em ashore."

Again the others nodded and fell silent. No one seemed to know what the next step should be. They had each of them worked on shipboard at some point in their lives, like most men of their sort, and they were not strangers to such things, but neither were any of them mariner enough to see clearly what needed to be done. Van Loudersong might — LeBoeuf had an inkling he had spent considerable time at sea — but none of the others did.

"Stay tackle's still there, looks well enough," Billy Solent offered. The stay tackle was a heavy arrangement of ropes and pulleys that hung directly over the main hatch, used chiefly for hoisting cargo in and out. LeBoeuf had noticed as they approached the ship that it had come loose and the lower end was hanging in the water, but otherwise it seemed intact.

"No," Van Loudersong said. "The ship, she's heeled too far over."

More nodding followed. "Maybe we can use the main yard tackle along with the stay tackle," Billy suggested next. But each of them had seen the damage the storm had done to the rig and it was clear that the yard tackle would be of no help.

LeBoeuf stood silent, watching the men, watching the consideration play out on their faces. Some were putting serious thought into the situation, others seemed incapable of doing so. It was Pierre le Chasseur who spoke next.

"Don't see as how we can get this cargo out with the ship lying such as she is," he said. "We should get her floating again, on an even keel. That's what needs done." The others nodded, seeing the truth in that.

Yes, yes, exactly, LeBoeuf thought. He was hoping one of the others would hit on that idea. He did not want to suggest it himself.

"Will it float, at all?" Billy Solent asked.

"Long enough to get the cargo off," Van Loudersong said. "After that it's LeBoeuf's worry, not ours."

That brought a chuckle from the gathered men. LeBoeuf opened his mouth to suggest the next move, then closed it again and waited. A moment later Van Loudersong said, "If we hope to stand the ship up, we'll need to get these barrels amidships. They're holding her down, as is."

"Reckon you're right," LeBoeuf said. "Tide's coming in now. We shift as much of the cargo as we can, the high water might lift her right off."

That was met with further agreement, and soon the men in the hold were working in small gangs to roll the various casks from the larboard side to a place as close to the centerline of the ship as they could. There were casks of all sizes: tuns, butts, hogsheads, barrels, which had all once been neatly stacked but were now dumped in a jumble on the low side of the hold. A number of the tuns, it was discovered, were filled with water, two hundred and forty gallons of it per cask, and the men saved themselves a bit of effort by staving in the heads of all but two and letting the contents run into the bilges. That done, the pumps were manned and the now brackish liquid was pumped overboard.

Slowly, as the pile of casks was heaved to the centerline and the tide crept in to give her a lift, the ship began to stand upright, her angle of heel becoming less severe. LeBoeuf could feel the vessel moving under foot. It felt to him like a baby kicking in its mother's womb, a once-motionless thing stirring to life. The incoming tide was lifting *Santiago* off the sand, not flooding her, and that told LeBoeuf that the hull was still sound, or at least sound enough that the ship could be kept afloat.

Henriette found the master's pantry and fetched wine and bread and meat, and once they had done all they could with regard to the cargo they gathered on the weather deck and shared it out. The breeze was blowing a steady ten knots and it felt delightful washing over their sweat-drenched skin and clothing. The sky was blue, dotted here and there with clouds piled up in great heaps. With the ship no longer tilted at so steep an angle it was much easier to move around the deck. For LeBoeuf, all seemed right with the world, more than it had in a long time.

As they ate they could feel *Santiago* standing straighter still as the sea lifted the turn of her bilge off the sandbar, and every once in a while there was a wave sufficient to make the ship rock on her keel.

"She lives!" Van Loudersong said, jubilant and clearly a bit surprised.

"She ain't sunk," Billy Solent said. "But she ain't free of the bar, and she's yet too far over to get the use of the stay tackle."

"I don't know as she'll come more upright than this," Le Chasseur offered. "She's sitting hard on the sandbar." That got the men looking around, nodding and considering their situation. LeBoeuf sat silent, chewing a mouthful of bread and cheese, watching the others, waiting for someone else to think of it.

"Be an hour or two until high water," said Levesque.

More nodding.

"We can haul her off the sand, I suppose," Le Chasseur said at length. "Lower that anchor into the periagua, carry it out some ways. Once we're at the top of the flood, if we lay into the capstan, we might haul her free."

We might, LeBoeuf thought, still chewing. The others continued to nod.

And so that was what they did. Once the wine and the food were gone the men turned to the next task, which was getting the massive best bower, the primary anchor, lowered down into the boat and then dropped a cable length away from the ship.

The anchor hung from its cathead, a stout beam that thrust out over the bow far enough so the anchor could be dropped without hitting the side of the ship as it went down. But that only worked when the ship was nearly upright, which it was not. Now, as they lowered the anchor, the flukes tore at the ship's side, gouging out great divots of wood that made LeBoeuf cringe as if they were being torn from his flesh. But it was a cosmetic wound only, and did no real damage to the hull.

At last the anchor was clear of the ship and hanging from two heavy poles rigged off the stern end of the periagua. LeBoeuf was about to lead the boat crew over the side and down when he stopped and looked back at the others.

"Thought just come to me," he said, as if this idea was a new revelation, which it was not. "Best run another cable out the stern there, bend that to the anchor as well. That way we can haul by the bow and the stern. Rock her right off the sand, if you see."

The others nodded as they saw the wisdom of that. If there were heavy ropes attached to the anchor from both the bow and stern then they could pull the ship from either direction. They hurried off to attend to it, and soon they had rousted out another anchor cable, run it through the hawse-hole in the stern and bent it to the ring at the end of the anchor's shank. That done, LeBoeuf and the others took their places on the thwarts of the periagua, took up their oars and began to row.

It was no easy task, rowing clear of the ship with the weight of the anchor and the pull of two cables at the periagua's stern. But the buccaneers were strong men, and capable enough, and they were soon tolerably far from the sandbar and able to set the best bower to advantage. Van Loudersong and Lessard stood and used their oars to lever the massive anchor off the poles from which it hung. It plunged into the clear water and the periagua rocked and bobbed as if pleased to be free of its weight.

They rowed back to *Santiago*'s side and climbed aboard. For ten minutes LeBoeuf stood leaning against the mainmast while the others argued about how best to rig the capstan for hauling on the anchor line. He looked outboard, toward the beach. The tide was near its crest. They did not have time to argue much longer.

LeBoeuf abandoned the men on deck and went below. Up in the bow on the 'tween decks he had seen various ropes and blocks and sundry bits of rigging hanging against the sides of the ship. He made his way forward and poked through the tangle of gear until he found a heavy, six-part block and tackle. He took it down and hefted it over his shoulder and made his way back on deck, where the discussion was still on going.

"See here what I found," LeBoeuf said as he dumped the heavy blocks and rope onto the deck. "Seems to me if we clap that on to the anchor cable, and use the capstan to take up the fall, it would be a lot quicker than rigging a messenger. Get more pull, too."

The others mumbled and looked around as if they were considering the unlikely possibility that it might work, which, LeBoeuf knew, they were only doing to save face. None cared to admit that a blockhead such as LeBoeuf had hit on exactly the right answer with the first thing out of his mouth. But once they had spent enough time nodding and muttering agreement they took up the block and tackle and stretched it out along the deck. Ten minutes later it was bent to the anchor cable, the fall wrapped around the barrel of the capstan, the capstan bars shipped and the men leaning against them.

"Very well, let us heave," Van Loudersong said, giving orders because he liked to give orders and because no one else seemed inclined to do so. The men pressed their bare feet against the wooden slats nailed to the deck for traction and leaned against the capstan bars. The bars were chest-high for most of the men, but LeBoeuf was forced to bend at the waist so that he was not pushing with his stomach. Still, with his hands wrapped around the bar and his feet pressed against the wooden slats he was able to exert a terrific amount of force.

The capstan turned easily at first, the pawls falling clack, clack, clack, as all the slack was worked out of the system, and then it slowed as the tension came on the line. The air was filled with the creaking and popping of straining rope, the groan of the capstan as the sideways pull tried to tear the barrel from the deck. The men grunted and the pawls clicked as they fell, slower and slower, as if the capstan itself was slowly dying.

And then it stopped.

"Heave!" Van Loudersong cried and the men dug in and pushed and grunted with the strain. LeBoeuf's eyes were on the deck, his full concentration on his legs and arms and the wooden bar pressed into his chest.

"Heave!"

An inch, maybe less. Not enough to make the pawls drop into the next catch. And then nothing at all. They could get no more from the rope.

"Avast heaving, we can't..." Van Loudersong began but LeBoeuf cut him short.

"No! Heave!" LeBoeuf shouted. He had felt it, felt it though the souls of his feet. Just the hint of a vibration, but he had felt it. The stirring of life.

"Heave!" LeBoeuf roared again and all the power of his legs and arms and back and shoulders went into that one word, and into the crushing force he was exerting as he drove himself into the wooden shaft.

"Heave!" And he knew they were heaving, every one of them. They were not grunting or groaning or making any sound — all their effort was going into that one last desperate thrust.

And then she moved. *Santiago* slewed a bit to starboard, her bow lifting and swinging a few degrees off the sand. And suddenly the capstan was turning free and the men nearly tumbled to the deck and they laughed as they turned the machine on its axis and took up the slack they had won.

The brigantine had shifted; she had not come free, but that one bit of movement was enough to tell them all that it was not hopeless. Indeed, it was enough to assure them that they would get the ship off the bar. So they heaved again and pulled her a few more degrees around. They shifted the block and tackle to the hawser that was run out the stern and hauled away on that and worked the aft end of the ship partway off the sand. And then back to the bow again.

The sun was dipping down in the west and the tide was falling with unsettling speed when they finally drove the capstan the last quarter of a turn and felt *Santiago*'s keel slide off the sandbar and into deep water. The men at the capstan bars straightened and gulped air as the current took the ship by its stern and swung her around until she was riding easily at the anchor they had set hours before.

The men were red-faced, dripping sweat, wet hair plastered to their heads and their faces, beards soaked through. But they were smiling. And they were laughing, those who still had energy enough to laugh. Laughing with exuberance at what they had done.

LeBoeuf did not laugh. He was tired, yes, but that was not the reason. The feelings swirling around inside him were too complex to be turned into something so simple as a laugh. The ship was floating. He could feel it underfoot, that old, familiar feel, the subtle motion of a ship riding at anchor. A living thing, a spiritual thing. His ship. Deep in the center of his massive frame, behind his all but emotionless face, his tangled beard, his sweat-drenched shirt, he was not laughing. He was singing.

"Well, we heaved her off," Pierre le Chasseur said. "I'd not have thought it. Well done there, Van Loudersong. Good seamanship, for a Dutchman."

"We Dutch are the best seamen," Van Loudersong said. "Damned country's so damned wet we'd drown in our homes, otherwise."

"So," D'Anton said. "Will she sink under us?" D'Anton, as was his wont, had been working like the devil and saying little. These were the first words LeBoeuf could recall him speaking that day.

"We best find out," Van Loudersong said and he led the way across the now-horizontal deck, down the ladder to the 'tween deck and then down into the hold. The casks had rolled farther to starboard as the ship had come upright, but they had done no damage as they jumbled themselves anew.

LeBoeuf let the others go first though he, of all of them, had the most interest in the state of *Santiago*'s hull. There was only eight feet or so of water under her keel where she rode at anchor. If she sank now her hold would fill nearly to the 'tween deck before she rested on the bottom, but the buccaneers would still be able to rescue the cargo. They would have to spend the whole night swaying it up from below as the ship sank under them, but they would still get their share of the salvage.

LeBoeuf, however, would get nothing. His share — the ship itself — would be lost. Even with most of her upper works sticking out from the water, high and dry, there would be no raising her off the bottom.

The sun was going down, but there was still enough light coming in through the open hatch for the men in the hold to get a good idea of the state of things, and they were happy with what they could see. There was a few feet of water in the bilge, which might well have been there even before they heaved her off the sand. There was undoubtedly water leaking in — all ships leaked, even ships fresh from the yard — but it was not pouring in at any prodigious or even detectable rate. Ten minutes at the pumps every hour or so should keep her reasonably empty.

Incredible... LeBoeuf thought. The hurricano had carried *Santiago* past the many ship-killing reefs and shoals that were strewn along the coast, past the jagged peninsulas that thrust out from the shores of Hispaniola, and set her down on the sandbar like someone laying a child in a crib.

This is a lucky ship, LeBoeuf thought next.

With the hull deemed reasonably sound, and the men exhausted from the efforts of the day, they decided the cargo could live in the hold for another night. In their earlier efforts they had come across a few barrels that seemed likely to contain wine, so they lowered the stay tackle down into the hold and hoisted one of them on deck. They stove in the head and found it did indeed contain a pungent red, seemingly of French vintage. Cups were located in the galley and the master's cabin, and soon the level of wine in the barrel began to drop faster than the ebbing tide.

It was a jovial moment, a bit of reprieve after finding the hurricano had stripped them of everything they had built. Soon, however, food, drink and weariness put an end to the merriment. The more ambitious of the men found blankets or bits of spare canvas or torn sails to make beds on the deck, but most went to sleep wherever they happened to fall.

LeBoeuf had spent most of the evening sitting on the steps that led from the waist to the raised quarterdeck, a pewter cup in his massive hand, pouring cupful after cupful of drink down his throat. He consumed enough of the wine — tangy, with just a hint of sweet fruit, very much to his liking — to put most men in the scuppers but it had little material effect on him, except, perhaps, to smooth out the course fabric of his thoughts.

But even without the wine, the mere act of sitting on a ship, *his* ship, and running his eyes over the sweep of her deck, the taught rigging holding the oiled masts aloft, settled his mood in a way that it had not been settled in some time.

At last he could feel his eyelids growing heavy, the strength in his body draining off like the contents of the near-empty wine barrel. He stood, his muscles making their displeasure clear. He stretched a bit. He debated going aft and sleeping in the master's cabin — his cabin — and wondered how the others would take that. He smiled to himself. It was a stupid thing to wonder. None of these men, *les boucaniers*, the hunters of Hispaniola, cared a tinker's cuss where he slept. Most of them were already passed out drunk.

Henriette was sitting on the deck nearby. She had stayed near LeBoeuf without ever giving the sense she was *with* him, and she, too, had been drinking wine prodigiously. He looked down at her now.

"I'm going to sleep. Aft, in the master's cabin," he said. His tone was flat. No suggestion, no invitation, no discouragement. A statement of fact. She nodded. He turned and ducked under the quarterdeck and, partially crouched, walked back through the semi-dark of the moonlit space.

Fifteen feet aft a bulkhead stretched across the deck, larboard to starboard, making up the forward wall of the master's cabin. It was barely visible in the dark, but LeBoeuf knew it was there. He reached out as he stepped forward and his fingertips brushed against the wood. He ran his hand along the bulkhead until he found the door, then felt his way down until his fingers fell on the latch. He lifted it and swung the door in.

The master's cabin was a tiny affair, as LeBoeuf knew it would be on a small merchant ship such as *Santiago*. It was small for a normal sized man; for LeBoeuf it was more like a closet, eight feet from the forward end to the settee under the stern windows, and ten feet wide at the bulkhead, growing more narrow toward the after end. A table took up a good portion of the deck, with a bunk to larboard and some sort of cabinet to starboard.

LeBoeuf drew a deep breath and held it. He could smell wine and rum and a hint of past meals. Some sort of perfume. The smell of a man's sea-borne home, a man LeBoeuf had never known, whose bones now rested some fathoms deep.

The moon was nearly overhead, but its light was coming in through the stern windows and casting bluish squares on the deck. LeBoeuf ran his eyes around the room. It looked as if the late master had staged a bear baiting in there. The table was lashed to the deck and so had remained in place, but that was about all that had. Bits of smashed crockery covered the deck and books and rolled up charts that had once been neatly stored were now scattered around. The rug on the deck was soaked through; LeBoeuf could feel it through the thick callouses on the soles of his bare feet.

More work for the morrow, he thought. He unfastened the belt that was around his waist and set it and the knives that hung from it down on the table. He grabbed the hem of his sweat-stained shirt and pulled it up over his head and set that on the table as well. It was a cool night and the air felt good on his skin and it felt good to be free of the shirt that carried on it the remnants of dirt and blood and sweat and salt crystals left behind as the ocean water dried.

He stepped around the table, sat on the edge of the master's bunk, then laid down and stretched out as best he could. The bunk was too short for him, of course, but he was well used to that. Save for those few occasions when he was able to demand a bunk special-built to accommodate his size, every such bed was too small for him.

Sleep was just washing over him when he heard the sound of the door latch lifting. He reached for his knife, his hand moving through mindless instinct. His fingers fell on the leather sheath and then he realized who it was. He pulled his arm back again.

In the moonlight streaming in through the stern windows he could make out Henriette's shape as she slipped through the door and closed it behind her. She moved toward the bunk, silent, graceful, unworldly as a specter.

"You asleep, LeBoeuf?" she asked. Her tone could not be called affectionate, or even particularly pleasant. But she no longer sounded angry. At least not very.

"Hmm," LeBoeuf said, a grunting sound that suggested he was awake but only a bit.

"There's but one bed in here," Henriette said. "I'll share it with you." She made it sound as if she was doing LeBoeuf a favor, a clever trick which LeBoeuf appreciated. And, indeed, lovely as she was, some men might have looked on her mere physical proximity as a favor akin to a gift from God.

"As you wish," LeBoeuf muttered. He pushed back closer to the side of the ship, making as much room as he could. It was not much, given his bulk, but Henriette was of no great size and the space was sufficient.

She laid down, her back to LeBoeuf, pressed gently against him, spoon-fashion. He could not tell if she was touching him on purpose or if there was simply not enough room for her to lie there without making any contact at all. He reached out an arm and draped it over her thin waist, in part because it was the most comfortable position for his arm. He waited to see if she tensed, or objected, or reacted in any way, but she did not.

Henriette had been waiting these past months for him to make some sort of advance on her. LeBoeuf understood that. She was waiting for him to demand carnal knowledge, or to attempt rape, as Le Rongeur had done, which she would resist, perhaps to the death. But he made no demands, and certainly made no attempt to rape her, because, despite his savage appearance and the company he kept, he was not at all the sort to rape a woman. Quite the opposite, actually.

Nor had LeBoeuf explored the possibility of carnal knowledge based on consent. He did not seem able to summon the enthusiasm. For a year and a half he had been drifting around with barely enough interest in his own life to continue drawing breath. Making love to a woman required considerably more *joie de vivre* than he thought he would ever muster again.

But now, for the first time in quite some time, he began to feel a stirring, a once common desire, all but quenched and now starting to rekindle. He did not know why that was. *Santiago* had given his spirit a lift, perhaps, or the fact that Henriette, young and lovely, was lying in his bunk, pressed against him, his arm around her.

He wondered if he should speak. He wondered if he should pull her close and kiss her lovely chestnut hair. He wondered what she might say, how she might react. And he was still wondering those things when he fell into a deep and impenetrable slumber.

Chapter Thirteen

To Benjamin Graves's knowledge, the Spanish had never troubled themselves with the Lesser Antilles, the string of islands that formed the eastern edge of the Caribbean Sea. The land was too small, too mountainous, too lacking in precious metals to be of much interest. Spain looked instead to the larger islands: Hispaniola, Puerto Rico, Cuba, Jamaica, and the Main. The Windward and Leeward Islands were left mostly undisturbed. And into that void came the English, the French and the Dutch.

Such encroachment, however, was not to be tolerated. The Spanish might have no interest in the Lesser Antilles, but neither would they allow any other nation to get a foothold there. Weak and overextended as the Spanish empire was, it could still project massive force to drive away the interlopers. Graves felt pretty certain that was what they were hearing now. Who else? English, French and Dutch might hate one another, but they were not likely to go to war with each other in the Caribbean, not when they all hated the Spanish even more.

Maja turned away from the direction of the sound. He looked out to the east. He looked up at the rigging overhead. The sails, furled to their yards, had an orange cast to them in the early morning light. The long banner at the main mast head hung straight down, motionless. There was not a bit of wind.

"Don't know why you'd wish to sail off," Graves called out. "You're Señor Corregidor's man. These Spaniards, they're your brothers in arms. Señor Corregidor will see no harm comes to you, I'm sure."

Maja glared at him again. "Shut your mouth," he said and Graves shut his mouth, but he was smiling as he did. Maja would not care to be taken by the Spanish. Whoever was leading this Spanish fleet was not likely to be impressed by his connection to Señor Corregidor, which Maja could not prove in any event.

Nor would Señor Corregidor offer Maja any help. He would, rather, deny any connection to the mulatto privateer. The Spanish would take both Graves and Maja's ships as prizes and likely take Maja, mixed race such as he was, as a slave. It would be the silver mines for him for the rest of his life, which at least would not be terribly long.

"See here," Graves said. "You cut me down, suffer me to get my ship underway. You go back aboard *Santa Rosa*, get her underway, and we sail right away from here. In company. We'll shape a course back to see Señor Corregidor if you like."

Now it was Maja's turn to smile. It was a weak try on Graves's part, but the best he could come up with, given the agony in his wrists and the proximity of a Spanish fleet and his complete lack of anything with which to bargain.

"Prithee, are you a witch of some sort?" Maja asked. "Can you bring on the wind?"

"We got sweeps," Graves said, nodding toward the twenty-five-foot oars lashed in the scuppers. "A fellow knows what he's doing, he can get this ship underway with the sweeps. There's like to be wind out there on the water. We just got to sweep out to it."

Maja looked down at the sweeps, up at the limp flag, off to the east and then back toward the sound of the guns, more frequent and determined now. Graves could well imagine the struggle going on in the man's head. He would be trying to calculate the greatest threat. Señor Corregidor? The Spaniards? Maybe something of which Graves was not even aware.

Then Maja made a decision. He turned and crossed the deck, pulling his dagger as he did. Graves felt his stomach twist. He pictured his belly being split open, his guts spilling out on the deck. Once again he considered puking. Maja stopped a foot in front of him and slashed up with the blade. The lashings holding Graves's wrists parted and Graves nearly fell to his knees.

"Cut them free!" Maja called to his men, gesturing with his knife toward the bound crewmen sitting on the deck. He turned to Graves. "Get them sweeps out, and you and your men mind them well," he ordered. "And them blackbirds, get them pulling too. If you can't sweep us out against the current I'll cut your throat. All your throats."

"Faith, you truly know how to inspire a man," Graves said as he rubbed his wrists and shook his hands to get the blood flowing, but Maja had already turned and was making his way forward.

When his men had been cut free, Graves ordered them to unlash the sweeps and wrestle them into the row ports between the guns. The three former slaves were standing in a little knot near the larboard rail, watching the goings-on, confused and uncertain. Graves called to them in his rudimentary Spanish and indicated they should help with the sweeps. They nodded, apparently relieved to be told what to do, and helped in deploying the long oars.

She was not a big ship, Graves's vessel, only about one hundred tons burthen, flush-decked and barque-rigged. Her name at the moment was *Charles Rex*, though that tended to change fairly often. She was small enough, and nimble enough, that she could be moved with the sweeps in the right conditions. Graves hoped very much that these were the right conditions, but he was not entirely certain.

He heard a dull chopping sound from forward. Maja had an ax and he was hacking away at the anchor cable, not willing to waste even what little time it would take to slip it overboard. Three powerful strokes and the thick rope parted. The cut end snaked slowly across the deck and out the hawse pipe and the ship began to turn slowly with the tide.

Might have waited until I said I was ready, dumb bastard, Graves thought. He looked around. There were six sweeps, three to a side, and two men on each, as good as it was likely to get.

"All right, now, pull! Pull, you whores' sons!" Graves shouted and the men dipped their oars and leaned back and took a few steps forward. Graves felt the motion of the ship change, just a bit, as the thrust of the oars stemmed the tide and perhaps even drove the ship slightly forward.

Graves looked out toward the island, trying to gauge the ship's motion against a fixed point on shore. *We'll be right up on that damned beach if the tide gets the better of us*, he thought, but there was nothing for it. Going aground, sinking the ship, setting the ship on fire, any of it was preferable to being taken by the Spanish. Or winding up in Señor Corregidor's hands, for that matter.

Stroke after stroke the men heaved back on the sweeps until their faces were red and the sweat was running down their foreheads and soaking their shirts, and yet the ship seemed fixed, going neither forward nor back, as if it was still firmly anchored to the bottom. Graves saw Maja look aloft again and then out toward the shore. His face betrayed no emotion, but there was an anxious quality to his movements.

I'll bet you're scared, you black-hearted son of a bitch, Graves thought. The Spanish were not known for their mercy, certainly not toward anyone who had the blood of a native savage. Or a Black man. Or, worse, both.

For another three long, agonizing strokes the ship seemed to hang there, motionless, caught between opposing forces. And then suddenly Graves felt a shift, a subtle change under foot. He sighted past the mizzen shrouds to the shore beyond and he could see the ship was moving at last, the pull of the sweeps driving it forward, foot by painful foot.

Tide's turned, Graves thought. At long last the tide had turned and now it was starting to carry the ship out to sea, aiding rather than hindering the men at the sweeps.

"Tide's turned!" Graves shouted out to the deck in general. He could feel a surge of relief, but Maja showed no reaction at all, as if he had not even heard.

The momentum of the ship built with each labored stroke. She was making headway now, her motion obvious in relation to the distant shore. Graves stepped aft and rested his hand on the tiller and looked down the length of the deck. He pressed his thigh against the tiller, shifting it to starboard a few inches, and watched as the bow turned slightly to larboard.

"What the devil you think you're about?" Maja said. Stealthy as the man was, and engrossed as Benjamin Graves had been in cunning the ship, he had not even noticed Maja coming aft, and the sound of his voice made Graves jump.

"Cunning the ship. Reckoned someone better do it," Graves said.

"I'll do any cunning needs doing," Maja said. "You stand fast, make ready for me to cut your throat."

Graves took a step aside but he remained aft, planted on his familiar quarterdeck, his hands clasped behind his back. He was not so worried about Maja's threats now. He was far more worried about this fresh danger coming up from the south. He wondered what they would see once *Charles Rex* left Stoney Point and Bloody Point astern and they could look past the shoreline in the direction from which the gunfire was coming.

The rowers were finding their rhythm now, taking two steps forward as they hauled on the oars, lifting the blades, taking two steps aft. *Charles Rex* was moving faster through the water, though for all the laboring at the oars Graves knew it was the tide that was doing a bulk of the work.

The gunfire had been building like a thunderstorm rolling down on them, one gun firing after another, an unbroken wall of sound. Graves knew there was but one great gun on Nevis, and he reckoned that was one of the guns he was hearing now. That meant that the rest had to be coming from a ship firing at the battery on shore. Or many ships, by the sound of it.

Stoney Point to the south was coming abeam, revealing Bloody Point behind it, which obstructed their view of the south end of St. Christopher and Nevis beyond. Maja looked toward the points of land. He looked aloft. He looked forward beyond the bow. He turned to Graves.

"Very well, you great filthy swine," Maja said to Graves. "I'm going to set sail, and you're the only one on deck who's of no use. So get your miserable hide up aloft and cast off the fore and main topsails. And make ready to set the courses."

"Delighted to be of help," Graves said. "But..." His voice trailed off with a skeptical note.

"What, are you grown too fat to get yourself up in the tops?" Maja asked.

"Most likely," Graves said. "But see here, we'll be headed once we've weathered Bloody Point. Best keep the sails in their gear until we're well clear of the shore."

Maja scowled at him. His hand reached around his back and Graves was sure his fingers were on the hilt of his dagger, but he could see the uncertainty on the man's face as well. Graves knew the waters around St. Christopher, and he knew his ship, and Maja was not so familiar with either.

"Just loosen off the sails," Maja said, withdrawing his hand. "I'll decide when we set them."

The hands at the sweeps continued to row and the ship continued to be borne out on the tide as Graves ambled off toward the foremast. He could feel a bit of his old cockiness returning. It was clear to him now that Maja had instructions to bring him back to Señor Corregidor unharmed. That meant he was safe for the moment. Safe, at least, from being dismembered by Maja and his long dagger.

He reached the foremast, put a foot on the pinrail, grabbed hold of the fore shrouds, swung himself onto the ratlines and began to climb. He was not fat, despite Maja's assessment, but he was no longer a lean, sinewy mariner either, and the climb aloft was more difficult than it would once have been. Still, he scaled the shrouds with respectable speed, determined to deny Maja the satisfaction of seeing him struggle.

He climbed up and over the edge of the round top and there untied the gaskets that held the topsail bound to the mast. That done, he climbed back down to the deck and headed aft to the mainmast. There was a time when he would have climbed ape-like along the rigging from one mast to the next, but those days were long past.

Up the main shrouds, up and over the edge of the main top, and once his breath had returned Graves unlashed the main topsail as he had done the fore, letting the gray canvas spill out of its tight bundle and into a great heap at his feet. He stood and looked to the south, his field of view much broader now that he was fifty feet off the deck. He sucked in his breath in surprise. Not a happy surprise.

The Spanish had indeed come.

He could see a cluster of sail off to the south, the ships' hulls lost in the cloud of their own gun smoke. And there were a lot of ships. Big ships, twenty heavy galleons at least. It had to be the plate fleet, the *galeones*, one of two well-armed convoys sent from Spain each year to collect up the riches of the New World and carry it back to the old. They would be just arriving after their ocean crossing, no doubt ordered to make a stop at the Leeward Islands, there to brush off the unwelcome French and English intruders. It was akin to using siege cannons to drive off a flock of sparrows.

A week earlier, Graves thought. *A week earlier and the hurricano would have wiped these bastards from the face of the earth.*

It was not the galleons that worried Graves. Powerful as they were, they could never catch the nimble *Charles Rex*, nor would they waste any effort trying. But the frigates were a different matter.

There were two of them, well-armed and fast. They were finding wind out on the open water and had all sail set and drawing, heeling over as they raced north, the water churning white around their bows. They were closer, much closer, than the galleons, and they were making right for *Charles Rex* as if they had no other thought in mind.

Chapter Fourteen

Santo Domingo. Most venerable of cities in the New World, rising up from the jungles of Hispaniola like some great monument to Old Spain, rendered in white stucco and yellow brick and red tile. By the Year of Our Lord 1629 it was already well more than a century old, its dominance ebbing away, its light eclipsed by those newer, grander cities on the Main: Veracruz, Portobello, Cartagena, all of which had been jungle, home to wild beasts and savages, when Santo Domingo first rose to greatness.

Cristoforo Colombo walked the ground where Santo Domingo stood. His brother Bartholomew established the first city there. Those who followed continued to impose civilization on the wilderness, laying out a grid of paved streets, and in the blocks between them building the Cathedral Santa María La Menor, the Alcázar de Colón, the massive Las Casas Reales, center of the royal government in the New World. There were hundreds of other buildings as well, great and small, all enclosed in mighty stone walls, lined with cannons trained toward the jungle as if holding at bay a besieging army of vegetation.

They had all passed that way *en route* to immortality: Ponce de León, Cortes, Balboa. The English pirate Francis Drake had taken the city and held it for ransom more than a decade before Don Alonso Menéndez was born. But Santo Domingo had survived Drake, just as Don Alonso had survived shipwreck.

And now it was Don Alonso's turn to take Santo Domingo and wrest from it what wealth he could. He would not use gunpowder and bare steel, as Drake had, but rather his wits and cunning, and with those he meant to have a much longer and more profitable tenure.

Alonso saw nothing of the city at first. For four days he and Francisca remained sequestered in the suite of rooms reserved for the lieutenant governor and his household in Las Casas Reales, fussed over by servants and priests and physicians who bled them and made them drink vile broth made from ingredients with names Don Alonso did not recognize or care to remember.

They had been taken there directly from the wreck site in a carriage which Governor Don Gabriel de Chávez y Osorio had wisely brought with him on his reconnoiter. It was a perfectly fine carriage, as good as one would find in Seville or Madrid. But the roads, if they could be called such, were as bad as anything Don Alonso had ever seen, and the trip was akin to enduring a second hurricano.

They propped Francisca up in her seat and secured her with ramparts of pillows and covered her in blankets. Don Alonso and his secretary, Juan Cardero, and Father Pedro and Gabriella had all crowded in around her.

Such irony… Don Alonso thought as they bucked and yawed their way down the jungle path, the air filled with the buzz of insects and the screaming of strange birds and the dull sound of the horses' hooves on the soft earth. *We live through the wreck only to be beaten to death in the carriage that takes us to safety.*

But the misery of the carriage did not kill them, and long after dark they rolled through the massive gate in the stone wall surrounding the city, rattling down cobbled streets by the light of torches borne by mounted soldiers on all sides. They were helped down from the carriage and escorted into their suite of rooms, save for Francisca, who was eased onto a litter spread with a down-filled silk mattress and carried to her quarters.

This attention, Alonso knew, was not in deference to his office as lieutenant governor or the position that the Menéndez de Aviles family held in Spanish society. It was not out of concern for his wife's delicate constitution. It was, rather, because of the wealth and importance of Francisca's father, Don Cristóbal de Seville, a man of great influence in both Old Spain and new.

It was Don Cristóbal who had secured Alonso's position as lieutenant governor. It was Alonso's connection to Don Cristóbal that would allow him to take the utmost advantage of his place in colonial government.

Alonso was not troubled by any of that. He was not ashamed of his own family. Theirs was an ancient and respectable line, even if it was not in the highest order of Spain's celestial hierarchy. But no matter. If Alonso could not be born to one of the most important of families, he could at least marry into it, and use that marriage to lift the Menéndez de Aviles family even higher.

The lieutenant governor's suite of rooms was well appointed, airy and spacious, which made the time Alonso and Francisca remained ensconced there more tolerable. Francisca's strength seemed to ebb and flow, but Don Alonso, young, strong and athletic, recovered quickly from the battering of the shipwreck and the lesser beating of the carriage ride. By the second day of their confinement he was pacing the red tiled floor, eager to be out of doors, away from the people who were employed to worry over him. For almost a year, since first hearing of his appointment as lieutenant governor, he had been placing his pieces on the board of Santo Domingo, and now he was eager to start moving them.

By the evening of the fourth day he could bear no more. He sat down at the oak desk in the big office that adjoined his suite of rooms and took up a pen and paper. He thought for a moment and then wrote:

> By the grace of God and the great kindness of Governor Don Gabriel de Chávez y Osorio and all the people of his household, I find I am much improved in my health, enough so that, in my zeal to be of utmost service to His Most Catholic Majesty, in my current office, I am most eager to begin the execution of my duties, in whatever form would be of greatest help to the esteemed Governor and his administration.

Greatest help to the esteemed Governor... Alonso reflected on his words. *Were I honest I should change that to 'greatest help to the* lieutenant *governor',* he thought and smiled.

Well, I shall just confess my dishonesty when next I see a priest.

He smiled wider with that thought. Sometimes he did enjoy being honest with his confessor, revealing the blackest marks on his soul. He enjoyed the priest's discomfort, and the fact that he could never speak a word of it. He enjoyed hearing the priest nearly choke as he granted absolution.

He folded the paper and sealed it. "Gabriella!" he called and a moment later his wife's maid appeared in the door. Alonso had found himself relying on her with increased frequency. She was smart, active and trustworthy. She was lovely to look upon.

"Yes, Don Alonso?" she asked. Alonso held up the sealed note.

"Pray take this note to the governor. Give it to his secretary, his manservant, whoever can get it to him most quickly. Before I go mad."

"Yes, Don Alonso," Gabriella said. She moved across the room, her silk petticoats making a rustling sound in the still night. The light of the numerous candles played off her smooth white skin, her full lips. She stopped a few feet away and reached out slowly for the note. Alonso tipped the edge of the paper toward her and she took it between thumb and forefinger. She held the note but did not move, and Alonso did not release his grip.

For a moment they remained that way, looking into one another's eyes. Then Alonso let go of the note and ran his fingers lightly up Gabriella's hand. His fingertips brushed the edge of her sleeve and he circled them around her wrist before drawing his hand back. He was sure he felt Gabriella give a little shudder. Neither spoke.

"I'll return directly," Gabriella said at last, her voice husky, thick, just above a whisper.

"Do that," Alonso said.

She nodded, turned, and sailed out of the room, and that, Alonso knew, would be an end to it for the night. When Gabriella returned she would turn her attention to Francisca, tending to her needs as was her duty. These little flirtations were nothing, just drops in a bucket. But at some point, Alonso knew, and he was certain that Gabriella understood, the bucket might overflow.

Gabriella would be his, he knew, if he wanted her. And he certainly wanted her. But he was not certain his desire outweighed the risk. There was always the chance that his wife might find out. That in itself was not a great problem. But it meant that Francisca's father might find out as well. And that could be a problem indeed.

The governor's reply came early the next morning and it was just what Alonso had hoped. He dressed carefully: knee-high leather boots, silk doublet and breeches, a wide-brimmed hat: functional, not too ornate, clothes that, despite their simplicity, left no doubt as to their quality, and the quality of the man who wore them. He stepped carefully into the bedroom he and Francisca would share once she was well enough to share a room.

She was in the tall bed, propped up with a great array of pillows and partially hidden by the fine linen curtains that draped down from the frame above. As he crossed the floor the nun who sat by her bed as nurse stood and bowed and Alonso gestured for her to sit.

"My sweet, how do you fare?" Alonso asked when he reached the side of Francisca's bed. He kept his voice soft so as not to startle her. Francisca opened her eyes and her head lolled in his direction. She seemed weaker and more pathetic than was entirely warranted, but Alonso kept the look of sympathy fixed on his face.

"I'm on the mend, husband," she said. "Thanks be to God, and to the Virgin Mary, and to you and Father Pedro for your prayers. God hears the prayers of faithful men."

"Of course, my dear one," Alonso said. "But I've come to tell you the governor has asked that I join him today. We're to inspect the city. See what progress has been made in repairing the damage from the hurricano."

"Oh, Alonso, sure you shouldn't be leaving your bed so soon! You're not strong enough to ride, I fear."

"Never you worry, my sweet," Alonso said. "We Menéndez de Aviles are stout as oak. As our sons will be. Just you wait."

That earned him a weak smile and a nod, and after a moment more of husbandly banter Alonso was able to take his leave. He made his way through the now all-too-familiar rooms and, for the first time, allowed one of the house servants to open the heavy oak door that led from the foyer onto the wide brick plaza beyond. He stepped out into the glare of early morning sun. He blinked and felt the tears run down his cheek. He wiped his eyes and looked out across the plaza.

The ramparts of the city wall were fifty feet away, built of the same cut stone as Las Casas Reales. They stood five feet high and stretched off to the north and south before they were lost from sight behind the buildings on the periphery of the Royal Houses. Cannons gleaming with fresh blacking sat evenly spaced along the wall, peering out through the embrasures, and soldiers moved slowly back and forth, keeping desultory lookout. Beyond the fortification Alonso could see the tops of palm trees swaying in the breeze, and beyond those, the wide, brown Rio Ozama, the river that connected Santo Domingo to the sea.

The governor's party was at the south end of the plaza, a dozen horses standing patiently, their reins in the hands of stable boys, a dozen men in clothing brighter than Alonso's milling about. A dozen mounted troops were waiting twenty feet off, half with tall lances held erect. Alonso hurried toward them across the open space.

He was still forty feet away when Gabriel de Chávez y Osorio, captain general and governor of Hispaniola, saw him coming. "Ah! Here is our castaway!" he called over the chatter, and the others fell silent and turned in Alonso's direction. Alonso paused as he came up with the crowd and swept his hat off in a courteous bow.

"Your Excellency!" he said. "Gentlemen."

"Thanks be to God you're well," Don Gabriel said. "I don't think you've had the pleasure of meeting these others. Gentlemen, this is our new lieutenant governor, Don Alonso Menéndez de Aviles, of the Order of Santiago. As I'm sure you know, he is married to the daughter of Don Cristóbal de Seville."

The other men removed their hats and bowed as Alonso had done, if perhaps with less enthusiasm, and muttered their pleasure at meeting him.

"Don Alonso, these gentlemen are of the *Real Audiencia*, and you'll come to know them well, I dare say, but please allow me to name them." With that Don Gabriel introduced Alonso to the comptroller-general, the chief magistrate, and several of the senior secretaries of the audiencia, to whom Alonso nodded his greetings.

Don Alonso considered himself an able judge of men, even on first meeting. He considered each of these officials in turn and he saw what he expected to see: idle men who enjoyed the leisure that came with offices such as theirs, men of decent connections and middling abilities.

Government men, biding their time. Men who posed no obstacle to his own ambitions. He did not think it likely that time would alter those opinions.

"And this fellow," Don Gabriel said, gesturing to a portly, florid man who stood a bit apart from the others. "This is Don Nicolás Pérez de Maldonaldo, who is mayor of this city." Alonso nodded his greeting to the mayor, and the mayor in turn bowed at the waist, to the extent that he could with his doublet tight around his ample belly. He straightened and smiled broadly. He wore a pointed goatee on his chin and over it a thick moustache, curled at the tips, that seemed to wave at Alonso as the mayor smiled.

"A pleasure to meet you, Don Alonso, and welcome to Santo Domingo. I have been amiss, failing to welcome you before, but I feared to disturb you after your...dramatic arrival."

"Never think on it," Alonso said, smiling at the genuine sincerity of Don Nicolás's welcome. Officials of the Spanish government were not always famous for their genuine sincerity.

"You're well now, I trust?" the mayor asked.

"Very, Don Nicolás, thank you," Alonso assured him.

"And your wife? How does she fare?" Don Nicolás asked next. "I've heard she suffered considerably." He shook his head in concern.

"She's weak, but she improves," Alonso said. "Thank you for asking. Do you know her father?"

"Her father?" the mayor asked. "I don't believe I do. Should I?"

"Señora Francisca's father is Don Cristóbal de Seville," the governor supplied.

"Of course he is!" Don Nicolás said. "You said so not a minute before." He smiled and shook his head again, this time in wonder at his own absent-mindedness. "No, I do not know that worthy man, but one hears his name."

"One does," Alonso agreed.

Introductions done, the men mounted their horses. A fine black stallion, a spirited animal fitted with a polished leather saddle and bridle tricked out with silver had been brought for Don Alonso's use. A stable-hand appeared with a wooden step to facilitate mounting. This Alonso waved away, setting his foot with ease in the stirrup and swinging himself up into the saddle. The boy next brought the step to the governor and then the mayor and then a number of the others, each of whom made use of it.

"Don Alonso, ride with me, pray," Don Gabriel shouted, and Alonso brought his horse up alongside the governor's as they rode out of the plaza, six of the mounted troops leading the way. The mayor came up on the governor's other side and the rest of the Real Audiencia followed behind, with the last of the troops making up the tail end of the parade.

They rode south down the straight, cobbled street, their view of the ramparts and the river blocked by the low stucco buildings that lined the eastern side of their route. Ahead, the high square tower of the fortress Fortaleza Ozama loomed over the lesser buildings and on its far side guarded the seaward approach to the city. Santo Domingo was one hundred and twenty-five years old, practically newborn by the standards of Old Spain. But those years were starting to show, the decay exacerbated by the paucity of resources devoted to Hispaniola and the attention paid, not to Santo Domingo, but to the newer, richer Spanish Colonial cities to the west and south.

But as they clattered down the road Alonso could see it was more than just neglect that had taken its toll there. Santo Domingo looked as if God, in a moment of extreme irritation, had brushed the city aside, like an angry man knocking a plate off a table. In the wake of the hurricano the streets were littered with shattered roof tiles and broken palm fronds already turning brown. There were overturned carts and debris tossed randomly about. Here and there buildings stood open to the sky, their roofs completely torn away.

"That hurricano that nearly killed you, Don Alonso," the mayor said, "you can see it did quite a bit of damage here. Not the worst I've seen, but bad enough."

"Bunch of lazy dogs," Don Gabriel said, making a broad, sweeping gesture with his arm. "We get the bottom of the barrel, I can assure you. All the rogues settle here in Santo Domingo. And the slaves. As lazy as they come, the laziest of a lazy breed. This should have all been cleaned up days ago."

Alonso nodded, but it did seem to him that a lot of work was being done. Gangs of men were throwing broken bits of tile and the debris from shattered buildings into carts, tossing shovelfuls of mud and crumbled stucco aside, collecting and stacking scattered bricks. The street was crowded with people: poor Spaniards and Black slaves and Indians and those who seemed a mix of all three. As they rode through intersections with other streets Don Alonso looked down each one, and all seemed similarly crowded and busy.

"Ha! Don't let this grumbling old man poison your mind, Don Alonso," the mayor said, his tone one of good-natured amusement. "It's true, to be sure, that most don't care to stay in Santo Domingo anymore. It's on to Veracruz or Cartagena or Portobelo with them. But we have decent enough men here, and our slaves work as hard as any. Which is not too terribly hard, I'll admit."

"Slaves require proper inducement to work hard," Don Alonso observed. "The poorer sort as well. That's always been my experience."

"Indeed," Don Nicolás agreed.

They rode on in silence, the hooves of their horses ringing loud on the cobblestones. The working people looked up as they rode by and some lifted their hats in a gesture of courtesy and some just watched them pass and some regarded them with a surliness that Alonso found annoying in the extreme.

Give me some time and I'll knock the cheek clean out of these curs, he thought. It seemed scandalous to him that Don Gabriel de Chávez y Osorio, captain general of Hispaniola, or even the mayor, Don Nicolás, would suffer such disrespect. He himself had never cared much about the attitude of the common people, but he was finding now that their silent aggression annoyed him, and he wished very much to address it.

But not yet. He had been in Santo Domingo all of four days, and in that time had not even left his apartment until now. He had to await his moment. He knew enough about accumulating power to understand that. And in the meantime, he had more pressing business. Considerably more pressing.

That thought reminded Alonso of something else, something which the shipwreck had all but driven from his mind: *Nostra Sennora de Santiago. Trois Frères.* The brigantine that had crossed the ocean with them, last seen standing off to the northwest in the teeth of the rising storm. Not all of his plans had been based on what that ship held, but many of them had.

And now she was gone. He was all but certain. If *Nostra Sennora de Regla*, that mighty gallion, had not survived the storm, than there was little chance the frail *Santiago* lived.

A setback, Alonso told himself. *Unfortunate, but no more than that.* And he knew, in his heart, that that was true. But it did little to settle the discomfort in his gut.

They passed another cross street then turned east and the mounted soldiers led them off the road and onto the well-trod parade ground that surrounded the Fortaleza Ozama.

"We'll climb to the top of the tower," Don Gabriel declared. "From there you can see all of Santo Domingo and the coast east and west. Finest view in the West Indies. That is, if your strength is returned enough that the steps won't tax you too greatly."

"I'm sure I'm equal to the effort," Don Alonso assured him, though he was not so certain about the portly Don Gabriel, or the considerably more portly mayor, Don Nicolás Pérez de Maldonaldo.

If Don Gabriel drops dead of the effort, Alonso mused, *then I am governor and captain general. Four days after my arrival.* Such a speedy advancement would be stunning. It was enough to make a man think.

They dismounted and the governor led the way to the fortress. Fortaleza Ozama had been built not long after Santo Domingo itself was established, back when Spain was gaining its first foothold in the New World, which made the feat of construction that much more impressive. The stone structure seemed to Don Alonso more like three buildings joined together: one that housed barracks and officers' quarters and kitchens, a larger one that consisted of prison cells and casemates sheltering heavy guns, and, most conspicuous of the three, the sixty foot tall square tower that loomed over all.

Don Gabriel led the way up the first two sets of stairs, built onto the exterior of the middle building, and then into the cool, dark interior of the tower. From there the stairs grew narrow and steep, making their zigzag way up to the roof. Don Alonso could feel the weariness in his legs and a subtle shortness of breath. It was not the result of the shipwreck, he knew, but rather the confinement of the sea voyage that had left him in that weakened state. But it was no matter. Don Gabriel was setting the pace, and even weak as he was Don Alonso could not fail to keep up with that old and well-fed man.

They stepped at last through the door that led onto the roof of Fortaleza Ozama: red brick laid out in a herringbone pattern, somewhere around thirty feet square and surrounded by low walls and embrasures built of the ubiquitous coral stone. The breeze was fresh and warm and it felt good on Alonso's now sweating face.

"Here, what did I tell you?" Don Gabriel said, gesturing with his arms. "Most excellent view in all the West Indies. At least that a man can get to. There might be better up in the mountains, but go up there and you're likely to be eaten by one of the savages that lives there. Isn't that right, Señor Mayor?"

"Right as ever, Don Gabriel," the mayor said.

Alonso nodded. He knew nothing of savages, but he could see that the view was indeed as fine as Don Gabriel had promised. He looked south. Less than a mile away he could see the wide mouth of the Rio Ozama, and beyond it the light blue water of the Caribbean, winking and sparkling in the sun.

Below them they could see all of Santo Domingo, the streets laid out in neat perpendiculars. The city's eastern side bordered the river, its southern side bordered the sea, and the boundaries to the west and north, each no more than half a mile long, had been carved from the jungle. All was enclosed by massive stone walls with cannons and parapets spaced at regular intervals. Across the river, on the eastern shore of the Rio Ozama, the jungle lay like a carpet over the flat country, terminating in a jagged line at the sea's edge.

Don Alonso turned slowly to his left, his eyes running up the length to the waterfront on the western bank of the river. From the top of the tower he could see buildings and docks and alleyways that seemed wedged in between the city wall and the riverbank, a section of Santo Domingo which at street level had been hidden by the city walls and the high ground on which they sat. He could see docks thrust out into the river, some intact, some looking as if they had been snapped like twigs.

"What is this place, there?" Don Alonso asked, pointing down toward the waterfront.

"Slums. Refuge of the worst of these villains," Don Gabriel said.

"Nonsense," said Don Nicolás. "Again, Don Alonso, I beg you do not listen to this miserable old man. It's a waterfront, like most the world over. Those buildings, they're chiefly warehouses and such. Some merchants have their counting rooms there. Sure, there are some rough characters. Miserable whorehouses. The sort of taverns a gentleman such as yourself should steer clear of. But what paltry trade we do here in Santo Domingo, it goes through there."

"I see," Don Alonso said, looking closer now at the tight-packed buildings. There were a few men moving around in the streets, a wagon pulled by a weary-looking mule rolling slowly north. But that was it. There were no ships at any of the docks, no signs of commerce of any sort.

"To be sure, there doesn't seem to be much trade," Alonso observed.

"Of course not," Don Nicolás said. "Hurricano saw to that. Being on the river, and not the sea, it protects us somewhat, but there was damage enough, I assure you."

"Damage enough for anyone," Don Gabriel said. "There were a dozen ships there last week, a dozen at least, anchored or tied to the docks. Once the weather started to turn the largest of them headed out to sea. The ones that stayed? Well, a couple are sunk in the river. One was beat to death against the pilings. Do you see those two warehouses just south of Las Casas Reales? The ones with their walls all fallen in?"

Alonso looked in the direction in which the mayor was pointing. He saw the warehouses in question and nodded.

"Two of the ships were driven ashore and dropped right on top of those damned places. Crushed the walls in. If you go down there you'll see half of one of the ships still laying right inside the building to the north. The other is in a thousand pieces. Scattered all over. Debris must cover half a mile."

Alonso shook his head. He might have had a hard time envisioning wind and waves with the power to do such damage, had those same wind and waves not nearly killed him as well.

"Speaking of merchants," Alonso said, "do any of you gentlemen know of a merchant here by the name of Carlos Hernández?"

The name brought a short, sharp laugh from the mayor and a grunt from Don Gabriel which Alonso took to mean that they did indeed know of the man.

"Sure, we know that flea-bitten cur!" Don Nicolás said with his usual amused inflection. "That big warehouse, the one a block to the south of the ones that are crushed in? That's his. His offices are in the back of the building."

"Hernández is a cur, as Don Nicolás says," Don Gabriel added. "A notorious criminal, but a clever one. What business would you have with him?"

"None," Don Alonso said. "But back in Madrid I often heard his name spoken whenever I mentioned I was coming out to Santo Domingo."

"No surprise there," Don Gabriel said. "He's no more than a puffed-up smuggler, but he wields a lot of power, in his own way. Knows everyone, has his hands in any number of enterprises."

"Some of them are even legal, I would venture," said Don Nicolás.

"Of course he does some legal business," the governor agreed. "He needs to, so that he has some way to explain his great wealth."

Alonso nodded. What he was hearing now about Carlos Hernández was just what he had been told, what he understood to be true. It was what he was counting on. It was not news, but it was confirmation. It was another piece in the complex mosaic that he was building, and it fit neatly in place.

Chapter Fifteen

Benjamin Graves stood in the main top, one hand on the shrouds, eyes fixed on the two frigates racing north on a course to head off any ship trying to flee from St. Christopher. There was little motion aloft, with the ship driven by sweeps and no sails set, and only the smallest of ocean swells rolling in, but Graves's thoughts were tossing about like a skiff in a tempest.

Now what in all hell shall we do? he wondered. He turned and looked north, hoping some answer would present itself. Perhaps if there were a number of other ships getting underway, ships slower than *Charles Rex*, the Spaniards would concentrate on the easier prey while his own ship made for the horizon.

But that was not going to work. He could see as much right off. There were only two other ships trying to get clear of the island, both being driven by sweeps. One was Maja's ship *Santa Rosa*, the one he had come in, the one now commanded by Maja's man Ortiz. The other one Graves did not recognize. Five ships rode at anchor and showed no sign of moving, their crews either ashore or passed out drunk. A dozen more lay scattered along the beach or driven into the trees by the hurricano's massive waves.

Graves sighed. There was nothing more to learn from his high perch, and no inspiration coming his way, so he swung himself over the edge of the top and climbed back down to deck. The men at the sweeps were still hard at it, sweat running down their faces and soaking their shirts as the sun climbed above the hills to the east and spread light and heat over the water. The ship was making two or three knots, at least, though Graves knew it was still mostly the ebbing tide that was driving them. And he knew the Spanish frigates were making twice that speed at least.

Maja had turned the tiller over to one of his men and climbed up on top of the bulwark, a hand on the mizzen shroud to steady himself. He was staring south, eyes on the Spanish frigates.

Graves strolled aft, a man seemingly without worries. "Here, Maja," he said. "There are two Spanish frigates to the southward and making for us. In case you didn't see them."

"Did I ask you?" Maja said, his eyes never leaving the distant ships.

"No," Graves said. "But I reckoned I'd tell you anyway. We'll be out of the lee of this island directly. Then we'll find the wind them Dons are finding and we can set sail. You best pray we're not too late."

He waited for Maja to say something but he did not.

Fine, Graves thought. *You don't want my advice, I'll keep my own council.* And for a minute or so he managed to do that, standing there in silence, waiting for Maja to speak, until he could stand it no longer.

"Once we set sail we can run off to leeward," Graves continued. "This ship's a fast one, but not so fast as the frigates. Hopefully them Spanish bastards aren't so determined to run us down, 'cause if they are, we're done for."

He looked up at Maja. Maja took his eyes off the frigates and looked down at Graves with an expression that showed a complete lack of interest and a healthy dose of contempt.

"I'm just looking to save all our skin," Graves said. "Mine, yours..." Maja looked out toward the horizon again. Graves shrugged and walked off forward.

Stupid bastard... Graves thought. His preference: let Maja and his men be crushed under the Spanish guns, killed or dragged off to the mines. But, alas, the consequences would not be Maja's alone. The two of them were quite literally in the same boat.

He reached the bow and stepped up on the base of the bowsprit and looked off toward the frigates south of Bloody Point. They were noticeably closer now, not a pleasing sight. But Graves could also see ruffles on the water ahead, which meant wind.

He considered turning and calling aft, telling Maja to send hands to make ready to set sail. He did not know Maja well — no one did, as far as he could tell — but he had the impression that the man was an indifferent mariner. Like so many in that part of the world, Maja understood the basic workings of a ship, knew how to set sail and take it in, knew how to steer and generally how to get from one place to another, but not much beyond that. A rudimentary knowledge of seamanship was essential for men in their trade, legal and otherwise.

But for Graves it was different. He had been a sailor since leaving home, had spent more time afloat than ashore. Seamanship was not just something he did, it was who he was. He had a gift for it, loved it even, though he would not admit as much, because he also loved to complain endlessly about the sailor's lot in life, as all seamen did.

Overhead the long banner hanging from the top of the mainmast flicked and stirred as the *Charles Rex* found breeze at last. Graves opened his mouth to call orders aft, hoping to humiliate Maja by showing more alacrity than him when it came to sail handling, but he was not quick enough.

"You men, get ready to make sail!" Maja called from atop the bulwark. "Fore and main, stand ready at the gear!"

Damn his eyes... Graves thought. He climbed down from the bowsprit and took the neat coils of rope off of the belaying pins from which they hung and laid them on the deck so they would run free.

On either side the men, red-faced, sweating, gratefully pulled the long sweeps in and set them down, then moved to the pinrails where the rigging was made off. The three former slaves stood together in a knot amidships, uncertain what to do next.

Graves shook his head and walked aft. He grabbed two of the Black men and led them over to the larboard side, then cast off the main sheet and put the heavy rope in their hands.

"*Recorrido!*" he said, which he believed meant "haul" in Spanish, and apparently it did because the two men began to pull with a will.

"No, no, when I say!" Graves said, quite unsure how to render that in Spanish. The two men stopped pulling and looked at Graves, confused. From behind them Maja called out a few words in Spanish and the men turned, listened and nodded.

"Get forward, Graves, and see to them foresails," Maja added. Graves waited for the next part, the insult or threat of bodily harm, but Maja seemed to have nothing more to add. Graves turned and walked forward again.

Bastard must be more worried than he lets on, Graves thought.

He stopped by the foremast, looked around, saw the coils of rope laid out on the deck, the clew garnets and buntlines and martnets cast off and held in hand.

Good, good, he thought.

"Let fall the foresail!" Maja called from aft. "Let fall the mainsail!" The ropes were let go and the heavy canvas sails fell like curtains, rippling and snapping in the gathering breeze. Graves hurried aft and took up the foresheet and pulled. The wind caught the sail and bellied it out, enough wind to fill the sail but not so much that Graves could not pull the corner in singlehanded.

He looked to the south. The frigates, which had been hard to see from deck just moments before, were frighteningly visible now, still driving ahead with their sails full and straining. He looked in the direction from which the wind was starting to blow.

Come along now, come along, he thought. He wrestled for a moment with a decision, then pursed his lips and began to whistle softly. It was a charm certain to bring up the wind, and though it could sometimes summon more wind than was wanted, far more, it was worth the risk just then.

Fore and mainsail set, the men sheeted home the topsails and hoisted the yards, then let go the triangle-shaped mizzen sail and sheeted that home as well. Last of all the spritsail under the bowsprit was cast off and the yard cocked at a sharp angle for the sail to fill.

Charles Rex was heeling to leeward now, her sails straining as the wind began to build, her motion changing from flaccid drifting to the lively pitch, yaw and roll of open water. The seas made a rippling sound down her sides and the wake stretched out astern. Graves nodded, smiled to himself, and stopped whistling.

The ship was moving fast. Not as fast as she could, but fast. The Spanish frigates bearing down on them, however, were moving faster still.

Graves's eyes moved from the banner at the mainmast head to the ships in pursuit, then out past the bow of the *Charles Rex* as he considered bearings and speed through the water and the relative sailing qualities of the ships involved. He turned and looked aft. Maja was still standing atop the bulwark, but he was not looking at the Spanish frigates now. Rather he was looking to the north where *Santa Rosa* was also setting sail, joining *Charles Rex* in its headlong flight.

Don't care to lose that one, do you, Graves thought.

Señor Corregidor had sent Maja in command of *Santa Rosa* to retrieve his stolen cargo and bring Benjamin Graves back for punishment. Maja might return with Graves as a prisoner and *Charles Rex* as a prize, but he had failed to recover Señor Corregidor's cargo. Now if he lost *Santa Rosa* as well it would likely go hard for him. Señor Corregidor was a hard man. Partial success did not please him.

Graves looked back at the Spanish frigates just in time to see the leeward vessel swing up into the wind, her sails flogging as she tacked about. A moment later she settled on a new course, heading northeast, breaking off the chase, making for the island and not for the fleeing ships. Graves smiled.

A bit of luck there, he thought, *at long last*. Now they had only one frigate with which to contend. A bad situation still, but only half as bad as it had been a moment before.

He headed aft again. Maja had come down off the bulwark and was standing by the man at the helm, his eyes fixed straight ahead. He did not look at Graves or acknowledge him in any way.

"So, Maja, I reckon you'll want to bring *Santa Rosa* back to Señor Corregidor," he said. "The man loves that ship. And of course you won't be bringing his cargo back, which is what he really wants."

"You're what he really wants," Maja said, still not looking at Graves. "And I have you. Señor Corregidor will probably want to carve you up himself, but I hope he asks me to do it." There was lack of conviction in Maja's *pro forma* threat. Graves could hear it. It was subtle — Maja gave almost nothing away — but it was there. The fate of Benjamin Graves was not the man's most immediate concern.

"We shouldn't keep this close to *Santa Rosa*," Graves continued. "Makes no sense. There's only one frigate coming for us now. We should split up, let them come after one or the other, but not both of us."

Maja half turned and looked at Graves, a steady, inscrutable look, as if he was trying to dig through Graves's flesh and see what was in his heart. It was unnerving, but Graves held Maja's gaze. He tried to remain silent and inscrutable as well, but those were not really qualities he possessed.

"See here, I don't want to be caught by them Spanish bastards any more than you do," Graves said. "I'd rather take my chances with Señor Corregidor. Señor Corregidor's like to be more reasonable than them. And you know that ain't saying much."

For a moment more Maja just stared at Graves. Then he nodded his head toward the tiller.

"Take the helm," he said. "You do anything I don't like, you lose an ear. To start."

"As you wish, my lord," Graves said. The man at the tiller stepped aside as Graves wrapped a hand around the wooden shaft. He leaned his thigh against it, gauging the pressure that the ship was exerting on the rudder.

"Maja!" Graves shouted. "I'm going to fall off some, put some distance between us and *Santa Rosa*. See who this bloody Spaniard chases. So you leave my damned ears be." Maja gave a barely perceptible nod.

Oh, you're a cool one, Graves thought. *Bloody savage...*

He pushed the tiller away with his hand and thigh, saw the bow start to swing to larboard. "Hands to the braces, hands to the braces!" he shouted. "Haul away your starboard braces!"

The men on deck moved fast. Every one of them, the freed slaves included, understood the danger they were in. As Graves turned the ship they cast off the braces and hauled the yards around, keeping the sails set at the most perfect angle to the wind, driving *Charles Rex* as fast as she could be driven.

"That's well! Belay!" Graves called. He pulled the tiller amidships and looked over his shoulder at the Spaniard. *Charles Rex* and *Santa Rosa* were drawing apart now with Graves's change of course. The Spaniard would have to choose which of the two he would chase. Graves hoped very much he would choose *Santa Rosa*.

But he did not. For a moment the Spanish frigate maintained its unwavering course, plowing its straight furrow through the water, heading for neither *Charles Rex* nor the other, as if wrestling with a decision. Then the ship's bow swung off to larboard, following in *Charles Rex*'s wake.

Damn... Graves thought. Maja was also looking at the Spaniard, watching the change of course. He turned and looked at Graves.

"Well, the bastards have to go after someone!" Graves, protested. "*Charles Rex*, she's a fast ship, might well out-sail these whores' sons yet."

Maja continued to stare at Graves, just long enough to make it clear that he thought Graves was a lying dog, then turned and looked forward again.

I'm going to enjoy watching them Spaniards beat you like a mule, Graves thought. He looked aloft, checking to see if the set of the sails could be improved in any way, but he did not think so. *Charles Rex* was going as fast through the water as she could under those conditions, and it was quite fast indeed. Just not as fast as the Spaniard.

It was a race, nothing more, hunter and prey, the hawk swooping down on the pigeon. It was a race that *Charles Rex* would invariably lose unless they met with some great bit of luck: the Spaniard lost a sail or a mast, or decided to give it up. Graves thought about saying a prayer, but he did not think God was much interested in helping his sort. He could only hope that the Almighty would look even less favorably on the Romish ship astern.

For half an hour, and then a full hour, the chase went on. The sun climbed high above St. Christopher and the Spanish frigate gained on *Charles Rex* with each passing moment, until she was no more than a cable length astern. Graves remained at the tiller, making small adjustments to the ship's heading, coaxing the tiniest extra speed out of her, an effort that he and everyone else understood was futile.

Maja remained silent, staring straight ahead and now and then looking astern at the ship in their wake. Finally he leaned against the bulwark ten feet from where Graves stood, folded his arms and stared at Graves.

Graves ignored him for as long as he could stand it. Which was not long. "What?" he demanded. "Prithee, what would you have me do?"

Maja shrugged.

"Exactly," Graves said. "There's naught I could do, save for run like the devil and hope these bastards give it up."

"They seem very determined," Maja said, the first words he had spoken in well over an hour.

"Well, sure, but if we can keep out of their hands a bit longer…" Graves said. He was struggling to come up with the second part of that sentence when they heard a dull, flat booming sound astern, followed by the high-pitched buzz of some sort of iron shot flying past. Graves turned and looked astern just as the cloud of gray smoke from the Spaniard's bow guns was whipped away by the breeze.

"Chain shot," Maja observed.

"Mayhaps. Or mayhaps crossbar shot," Graves said. Either way it was an unhappy development. Chain or crossbar, a well-placed round could bring *Charles Rex*'s rig down around their ears, and that would put an end to their flight very quickly.

Maja shook his head. "You are not a lucky man, Benjamin Graves," he said again, and this time Graves found it particularly irksome. Perhaps because he feared it was true.

Luck... Graves thought. *Luck favors the bold...*

And that was true. Graves knew it. The times he had been most lucky were the times he had been most bold. Good luck did not happen to those who just sat on their buttocks and hoped it would come to them.

"Hands to the braces! Hands to the braces!" Graves shouted with enough urgency to get the men racing to the pinrails. "Stand ready to get larboard tacks aboard!"

Maja straightened. "What fool thing do you propose now?" he asked.

"I don't know," Graves said, which was true enough. He was just letting the boldness — boldness bordering on madness — carry him along now. He shoved the tiller hard over to starboard and *Charles Rex* swung hard a-larboard, heeling as she turned.

"Let go and haul! Let go and haul! Board your larboard tacks! Haul, you whores' sons!" Graves shouted and Maja repeated the words in Spanish and the men, stunned and confused as they were, did as they were told.

The horizon seemed to spin past as Graves turned the ship through nearly one hundred and eighty degrees. Nevis to the south and then the island of St. Christopher appeared dead ahead. And then the Spanish frigate lay under their bow, as she and *Charles Rex* charged at one another like knights in the list.

"If you mean to ram her, I reckon we'll get the worst of it," Maja observed.

"We'll see," Graves said. His eyes were on the Spaniard now. With the two ships converging the distance between them was falling away fast. A puff of smoke appeared at the Spaniard's bow, and then the sound of the gun and in the same instant the scream of the shot passing overhead. Graves saw the starboard main brace part, the ends of the severed rope falling to the deck, and one of the men racing aloft to repair it before he could even give the order.

Two hundred feet separated the ships now. Graves could see the water piling up under the Spaniard's bow. He could see the crew running around on her deck: he even thought he could hear the excited gibberish of those confused men shouting fore and aft. On this course the two ships would indeed hit head-on, and there was no doubt that the man-of-war would stave in *Charles Rex*'s bow like an egg.

No, I reckon not... Graves thought. He really did not know what he would do next, but he knew that ramming the Spaniard would not be it. He pulled the tiller toward him and watched the ship's bow turn to starboard, settling on a course that would take them down the Spaniard's larboard side, her leeward side, as they passed.

Though he had not actually thought it through, Graves realized he was counting on two things. One was that the Spaniard did not wish to collide with *Charles Rex* any more than Graves wished to collide with the Spaniard.

Because if the Spaniard did wish to hit *Charles Rex* he could do so easily enough. One slight twist of the rudder and the two ships would become one.

The second was that the Spaniard would not fire his great guns into them. The frigate's cannons would be loaded of course, going into battle as they were. The two ships would pass with no more than fifty feet of water between them. If the Spaniard loosened a broadside then that would be the end of Graves's dubious career, and likely the end of his ship as well. Their only hope was that the Spanish captain would not risk sinking his ship by opening his gunports on the downwind side.

We'll find out directly, Graves thought. He did not even consider loading and firing *Charles Rex*'s four-pounder guns. A broadside from *Rex* would be as effective as hurling ships' biscuits at the frigate.

A gust of wind heeled both ships and drove them on and then they were alongside one another with a stone's throw of distance between them, and Graves's first concern was answered. The Spaniard did not alter course, did not make any effort to turn into the path of *Charles Rex* and smash the smaller ship under her superior size and weight.

Across the water Graves could see men racing around the Spaniard's deck. He could see the officers aft in their bright-colored clothing, he could see arms waving and pointing.

He looked down at the dark hull with its bands of yellow and red paint, geometric chevrons and intricate vine patterns. The gunports were closed, and with the ship heeling as steeply as she was Graves doubted the captain would dare open them. One hard roll and the seas would come pouring in and the ship would go down in minutes. It had happened often enough in the past.

And what now? Graves thought. What would they do once they had shot past the Spaniard? The frigate could turn and bring her guns to bear and that would be an end to it. The guns might not be run out now, but that could change in an instant.

"Hands to wear ship!" Graves shouted. He looked over at Maja who had not spoken or even moved since Graves had spun *Charles Rex* around. Maja turned his head and looked at Graves now, raised his eyebrows, then looked forward again.

The frigate plunged on past, the high, ornate stern with its gilded carvings around the aft windows sweeping past *Charles Rex*'s quarterdeck. Graves pulled the tiller toward him and the ship slewed around to starboard, the horizon sweeping past her bow as the men forward hauled on the braces to keep her sails square to the easterly wind.

The ship rolled through the turn, reversing course once again, and Graves pushed the tiller back amidships. The Spaniard was directly ahead of them now and three hundred feet off. They were banging into the ship's wake, following her elaborately decorated transom west, the two ships running in a straight line almost directly downwind. The Spaniard had no cannons pointing aft. As long as *Charles Rex* remained exactly astern, none of their guns would bear.

"You have the lion by the tail now," Maja said. "A safe place, methinks. Until you let go."

Graves was grinning despite himself, despite the truth of Maja's words. They were safe for now, but they could not stay there forever, and the Spaniard would certainly do something directly to shake them off.

"Let us wait and see what the lion does," Graves said.

They did not wait long. The two ships charged on for another quarter mile, *Charles Rex* racing along behind the frigate like a mouse chasing a cat. Graves could see heads appear over the high stern as the officers looked back at the strange ship in their wake and no doubt debated what to do about it. He could just envision them shouting at one another in their absurd Spanish and waving their arms around as if they were in the midst of a swarm of bees. The English ship was a threat to nothing but their egos, but for officers of Spain that was at least as important as their lives.

Then with no warning the frigate turned hard to larboard, her yards bracing around, the gunports along her side swinging open, the long barrels of the guns running out. She was turning on her tormentor, hoping to spin around quick and catch them by surprise.

Graves knew Maja was looking at him but he kept his eyes straight ahead, fixed on the Spanish frigate and the curving wake behind it. If he panicked and turned now, which the Spanish captain doubtless hoped he would, *Charles Rex* would be right under the Spanish guns and they would not live there long. But Graves did not panic. He held his course as the frigate came around, keeping *Charles Rex* on the Spaniard's stern.

"Stand ready with them braces!" he shouted forward. "Stand ready to brace up, larboard tack!"

The aftermost gun in the Spaniard's broadside went off, a billow of smoke shot out over the water, and the round shot screamed by, thirty feet astern. The Spanish gunners had become over-eager: their ship had not turned enough for the guns to bear.

"Haul away your braces!" Graves shouted as he pushed the tiller away and watched *Charles Rex*'s bow swing around, following the Spaniard through the turn. The men pulled with a will and overhead the yards pivoted around the masts as *Charles Rex* reversed course again, turning from her downwind run to sailing full and bye. And once more they were directly behind the Spanish frigate. The lion had tried to shake them, but they were still holding tight to its tail.

"How long you reckon we can play at this game?" Maja asked.

"Not sure," Graves said. "Until them Spaniards grow bored, or make some mistake."

"Or until you make some mistake."

"Fear not," Graves said. "You'll die of old age afore that happens."

But the Spaniard was not bored, not yet. He was turning once again, his bow swinging to pass through the eye of the wind as he tried again to get his teeth into the elusive prey astern.

Uh oh... Graves thought.

"They're tacking!" he shouted. "Stand ready to come about!"

Rather than wearing ship, turning with the wind astern, the Spaniard was going to tack, turning the ship's bow through the wind, an altogether trickier proposition. For a moment the ship would point straight into the wind like a weather vane, with the chance that she could stop right there, stuck, failing to complete the turn. "In irons," it was called.

Now Graves had to tack as well, or he would be under the Spaniard's guns for certain.

Damn it, damn it... Grave thought. The Spaniard would have a large crew, well-trained at this maneuver, whereas he had just a handful of men who spoke two different languages, most of whom he did not know, some of whom knew nothing of ships and sailing. If the Spaniard was in danger of getting in irons, he was even more so.

The frigate continued its turn, coming up into the wind. The sails started to shiver as the wind blew down both sides of the canvas, then came aback, flattened against the masts as the wind struck them on the forward side.

Wait...wait... Graves thought. He had to time this perfectly. He had to turn in time to keep astern of the frigate but not so soon that he ran the risk of smashing into her. Ahead of them he could see the yards on the frigate's main and mizzen mast start to swing around as the wind continued to press against the sails on the foremast.

Graves pulled his eyes from the Spaniard and looked down the deck of his own ship. The men were ready, braces in hand, looking aft at him.

"Very well, you whores' sons," he shouted. "Get ready to haul when I tell you, and not a second before or after!"

"I think the Spaniard is in irons," Maja said.

Graves looked up quick. In the few seconds he had been looking away the Spanish frigate seemed to have plunged into chaos. The sails were flogging and snapping in the breeze, yards were bracing this way and that, and the bow was pointed directly into the eye of the wind. Most crucially, the ship had stopped. She hung there, held in the invisible hand of the easterly wind.

"Ha!" Graves shouted in delight, and then said, "Oh, damn my eyes," as he realized *Charles Rex* was two hundred feet and ten seconds away from smashing into the Spaniard's stern. He pulled the tiller toward him and watched the ship's bow turn to starboard, turning to run down the Spaniard's starboard side.

Charles Rex came hurdling down on the frigate's tall stern, passing so close that Graves had to look up at it. He could see the officers in their brilliant silks looking down at him. They were so close he could see their moustaches and neat goatees and the red and yellow stripes of their doublets. The madness was still on him and he could not resist giving them a friendly wave.

The gesture was greeted by the roar of a cannon right underfoot, and the shudder of the deck below him as the Spaniard blasted round shot into *Charles Rex*'s hull from twenty feet away.

"Oh, damn my eyes!" Graves shouted again, much louder this time. On this heading they would pass down the full length of the Spaniard's side, giving each of their heavy guns an easy shot at point blank range.

He pulled the tiller toward him, hard, and *Rex* turned to starboard, turning away from the Spaniard just as two more guns went off. Graves could feel the concussion from the cannons' muzzles. He felt the deck jump as the shot struck the hull. He saw a burst of splinters and the dark streaks of the balls in flight as they passed right through *Charles Rex* and smashed out the other side, flying another hundred feet before plunging into the sea.

"Haul away your larboard braces, haul away!" Graves shouted and the men forward pulled and the yards overhead turned. They were sailing directly away from the Spaniard, the wind coming over the beam, racing to get clear of the reach of the guns. They were still well within range, but the Spaniards had only the stern of *Charles Rex* to shoot at now, a considerably smaller target.

One after another the Spanish guns fired, jetting smoke out over the water. The round shot shrieked by, some close enough to feel the wind of its passing, some so far off the mark they could not even see where it fell. One ball passed through first the mainsail and then the foresail, leaving ragged holes in the canvas, before plunging into the sea ahead. But that was as close as any came.

By the time *Charles Rex* was beyond range of her guns, the frigate was still struggling to straighten out her mess aloft, to get out of irons and underway. Benjamin Graves altered course again, sailing with the wind astern and St. Christopher's and Nevis in their wake. They could hear the sound of heavy cannons, muted and soft, as the galleons closed in on Old Road Bay, where *Charles Rex* and *Santa Rosa* had lain at anchor just that morning. Already they could see great columns of smoke rising off the land, marking where the Spanish troops ashore had begun their devastation.

"There," Graves said. "You still reckon I'm unlucky?"

Maja shrugged. "Not sure," he said. "We'll see if Señor Corregidor decides to kill you quick. Then we'll know."

Chapter Sixteen

The sun was streaming in through the stern windows when LeBoeuf came awake. *Santiago* was rocking gently at anchor. Henriette was gone.

Those things he knew even before he opened his eyes. He could feel the warmth of the sun on his face and the brilliant light against his closed eyelids. He could feel the motion, the blessed motion, of a ship under him, rocking him, cradle-like.

He could not feel Henriette under his arm or pressed gently against him, as she had been all through the night. He stirred a bit, held his hand up to shield his eyes and then opened them. The cabin was indeed filled with light, and tiny bits of dust floated in the shafts coming through the glass. Henriette was sitting on the settee aft, her feet drawn up under her petticoats, her arms hugging her legs.

"So," she said. "Do you like girls?"

LeBoeuf pushed himself up on one elbow and found a place where the sun was not in his eyes. He dropped his hand. "I like them well enough," he said.

Henriette nodded. LeBoeuf wondered if she would continue that line of questioning, but she seemed satisfied with that answer. She looked around the cabin. "Whoever the bastard was that was master of this ship, he was no pauper, I can see that," she said.

LeBoeuf looked around as well, the first time he had seen the cabin in the daylight, and he could see that Henriette was right. Either *Santiago*'s master or her owner — and they might have been one and the same — had money enough to fit the cabin out well, tiny though it may might be.

The curtains that hung down over the stern windows, now pushed aside, were fine white linen with lace edges and embroidery in the corners. The table was mahogany, polished so it shone like a coat of ice on a sunny winter morning after the rain. The cabinet that took up most of the starboard side was mahogany as well, clearly made to match the table in color and style. The deck was covered with a carpet. It was still soaked through from the seas that must have washed through the place, but LeBoeuf could make out the intricate patterns woven into the fabric, the delicate fringe around the edges.

"Find anything of worth?" LeBoeuf asked.

"What do you mean?"

"You were in here yesterday, fetching the food and drink. I imagine you had a bit of a look around."

Henriette's eyebrows came together. "What are you saying? Are you saying I'm a thief?"

LeBoeuf shrugged. Henriette's denial, feigned though it was, was rendered in a very believable manner. She was skillful and quick. That was certainly why she had risen to the heights she had, and not ended up as some broken, poxed whore on the streets of Paris.

Still, LeBoeuf did not doubt she had explored the cabin thoroughly and laid claim to anything worth having that she could hide.

"Of course I'm not saying you're a thief," LeBoeuf said. "You were lady in waiting to the queen. But, prithee…this ship…she's mine. You know that. I traded my part of the cargo for her."

"I know," Henriette said. "Clever bargain. With such wily deal-making, it's little wonder you are the great man you are today."

"The rest of it, all the contents of the ship, it all belongs to the others," LeBoeuf continued, ignoring Henriette's observation. "These boucaniers, they're a lawless crowd. But there are a few rules they do not break, and one is that they never steal from their kind."

"I'm not their kind. And I do not steal."

"No, you're not their kind, I'll warrant. But it would not go well for you if you was found to have taken something. So if you have, don't get caught."

Henriette glared at him for a moment. Then she made a *humph* sound and looked away.

LeBoeuf swung his legs over the edge of the bunk and sat for a moment, then stood with care. He was accustomed to low overheads and had learned through hard use to avoid smashing his head into deck beams and such. He often wondered how much smarter he might have been if he had not bashed his brains as often as he had.

His shirt was still heaped on top of the table and LeBoeuf considered pulling it on again but he could not bear it, so he left it there. He hoped that in doing so Henriette might take it upon herself to launder it as she had taken to doing with some of his other clothing those past weeks. Of course, implying she was a thief might not have inspired the helpmate in her.

"How did you get that scar?" Henriette asked. LeBoeuf looked down at jagged line of healed pink flesh that ran diagonally across his belly.

"Not that one, the one on your face," Henriette said.

LeBoeuf resisted the urge to touch it. He knew what it looked like, lighter than the rest of his deeply burned skin, a neat slash from just below his right eye that disappeared into his tangle of beard.

"Sea fight," LeBoeuf said. "I was boatswain aboard a privateer. British frigate shot down our foremast. Broken end of the fore topsail yard nearly took my head off, but it settled for leaving a scar."

Henriette nodded. The sun was mostly behind her and she was hard to see and LeBoeuf could not tell if she believed him or not. Or if she really cared.

"I'm going on deck now," he said. "We'll be getting the cargo out. Which is the property of them others, as I mentioned."

"I wish you joy in your labors," Henriette said.

"One more thing," LeBoeuf continued. "Later, me and some of the others...Van Loudersong for one, I'm sure...will come back and search this cabin for anything of worth, because that would be part of what the others claimed. Most ship's masters, they have some specie, gold or silver, tucked away in their cabins. For buying supplies, hiring shipwrights, that sort of thing. The other men, they would be very surprised if they found nothing. Very surprised. And unhappy."

He looked Henriette in the eyes and she looked back, unflinching, unwavering, her lips pressed tightly together. They remained that way for a moment, swords locked, before she spoke.

"Then let us hope they find something," she said.

"Let us hope," LeBoeuf agreed. He picked up his belt and knives and stepped through the door. He walked crouching under the quarterdeck then straightened to his full height and strapped the belt around his waist. He looked up at the sun. It was early and the others were still sprawled out on the deck.

The evening before, they had managed to locate some ships' biscuits and a few hams and had made a decent supper of them. Now LeBoeuf drew a knife and cut off a chunk of meat, found the better part of a biscuit and took his place on the quarterdeck steps once again. He ate in silence and looked around and started forming a list in his head.

Pump the bilge dry, overhaul the stay tackle and see it's not about to carry away. Get this wreckage cleared off. Send some hands ashore to find some more boats and men...we won't get this cargo ashore with the men we have here and just the one periagua.

He was already issuing orders in his mind when he recalled that he had no business issuing orders at all. *Santiago* might be his ship, but these men were not his crew. He was no more captain over them than he was captain over the savages who lived in the mountains. If there was one thing that drove a man to live the life of a boucanier, it was that he would suffer no one to have authority over him.

LeBoeuf sighed. He would need to use diplomacy where once he would have simply used cold command.

He finished his breakfast, took a deep drink of the ale they had hoisted up on deck, and ambled over to the pinrail on the starboard side. He took the fall of the stay tackle off its belaying pin and let the heavy block with its iron hook drop to the deck. It hit with a jarring thump which he hoped would wake the others, but it did not, so he continued on with his task, inspecting the rope to see that it would not break under the strain of hoisting the barrels up from below.

That done, he went forward and found a handspike and tried the windlass to see that it still turned. He climbed up the main shrouds and out onto the main yard and freed the end of the yard tackle, then brought it back to deck. By that time the others were beginning to stir, some awake enough to start quaffing more of the wine and brandy they had found in the hold.

"LeBoeuf, what are you about?" Van Loudersong said, sitting on the main hatch and shielding his eyes as he looked up.

"Getting the stay tackle and yard tackle ready. Reckoned the lot of you'd want to get your cargo ashore. In case the ship decides to sink after all."

Van Loudersong nodded. He looked around. He looked back at LeBoeuf. "We'll have to fetch some of the men still ashore. If they want part of this cargo they can work for it. And more boats. We won't get all this ashore with just the one periagua."

"Right," LeBoeuf said, nodding. "Good thought, that." He half turned from Van Loudersong and looked aloft. The topmasts had cracked just above the caps and were hanging like broken arms, and with them the topsail yards.

"Huh…" LeBoeuf said with an uncertain tone.

"What?" Van Loudersong asked.

"Well, seems to me, all this wrecked top-hamper, it's in the way of getting the cargo out. Don't know how we sway anything overboard with those topmasts and the yards just hanging like that."

The Dutchman looked up as if noticing the smashed spars and torn rigging and sails for the first time. He sighed. "Reckon you're right," he said, his tone one of resignation. LeBoeuf had just added another two hours to their labors, but there was nothing for it.

Van Loudersong stood and took a long drink of wine and then took command as LeBoeuf knew he would. He ordered those still asleep to wake up, to have some breakfast, some wine. He ordered a handful of men to row ashore and round up the others and all the boats they could find. He ordered men up aloft to start straightening out the tangled nightmare that the hurricano had made of the rig.

LeBoeuf stood back, watched, said nothing. The boucaniers needed some organizing, and they seemed willing to let the Dutchman do it. And since Van Loudersong was ordering the men to do what he, LeBoeuf, wanted them to do anyway, LeBoeuf was also willing to let the man have at it.

It was possible, of course, that the others would start to resent having someone assume command over them. If so, better that their resentment be directed at Van Loudersong then at LeBoeuf.

The *ad hoc* crew worked through the morning hours and they worked quickly. The hunters were men used to hard labor — they could work with a will when they wanted to — and when it came to securing their newfound wealth, they very much wanted to. They cast off the rigging, with LeBoeuf insisting that they save what they could. They lowered the ropes to deck, and with it the broken masts and yards. They untangled lines which the storm had twisted into fantastic knots. They freed bits of torn sail and dropped them fluttering down.

The sun reached its zenith and the men stopped briefly for a dinner of ham and biscuit and ale from a barrel they had overlooked earlier. Their meal finished, they decided to search the master's cabin to see if there was anything there worth taking. Van Loudersong led the way, and in short order they found a small leather sack filled with sixty doubloons. It was a decent enough haul, enough to prevent them from wondering, as LeBoeuf did, how much had been in the sack originally.

The search of the cabin done, they turned back to emptying the hold. Slings were fastened to the casks and one by one they were hoisted up from below, swayed over the side and set gently down into the waiting boats. The men ashore had managed to find four of them large enough to bear the weight of a barrel or two, all that the hurricano had left behind. Oars manned, they moved back and forth between the ship and the beach carrying the salvaged cargo to the land and then coming back for more.

And they discovered, as they dug into *Santiago*'s hold, that the ship was more richly laden than they had first realized. Along with the butts of wine and barrels of brandy and hogsheads of olive oil and flour and such they found firkins of musket balls, barrels of gunpowder; they discovered crates filled with muskets, flintlock muskets, and not the matchlocks of expiring vintage. They found bolts of cloth, fine linen and even silk.

LeBoeuf realized that he had traded away a small fortune. And still he felt he had the best of it.

There was ample daylight left by the time the last of the cargo had been hoisted out of the hold, over the bulwark and down to the waiting boat.

"Here you are, LeBoeuf," Pierre le Chasseur said. "We leave you an empty ship. May she serve you well."

LeBoeuf nodded. He was tired and filthy from the work of the day, but he was also profoundly satisfied, and even Le Chasseur's tone, which clearly suggested that LeBoeuf had made a fool's bargain, could not undermine his good humor.

"I've no doubt she will," LeBoeuf said. "And any of you wishes to stay aboard, help me get her ready for sea, well, I would be grateful."

He saw amused glances pass from man to man. Billy Solent spoke next. "And what would be our reward for that?" he asked.

"My gratitude. That's what I said."

More glances, and those even more amused. "Well," Billy said, "your gratitude and a purse full of gold might be something, but I don't reckon the one without the other will move too many of us."

He was right, of course, and LeBoeuf knew it. One by one the buccaneers climbed down *Santiago*'s boarding steps and settled in the boats and rowed ashore. The sun went down and they lit a fire on the beach and set in to eating and drinking. The flames illuminated the great store of salvage they had taken from the hold and piled nearby.

LeBoeuf stayed aboard, as did Henriette. Le Rongeur remained as well, which was no surprise. He would find no welcome among the men on the beach. He had never been well liked, and after having abandoned LeBoeuf to the lanceros and having tried to have his way with Henriette, he was liked even less.

Le Rongeur certainly knew that, and he knew LeBoeuf despised him as well. But he also knew that LeBoeuf needed every able body he could find to make *Santiago* ready for sea and so would at least tolerate him. And in that, Le Rongeur was correct.

The bacchanal on the beach was still at full strength when they turned in for the night. Once again LeBoeuf retreated to the master's cabin — his cabin — and once again Henriette followed him there. She laid down beside him as she had done the night before. And like the night before, LeBoeuf was debating whether or not to make some amorous advance when he fell fast asleep. He wondered, as he felt himself drifting off, whether this second failure to stay awake would convince Henriette that women were indeed not to his liking.

LeBoeuf woke the next morning to the sensation of something soft and warm hitting his face. He opened his eyes. The cabin was dim-lit, the tide having swung the stern away from the rising sun. Henriette was no longer in bed, but his shirt was, laying crumpled by his head where she had thrown it at him. He looked up. Henriette was sitting on the settee as she had been the morning before.

"I washed your shirt," she said. "Maybe now I won't want to puke every time I smell it."

"Thank you," LeBoeuf said, sitting up. He took a moment to get his bearings, then picked up the shirt and slipped it on. It was warm from having dried in the morning sun, slightly crisp and smelling of soap. It was heavenly.

"Thank you," LeBoeuf said again. He stood, careful not to hit his head. "Now, we must repair the ship."

Henriette frowned. "What do I know of repairing ships?" she asked.

"There are things you can do," LeBoeuf said. "You can help by tending the sheets. I'm sure you've tended plenty of sheets."

"Go to hell," Henriette said.

"In due time," LeBoeuf said.

He stepped through the door and out to the waist. Le Rongeur was lying on the deck forward, using a coil of rope as a pillow and LeBoeuf left him alone for the moment. He looked aloft. A great deal of work had already been done in preparation for getting the cargo out. The fore and main topmasts were down, and the topsail yards as well, all of them lying on deck with rigging and bits of sail still attached. And all were damaged nearly to the point of uselessness.

The topmasts had both snapped about ten feet up from their heels. They had not broken clean apart but rather had shattered, the two parts still clinging together like a green twig bent in half. The fore topsail yard was in similar shape, shattered in the slings with the larboard yardarm snapped clean off. Much of the rigging had been shredded, the frayed ends lying like cat-o'-nine-tails on the deck. The main topsail yard was a bit better than the fore, but not by much.

Still, it was incredible that the ship, the masts, the yards, the hull had survived to the extent that they had. But hurricanos were like that. LeBoeuf had seen it before. One thing was destroyed, another saved, for no reason this side of Heaven.

Le Rongeur came ambling over, clearly unsure of what reception he might expect. Gratitude for his staying? Continued fury for his attack on Henriette? Or the same utter indifference with which LeBoeuf had treated him during most of their time together?

"Get up aloft, start casting off the robands on the foresail," LeBoeuf said. He was not in the mood for idle chatter. He never was.

"What the devil's a 'roband'?"

"The small lines that tie the sail to the yard. Start at the yardarms and work your way in to the middle."

"Cast off… You mean untie? Why don't I just cut them?"

"Don't cut anything I don't tell you to cut," LeBoeuf said. Le Rongeur nodded. He knew better than to question. He started to turn away, then stopped.

"How…" he began and stopped again.

"How what?" LeBoeuf asked in a tone that did not invite continued discussion.

"Nothing," Le Rongeur. He turned and walked off toward the foremast, clambered onto the shrouds and began to climb aloft like a man unaccustomed to doing so. Le Rongeur had told LeBoeuf a bit about his past life, but LeBoeuf had not really paid attention. He could not recall if Le Rongeur ever claimed to have gone to sea.

How...?

That was the start of the question Le Rongeur wanted to ask. And LeBoeuf knew what the rest of the question would have been, if the man had been allowed to continue.

How can we possibly get this ship ready for sea? Two men and a woman, by themselves?

It was a good question. The answer was, they could not.

The other answer was, they would not have to.

But for that day, and for the next few days, the three of them did work alone, the hours settling into their own routine. Henriette grew more domestic by the day. She would rise early and stoke a fire in the brick hearth LeBoeuf had put together on the deck. She would make a porridge out of oats and molasses which LeBoeuf purchased from the men on the beach. The food had once been part of *Santiago*'s cargo, but now was the property of the buccaneers.

The three of them would eat and then they would get to work, and for people whose lives had long been marked by turmoil and uncertainty, such sameness was not at all unpleasant. LeBoeuf and Le Rongeur worked up aloft, generally, and on separate masts if LeBoeuf could arrange it. Henriette would busy herself removing the rigging from the yards on the deck, or making piles of gear, or wrestling up supplies from the boatswain's stores and tools from the carpenter's, or readying the next meal.

With the masts and yards on deck LeBoeuf was able to better assess what needed doing, what was salvageable and what was beyond redemption. The topmasts, he realized, could not be repaired in any way, but their cause was not lost: he could simply cut off the broken ends and reuse what was left. They would look odd, to be sure, like withered limbs, but that was the least of his concerns. He wanted only to get the ship in such condition that he could sail her to someplace where a Frenchman might find help, and not a Spanish prison. Tortuga, perhaps, or St. Christopher's.

Shortening the masts, of course, meant shortening the rigging as well, so LeBoeuf set up a makeshift rigging loft on *Santiago*'s quarterdeck, where he could carry out those alterations, along with the numerous other repairs that the rigging required. He taught Henriette some of the basic techniques of the rigger's art and set her to it, as she in turn complained bitterly and bemoaned the abuse.

"You expect me to do that?" she asked as LeBoeuf showed her how to haul a length of marline tight. "Are you mad? A day of that and my hands will look like some damned fishmonger's wife. And my petticoats will be thick with tar. You think I want to look like the jolly, sheep-biting Sailor Lad?"

"I think your days of serving m'lady are well past," LeBoeuf said.

"And I think your plans, if you have any, are a fool's dream," she spat. "As if the three of us could repair and sail this ship! Even if we had another three men here, men who were twice as smart and able as you...which would not be very hard to find, I can assure you...even then we would not be able to set this wreck to rights."

"You know better than me, of course," LeBoeuf said.

"You're like Noah, building your ark all by yourself while everyone laughs at you."

LeBoeuf nodded. He wondered if she knew how things had worked out for the people who laughed at Noah.

"Look at them," Henriette said, nodding her head toward the men and women on the beach. "Even I know the cargo from this wreck was worth a fortune. And you just gave it all away. So now we work at this pointless task, and the rest, they sit idle and wait to sell their booty and walk off with the gold."

"Yes," LeBoeuf agreed. "Yes, they do." He held up the tarred marline in his hand. "Now let me show you how we finish off this round seizing."

The rigging required some skill and knowledge, but sawing the masts in two and cutting holes for the fids and mast ropes were mindless, tedious jobs, so LeBoeuf set Le Rongeur to them. Le Rongeur was no more enthusiastic or willing than Henriette, but happily he did not dare push LeBoeuf too far. He grumbled as he worked, cursed under his breath, shot ugly glances aft at LeBoeuf and Henriette, but he did no more than that. He knew that LeBoeuf would be perfectly happy to set him ashore, where he would be at even greater risk. He had no friends among the men there. What's more, things on the beach did not seem to be going terribly well.

The first few nights after the cargo had been hauled ashore were marked by impressive bonfires, the hurricano having left considerable fuel in its wake, and the sounds of raucous celebrations. But the celebrations grew more muted as the week wore on, until finally the bacchanal seemed to devolve into shouting and screaming and then gunfire. The following night there were not one but two bonfires, a hundred yards apart.

LeBoeuf stood on his quarterdeck, looked at the two fires and the great pile of booty midway between them, just visible at the edge of the firelight. He shook his head.

This is not good... he thought. Things seemed to be falling apart even quicker than he had imagined they would.

Chapter Seventeen

At the southern end of the city of Santo Domingo, where the river met the sea, the city wall made a sharp turn to the west, following the island's shoreline. It was the least respectable part of the upper town. It was where the tradesmen and the laborers and the sailors and the shopkeepers lived and did their business and took their leisure. It was where the merchants who catered to the lower sort sold their wares and the tavern keepers sold drink and the prostitutes sold pleasure.

It was not, to be sure, some thoroughly depraved region of squalor and vice, not like the slums of Madrid or Seville or even the waterfront of Santo Domingo that lay outside the walls. Or so Don Alonso imagined — he had not visited any of those other places. But compared to the neighborhoods surrounding Las Casas Reales, the south end of Santo Domingo was something far more unsavory, far more base. It was just dangerous enough to give Alonso a bit of thrill as he moved through the dark, narrow, crowded streets.

He kept his right hand tucked under his cloak, inches from the pistol hidden there. That precaution was not entirely necessary, he knew, but it helped sharpen the sensation.

Don Alonso had taken his clandestine leave from Las Casas Reales an hour before, after apologizing to Francisca for having to work late on official business. He instructed the servant waiting outside his office to summon his secretary, Juan Cardero, then he stepped into the big room and closed the door behind him. A large table which served as a desk occupied much of the floor. There was a sitting area with a few oak and leather chairs, and discreetly to one side a small bed, because Don Alonso enjoyed a siesta on occasion and did not wish to leave the blessed privacy of his office just to take a short nap.

Alonso crossed the room to a heavy trunk that sat near the bed. He opened the lid and let it rest against the wall. Inside were, among other things, a plain suit of clothes, a dark wool cape and a black, wide-brimmed hat. These he removed and spread out on the desk.

A knock at the door and Alonso said, "Come."

Juan Cardero stepped in and shut the door behind him. The secretary was pale and quiet, furtive, always on the lookout for the main chance, and Don Alonso did not particularly like him. Nor did he trust the man, and he was certain Cardero took every opportunity to enrich himself at his master's expense.

But Juan was also clever and capable. He had a near complete knowledge of all of Don Alonso's business and a great facility for keeping it all organized, which was invaluable. Cardero kept secrets well because it was in his interest to do so. His thefts were minor, and as long as he saw Don Alonso as his best chance for wealth and advancement then he could be trusted, after a fashion.

And there in Santo Domingo, a thousand leagues from anyone or anything that was familiar to him, Juan Cardero needed Don Alonso too much to betray him completely.

"Cardero, I'll be going out," Alonso said. "Help me shift my clothes."

"Yes, sir," Cardero said, no surprise, no question in his voice. He crossed the room and Don Alonso lifted his arms and Cardero began to undo the hooks that held Alonso's breeches to his silk and brocade doublet. Alonso kicked off his shoes, and once the breeches were free Cardero let them fall to the floor and Alonso stepped out of them. Alonso turned to face Cardero and Cardero began to undo the row of small, silk-covered buttons that ran down Alonso's chest.

With Cardero's help, Alonso traded the fine clothing of a lieutenant governor for something more earthy: leather breeches and a plain wool doublet and boots that reached up to his knees. The clothes were well-worn and familiar, veterans of dozens of quiet assignations of various sorts.

Alonso reached back into the chest and pulled out a small box that contained a pistol and powder, ball and priming and held it out to Cardero.

"Load this," he said. "And do it properly, if you know what's good for you."

"Yes, sir," Cardero said. He set the box on the desk and flipped open the lid. Alonso reached into the chest once again and pulled out a rapier with scabbard and shoulder belt, something far more plain than he was wont to carry. He draped the leather belt over his shoulder and adjusted the way it hung.

"Here, Don Alonso," Cardero said, turning back to Alonso and handing him the pistol and the small flask of powder and a leather bag heavy with bullets. Alonso took them. He slipped the pistol into a loop on the shoulder belt where it would be hidden by his cape and hung the flask and the bag from the baldric of his sword and he relished the thrill he always felt at being armed in that way.

He swept his hat up off the desk and set it on his head. "I shall be gone a few hours," he said.

"Yes, sir," Cardero said, a hint of worry on his face. This sort of thing was not unusual for Don Alonso, but they were not in Spain anymore. Now they were in a city in a part of the world that was not familiar to either man. Still, Cardero knew better than to ask questions or protest.

"No one is to know I'm away," Alonso said, looking Cardero in the eye. "But I need not tell you that."

"Of course, Don Alonso," Cardero said. He met Alonso's eyes and did not flinch.

Transformation complete, Cardero stepped out into the foyer and called the servant to him. He told the man to inform Lady Francisca's maid that Don Alonso would be at his work for several hours more. The servant hurried off, and once the way was cleared Alonso slipped out of his office and then out a little-used door off one of the side rooms and out into the warm night.

He walked quickly south, his hat pulled low over his head. He had not been long in Santo Domingo, and there was little chance of his being recognized anywhere, but if he was, it would most likely be in the neighborhood of Las Casas Reales.

When he was a few blocks away he turned off the wide street and made his way along an alleyway that terminated at the city wall, a dark place where no sentries patrolled. He stopped there and looked down at the tangle of warehouses below and the Rio Ozama beyond, all of it illuminated by a quarter moon. There were a few pinpoints of light scattered around the streets and alleys of the lower town, some fixed, some moving, lanterns hanging from hooks or carried by people hurrying about their late-night business.

At the river's edge a single ship lay tied to a dock, a lantern illuminating a small patch of its deck. Alonso could see no one moving on board, but he imagined there was at least one man there, some sailor keeping the night watch.

Asleep in the scuppers, he thought. *Or dead drunk.*

But it did not matter. There was nothing there on the ship to protect, save for the ship itself, and Alonso did not care about that. Everything he did care about was already ashore. Or at least it was supposed to be. That was the purpose of this clandestine foray into town: to make certain that things had been attended to, to assure himself that all was stowed safe and ready for its second act.

He took one last long look at the ship and at the crowd of buildings below and then turned and continued south. He kept to the road that ran along the wall because it was darker and there were fewer people there than on the wider, more well-lit roads farther inland from the river.

At the southern end of the city he walked west down the wider streets there, pushing through the crowds, an unsavory mix of soldiers and sailors and whores and drunks and sundry other villains. He kept his hand under his cape and his hat pulled low, glancing up as he walked. He was looking out for a particular tavern, and two blocks later he found it, a building of whitewashed stucco intersected by heavy black timbers. Over the door a carved sign depicted a strutting bird painted in dull gold, head thrown back in full cry. The tavern Gallo de Oro. The Golden Cock.

He paused on the cobbled street outside the tavern, the crowd walking past parting around him like he was a stone in a river. The door to the tavern was open and he could see hints of people in the light of the few lanterns inside. He glanced left and right: no one was paying the least bit of attention to him. He crossed the street and walked through the door.

The Gallo de Oro was small and crowded and hot on that warm West Indies night. It smelled of fried onions and tobacco smoke and the sweat and dirt of men. No one was speaking particularly loud, but the cumulative sound, like the fetid air, was oppressive.

Alonso moved slowly into the tavern room, alert for anyone who might find him suspect, anyone who might question his presence there, but no one even looked up as he entered. He stopped near the middle of the room, uncertain. Arrangements had been made as to time and place, but now that he was there he did not know what to do next. He was still considering the question when he felt a tug on his sleeve. He looked down at the face of a young boy, eight or nine years old by the look of him.

"Señor..." the boy said and jerked his head toward the far corner of the tavern, then pulled harder on Alonso's sleeve. Alonso nodded and followed and the boy led him to a small table in the back of the tavern, a crude, pock-marked thing with two chairs and a pitcher and two cups.

One of the chairs was occupied by a man with long dark hair, tied back, a dark moustache and goatee. His clothes were simple but not poorly made and not filthy like those worn by the working men who crowded the place. He was not an unpleasant looking man, though there was a suggestion of portliness about his face and stomach, like a man half-way between the lean vigor of active youth and the softness of a more sedentary middle age.

The man looked up as Alonso and the boy approached. He looked at Alonso, looked into his eyes, and for a moment he said nothing.

"Don Alonso," he said at last, a statement, not a question.

"Señor Carlos Hernández," Alonso said, also a statement.

Hernández gestured toward the other chair. "Sit, Don Alonso," he said. There was no deference in his tone, no acknowledgement of Alonso's considerably superior station, which did not please Alonso, but he chose to ignore it. He sat, and Hernández picked up the pitcher and filled the two cups.

"So, how do you like Santo Domingo?" Hernández asked.

"It is not Madrid," Alonso said.

"No, it is not," Hernández said. He lifted his cup and took a long drink, then added, "In some ways that is bad, and in some that is very good."

Alonso looked at his cup but did not reach for it. He had no interest in drinking any offerings of the Gallo de Oro, nor had he any interest in idle talk, certainly not with the likes of Carlos Hernández, considered a cur by men of quality.

"The ship tied to the wharf, that is the *Lion de Bilbao*?" Alonso asked, though he knew the answer.

"It is," Carlos Hernández said. Alonso waited for him to say more, but he did not. Alonso cleared his throat to fill the silence between them.

"And all was in order?" Alonso asked.

"It was." Again, Hernández said no more. In the silence Alonso considered what he would say next, but before he could speak Hernández did.

"You are a very lucky man, Don Alonso," he said. "That's good. I like to do business with lucky men."

"Prithee, tell, how am I lucky?" Alonso asked. He had done a great deal to improve his situation, and he considered his success a product of his own boldness and cunning, and not of luck.

Hernández shrugged. "If the *Lion* had sailed a few days earlier, she would have been sunk by the hurricano. As your galleon nearly was. Instead, she missed the hurricano and arrived at a time when there is great need. Everything in her hold is worth ten times what it would normally be worth. But had she sailed a few days later she would have arrived after Toledo and his fleet, and then there would be little demand for what she carried. In truth, Toledo might have simply taken her."

"Toledo?" Alonso said.

"Don Fadrique de Toledo?"

"Don...Fadrique Álvarez de Toledo y Mendoza?" Alonso clarified. "He is coming here?"

Hernández nodded and gave Alonso a quizzical look. "You did not know? The lieutenant governor?"

Alonso felt himself flush with anger but he kept his voice even. "I did not. When is he supposed to arrive?"

"Soon," Hernández said. "He has already come ashore on St. Christopher's, I hear. Driven off many of those French and English dogs. Took the rest to work the silver mines. I believe he will sail for Santo Domingo once he has settled things there."

Alonso stared down at the dark liquid in the cup on the table in front of him. *Fadrique Álvarez de Toledo y Mendoza...*

He knew of Don Fadrique, of course. Captain General of the Ocean Sea Navy, a man close to the king, much admired in court. He and Alonso were fellow knights of the Order of Santiago and had met on a few occasions, though Alonso was not at all certain Don Fadrique would remember him.

Don Fadrique would certainly remember Alonso's father-in-law, Don Cristóbal de Seville, however. They were old friends, as Don Alonso understood it.

Does this change anything? Alonso wondered. He could not see how it would, but he would have to think more on it, when he had a moment to genuinely think.

"Is this a problem, señor?" Hernández asked and Alonso was certain he heard a note of amusement in the question.

"Not at all," Alonso said. "Don Fadrique Álvarez is an old friend from court. It will be good to see him again. But I understand your concern about what might happen when his fleet arrives. It will be very hard to do anything…privately. We must act before then."

"Agreed," Hernández said. "But we have only *Lion de Bilbao* afloat to move your merchandise. That could be problem. I thought you would have another ship for that."

"I thought so as well," Alonso said. "But I think she was lost in the hurricano."

"I see," Hernández said. He frowned. "This is a complication. But I may be able to assist."

"Good," Alonso said. "Now, I would like to see it."

"See it?"

"My cargo, I would like to see it."

Hernández frowned deeper and cocked his head. "It's in my warehouse, señor," he said.

"I know," Alonso said. "And I would like to see it."

Hernández was silent for a moment, his eyes on Alonso's, and Alonso held his gaze without wavering. "You do not trust me?" Hernández said at last.

"It's the merchants in Madrid I do not trust. I wish to see that they shipped what I paid for."

Again Hernández was silent for a long moment. He looked at Don Alonso but there was no expression on his face. Then he shrugged.

"Very well, Don Alonso. We go to my warehouse. It's not the sort of neighborhood a man like you might frequent." Hernández gave a hint of a smile. "You best keep a hand on that pistol hidden under your cape."

Alonso felt himself flush. "I'm not concerned about the villains who might lurk around your warehouse," he said. He stood and Hernández stood and they worked their way through the packed tavern room and back onto the street, where the air smelled fresh and cool despite the crowd of people and horses there.

Hernández led the way back toward the eastern wall, toward the heavy oak gate that led to the lower part of Santo Domingo. The gate was closed now, but a smaller door beside it stood open, flanked by guards in steel breastplates and peaked helmets and holding tall halberds straight up like ships' masts.

Alonso pulled the brim of his hat a bit farther down but Hernández did not break his stride as he approached. The guards looked at him and nodded in familiarity and Hernández nodded back as he stepped through the door, Alonso right behind. The guards did not say a word.

Outside the gate a flight of crude granite steps led from the wall down the embankment to the streets and alleys and warehouses below. A few lanterns hung from iron poles at irregular intervals and they cast a weak light on the steps, but still it took all of Alonso's concentration to make his way down without tumbling head first. At the bottom step Hernández took one of the lanterns in hand and led the way into a narrow alley.

Alonso could feel something soft underfoot coating the cobblestones, and just as he was trying to guess at its nature he felt himself slip. He cursed and stumbled and just managed to avoid a humiliating fall.

"Careful," Hernández said in a harsh whisper. "The hurricano, it flooded this whole place. Left half a foot of mud on the streets. Much of it is still here."

"I see," Alonso said.

"Damned storm dropped a ship right on my warehouse, can you believe that?" Hernández said with a note of amusement.

"I heard," Alonso said. "But I didn't think it was *your* warehouse that the ship fell on."

"I have many warehouses," Hernández said. "But I don't admit to all of them. If one man owns too much it can make the wrong people nervous."

They continued on, Hernández leading the way through a maze of alleys and streets that left Alonso baffled and gave him an uneasy, vulnerable feeling. He was completely at Hernández' mercy now. If Hernández abandoned him he would never find his way back, at least not before sunrise, and from the furtive sounds of people moving in the dark, the occasional cry from some hidden place, the light of lanterns appearing and disappearing, Alonso did not think he would last that long. His rapier and one pistol would not be enough to save him in that part of Santo Domingo.

At last Hernández stopped by a wooden door set into a rough stucco wall. He handed the lantern to Alonso and pulled a ring holding a dozen keys from a hook on his belt. He found the one he wanted and unlocked the heavy padlock hanging from the bar across the door. He removed the lock, lifted the bar, swung the door open and gestured for Alonso to enter.

Alonso stepped inside. The lantern in his hand cast a circle of light that was soon swallowed up by the darkness in the big warehouse, but the light around him fell on great stacks of barrels and bundles of cloth and sacks of wheat and other grains. The cavernous space was jammed with goods, and from what Alonso could see he was looking at only a small portion of its contents.

Behind him he heard the bar on the door drop and the lock snap shut. Hernández stepped up beside him. "This is not all yours, of course, Don Alonso. But much of it is. Here, come with me." He stepped off to the right and Alonso followed. They made their way around the barrels stacked up near the door and down a narrow passage between them and a mound of bulging sacks. Hernández stopped.

"Here, señor," Hernández said, spreading his arms. "This is the cargo that was carried aboard *Lion de Bilbao*."

Alonso nodded and stepped forward, holding the lantern high. In his mind he could see the manifest he had approved back in Madrid: fifty barrels of ale, fifty of a cheap wine, one hundred sacks of flour...

The government of Spain allowed no trade in the West Indies with any nation other than itself, and the tariffs were absurdly high. At the same time, Spain could not export anything close to the quantity of goods that the region required, since the Spanish economy was kept alive by the gold and silver flowing from the New World and not through any sort of useful industry. That meant there was little Spanish merchandise to trade, and what there was was absurdly expensive.

It also meant that an enterprising man who could import goods and avoid the tariffs, and who was willing to sell to anyone, Spanish, English, French, Dutch, all the vermin invading that part of the world, could make a fortune quickly and many times over.

When it came to importing – smuggling – however, it was mostly the vermin themselves, the English, French and Dutch, who were doing it and reaping the benefits in gold. Few Spaniards indulged in the trade because few had the connections, the zeal or the courage to undertake such an enterprise.

But Don Alonso Menéndez de Aviles, knight of the Order of Santiago, did.

He ran his eyes over the stacks of goods. He took a few steps forward and examined what fell under the light of the lantern. He turned to Hernández.

"This is not all of it."

"No," Hernández said. "This is the part that will make no one suspicious. Come." He took the lantern from Alonso's hand and led the way farther into the warehouse. He paused in front of a stack of barrels two high and handed the lantern back to Alonso. He reached up and wrapped his arms around one of the barrels on the upper tier, lifted it up and set it on the floor to one side. Then he grabbed another and set that aside as well.

"Those barrels seem light," Alonso said. "Are things so dire here that you've taken to importing air?"

"Barrels can be useful for more than just holding things," Hernández said. "They also serve well for hiding things." With the upper tier gone he rolled the lower tier of barrels clear to reveal a small door in what Alonso had thought was an exterior wall. Hernández lifted the latch and pushed the door open. He took the lantern again and bending nearly double led the way through, Alonso following behind.

Once through Alonso straightened and found himself in another warehouse a quarter the size of the one they had left. This one, like the first, was filled to near capacity with barrels and stacks and bundles of this and that.

"Here," Hernández said, spreading his arms wide. "Here is where we keep the things we do not wish to be found."

Alonso nodded and began to walk slowly around. Here were a dozen barrels of fine Rioja wine, complete with the seals that proved their authenticity. And here were firkins of Manzanilla olives in savory oil and crates that Alonso knew contained rapiers of the finest Toledo steel. Bolts of cloth. Alonso pulled a corner free and saw in the lantern light a rich red and gold brocade, and in his mind he could see the description of that very cloth written on the bill of sale he had signed in Madrid.

"Good," Alonso said. And he meant it, and he felt a small surge of excitement as he examined these wares. There was money to be made importing ale and wine and flour, certainly. But the real profit was in bringing over the finest things that Spain produced to a country starved of such luxury and selling it to whoever had taste enough to want it and gold enough to purchase it.

One could not lade an entire ship with such fine goods without attracting unwanted attention, and with it suspicion, so *Lion de Bilbao* had sailed with her pedestrian cargo between decks and the truly valuable things hidden in the darker recesses of her hold. And now here those fine things were, safely ashore and ready to go off to the many eager buyers in the West Indies, men who had accumulated great wealth and had little to purchase with it.

Alonso felt his lips spread involuntarily into a wide grin. He had spent a small fortune on that cargo and he anticipated making a great fortune as a result. He looked up at Hernández. "Good," he said again. "I am pleased. Now we must see about getting it to market."

Hernández nodded but he wore an uncertain expression. "Don Alonso…." he said and paused.

"What?"

"Forgive me, Don Alonso, but there is something I must say. As a Christian. You have not been long in Santo Domingo. There's much about this city…and the West Indies…that you do not yet understand."

Alonso felt a flush of anger at the man's impertinence. Carlos Hernández might be a fixture in Santo Domingo, he might be well known to the lower sort, he might even be a man of wealth, but he was still nothing but a merchant and a cur, while he, Don Alonso, was a knight of the Order of Santiago, scion of the family Menéndez of Aviles, son-in-law to Don Cristóbal de Seville. Lieutenant Governor of Hispaniola.

"I mean no disrespect, Don Alonso," Hernández said quickly, reading the reaction on Alonso's face. "But you must know, there are many powerful men here in Santo Domingo. Men who should not be crossed."

"I see," said Alonso. "And the governor, is he one I should worry about?"

"The governor? No. He's a good man. Perhaps not the most clever of men, but a good man. He's of no concern."

"Well, there you have it," Alonso said. "I need not fear the governor, and he is the only man in Santo Domingo who's more powerful than me. Which means, Señor Hernández, there is no one I need fear. So pray, let us discuss how we will get these things from your warehouse to those who would lay down gold to have them."

Carlos Hernández was quiet for a moment, and he seemed to be studying Don Alonso, though in the dim light of the lantern it was difficult to tell. And then, apparently, he understood the truth of Don Alonso's words. He nodded.

"Very well, señor," he said.

Chapter Eighteen

The morning after the second bonfire appeared on the beach, Van Loudersong and a dozen others loaded into a periagua and rowed out to where *Santiago* swung on her anchor. LeBoeuf was fastening a deadeye to one of the topmast shrouds, Henriette was cursing about tar on her petticoat and Le Rongeur was alternately grumbling and striking a chisel with a mallet when the boat came alongside.

"May we come aboard?" Van Loudersong called. LeBoeuf nodded and the Dutchman, along with D'Anton, Levesque, Lessard, and the others who had come with them, came climbing up the side. They spread out along the deck, eyes running over the work going on there and up aloft.

LeBoeuf climbed down the half-dozen steps from the quarterdeck to the waist. "Welcome aboard," he said. "What brings you?"

"Nothing...nothing, really," Van Loudersong said. "Just curious, I suppose, as to how it goes with you."

LeBoeuf looked around as if just noticing the ship for the first time. "Good," he said. "It goes good. How go things on shore?"

"Good," Van Loudersong said. "All's well."

"I saw two fires last night," LeBoeuf said. "Used to be just one."

"It's that whore's son Le Chasseur," Levesque offered. "We disagreed on when to split up the cargo there. How it was to be done. Le Chasseur, he wants to do it now. We say wait until it's sold and split up the gold and silver. Much simpler. Less chance for mischief."

"So...you broke into two camps? Those who favor your plan and those who favor Le Chasseur?"

Van Loudersong shrugged. "You know how it goes. With any men, but doubly with these boucaniers. Words fly."

"Seems I heard bullets fly as well," LeBoeuf said.

"Too much brandy, too much time on their hands," Van Loudersong said. "Men play the fool."

LeBoeuf nodded.

"Once the ships return, like they did before the hurricano, then we sell the cargo and we split up the company," Van Loudersong continued. "Each

153

man will have enough to set himself up nice, I should think. On Tortuga or Barbados. Maybe get a plantation, if a fellow's so inclined."

LeBoeuf nodded.

"Shouldn't be long," Van Loudersong said. "You saw that ship two days ago?"

"I did," LeBoeuf said. A barque of tolerable size, a bit larger than *Santiago*. She had been a few miles off shore, heading west, but changed course and stood in close, approaching within half a mile or so. LeBoeuf thought she might come to anchor, but instead she turned and headed back out to sea.

LeBoeuf had watched her warily. Whatever she intended, it was not clear. Trade for smoked meat, perhaps, like the ships that came before the hurricano, but she did not really have the look of a merchantman about her.

In truth he had taken her for one of the Spanish *guarda coasta*, one of the armed vessels sent out from Santo Domingo to attack the boucaniers when opportunity presented itself. They were the sea-borne equivalent of the lanceros, and LeBoeuf wondered if the men on the beach would come out and fight if the Spanish decided to try the bold move and attack his ship. He did not think so. But in any event, she hauled her wind and sailed off and LeBoeuf had not seen her again since.

"I thought the ship was coming to trade," Van Loudersong said. "And wouldn't they have been surprised to find what we had to offer? But she did not stop."

"Methinks it's not healthy, the lot of you lying about on the beach, drinking all day," LeBoeuf said. "Tempers flare when men have too much time on their hands. Why don't you hunt in the meantime? You could lay in some smoked meat, have that to sell, too. Once the ships return."

Van Loudersong did not answer at first. He seemed to be considering the question. D'Anton answered instead.

"None dare leave the beach," he said. "Each man, he's starting to think the others will take his share. No one dares leave the cargo and go inland for fear it won't be there when he returns."

"Hmm," LeBoeuf said.

"So," Van Loudersong said, his voice suddenly brighter. "What do you mean to call your yacht? Can't leave the Dago name in place, I wouldn't think."

"Don't know," LeBoeuf said. "Maybe *Henriette*." He turned and called back to the quarterdeck. "What say you? Should we call the ship *Henriette*?"

"Name it after yourself," Henriette said. "Call it *Big Dumb Ox*."

LeBoeuf turned back to Van Loudersong and shrugged. "Haven't decided," he said.

"Looks like you've done quite a job here," Levasseur said. "Got all this down, the masts and yards and such. Of course, getting it back up will not be so easy."

"Not so hard," LeBoeuf said. "Capstan, blocks and tackle. Up they go."

The men looked around at the spars and gear on deck. LeBoeuf wondered if they understood that his words were not at all true. The lot of them had helped take it down so they could get at the cargo, but even then, with gravity as their assistant, it had taken considerable effort. Sending it back up with just two men and a woman, and only one of them understanding the business, would be all but impossible.

"If you like, I suppose we could lend a hand," D'Anton said, and the others nodded. LeBoeuf could see there was genuine interest. Lounging on the beach, drinking brandy and wine, eating roast meat, fornicating: it was the pinnacle of existence for the men who became buccaneers, but even they were bound to grow tired of that life. It had been weeks now, by LeBoeuf's estimate, and he could see they were ready for something new.

Le Rongeur, who was no one's idea of a speedy worker, had mostly finished with the fore topmast and had yet to start in on the main, so others took up the tools and set to work. The buccaneers were not sailors, necessarily, but most had been to sea for some period of time and the work that needed doing was not foreign to them. At LeBoeuf's direction the topmast shrouds were repaired and shortened, deadeyes seized on, topmast forestays altered to fit properly, all the rigging made ready to be set in place. Others, those who knew their way around a ship's rig, went aloft to set up mast ropes and yard ropes for hoisting the heavy spars up into place.

With just a few hours of daylight left they hauled the fore topmast rigging up into the foretop and ran the mast rope to the capstan. Then, on LeBoeuf's command, they leaned into the capstan bars and began to turn the capstan around, the pawls making their clack clack clack sound as they fell. The fore topmast lifted off the deck and rose up aloft, with men on the shrouds and in the foretop to guide it. Once the top of the mast was half way up they draped the rigging over the masthead and set the crosstrees in place. Then they leaned into the capstan bars again and sent the topmast up the rest of the way.

"Fid's in!" Levasseur called from aloft to indicate the mast was secured. The men at the capstan bars eased off and stepped back. They were smiling.

"Good day's work," LeBoeuf said. He nodded and the others nodded.

"Good day's work," Van Loudersong agreed. In the gathering darkness they could see the first flames of a bonfire in what LeBoeuf assumed was Le Chasseur's camp. They heard someone shout and a woman scream, though whether it was in fear or exuberance they could not tell.

"We best get back ashore," Van Loudersong said. And with that the buccaneers climbed back over the side and down into the periagua, then took up the oars and rowed for the beach.

"There, you see," Henriette said as they watched the boat head toward shore.

"What?" LeBoeuf asked.

"I told you, you fool, you wouldn't be able to put these masts and such back up without help."

"I guess you were right," LeBoeuf said. "Like you usually are." He looked up at the fore topmast, rising high above, black against the red and orange of sunset. He wondered if it would occur to Henriette that he *did* get help, without even asking for it.

As the last of the daylight faded away, Le Rongeur lit a lantern, Henriette attended to supper and LeBoeuf wrestled with opening a fresh firkin of wine; the evening routine of their odd little family, part convivial, part disdainful, part indifferent.

It was a strange dynamic, to say the least, and it amused LeBoeuf to watch it play out. It was like theater, and though he was an actor in the drama he felt more as if he was part of the audience, a groundling, an observer who had no personal stake in how the story played out. The only plot of interest to him now concerned his ship's rebirth, and how *Santiago* would carry him back to sea.

Not *Santiago*, he thought. *Roumois*…

Van Loudersong was right. He could not keep the Don Diego name. He would call her *Roumois*, after the region of France where he had been born and raised.

He smiled. He liked that name. But then again, people would ask why he had chosen it. On the few occasions when the question arose, he had named La Rochelle as his home, and perhaps some other places he did not recall, but never Roumois. He did not like to spark curiosity.

"Well, we got the one mast up," Le Rongeur said. He had a biscuit and a chunk of meat in one hand, a cup filled to the brim in the other. He was sitting on the pinrail about ten feet from where LeBoeuf sat on the quarterdeck steps. That was the distance Le Rongeur always maintained, about ten feet. He seemed to think it was the minimum LeBoeuf would tolerate, and he was right. Two fathoms would have been preferable.

"It was lucky Van Loudersong and the rest come out to help," Le Rongeur continued. "Still got this other mast to go. Yards, too. Don't know how we get them up."

"We'll see," LeBoeuf said. He actually knew exactly how they would get the last of the spars and rigging up, but he had no intention of discussing it with anyone, least of all Le Rongeur.

"'We'll see'," Henriette repeated, giving her scorn free range. She was sitting on the fife rail at the base of the main mast, only a few feet away from LeBoeuf.

"Those drunken fools on the beach might come back, offer more help," she continued, "just so they can have their laughs at your expense. But you still have no one to sail this miserable cockleshell. Even I know it takes more than one dumb ox, one miserable rodent and a woman to sail a ship."

"I guess you were right," LeBoeuf said. "Like you usually are."

Henriette was not done, LeBoeuf could see that. Her temper was like a barrel rolling down hill, building up speed and momentum. But before she could continue she was cut short by a scream from the shore, a gunshot, then another, and then a burst of shouting.

"You see," Henriette said, her line of attack changing direction faster than any rolling barrel could hope to do. "There's no more help coming from there. Those fools will all kill each other before they can lift another finger."

LeBoeuf was on his feet before she had finished and was walking forward, his eyes on the dark shoreline. In the light of the two fires he could see figures moving here and there with the disjointed, disorganized quality of a mob. The shouting had not diminished, and the voices were still punctuated by gunfire, the muzzle flashes making bright bursts of flame even in the light of the bonfires.

Bâtard... LeBoeuf thought. The situation on the beach was volatile and nearing combustion. He turned to Henriette and Le Rongeur.

"I'm going ashore," he said.

"What?" Le Rongeur said. "Are you mad? They've started shooting each other over there."

LeBoeuf ignored him as he pushed past, heading aft. He threw open the door of the great cabin and grabbed up his musket and belt and cartridge box. He considered for a second grabbing his prize sword as well but dismissed the idea. He turned and rushed back to the waist as fast as he could move while bent nearly double.

"You're going to leave me here with this miserable turd?" Henriette asked as he emerged onto the deck.

"Come if you wish, or stay, I care not," he said, which was true. He moved toward the gangway and grabbed up the painter made fast to the bow of the canoe that drifted alongside, the only boat they had. He pulled the canoe up to the bottom of the boarding steps bolted to the ship's side and then turned backward and began to climb down.

Henriette was standing there and their eyes met. LeBoeuf could see the anger in her expression, which was usually there, and the uncertainty, which was not.

"I don't know what you think…" she began, but he cut her off, his patience exhausted, even as he continued to descend.

"I told you, come or don't," he said, "but either way, pray, shut up."

He reached the last rung and leaned down and set his musket and cartridge box in the bottom of the canoe. Then he stretched out his leg and caught the edge of the canoe with his foot. It was a tricky business, getting his great bulk into the unstable craft, and he did not need Henriette's sharp words to distract him.

He planted his foot on the bottom, and holding tight to the steps on the ship's side eased himself down until he was seated on the thwart, the boat as stable as it was going to get. He looked up and found himself staring up Henriette's smock and petticoat as she climbed down after him, but he could see no more than her calf — the rest was lost in the dark folds of cloth.

More nimbly than he had done she set herself down on the forward thwart. "Catch a fine look, did you?" she asked.

"A disappointment," he said, leaving her to wonder if he was disappointed by what he saw or how little he was able to see. He looked up again. Le Rongeur was looking down at him, clearly trying to think of some clever quip, but failing, since he was not a clever man.

"Cast off the painter," LeBoeuf said and without a word Le Rongeur untied the painter and dropped it into the canoe. LeBoeuf picked up the paddle and pushed off against the side of the ship and took a stroke, the canoe moving easily under him.

"Reckon the ship's my after they kill you on shore!" Le Rongeur called, apparently the best he could manage. LeBoeuf ignored him, took another stroke. "Reckon I'll just go settle in the great cabin now!"

"You're not afraid of what he'll do, with you gone?" Henriette asked.

LeBoeuf shrugged. "What can he do? We have the only boat. He can't go anywhere. Which means he'll have to answer to me when I return."

"Does he know that?"

"He'll figure it out."

"Makes me sick, the thought of him in the great cabin. He better not lie down in that bed."

"He won't," LeBoeuf said. "He doesn't have courage enough."

The shouting on the beach was getting louder, the gunfire, while still sporadic, was getting more frequent. LeBoeuf paddled harder. This conflict ashore, he knew, was like a fire on shipboard. Catch it quick and it's easily extinguished. Let it spread too far and there's no chance of stopping it before the destruction is complete.

The bow of the canoe ran up on the sand and LeBoeuf swung a leg over the side and stepped out into water a foot deep. He grabbed his musket and cartridge box and hurried up the beach. He heard Henriette make some sound of protest but he ignored her as he raced toward the nearest fire. Van Loudersong's fire.

The flames were reaching seven feet in the air and there were bodies scattered around at the edge of the light, but LeBoeuf was fairly certain they were passed out from drink, not dead. There were some women as well, some upright, some likewise sprawled in the sand. There were no still-conscious men that he could see.

"Merde," he said out loud. He looked over at the other fire a couple hundred feet away. He could see people upright and moving, their dark shapes sharp against the bright flames. He could see weapons in hands.

"Merde!" he said again and ran off in that direction. He could hear voices building in volume and pitch. He could not make out any specific words, but the fury behind them was clear.

Idiots, damned idiots, he thought.

The men at the other fire stood clustered in a wide circle as if they were gathered around a cockfighting ring, and LeBoeuf had a pretty good idea of who was at the center of the crowd. He reached the periphery and shouldered his way through, then grabbed handfuls of coats and shirts and shoved people aside and as the pack of men became too dense to part with his shoulder.

He broke through to the center of the crowd and, as he guessed, the two cocks, Van Loudersong and Pierre le Chasseur, stood shouting at one another, five feet between them. They each held muskets, each pointing their weapon in the general direction of the other. Their faces were red and contorted in fury. Neither man was listening to what the other was saying. Van Loudersong, LeBoeuf realized, was actually yelling in Dutch.

Both men stopped, mid-shout, and looked over at LeBoeuf as he came bursting into their stand-off, and instinctively they began to swing their muskets in LeBoeuf's direction. That, LeBoeuf knew, was the first problem that needed solving. There was untold mischief the two might cause with loaded weapons.

LeBoeuf dropped his own musket to the ground but did not slow in his advance. In two steps and he was on them, left hand on the barrel of Van Loudersong's musket, right hand on Le Chasseur's, and with one quick, powerful jerk he pulled both guns from the men's hands and flung them back over his shoulders into the dark.

There was silence on the beach where an instant before there had been a madness of noise. Van Loudersong and Le Chasseur, mouths still open, looked down at their empty hands and then back up at LeBoeuf as if he had used a witch's trick to make their muskets disappear.

"You damned idiots!" LeBoeuf shouted. "What the devil do you think you're doing?"

LeBoeuf's voice broke the spell. Both men exploded with words, yelling at LeBoeuf, gesturing wildly with hands now free. All around them the on-lookers joined in, so the great wave of noise rolled over them all, drowning them like some massive boarding sea.

Le Chasseur was the first to abandon words in favor of force. Though LeBoeuf could not make out what any one person was saying, apparently Le Chasseur could. He turned toward Van Loudersong and all but leaped the five feet between them. He grabbed the Dutchman by the collar of his doublet, drew back his fist, and might have delivered an ugly blow to the surprised man's face had he been just a bit quicker.

But he was not quick enough. LeBoeuf's arms shot out and he grabbed Le Chasseur by the shirt and Van Loudersong by the arm and pulled them apart, then shoved them hard. They stumbled back, arms wheeling, legs searching for balance, and to their credit they managed to remain on their feet.

Around them the crowd roared their approval, and LeBoeuf wondered how many of them actually cared about the point being argued, and how many were just there for the cock-fighting. He was certain that bets had been placed.

"Enough, I say!" LeBoeuf bellowed, and his voice was as powerful as his arms, powerful enough to stamp down the raucous crowd and the howls of furious protests from the mouths of Van Loudersong and Le Chasseur.

"Not your fight, LeBoeuf!" Le Chasseur shouted, the first to recover enough to form words. "It's me and Van Loudersong, and there's none will make me…"

"Enough!" LeBoeuf roared again and that was an end to it. Le Chasseur, Van Loudersong, the men gathered around, they were all silent now. He looked at Le Chasseur. "You want to split the plunder up now? Do it. Split it up. Each man of you can sit by his little pile of plunder here on the beach until the gulls are picking at your bones."

There was silence for a moment, then Van Loudersong spoke. "When the ships come to trade…" he began but LeBoeuf could not bear to hear the rest.

"The ships are not coming to trade!" he roared. "Are you such fools that you don't see that? No ships are coming! Look around you!" He spread his arms to indicate the island beyond the light of the fire. "The hurricano destroyed everything! If it did this much hurt to us, it did as much to all the West Indies, and beyond! You think there's anyone out there who means to come here to trade? For smoked meat? Do you think there's anyone out there who's thinking about smoked meat? If one ship in a hundred lived through that storm it will be God's own miracle!"

That was met by further silence. As LeBoeuf knew it would be. He knew that this had not occurred to the boucaniers, who were not always the most insightful of men. The ships had always come. The men on the beach just assumed they would continue to come.

"So...what? What do we do?" It was Billy Solent who spoke in his strange, English-tainted French.

"We got brandy enough," someone offered. "For a while."

More silence. Then from out of the dark someone else said, "LeBoeuf's got a ship. Could bring our wares to market in LeBoeuf's ship."

Ahh... LeBoeuf thought. *It comes to them at last....*

An undercurrent of muttering followed that suggestion. Van Loudersong and Le Chasseur exchanged glances. LeBoeuf remained silent, his expression offering nothing.

"Well?" Van Loudersong said. "What say you, LeBoeuf?"

LeBoeuf frowned and nodded and appeared to be considering this for the first time. "I suppose that could be just the thing," he said. "Of course, the ship's not near ready for sea. All the main top-hamper's still on deck. It would be much to our advantage to make new topsail masts and yards..."

"No great hardship there," Le Chasseur said. He seemed to be warming to the idea of using LeBoeuf's ship to get off that desolate beach, and doing so quickly. "Plenty of men among us have followed the sea, and plenty with skill enough to fashion masts and such. Hell, we don't even have to cut down trees, there's a thousand on the ground already. Wouldn't take much time at all to have LeBoeuf's little ship ready to sail."

Heads were nodding now, men looking around at their fellows, the anger starting to dissipate.

"What more will you demand, LeBoeuf?" Van Loudersong asked. "Besides the repair of your ship?"

"One percent," LeBoeuf said. "One percent of the worth of the cargo, and men enough to sail the ship to St. Christopher after the cargo's sold."

Van Loudersong frowned and looked down at the sand. He was silent for a moment, but then he nodded and LeBoeuf was glad for that. Skin-flint Dutchman, he had worried that Van Loudersong of all of them might try to haggle. He looked up at LeBoeuf.

"Tortuga?" he asked.

"Tortuga." If they were going to find a market for their plunder anywhere, it would be Tortuga. The island was just a few miles to the northwest of where they stood. The Spanish claimed it as their own, as they did all that part of the world, but they had made no effort to settle it. And in their absence others had moved in: the English and the French and sundry other cast-aways from the civilized world, sailors and run-away slaves and boucaniers.

The first of the settlers had dropped anchor in Tortuga's one decent harbor just a few years before, but already the island enjoyed a unique reputation. It was known as a place where business or recreation could happen with no sort of government or law to interfere. It was a place where men who made their living on the periphery could go to buy or sell and not concern themselves with licenses or tariffs or bills of lading or any such nonsense.

LeBoeuf leaned down and picked up his musket and wiped the sand off the lock. The mob on the beach, which just moments before had been howling for blood, began to drift away, back to their fires and their broached barrels of wine and brandy. The buccaneers were men who were largely shunned by the world, and for that reason they did not trend to shun one another. The sharp disagreement over dividing the salvage had been like a splinter in the foot, and once it was removed a sense of relief and a spirit of comradeship reasserted itself. The bonfire that marked Le Chasseur's camp was largely abandoned as the men returned to the first and more substantial fire closer to the water.

"Well, God loves a fool," Henriette said a little while after. "And there's proof of it." They were standing ten feet from Van Loudersong's fire, the heat of the flames making their skin feel flush.

"What?" LeBoeuf asked.

"You do such stupid things, and every time it seems there's God's luck to bail you out. Trade away a fortune in cargo for some half rotten ship...and you not even able to put the masts back up... and now all of a sudden you have all these men willing to do whatever job of work you need."

"I'm a lucky man," LeBoeuf agreed. "I guess God smiles of the righteous."

Henriette gave a snort of derision but said nothing more.

Chapter Nineteen

Charles Rex plowed on west, coming a little north as she did, until *Santa Rosa's* topsails came into sight. An hour later the two ships were sailing in consort.

Graves had put nearly a mile of water between *Charles Rex* and the Spanish frigate by the time the Spaniard managed to get her yards and sails straightened out and get underway again, but she had not turned in pursuit. Rather she got her larboard tacks aboard and stood in toward the island of St. Christopher's, a bull weary of chasing after the little dog at its heels. Graves did not think the frigate's captain would be reporting that morning's dance to whomever he reported to.

Even before the Spanish frigate was out of irons, Graves raced below to assess the damage they had done to *Charles Rex's* hull with their great guns. It was entirely possible that his deft maneuvering had been for naught. One well-placed shot from the eighteen pounder guns in the Spanish broadside (Graves felt certain they were eighteen pounders) would send *Charles Rex* to the bottom in little time.

He hurried down the ladder to the 'tween decks, stopped, looked side to side and then let out a low whistle. *Charles Rex* had been built to be fast, she had not been built to withstand cannon fire, and it showed. The Spaniard's cannon balls had struck the larboard side, making relatively neat holes as they passed through, then flown clean across the deck and smashed out the starboard, leaving larger, more jagged holes in their wake.

Normally the 'tween decks would have been packed with cargo and the round shot would have made a hash of it, but Graves had off-loaded Señor Corregidor's goods before the hurricano struck. *Charles Rex* was all but empty. There had been nothing but air in the way of the cannon balls.

Graves walked slowly forward. Three of the Spaniard's shots had struck home, just as he thought. Daylight streamed in through the three matching sets of holes, larboard and starboard. One of the balls had taken a chunk out of the main mast, just clipping it as it passed on by. Graves reached out and touched the splintered wood. He shook his head.

That was bloody close… he thought. Did such a near miss suggest he was a lucky man? He did not know.

But he did know he was lucky on one count: that the Spaniard had been so close when he had fired on them. Had the ships been farther apart there was every chance that the shot would have hit near the *Charles Rex*'s waterline, which would have sent the seas rushing in. Close as they had been, the Spanish gunners could not depress their guns far enough to strike lower than the level of the 'tween deck. The damage they had done could be easily repaired, and unless they were suddenly beset with foul weather, which Graves doubted they would be, then his ship could still swim perfectly well as it was.

Señor Corregidor will be happy, in any event, Graves thought. *Charles Rex* was Señor Corregidor's ship now. Graves still hoped that Señor Corregidor would not take his life, but he was resigned to the fact that he would take his ship.

He finished his inspection then made his way back to the quarterdeck where Maja was leaning on the bulwark, one of his men manning the tiller.

"Well?" Maja asked.

"Damndest thing," Graves said. "Damn Spaniard, their shot come right in one side and right out the other. Six holes, neat as can be."

Maja made a grunting sound but said no more. Graves looked aft. The Spanish frigate was lost to sight now, and just the upper half of St. Christopher's was still visible above the horizon, along with the thick columns of smoke rising up from the island. Graves stared at the steep, tree-covered mountains in their wake. He waited for some further word from Maja, but after a moment or two it was clear that none was coming.

"So, you want to get some hands on fixing the damage from that round shot?" Graves asked. "It's no real danger right now, but generally you don't want to be sailing about with six big holes in the side of your ship."

Maja turned and looked at Graves, silent, then finally he nodded. "Get your men and get below and see what you can do," he said.

Graves nodded and called to his men, the original members of *Charles Rex*'s crew, who looked grudgingly aft at him. They were not very happy with Benjamin Graves just then. Graves had assured them that they could make their fortunes absconding with Señor Corregidor's cargo. Instead they might well have forfeited their lives.

Nonetheless, when Graves called to them they stood and shuffled aft. It was not out of loyalty to him, however, that they did as they were told. It was to get in Maja's good graces, as best they might.

"Díez," Maja called forward to one of his own men, and followed that up with a burst of Spanish too fast for Graves to understand entirely. He thought perhaps Maja had told his man to go below and keep an eye on the work, to see that the English did not play any tricks. Soon after, when Graves led the men below, and Díez followed and took his place on an old chest and glared at the Englishmen with arms folded, Graves was certain of it.

They worked through the afternoon, finding boards and bits of dunnage and nailing them over the holes in the ship's side. When that ugly but serviceable work was done they found old canvas and soaked it in a tar and varnish mixture and spread it over the holes on the exterior of the ship, securing it in place with nails and wooden battens. It was hot work on the lower deck, but not so bad when they came up from below and were able to work in the embrace of the afternoon breeze.

The actually sailing of the ship required very little effort. The trade winds blew steady and consistent, ten knots or so out of the east, and they rarely faltered. *Charles Rex* and *Santa Rosa* had all plain sail set and drawing as they rolled along at an easy six knots, with one man at the helm and no need to adjust the sails in any manner. Driving a ship in the Caribbean was some of the easiest sailing to be had in the world. As long as you were going to leeward, heading west.

Once the temporary repairs were done, Graves and his men washed themselves with turpentine and sea water, then pulled their clothes back on again, Graves his well-worn, faded doublet and the sailors their long shirts, belted at the waist. Graves ran his fingers through his wet hair, looked forward and was surprised to see *Santa Rosa* just a quarter mile ahead and hove-to. Her foresails were aback and the sails on her mainmast filled with wind and in that configuration she was stopped dead in the water, apparently waiting for *Charles Rex* to catch up to her.

Graves walked aft to where Maja stood, where he had been standing all along, as if his feet were nailed to the deck. "What's acting?" he said. It had become a game to him now, asking Maja a question, placing a silent bet on whether or not the man would answer.

"Shifting over to *Santa Rosa*," Maja said. Graves nodded. He had guessed wrong that time — Maja had answered — though the answer did not actually tell him that much. For a moment they stood in silence, then Graves started in again.

"Well, I reckon you're making a good choice. You should see to Señor Corregidor's ship. I'll take command here, and we sail in company that way. Both ships'll be in the best hands."

Maja turned his head and looked at him, fixed him with his bird-of-prey eyes. "You say one more fool thing like that I'll have you triced up again and I'll flog you on the hour."

"You mean...what? I'm to go with you?"

Maja turned his head away. Graves guessed, correctly this time, that the man would give no answer.

"Can I at least fetch some of my things from the cabin?" Graves asked.

"No," Maja said simply, closing the door to further protest.

Charles Rex came up to leeward of *Santa Rosa* and when she was a couple hundred feet off Maja ordered the helm over and the foresails aback and soon she, too, was hanging motionless, caught between the opposing forces on the sails. The boat towing astern was pulled around and four of the men, two of Maja's and two of Graves's, climbed down and took up the oars. Maja gestured for Graves to go next, which he did, without a word, as words were clearly useless at that point.

The four men rowed the boat over the low rolling swells and pulled up alongside *Santa Rosa*. Maja sent Graves up the side first and then followed behind. He barked a couple of orders to his man Ortiz, who had been commanding *Santa Rosa*, and Ortiz climbed down into the boat to be rowed back to *Charles Rex* to take command of that ship.

Ten minutes later they were moving again, *Santa Rosa* filling away under easy sail, *Charles Rex* following behind a few cable-lengths astern and down to leeward. The sun was dropping in the west, the ships following the track of brilliant light that spread from west to east.

They had been underway for not more than twenty minutes when the call came down from on high.

"¡Barco a la vista!"

The lookout was perched on the main topsail yard where he had the clearest view of the horizon. He hailed in Spanish, but Graves understood those words, knew them in several languages: sail ho.

The man at the masthead followed his call with a stream of Spanish that Graves did not understand, but every head aboard shifted from looking aloft to looking astern, so Graves surmised that it was astern that the strange sail was to be found. He looked as well but could see nothing but ocean, so he also surmised that the stranger was still too far off to be seen from the deck's height of eye.

"Maja, what does your man aloft say?" Graves asked.

Maja looked at him with the expression usually reserved for some loathsome insect. Finally he said, "Sail on the horizon. Same heading as us. Hull down."

Graves nodded. These were well-traveled waters. The ship on the horizon could be anything. But they were dangerous waters as well, and when a ship spotted another it would often keep its distance. If this ship was following astern then it did not seem overly concerned about the danger another ship or two might present. That could mean it was Spanish navy, maybe a dispatch vessel sent from the fleet at St. Christopher. Or it could mean a *filibustero*, a freebooter. A pirate.

"Well, I doubt they'll overhaul us in the dark," Graves said as if he had been asked. "Still, we best be ready. If it's a filibusteros they'll keep the same course through the night, hope we're still there come dawn. They'll have the sun and the wind astern, be able to sweep right down on us. That's when we got to look sharp for them. Got them silly four pounders aboard *Rex*, you best send word to your man Ortiz to see 'em loaded. Or if you need me to go take command there I'm willing to do it, though why I'd do you any favor I don't know."

Maja half turned and looked at Graves with an inquisitive expression. Then he turned the rest of the way and stared forward, beyond the bow and the sharply angled spritsail.

"See here, Maja," Graves started in again, "this is no time to have greenhorns standing the watch, and you can't keep the deck all night yourself. I'm willing to stand a watch as well, keep the deck, if you wish. So you may rest."

At that Maja turned and looked at him again, and Graves thought he saw, rarest of rare, a hint of amusement on Maja's dark face. "You're *willing* to stand a watch?" he asked.

"Ah…yes. Yes, I am," Graves said.

"Good," Maja said. "I hoped you might." He stepped over to the mizzen shrouds where a spare length of cordage was hitched to a ratline. He unhitched it and crossed back to where Graves was standing. He grabbed Graves by the shoulder and turned him around and then pulled his hands behind his back.

"Now, see here, Maja, I don't reckon…" Graves said as the coarse rope was wrapped around his wrists and hauled taut.

"More you talk the tighter this gets," Maja said, and Graves, knowing he was quite serious, clamped his lips tight.

Once his hands were bound Maja pushed him back against the bulwark, then yanked up on the bitter end of the cord around his wrists, pulling his arms up and back and forcing him to bend forward at the waist. Graves could feel that Maja was tying the end to the shroud over his head.

"Now, look here, Maja, what the hell you reckon I can do tied up like this?" Graves protested.

"Nothing," Maja said. "It's what I want you to do."

"I said I was going to keep the watch for you."

"So…" Maja said. "Keep the watch. You can do it from here."

"I don't think you…" Graves began but in that instant he saw all of the humor drain out of Maja's face, leaving something much darker in its place. Graves shut his mouth.

"You want me to tighten the cord?" Maja asked. Graves shook his head. Maja nodded and stepped off to the other side of the deck, leaning on the bulwark opposite Graves and staring out to sea, Benjamin Graves entirely forgotten.

Graves, in his life as a seafarer, had spent far more nights in misery than he could recall, but that night was certainly among the worst. Maja had adjusted the lashing with perfection: there was nothing that Graves could do but stand there, bent forward, arms pulled up behind him. He could raise his arms a bit higher, which took the strain off his wrists, but he could not hold them that way for very long. When he lowered them again the pain seemed to redouble, enough that he wanted to gasp, but he would not give Maja that pleasure.

Sometimes he drifted off to sleep, and when he did he would stumble forward and the rope would yank his arms and the pain would shoot up from his wrists right through his shoulders and neck. Sometimes he would try to lean back against the bulwark, but doing that put too much tension on the bindings and sent the pain shooting though his limbs again.

He tried to distract himself by thinking of those times he had been even more miserable. Up aloft in a January storm off the Lizard, pounding ice out of a frozen topsail just to get enough of a handhold to furl the thing, certain they were going to pile up on the coast in that impenetrable night.

Three days off the Azores clinging to the fife rail aboard a merchantman that had gone over on its beam ends in a storm and stayed there, masts gone, all but eight of her crew washed away. Three days without a drink of water and Graves, crazed and desperate, was ready to let himself slide into the sea, certain, in his fevered imagination, that he could safely drink his fill of salt water. He was just easing himself off the rail when a sail appeared over the horizon.

Adrift for a week in a long boat about twenty leagues from where he was now after the rotten tub he had shipped in sunk under their feet. No storm, no reef or shoal: the beastly ship had just gone down as if it had given up on life. There had been five men with him then, and food and water enough for three days on half rations. Which might have been enough if one of them had not gone mad on the second night while keeping the watch and eaten and drank the lot of it as the others slept.

After that they had subsisted on a single gull and the three fish they managed to snag. That largess, however, only had to feed the four of them after they had tossed their well-fed shipmate over the side.

At least the weather's fine, Graves thought, scrambling to find something good about his current situation. It was one of the few advantages of the West Indies. The weather was generally excellent. Save for the odd hurricano.

All through the dark hours Graves stood, hands behind his back, his wrists and arms in agonizing pain until they began to grow numb. He lapsed between half asleep and fully awake and near blacking out. His thoughts were sometimes clear, sometimes jumbled and random. It occurred to him, during one of the clear moments, that he would lose the use of his hands and arms if he was subjected to much more of Maja's tender ministrations. He had thought back at St. Christopher that being triced up then would be the end of it.

Then he wondered how much longer he would need his hands and arms. Not long, most likely, so it probably did not matter.

He was nearly lost in his fog of pain and jumbled thoughts when he noticed the first light creeping over the deck. He shook his head and looked up. Maja was standing at the bulwark opposite him, in the same spot he had been standing when the darkness had hidden him the evening before. As far as Graves could tell he had remained fixed to that spot all night.

Without a word, without even looking at Graves, Maja crossed the deck, reached up and jerked the cord around Graves's wrists free from the shroud. Graves's arms dropped and his knees buckled and he collapsed to the deck, twisting just enough to hit with his shoulder and not his face. The impact sent a shudder through his body followed by wave after wave of pain. He gasped despite himself. His eyes and mouth were open wide and he sucked in lungful's of air.

He felt steel on his wrists and pressure on the bindings and then Maja's sharp knife cut the cordage away. The sensation was agonizing and delicious all at once. From his position on the deck, laying sprawled out on his side, he found himself staring at Maja's dark calves and splayed bare feet and his worn, tar-stained canvas slop trousers as he crossed back to where had been standing a moment before.

Son of a bitch... Graves thought. He could not get the measure of Maja and it annoyed him. He prided himself on understanding the workings of men, considered it as crucial to his profession as ship-handling or navigation. But Maja eluded him.

He could not fathom, for instance, if Maja enjoyed hurting people in general, or just him, or if he only did it because Señor Corregidor expected him to. He could not imagine that Maja had much love for Señor Corregidor. But he seemed unwilling to betray the man, or even waver from the orders Señor Corregidor had given him.

All this Graves pondered as he lay on his side and let the blood flow back into his hands, which tingled and ached and burned with the sensation. He laid there for a full ten minutes before he could gather the energy or the courage to bring his arms and hands around in front of him. Finally he grit his teeth, took a deep breath, and did it.

The pain was not as bad as he feared it would be, but the sight of his wrists was worse. The cord had cut deep, leaving his skin torn up and slick with blood. The bruising extended halfway up his forearms and nearly covered his hands. Slowly, carefully, he flexed his fingers and worked his wrists back and forth. Both seemed to still function reasonably well, and he was surprised by that.

One of Maja's men stepped up, a wooden mug in his hand. Graves guessed it was filled with water and he realized that he wanted it more than he wanted anything else in the world at that moment. He had a sudden terror that Maja had sent the man to torment him, to stand there and drink the water in front of him. Or worse, pour it on the deck, because if he did Graves knew he would not hesitate to lap it up.

But rather than do that, the man reached down and grabbed Graves under the arm and lifted him to a sitting position, then handed him the cup. Graves took it in his trembling hands and lifted it to his lips, ignoring the pain, and drank. He gulped the warm, fetid liquid down and let it run over his chin and through his beard. When he was done he held the cup up like a priest raising a chalice.

"More?" he said. The man paused, then turned and looked at Maja. Maja gave the slightest of nods and the man took the cup from Graves's hands and walked off forward.

"¡Barco a la vista!" The upper rim of the sun had just topped the horizon, the dark night yielding to pale blue as the lookout called from aloft.

Maja leaned back and shouted up to the man, jabbering in Spanish, but Graves neither understood nor cared. His only thoughts were on that second cup of water that was in theory being brought to him now. And indeed it was, the Spanish sailor coming up from below bearing the wooden cup. Once again Graves took it in his eager grip and drained it away, this time letting go a deep sigh as the last of the liquid went down his throat.

He closed his eyes and leaned back against the bulwark. He felt the warm deck under him and the gentle motion of the ship in the long swells. He felt his head swimming with exhaustion. He heard the increasingly loud and excited talk fore and aft and aloft, the sailors yammering away in their monkey language.

And then his eyes were open again.

Barco…

He wondered if it was the same ship that had been following them the night before. He wondered if they could tell. He looked around at the men on deck and the men aloft. A few had jumped up into the shrouds and were climbing, no doubt hoping to get a look at this stranger.

Must be the same ship, Graves thought. *These apes wouldn't be getting so excited otherwise.* Seeing sundry ships in those waters was not so unusual. Having a ship trail you through the night meant something else altogether.

Graves closed his eyes again and let the sound and the motion and the warm wood and tar smells swirl around him, but the sleep that had been engulfing him was washed away. His rejuvenated mind was twisting and turning, filled with thoughts of the ship astern.

*Pirate…bastard must be a pirate…*he thought. The strange sail had followed them all through the night, and even though Graves could not decipher what the Spanish lookout was saying he suspected the ship was even closer now than it had been at sunset. How else could the man aloft have seen it so easily?

Benjamin Graves's mind began to poke and tear at the situation, looking for ways that it might be of benefit to Benjamin Graves. He could see several possibilities now, and sundry ways to capitalize on them. But before he could do anything — and this was the most difficult and frustrating part — he had to get Maja on board.

Graves put his hand down on the deck, meaning to push himself to his feet, and realized right off that that was a bad idea. Instead he reached overhead and wrapped a forearm over one of the belaying pins on the rail and pulled himself up that way, gasping and cursing as he did.

Having spent all night standing bent at the waist, and then laying on the deck for the past hour, his muscles were cramped and tight and it took him a moment of effort to straighten up. He reached full height at last, and stood there shaking his arms and hands as much as he dared. When he felt as recovered as he was likely to get he crossed the deck to where Maja had positioned himself, gargoyle-like, at the larboard bulwark.

Graves stopped five feet away and remained there, silent. As usual, he had no idea what to expect from Maja so he waited and Maja ignored him, which was the most common reaction. After a moment, when he was certain Maja would not speak, Graves took it upon himself.

"This bastard astern of us...same one as last night?" he asked, as casually as he could.

Maja turned his head and looked at Graves and at first he did not speak.

Just talk, you dumb bastard, why do you have to give me the snake stare every time? Graves thought, but he set a neutral expression on his face and waited. Finally Maja spoke.

"Looks like," he said.

Graves nodded as if he was thinking about that. "Bold fellow," he said. "If he was a merchantman he'd be running for the horizon, methinks. Spanish man-of-war, well, he'd be on top of us by now. So I'm thinking... pirate."

He waited patiently as Maja gave him the silent consideration. "Ain't you the clever one," he said at last.

"So, what are you going to do about it? Pirate stalking you and all?"

"You afraid?"

"No, curious."

A moment of silence and then, "I'm going to keep doing what I'm doing."

"Which is?" Graves asked.

"Sailing west. Taking you to see Señor Corregidor. Bastard astern, he'll go away. He won't like the idea of fighting two ships. Those cowardly dogs don't."

"Sure, sure," Graves agreed. "But see here, maybe it would be best if he don't go away."

Maja looked at him and gave him the slight cock of an eyebrow.

"No, hear me out," Graves said. "If this whore's son following us has had any luck he could have…the Lord knows what aboard. Cargo, booty. Could be worth a lot. How about instead of him plunder us, we plunder him?"

"And then I sail off one way, and I let you sail off another? And we forget about Señor Corregidor?"

"No, no, of course not," Graves said, though that was in fact exactly what he had in mind. "But the thing is, you're coming back without Señor Corregidor's cargo. Now, you come back with this ship astern of us and all its got in its hold, well, Señor Corregidor might feel more forgiving. Generous, even. When a privateer takes a prize, it's the usual custom he gets his share. Even Señor Corregidor might think so."

"He might," Maja agreed. "And you reckon he'll be generous to you as well?"

"I won't lie," Graves said and Maja could not resist giving the hint of a smile at that statement, but Graves ignored it. "Could be I help with taking this son of a bitch, help make Señor Corregidor a bit richer, he might be in a more forgiving mood."

Maja nodded, and Graves was pleased to see he was thinking about it. "Makes sense, what you say," he said. "Hard to believe, but there it is. Thing is, we could never catch that bastard. He'll be too fast. And I don't think he'll come after us. Not two ships to his one."

"Ah," Graves said. "He might. See, as it happens, I have an idea about that, too."

Chapter Twenty

The knock came at the door, soft and tentative, just as Alonso pushed Gabriella onto her back and shifted himself on top of her. Another knock, a little more insistent, but Alonso ignored that one as well. He felt Gabriella spreading her legs under him and he pushed himself into her. She gasped and threw her head back and bit down on her finger. Alonso could not tell if her reaction was exaggerated or genuine and he did not actually care.

He thrust slowly at first and listened for another knock at the door, though he did not think there would be one. It was early morning, just past dawn, and he and Gabriella were on the small bed in Alonso's office, the siesta bed. The only person who would dare knock on the door just then was Alonso's secretary, Juan Cardero. Cardero knew with certainty that Alonso was within, and he knew as well that if Alonso did not answer after two knocks he had better not knock a third time.

Gabriella wrapped her legs around Alonso's waist and dug her heels into the small of his back. Her hair, her beautiful dark hair, lay fanned out on the pillow. Alonso leaned down and ran his lips along her neck and increased his pace and soon they were moving together with a beautiful rhythm, moving to the metronome creaking of the bedframe and the syncopated notes of their stifled moans.

"Oh, Don Alonso…" Gabriella gasped, her voice soft, husky, alluring in a way that made Alonso's head swim.

"Mmm…" Alonso replied. He was not really one for talking in such situations.

"Was someone at the door?" Gabriella gasped.

"No one," Alonso said. "Just Cardero."

If he thought there was someone else at the door he would not be so sanguine, nor would he still be on top of Gabriella. It would be bad if they were caught at this, bad for both of them, because neither of them could afford Francisca's wrath. For Gabriella it would mean dismissal, with little chance of ever finding decent employment again, and certainly not if she was out on the streets in the strange city of Santo Domingo. She would end as she was now, on her back, again and again, but she would not be giving her charms away *gratis*.

Francisca could not dismiss Alonso, of course, could not toss him out of the Casas Reales. There was not much that Francisca could do personally to harm him. But she could, and certainly would, relate her displeasure to her father, and her father could break Alonso like a reed.

Concerning as that was, Alonso's mind was elsewhere, swept up in the sensation of Gabriella's thin, muscular body moving under him, the smell of her skin, the sound of her ragged breath, the feeling of being inside her. He marveled at the intensity of it, and he wondered if that intensity was heightened by the risk he was taking.

Perhaps, though certainly his recent abstinence played a part. He had not been with Francisca in months, not since stepping aboard *Nostra Sennora de Regla* in the port of Seville. And even before that, when they had made love, it was generally a dull affair that Francisca looked on more as a duty than a pleasure and which involved a lot of praying and such.

That was not the case with Gabriella. In Francisca's company Gabriella prayed quite a bit, but otherwise she was not really the praying type, her current cries of "*Oh Dios mio!*" notwithstanding.

Alonso finished at last and he assumed Gabriella was finished as well so he rolled off of her and lay on his back, sucking in the cool morning air. He felt Gabriella's arm across his chest: thin, almost weightless, like a bird's wing. Her breath, like his, was settling back to normal. They lay like that for a moment more, then Alonso rolled over and sat up, the tiles of the floor cool under his bare feet.

"Pray, help me dress," he said. "I must breakfast with the governor."

"Yes, Don Alonso," Gabriella said. He watched her climb out of bed, enjoyed the sight of her smooth skin, her shapely body, the feline way that she moved. He considered insisting she remain naked as she dressed him, but in the end he allowed her to put on her smock while he pulled his own linen shirt over his head and settled it in place.

Gabriella picked up Alonso's doublet from the floor and helped ease it over his head, then retrieved his breeches and held them out for him to step into. In short order Alonso's clothes were returned to the same state they had been in when he left his and Francisca's apartment an hour before. He stepped around the desk and gathered up some papers while Gabriella finished dressing herself.

When she was done, Alonso nodded toward the door. Gabriella sailed across the room and opened it. Juan Cardero was standing there, as Alonso knew he would be, and he showed not the least bit of surprise or curiosity at Gabriella's presence.

"Is that all you need of me, Don Alonso?" Gabriella called as Cardero brushed past.

"Yes, Gabriella, thank you," Alonso called without looking up. "Pray, go attend to your mistress." Gabriella nodded, gave a quick bow and was gone, closing the door behind her.

"Breakfast, Don Alonso, with the governor and the Real Audiencia," Cardero said. "And the mayor and his people. We are running a bit behind this morning."

"Yes, yes," Alonso said.

"Shall I bring the plantation accounts, señor?" Cardero asked. One of the duties of the lieutenant governor, Alonso had discovered, was collecting accounts of the production from the plantations clustered around Santo Domingo and beyond.

"Did you bring them last time?" Alonso asked.

"Yes, Don Alonso."

"And did anyone ask to see them? Or even ask what was in them?"

"No, señor. And they did not at the breakfast before that, or the one before that."

Alonso nodded. The leaders of Santo Domingo gathered for their breakfast meetings about every two weeks, and Alonso had dutifully brought with him all the reports and sundry other material that were in his purview. And no one ever inquired after it, or mentioned it in any way.

What's more, Alonso was nearly certain the reports submitted by the plantation owners were pure fabrication, crafted to minimize their taxes. This led Alonso to conclude that the entire exercise was pointless. As, he was coming to understand, was much of what the government officials in the New World did.

He sighed. "Yes, Cardero, bring the reports," he said. It would be just his luck that the governor would chose that morning to ask for them, and Alonso did not care to be found wanting.

They collected up whatever they thought might be needed, and quite a bit more besides, and left the office, locking the door behind. They made their way through the lieutenant governor's quarters and down the columned walkway that bordered the central courtyard to the far side of the sprawling building.

Once inside again they walked down a long hall of high whitewashed plaster walls hung with magnificent paintings of governors and generals and admirals past. Thirty feet above them the hall was crowned with a ceiling made up of an intricate crosshatch of dark stained wood beams. In Seville or Madrid such a home would have been impressive: in Santo Domingo, on the edge of the civilized world, it was astounding.

Two Black servants in silk livery flanked the big doors that opened onto the governor's dining room, and they opened the doors as the two men approached so that neither had to break stride as they entered. Most of the room was taken up by three long tables arranged in a U shape and covered with silver: silver candelabras and silver goblets and silver pitchers and silver platters and silverware.

Alonso looked at the gleaming display and smiled with amusement. All of this silver had been dug from the ground here in the New World, sent to Spain, likely passing through Santo Domingo *en route*, and then once it had been turned into something useful, sent back. Nothing of any value was actually made in those far reaches of the Spanish Empire. For that matter, not much of use was made in old Spain, either. Not anymore.

The chairs that lined the tables were half occupied now, mostly with the minor officials of the Real Audiencia who did not dare arrive after those of higher office. The governor was not yet there, nor was the mayor or any of their key people. Juan Cardero had, as usual, timed their arrival perfectly.

Yet another servant approached, bowed, and escorted Alonso to his seat, an unnecessary courtesy since he always sat in the same place — two seats to the right of the governor's chair at the center of the head table — and knew perfectly well where it was. The servant held his chair and Alonso sat. Cardero handed him the sheaf of papers they had brought with them, the papers about which no one would inquire, then took his seat on one of the chairs against the wall, from where he would watch his betters dine.

The bells of the cathedral, three blocks west of Casas Reales, came softly through the windows of the dining room, and soon after the rest of the people began to drift in, taking their seats, snapping fingers at the servants, talking among themselves. Last of all came Gabriel de Chávez y Osorio, Governor General of Hispaniola, and with him the mayor of Santo Domingo, Don Nicolás Pérez de Maldonaldo.

"Ah, Don Alonso!" the governor said as he walked past Alonso's chair to take his own seat. "I trust you've not been waiting long?"

"No, Señor Governor," Alonso said.

"Forgive me," Don Gabriel said, smiling, speaking overly loud and gesturing toward the mayor who was taking his seat on the governor's other side. "This old fool Don Nicolás prattles on and on. There's no escaping him, he's getting soft in the head."

"I only appear to prattle," the mayor said. "In truth I must say everything three times before Don Gabriel understands."

"I am certain you are both mistaken," Alonso said. "We must pray so. Hispaniola would be lost without you two such distinguished gentlemen to guide it."

"Ha, you hear that, Don Nicolás?" the governor cried. "The boy will go far in government with such a fine tongue for flattery!"

The mayor laughed and Alonso smiled. The two of them could be brothers, Alonso thought, Don Gabriel the older, Don Nicolás the younger. They were not too far apart in age, less than ten years, Alonso guessed. Don Gabriel was grayer but Don Nicolás was fatter. They both enjoyed the trappings of their offices, if not the work, such that it was. They enjoyed their food and drink, and whoring as well, Alonso imagined, though that he did not know that for certain.

He did know that both men were fine examples of Spanish officialdom in the New World: self-interested, wary of responsibility, lazy, not terribly clever. It was what Alonso had expected. What he had been counting on. There was opportunity there in the West Indies, and men such as the governor and the mayor were no impediment to a smart, ambitious, and well-connected man.

Don Gabriel took his seat. As he did, the bishop of Santo Domingo, sitting two seats past the mayor, rose and the room fell silent. The bishop crossed himself and everyone else did likewise. Then, in his ecclesiastical voice, half spoken, half chanted, the bishop began.

"In nomine patris et filii et spiritus sancti..." The others in the room joined in with him, forty or more officials representing every strata of colonial government mouthing the ancient Latin blessing. When it was done everyone crossed themselves again and the bishop sat once more.

The bishop's sitting seemed to unleash a torrent of platter-wielding servants. They streamed in from the side doors, each bearing silver trays with roast beef and chicken and fish, cheese and fruit, fine white bread soft as cotton, bottles of wine and ale, cups of chocolate, puddings and pies. Each dish was offered in turn to the men at the tables, a carefully choreographed presentation that brought the most desirable dishes first to the most important of the guests. As lieutenant governor, Don Alonso Menéndez de Aviles was among them, which would have been nice if Alonso had much desire to eat at that hour of the morning, which he did not.

The others, the governor and the mayor most notably, did not suffer a similar lack of appetite. They heaped their plates with the servants' offerings and allowed their wine glasses to be filled. Most of the other men at table did likewise. Some of the minor officials, Alonso guessed, looked on this as a chance to augment their poor salaries with an abundance of free food.

Alonso took just a few slices of mango in thick syrup and a slab of bread, which was all that he thought he could manage. He was not a great eater at any time, least of all at breakfast, nor had he any great love for the sort of loud, jovial *bon homie* that the governor and mayor and some of the other, older senior officials so enjoyed. Had it been up to him he would have dispensed with the whole thing entirely, or at least conducted the morning's business while they ate and so be done with both things all the quicker. But it was not up to him.

It was, rather, up to the governor, Don Gabriel, who was very much a great eater, and a great talker and raconteur, and who would conduct this affair in his own way. These breakfasts long predated Alonso's arrival at

Santo Domingo, and even Don Gabriel's. They were part of the elaborate ritual that surrounded government there, and Don Alonso knew that as long as he was only the lieutenant governor he could do nothing but endure it. So he poked at his mango and let his thoughts travel back to his morning with Gabriella as the minutes crawled by and the sounds of eating and talking and laughing swirled around him.

So lost was Alonso in his memories that the governor's announcement of the end of breakfast and the beginning of the morning's business took him by surprise.

"Very well, now, let us attend to our affairs," Don Gabriel said, his tone more formal, less jovial. He picked up a silver knife and tapped it against a glass. The high, sharp ringing sound seemed to kill the undercurrent of noise until all eyes were turned the governor's way.

Alonso straightened and tried to look attentive. He found this part of these breakfast meetings no more satisfying or enlightening than the part that involved eating, and he knew it would be no more productive. Don Gabriel's secretary would read various letters from government officials back in Madrid. They would hear the latest news of the *gallions*, which would not be markedly different from the previous news. Various new laws and decrees would be announced and then largely ignored.

"Now, we must first discuss the latest blessings from God who smiles on our work here in the New World," the governor began. "I speak of course of the successful conquest of the islands of St. Christopher and Nevis by the estimable Captain General of the Ocean Sea Navy, Don Fadrique Álvarez de Toledo y Mendoza. You have no doubt all of you heard something of this enterprise. Now I can tell you I've had correspondence of late from Don Fadrique himself and I will relate to you the latest news, right from the horse's mouth, as it were, or the admiral's pen. Ha!"

This, at least, might have been of interest to Alonso, had he not already known everything that Don Gabriel was about to say. He had first heard of Don Fadrique's conquest from Carlos Hernández, but since then he had received many reports in his official capacity. He had been in attendance when Don Fadrique's letter was read to the most senior officials at Las Casas Reals. But now he listened again to how Don Fadrique and his magnificent fleet had caught the English and French dogs quite unawares, how he had laid waste to them with his great guns before leading his men ashore in complete subjugation of the islands.

"So the islands are once again in the hands of Spain as they should be," the governor concluded, "and any French or English interlopers who are not dead...and those who are dead are the fortunate ones, I assure you...but those who are not are bound off for the silver mines on the Main."

This part of the report was greeted with heads nodding in approval. The next part, Alonso knew, would be met with considerably less enthusiasm, though it could hardly come as a surprise.

"Once Don Fadrique has finished with his business in Saint Christopher," Don Gabriel continued, "his fleet will come here, of course, and we look forward to welcoming him, the great conqueror."

Alonso could see the subtle looks of chagrin on the faces of the men around the table. Don Fadrique's fleet, conquering heroes though they might be, would bring with them a heavenly host of problems. There would be captains and generals and their officers, not to mention the admiral himself, to be fêted, housed, fed and entertained. There would be ships to resupply and repair, prisoners to guard, sick and wounded to tend.

Thousands of soldiers and sailors, confined on shipboard for months and now fresh from battle, would descend on Santo Dominigo. It would be a boon for the tavern keepers and whores, a nightmare for everyone else.

Further discussion of the fleet's arrival followed, but nothing of real consequence was said because no one dared be the first to express the concern that everyone felt. That done, the meeting moved on to the more mundane aspects of government.

Don Alonso kept his mouth shut. He had not been long in Santo Domingo, had not been long in his current office, but long enough for him to understand the futility of offering any thoughts or opinions.

He had tried at first, once he had seen how things operated. He gave suggestions as to how the plantations might be better managed, how the slaves better controlled, how the city might be improved, the soldiers better organized. He did it not so much because he cared but because he wished to appear as if he cared. He did it because he could see the glaring deficiencies and because he was bored.

It did no good at all.

No one in Santo Domingo wished to make a decision or take any responsibility, and Alonso suspected that was true in the rest of the New World as well. Nor did Madrid encourage any sort of independence. Matters of consequence had to be routed back to Spain, where, more often than not, they were ignored. Generally, the officials of the New World saved time and effort by not bothering to ask in the first place.

Soon Alonso found himself doing what the other office holders did, which was just enough to appear to be doing his job, just enough to keep the government functioning at a subsistence level, to keep the infrastructure intact and the island relatively free of criminals and run-away slaves and the French and English and Dutch filibusteros.

With little governing to do, men such as Don Gabriel and the mayor, Don Nicolás, worried most about taking their pleasure. Don Alonso, however, had greater ambitions. He was there to build great wealth and power in his own right. He was there to build his empire. The arrival of *Lion de Bilbao*, her tariff-free cargo stored down in the warehouse of Carlos Hernández and soon to be sold throughout the New World, these were the first steps on that road.

For the next hour and more Alonso tried to pay attention as various officials of the Real Audiencia made their reports and secretaries read correspondence. Finally Don Gabriel cleared his throat.

"Very well, I believe that concludes…" the governor began, words that Alonso longed to hear, but before the governor finished he was cut off by one of the men on the table to his right, a man named Antón Nuñez who was captain of the port.

"Don Gabriel, I beg your pardon, but there is one thing I wish to report," Nuñez said.

"Yes, Señor Antón?" the governor said as Alonso silently cursed the man.

"The gentlemen know we had but one guarda coasta ship which survived the hurricano," Nuñez said. "I ordered it to make a circumnavigation of the island, to see what damage had been done, to see if there was any shipping left at all. In particular I ordered that they look in on those miserable dogs along the northwest shore, the hunters and filibusteros."

Heads turned, eyes on the captain of the port. Here at last was new information that was potentially of interest to the men in the room.

"The master of the guarda coasta, he returned last night and reported to me," Nuñez continued. He shook his head. "Terrible, terrible…. There is much damage all over the island. Several of the plantations farther out are just gone. Forests laid flat. He saw a dozen wrecks piled up on all coasts. Nothing salvageable on the least of them. Not a man of their crews left alive that he could find."

The men around the tables nodded as they listened to the report. Grim as it was, it was nothing that they would not have expected to hear. They had all witnessed the fury of the storm, none more so than Don Alonso.

"And the filibusteros, what of them?" the governor asked. "I hope the hurricano swept them all to the devil."

"One would wish, but it seems not," Nuñez said. "They are like the cockroaches, very hard to be rid of them. The master, he sailed in near the shore. He could see there were fires burning so he guessed the filibusteros were still there, but the guarda coasta is a small ship, governor, and a small crew, and he dared not get too close ashore."

"Of course, of course," Don Gabriel said. "One doesn't wander in close to a pack of hungry wolves."

"The master did report one thing that was a surprise," Nuñez continued. "As I said, there were ships wrecked all around the island. Save for one.

Where the filibusteros make their camp just east of Tortuga the master saw a ship at anchor. From what he could see some of the upper masts and rigging was damaged but otherwise it was floating on its lines."

"What sort of ship was this?" asked Don Nicolás. He sounded like a man who was asking because he felt he should ask, not because he cared.

"Nothing of any consequence, Señor Mayor," Nuñez said. "A brigantine of one hundred, two hundred tons. No more."

Alonso, who had only been half listening at best, looked up quick.

Brigantine...he thought, but before the next thought was even fully formed in his mind he dismissed it.

Ridiculous...it's not possible...

But again...

It was possible. The guarda coasta had seen a ship which had apparently survived the hurricano. It was someone's ship. It could be his ship. There was nothing in Nuñez's brief description it prove it was not. It was unlikely, to be sure, but it was not impossible.

Alonso sat up straighter, opened his mouth, then closed it again. This was not the time, not the place to ask the many questions that were roiling around in his head. So he sat quietly and considered them, and considered his best move, as the governor made his last few superfluous comments about the morning's affairs.

Don Gabriel gave a deep sigh and stood, the official end of the business, and Alonso stood as well. Juan Cardero appeared at Alonso's side and began to organize the papers they had brought with them as Alonso said his goodbyes to the men around him. That done, he and Cardero made their way out of the dining room and back out into the walkway that bordered the courtyard. Alonso had made several decisions in the past few moments, and now it was time to act.

He looked back over his shoulder, saw that no one was behind them, no one within earshot. He understood that there was no reason for the urgency he felt. His instructions to Cardero could wait until they reached his office. They could wait another day or two, for that matter and it probably would make no difference. But Alonso's thoughts had been whirling, building like a storm, since he had heard Nuñez's words: *a brigantine of one hundred, two hundred tons. No more.*

A brigantine, like *Nostra Sennora de Santiago*, née *Trois Frères*. At anchor just east of Tortuga. The very place to which *Trois Frères* was bound.

"Cardero," Alonso said in something a bit louder than a whisper. "I'll need you to arrange a meeting for me. With Carlos Hernández. Discreet. You understand."

"Yes," Juan Cardero said. "I most certainly understand."

Chapter Twenty-One

The guns that lined *Santa Rosa*'s deck, eight six-pounders, made a great noise as they blasted away, one after the other, jetting flame and gray smoke out over the water. *Charles Rex* was firing back as fast as she could, the roar of her less impressive four-pounders less throaty and deep. But it was a good show. Effective. Believable.

There was a quarter mile between the two ships and they were sailing slow. For the past hour they had been running with their fore and main sheets eased, spilling wind from their big lower sails. As a result the stranger in their wake had been slowly overhauling them, so slowly he was likely not even aware of it at first. But he certainly was now, hull-up and just a little over a mile astern. Like a vulture, circling, he was hanging back, waiting to see what he could devour.

Benjamin Graves stood aft, as near as he dared to Maja, watching the action. *Santa Rosa* was turning to larboard and starboard, bringing her broadsides to bear, making all the noise she could, and *Charles Rex* was doing the same. Had they been loading their guns with round shot on top of the gunpowder they might have done real hurt to one another, but as it was they were firing only smoke.

"That bastard filibustero, he's not coming any closer," Maja said, his first words in half an hour. "We don't fool him. He has to wonder why we just started shooting now."

"No, no," Graves said, shaking his head. "That whore's son will see what he wants to see, and what he wants to see is two fat ships beating each other to death. He ain't going to think too deep on it. You'll see."

Maja grunted and did not reply.

Hope to hell I'm right on this, Graves thought.

It had been his idea, coming into his head like a figure emerging from the dark, growing more distinct as it stepped into the light. The pirate would be shy about attacking two ships at once, Maja was right about that. The filibusteros did not care to take inordinate risks. But if the two ships were to tear each other up a bit first, knock the fight out of one another before the pirate even came up with them? Those were the sort of odds a cowardly villain like that might favor.

Graves had laid it all out for Maja and to his surprise Maja did not dismiss the suggestion out of hand. That made Graves think that Maja was more concerned about returning to Señor Corregidor *sans* cargo than he let on.

They worked out the details quickly because there were not too many details to work out. Graves considered suggesting that he himself take command of *Charles Rex*, but he dropped the idea before even voicing it. Maja would laugh in his face, or worse.

Instead a few trusted men were sent in the ship's boat to Ortiz who remained in command of *Rex*, and they brought him Maja's instructions. *Santa Rosa* would start in firing with unshotted guns and then *Charles Rex* would do the same. They would keep it up, with a few other bits of play-acting and signals added to it, until *Santa Rosa* hoisted a red flag up her mainmast. Then, when the pirate came down to scoop up what was left, the two ships would turn and fight as one, and fight for real.

Simple. The best plans were. It only required that the pirate play along, and Graves wished he felt more confident that the bastard would do so.

No matter... Graves thought. If it worked out then the benefits might be enormous, but the consequences if they failed were small: they had nothing to lose from this charade beyond a barrel or two of gunpowder. Graves figured that was why Maja had agreed to the idea.

But for all that, Graves very much wanted to succeed. It was the one chance he had, tiny as it might be, to appease Señor Corregidor. Besides, Benjamin Graves had assured Maja it would work, and Benjamin Graves did not like to be wrong.

"Reckon it's time we hoist the white one to the mizzen peak," Graves said. Maja nodded and shouted an order aft. The sailor standing ready with the white flag hauled away on the halyard and the flag fluttered up to the peak of the mizzen yard.

Graves turned his attention to *Charles Rex*. For a moment she just sailed on, firing her guns, her sails set and drawing. Then suddenly the main yard dropped, plunging down to the deck as if it had been shot away, coming to a stop inches before it would have crushed the bulwark.

Easy, Don Diego, you dumb bastard, Graves thought. *You'll shiver that damned yard to pieces.* But he had to admit it was a good bit of theater. Any ship watching for a distance could well think *Charles Rex* had been disabled by a well-placed shot.

With her mainsail gone and the main topsail flapping in the breeze *Charles Rex*'s was doing little more than drifting. Maja turned forward and shouted out a few orders and *Santa Rosa*'s fore and mainsail were hauled up to the yard, reducing her speed as well. The helmsman put the helm over and the ship came broadside to the wind, broadside to the apparently crippled *Charles Rex*, and continued to fire away, with *Charles Rex* returning fire as best as she could.

From the main topsail yard the lookout called down, a touch of excitement in his tone. The lookout and Maja exchanged a few words, then Maja nodded his head and looked aft. Graves did not bother even hoping that Maja would tell him what the man had said.

"Well?" Graves asked.

"The pirate, he's set his foresail. He had it clewed up but now he's set it."

Graves smiled. "There! See?" he said. The filibusteros had been trailing behind, watching from a distance. Now he was setting more sail, ready to close with the two ships doing battle, now that one had taken a significant hit.

"Bastard's not here yet," Maja said.

He will be, Graves thought but he kept the thought to himself because saying it would be bad luck and because he could still be wrong. But every passing moment suggested that he was not wrong, as the strange ship astern continued to close with them, cutting the distance to half a mile, racing to get in the middle of the fight he was witnessing and claim all for himself.

Maja called out an order. The man who stood ready with the red flag hauled it up to the top of the mainmast. Maja called another order. The men loading and firing the guns stopped, stepped back and waited.

A hundred yards to windward hands aboard the *Charles Rex* hauled away on the larboard fore yard lift until the foreyard was cockbilled at an odd and unsightly angle, an angle that would appear to the filibusteros to be further damage. The *Rex*'s guns fell silent as well.

Two wooden tubs had been brought on deck, each holding a smattering of cutlasses and pikes and boarding axes and a few pistols, the sum total of all the weapons aboard *Santa Rosa*. On Maja's word the men grabbed up their weapons of choice, thrusting them through belts around their waists or draping shoulder belts over their heads.

Not too damned many men aboard, are there? Graves thought. All told, including Maja's men, his men, and the freed slaves, there were sixteen on *Santa Rosa*'s crew. *Charles Rex* likely had around ten. The pirate could be counted on to have twice that number at least, and not these miserable Spanish sailors but rather English or French or Dutch filibusteros. They were badly outnumbered and likely outmatched in fighting prowess. This was a fact that Graves had failed to take into account. At least until that moment.

No matter, we have surprise going for us, Graves thought. He tried to think it emphatically enough that he would actually believe it.

Maja shouted out yet another order and the men set to reloading the great guns. Flannel cartridges of gunpowder went down the barrels, but this time round shot went down as well, and grape shot after the round shot and then wadding over the entire load. This would not be an impotent broadside for dumb show. The guns were loaded to dole out real damage now.

Maja disappeared below and was back a moment later with a heavy cutlass at his waist, suspended from a black leather shoulder strap and hanging at his right side, and two braces of pistols hanging from ribbons around his neck. In his right hand he held a sort of club, two and a half feet long and rectangular in cross-section. It was narrow enough at the base for Maja to wrap his fingers around it, but it flared out toward the end, and the flat surfaces were covered with intricate carvings.

"What do you call that?" Graves asked, nodding toward the weapon.

"*Boutou*," Maja said, biting the word off, killing any further inquiry before it began.

Graves looked forward. The men had loaded the guns and run them out and now stood ready with the smoldering match to light the priming in the touchholes. A few others knelt behind the bulwark inserting fuses in the round grenadoes they would toss aboard the pirate vessel before going over the side.

That was the plan. As the pirate closed with them, *Santa Rosa* and *Charles Rex* would set sail, turn, and come up on either side of the filibusteros. A broadside from each ship, grenadoes on the enemy's deck and then over the side with pistols and cutlasses. And a war club, apparently. It was a good strategy, an effective strategy. Which was why they had no doubt the filibusteros intended to do the same to them.

"Here, Maja, what say you let me have a weapon?" Graves said. "I know the use of one well enough. Can't waste a man in this fight."

Maja looked at him and there was something smoldering in his eyes that Graves had not seen before, something frightening, dangerous and ugly. His face looked like the visage of an angry Carib god.

"You pick up a weapon I'll slit your throat," he said, his voice gravelly and low and Graves just nodded.

The two men turned their attention now over the larboard side. *Charles Rex* was still one hundred yards to windward, her main yard still down, her foreyard cockbilled and Graves hoped to hell that they had seen the red flag that told them to make ready to turn and fight. There was not an awful lot of time left. The pirate had all sail set and was coming down on them fast. No more than a quarter mile now separated the filibusteros from *Charles Rex*.

Come along, get your arse moving, Graves thought as he watched for any sign that *Charles Rex* was about to get underway, but as far as he could see she was just drifting on her spot of ocean.

Maja barked some orders. The helm came over and the sails braced around and *Santa Rosa* turned half around until she was sailing as close to the wind as she could, which was not too close. Worse, she was on a larboard tack now, sailing away from *Charles Rex*, not toward her. Ortiz was supposed to have turned *Rex* when Maja turned *Santa Rosa* and the two ships would come at the pirate together, on the same tack. But still *Charles Rex* showed no sign of moving.

"Come along you dumb bastard!" Graves shouted, unable to contain himself now. "Set your bloody sails!" There was little chance that Ortiz would actually hear him, and no chance his English would be understood, which Graves knew. He was shouting out of frustration alone.

He looked over at Maja who remained expressionless, unmoving, watching the thing play out to windward. The filibustero had altered his heading so that he was making straight for *Charles Rex*. Rather than having to contend with two ships at once, the pirate could split the two now, taking them one at a time. He might kill every man aboard *Charles Rex* before *Santa Rosa* could tack around and join in the fight.

Just then *Charles Rex*'s main yard gave a jerk and started to rise up the mast as the hands aboard her turned to setting the sail at last.

"Too late!" Graves shouted, and indeed it was. The filibustero was no more than a hundred yards to windward. He would be on top of *Charles Rex* before she even began to gather way.

"*Disparáis!*" Maja shouted, which Graves guessed mean *fire* in Spanish because the men at the guns brought their match down on the priming powder and nearly as one the four great guns on the larboard side went off with a deafening roar that made the entire ship shudder as if it had struck a rock. Graves could see a few holes smashed into the pirate's side and he thought he saw a swath cut through the men on deck by a passing spray of grapeshot.

Damn my eyes, there's a lot of them... Graves thought. The deck of the filibustero was crowded with men — white men, swarthy men, black men — and more were standing in the shrouds. They were shouting and waving swords and axes, some bare-chested, some wearing shirts and jerkins and some wearing bright-colored doublets.

Maja shouted again. The helmsman pushed the helm over and *Santa Rosa* turned up into the wind. Maja was tacking, turning the ship's head around so they could join in the fighting as the pirate ship covered the last few dozen yards to the side of *Charles Rex*.

Graves dashed off to the starboard rail and cast off the main sheet, then hauled away on the clew garnet as the ship's bow turned up into the wind. He looked aloft as the sails on the fore mast fluttered and came aback.

Please Lord, please see us through, he thought. Tacking in light air was no simple matter. If *Santa Rosa* got caught in irons then the filibusteros could

take their time with *Charles Rex* and still have more than enough fight in
them to subdue *Santa Rose* as well. Graves realized then that when he had
thought there was little risk in trying this caper it had not occurred to him
that the filibusteros might kill them all.

But *Santa Rosa* did not get caught in irons. With agonizing slowness her
bow turned through the wind, foot by foot, until at last the breeze was
coming over the starboard bow. The men braced the yards around and the
sails snapped and filled and *Santa Rosa* heeled a bit as she gathered way
again, heading toward *Charles Rex* now, and not away.

Graves made the main sheet fast and looked up, shocked by how
quickly things had changed. The filibustero had come alongside *Charles Rex*,
which had managed to get her mainsail hoisted part way but no more. The
pop pop sound of pistols and muskets came over the water, and the shouts
of men and the clash of steel blades. And then screaming as the first of the
victims fell.

Maja still had not moved, still had not spoken, save for the few orders
he had given. Now he watched, stolid and bloodless as a statue, as the
pirates poured onto the deck of *Charles Rex* and her crew died under their
swords.

From behind them the helmsman called a question, an edge of
excitement and perhaps fear in the words. The pirate's starboard side was
hard against *Charles Rex*. *Santa Rosa* was driving at their larboard side, their
unengaged side, with building speed. Maja replied to the helmsman, his
answer short, sharp and definitive, and whatever it was Graves guessed it
was not what the helmsman wanted to hear.

Next Maja shouted forward. The two men who had been arming the
grenadoes looked up and Maja barked a quick order at them, but rather
than obey, or even move, they just stared back at him. Maja took a step
forward and pointed at the filibusteros's ship and gave his order again, and
this time the men pointed as well and began to argue, which Graves
thought was perhaps not a good idea.

Maja turned and pointed at the helmsman with his boutou and spoke a
half dozen words, then turned and advanced on the men at the grenadoes.
One of them was still arguing as he approached, pointing at the grenadoes,
pointing at the two ships locked in battle. Without missing a step Maja
swung his boutou backhand and caught the man on the side of his head. A
spray of blood followed the swing of the club and the man lifted off the
deck as he was flung sideways and then collapsed, motionless.

The second man was backing away, hands up in a pointless gesture of
defense, when Maja's hand shot out like a snake making a strike. But rather
than hit the man Maja snatched the coil of smoldering match from his
hand. He shoved his boutou into his belt, grabbed a grenado from the box
and touched the match to the fuse. He held it there for a second and when

it started to sputter he cocked his arm and flung the iron globe across the stretch of water and onto the deck of the filibustero.

It was chaos there. The pirates who had not boarded *Charles Rex* were crowded at the rail, hacking and cutting, but through the press of rogues Graves could see some of the *Charles Rex*'s crew fighting back, swinging cutlasses and jabbing with pikes. Edged weapons and boarding axes were flailing in the air, pistols banging out here and there, men shouting and screaming. It was into that madness that the grenado flew, bounced, and then exploded.

It was an indiscriminate killer. The black sphere burst with a sound like a cannon shot, but higher, sharper, punctuated by the scream of fragmented iron flying in every direction. The four men closest to the explosion were nearly shredded as they were tossed aside, bellies torn open, limbs ripped apart. They took the brunt of the blast, but there were still fragments enough with force enough to fell men farther off, dropping them to the deck clutching wounds.

Graves took a deep breath and looked away and swallowed to keep from puking. He figured he had seen worse things in his life but he could not recall what. The grenado had blasted a hole in the line of fighting men, and it must have killed some of the crew of *Charles Rex* along with the filibusteros. Graves guessed that was what Maja's men had been arguing about, throwing a grenado that would kill some of their shipmates. For all the good it did any of them.

He looked up again. The fighting was still going on, but the filibusteros amidships had turned to see where this new, surprise threat was coming from, and as they did Maja tossed another grenado into their midst.

This one they saw coming and they turned and pushed and stampeded away, but there were too many of them and they were packed too tight to get clear before the bomb exploded. Once again the fragments of iron tore through the crowd of men, turning those in the way into bloody corpses flung randomly about. And before the last of them had even hit the deck *Santa Rosa* ran hard into the side of the filibusteros's ship, so hard that Graves staggered and nearly fell.

They hit just aft of the main mast. *Santa Rosa*'s bowsprit came sailing over pirate's rail and her spritsail yard hit its shrouds. For a second it was unclear which would give way first, but then the spritsail yard yielded, snapping near the center like a broken wing and collapsing in a heap of torn rigging and canvas.

Santa Rosa's bow hit the pirate's bulwark with a cracking, snapping sound as it crushed the ship's upper side with its slow, grinding momentum. The men on the pirate's deck staggered just as Graves had done, turning to meet this attack from behind. Maja hurled another grenado, this one toward the filibusteros's bow, where the men were still packed close and fighting.

Graves expected Maja to turn, to wave with his arm at the enemy on the other ship, to call for his men to follow him into the fight, but he did not. Instead he bounded forward down *Santa Rosa*'s deck to where the two ships were locked together. Without missing a stride he stepped up on the pinrail, stepped across to the filibusteros's bulwark and leapt from there onto the pirate's deck. It was as if Maja had forgotten that there were any fighting men aboard *Santa Rosa* beside himself.

Maja hit the deck just as the third grenado exploded, ratcheting the madness up even more, but Maja's presence did not go unnoticed. A handful of the filibusteros saw his leap and charged him in their unsubtle way, cutlasses raised like axes ready to chop wood. Maja grabbed up two of the pistols hanging around his neck, one in each hand, and thumbed the locks back as he lifted them.

The nearest of the filibusteros were four feet away when Maja discharged the guns into their chests, knocking them back into the men behind. He whipped the brace of pistols off from around his neck and flung them at the others, then snatched up the second pair. Those pirates still standing did not turn and run, despite that threat. Instead, they charged, trying to hack Maja down before he could cock and fire his second brace of pistols.

Graves, watching from *Santa Rosa*'s deck, was impressed. No cowards, they. But he was not surprised when two more were blown back into their comrades, arms flung up, weapons flying.

Now what, Maja, you dumb bastard? Graves thought. Maja was alone in the face of half the pirate horde. Graves's first impulse was to rally the men aboard *Santa Rosa* and lead them into the fight. He actually had his mouth open, ready to call to the others, when it occurred to him that it might be better if he did not. It could be very much in his interest to see Maja cut down then and there. Extracting himself from the current unpleasantness with Señor Corregidor would be considerably easier with Maja dead.

He closed his mouth and continued watching. A dozen of the filibusteros had broken off from the fighting at the rail and were turning on Maja, coming at him from every direction, the first of them just steps away.

This should do for him, Graves thought. But he was wrong.

With his left hand Maja pulled the cutlass from its scabbard and raised it to stop a blade coming down at his skull and with his right he jerked the boutou from his belt. Maja's cutlass and the pirate's were locked overhead as Maja swung the boutou sideways, striking the filibustero on the neck. The man crumpled as if his legs had been shot away under him and Maja swung the club back the other way, catching another square in the face. The man's head whipped sideways in a spray of blood and, Graves was all but certain, teeth.

It was an extraordinary thing to behold. Maja seemed not to know or care that he was alone on the deck, with a score of pirates, all those not fighting with the men aboard *Charles Rex*, pushing to get at him. He worked his cutlass and boutou in perfect concert, offense and defense, knocking weapons aside, thrusting, clubbing, creating an empty patch of deck around him with men writhing in pain scattered around its periphery.

An arm pushed through the crowd, pistol extended, pointed at Maja. Graves saw the twin flash of priming and muzzle and heard the sharp crack of the gun. Maja jerked to the side but Graves could not tell if he was turning away from the gun or if he had been shot. Either way he did not slow in the least as he plowed his way through the packed men in front of him.

Guess we better go help this bastard, Graves thought, somewhat grudgingly.

Benjamin Graves was not the sort who craved a fight, but neither did he shy from one, and he had been in plenty. This battle with the filibusteros was largely his doing — they were acting on his plan — and he did not feel right sitting it out. What's more, though he would not admit it, it annoyed him to see Maja displaying such fighting prowess as he stood idle by.

"*Via! Via!*" Graves shouted because he thought it meant "Go!" in Spanish and it was all he could think to say. He ran forward, grabbing a cutlass from one of the tubs as he did. He looked over his shoulder, happy to see the others following behind. He was willing to lead men into battle. Unlike Maja he did not care to plunge in by himself.

He climbed up on the bulwark using the fore shrouds to steady himself, then reached across to the pirate's mizzen shrouds, found his grip and swung himself over. He stepped on the rail of the pirate ship and dropped to the deck, stumbled, found his footing and looked fore and aft.

Maja seemed to be holding his own and Graves was inclined to let him be, since he was still not so certain he wanted the man to live through this. The deck was littered with filibusteros wounded and killed by Maja and the grenadoes. The rest of the fighting was going on aboard *Charles Rex* where the pirates had swarmed over the rail and pushed the *Rex*'s crew back across the deck. Graves was surprised that any of the *Rex*'s men were still alive, but apparently they were. He could not actually see them through the press of men, but he reckoned the filibusteros had to be fighting someone.

He glanced to his left and right. The Spanish crew, his own crew, the freed slaves had all come over the rail behind him. He waved his cutlass and raced across the deck, past where Maja was fighting off a half dozen men, and then over the pirate's starboard side and down onto the deck of what had been, until recently, his own ship.

Good, good... he thought as he straightened and refreshed the grip on his weapon. The filibusteros were turned with their backs to him and his men: they had not even seen them come aboard. That gave Graves and the others maybe twenty seconds worth of surprise, but Graves knew well what could be accomplished in twenty seconds.

He ran directly at the man closest to him, a big, dark-skinned brute, shirtless, bringing an ax back over his head. Graves caught a glimpse of Ortiz pressed against the bulwark, blood running down his face, the ax-man ready to split his skull.

Graves stopped three feet behind the man and drew his cutlass back, his eyes on the man's skin, glistening with sweat, rippling with muscle. The filibustero did not even know that Graves was there. One thrust, right between the ribs, and the thing was done.

He hesitated. He was accustomed to the hack and slash variety of fighting, the brawl-like melee where one flailed out at random at a packed enemy and it was not clear what sort of hurt you were doling out. Now he was looking at plunging his cutlass right into a man's back, seeing the point enter his body, using his force of arm to push the blade deep while blood came gushing as if he had stabbed a wineskin.

Suddenly he was not so certain he could do it.

Then the filibustero hacked down with the ax. Graves caught a glimpse of the terror on Ortiz's face and he lunged. The point entered the man's back and drove on through, an inch, two, and then Graves pulled the weapon back.

*Damn it, damn it…*Graves thought. He had lost his nerve in mid-thrust, pulled the weapon free before he had done any real hurt. The dark filibustero arched his back, roared and spun around, eyes wide, teeth barred like a wolf. Graves had saved Ortiz's life but otherwise had done nothing but enrage the ax-wielding beast.

The heart, the heart… Graves thought. A stab to the man's heart and it was over, but when Graves thrust again the point was aimed at the man's belly. Still, he drove it in with greater force, three inches, four inches.

The filibustero swung his arm down and knocked the blade free, tearing a gash in his flesh and sending a spray of blood across the deck, but painful as that had to be, it gave him no pause. He took a step forward and raised his ax and hacked down at Graves, a clumsy and obvious move and Graves stepped aside as the blade came down.

The ax head missed him by two inches — he could feel the wind of its passing — then the blade hit the deck and stuck. Graves chopped down on the pirate's wrist. He felt his cutlass strike bone but did not stop to look at what damage he had done. The man's shriek as he reared up, ax still stuck in the deck, his left hand clasping his spurting wrist, was enough for Graves to know that the fight was out of him.

He turned to his right. His men, the Spaniards, the freed slaves had made good use of their few seconds of surprise. They had not hesitated in their attack. They had caught the filibusteros from behind and killed them outright, or nearly so, or forced them to turn and fight, leaving it to the men of *Charles Rex*, pressed against the rail, to drive weapons into their exposed backs.

Half a dozen of them lay writhing on the deck. A few more lay motionless, dead or pretending to be. Three others, unhurt, apparently, were on their knees, hands held up, eyes wide and pleading.

"Very well," Graves said, loud, nearly shouting, "we'll leave these others to…"

Before he could finish, one of the Black men, one of the freed slaves, brought his cutlass down on the head of the pirate kneeling before him, straight down with a force that split the man's skull in a welter of blood and brains. The pirate remained as he was for a second more, upright on his knees, the cutlass wedged between the two parts of his head, and then he fell sideways. The Black man let go of the cutlass and let it fall, still stuck in the dead man's head.

"Enough! Enough of that, the bastards have given up!" Graves said, speaking quickly to keep from vomiting at the sight, unsure if the freed slaves or the Spaniards understood his words or cared.

"Very well. Now let us…" Graves continued, but he was interrupted again, this time by the startling sensation of steel, warm and slick, pressed under his chin.

"You have a cutlass," Maja said. "Do you think you can kill me with it? Before I cut your throat?"

Chapter Twenty-Two

Graves's fingers spread apart and the cutlass dropped from his hand and bounced on the deck. A hundred replies raced through his head, protests that he had to do his part in the fight, that he had to come to the aid of Maja's men, that the filibusteros would have gone after Maja *en mass* and overwhelmed him if Graves and the others had not stopped them.

Just shut your mouth, Ben, shut your bloody mouth, Graves thought, and for once he took his own advice. For a long moment, a very long moment, he stood silent and motionless with the steady pressure of Maja's bloody steel against his throat. Then Maja lowered the blade.

"You sorry I'm still alive?" Maja asked.

Graves turned just enough so that he could look at the man. There was no expression on Maja's face, but there were various rents in his clothes and an ugly laceration on his left shoulder where the pistol ball had apparently grazed him. There was a hole in his filthy shirt, just at his belly, framed by a wide and spreading patch of fresh blood. He held his cutlass in one hand, his boutou in the other. Both were dripping.

"Am I sorry?" Graves asked, sounding genuinely incredulous. "If I wanted you dead I could have let them filibusteros kill you. Instead, me and the others, we come to your aid."

Maja nodded, his face still expressionless. The filibustero whom Graves had wounded was lying at their feet in a spreading pool of blood, twisting in pain. Graves could see that he had nearly severed the man's hand with the stroke of his cutlass.

The pirate groaned and cursed and Maja lifted his boutou and brought it down hard. There was a thump as the pirate's head hit the deck and a sickening crack where club met skull, and then the man was silent and he did not move.

Maja stepped back and looked around the deck, at the dead and wounded and those who had managed to come through unscathed. Ortiz was still pressed against the rail, trembling, pale under his olive complexion, streaked with blood but apparently unhurt.

"Ortiz," Maja barked, then shouted a string of orders in Spanish. He turned to Graves. "I told Ortiz to get some men and bind these bastards' hands. Wounded or not, tie them up. You and your men help. Be quick and I'll hold off cutting your throat."

Graves nodded. He went below and found a sack full of short bits of cordage and brought it on deck, then he and the others set about tying the hands of the filibusteros, wounded or otherwise. None put up much resistance. Those with minor wounds were angry and sullen and needed their arms forced back behind them. Others were so close to death that binding them seemed pointless to Graves, but he was most certainly not going to argue the point.

When the last of the filibusteros was made fast Graves straightened and looked around. Maja was gone, where, Graves did not know. The Spaniards and English and Black men were standing around in a dazed confusion, which Graves knew always followed the wild exuberance of living through such a fight. But not all were standing. Some were lying on the deck, ignored by their shipmates, dead or wounded.

Guilford, late of the crew of *Charles Rex*, was standing off by the mainmast. He still held a short sword in his hand and his face was smeared with blood but he was upright seemed to be in generally good shape.

"Guilford!" Graves called and Guilford looked up at him. "Go get those bandages and such…the surgeon's kit…out of the master's cabin. Let's see about helping these poor sods."

Guilford nodded, tossed the short sword away and headed below. A moment later he was back with the familiar wooden chest that held *Charles Rex's* medical supplies. Graves had bought it himself in Portsmouth several years back and it had come in very handy, even if he did not know the use of half of the compounds in the various glass vials.

The Spaniards were watching as Guilford set the box down. "*Médico*," Graves said, pointing to the box and to the wounded men lying at various places around the deck. A few of the Spaniards nodded and a few of those moved to help their fallen shipmates, rolling them groaning on their backs, tearing bloody clothes away, examining wounds, deciding which were worth putting the effort into helping.

Graves was kneeling beside one of the Spaniards and wrapping a bandage around his thigh when Maja appeared just a few feet away. Graves tied the cloth off and looked up. He expected Maja to make some threat, offer some insult, but he did not. There was an odd look on his face. The same look was on the faces of the men beside him.

"Just looked down in the bastard filibusteros' hold," Maja said.

"That so?" Graves said. He stood so he would not feel as if he was supplicating to Maja. "What'd you find?"

Maja nodded. "It's good," he said. "It's good." He looked down at the wounded man at their feet, then around at the others. He turned and yammered in Spanish to the men behind him, then called out to Ortiz as well. Graves, whose rudimentary Spanish was starting to return, understood him to order the dead thrown overboard and the pirates who could still stand driven back aboard their ship. The men shuffled across the deck and Maja turned to Graves.

"You help them," Maja said, nodding toward his men. "You and your English."

"Oh…" Grave said. He turned and called a few orders to his men and they set about locating the dead among the filibusteros. They stripped weapons and jewelry from the bloody corpses, and any clothing worth keeping, though there was little of that. All plunder was piled by the main mast. Maja would decide how to distribute it, but taking anything before then would certainly earn a man a boutou strike to the side of the head.

Once the dead were made ready Graves directed his men to heave them over the unengaged side of *Charles Rex*. He tried to ignore the unsettling splash as their bodies hit the water. He hoped that the sharks would not come. That was something he did not care to see.

He found one of the filibusteros by the main hatch, face down, motionless. He hooked his toe under the man's shoulder and rolled him over and to his surprise the man let out a moan and made a weak gesture with his hand.

Son of a bitch…bastard's still alive, Graves thought. But not for long, he could see that. There was an ugly wound in the man's chest: the great quantity of blood soaking his shirt was a testament to how much of the life had drained from him.

"Graves! What in hell you about?" Maja called. He was standing on the deck of the filibusteros's ship, where the pirates who were still whole enough to move had been gathered, along with the crew of Maja's two ships.

Graves looked down at the man at his feet and realized that Maja could not see him behind the hatch combing. He realized as well that Maja would tell Graves to toss him overboard, living or no, if he knew he was there.

"I'm coming, Maja, I'm coming," Graves said, stepping up on the hatch and crossing to the other side, hoping that the dying man did not groan and give himself away.

It was a foolish thing to worry about, Graves knew. The man was a filibustero, and either way he would be dead very soon. Still, much as Graves did not want Maja thinking him soft-hearted or weak, throwing a living man overboard did not sit right with him.

Graves climbed over the rail and onto the deck of the filibustero. The three ships had been lashed together, and now they rolled and ground against one another in the long, easy swell. Graves had not actually looked close at the pirate's ship, but he saw now that the vessel was much as he would have expected. Coils of rope and sundry gear were scattered haphazardly around, and bones and other remnants of meals past littered the corners of the deck. Dark, discolored stains on the sun-bleached wood told where wine or rumbullian or perhaps blood had spilled and was left to dry.

The filibusteros, fourteen of them, still bound, were seated on the deck. Some were big men, some small and wiry. Some were light skinned, English or French or Dutch. Six of them were Black, escaped slaves, undoubtedly. The most dangerous of all since they could expect no mercy from any quarter if they were taken. Graves wondered if perhaps this was their lucky day.

By way of answer Maja stepped over to the first of the Black men and stood over him as the filibustero glared defiantly up. Then Maja reached down and grabbed the man under the arm, heaved him to his feet and pushed him aside, so hard the bound man stumbled and nearly fell. Then Maja did the same to the next of the Black men, then the next and the next until all half dozen were standing in a small knot by the larboard side.

They stared at Maja, wary and furious as he approached. He spoke to them in a voice low, and in what language Graves could only guess. He spoke for some time, a minute or so, which for Maja was a very long speech indeed. When he was done the men exchanged glances, and then, as if on cue, they all nodded.

Maja pulled his knife and stepped around behind the men and cut their bonds away. He looked in the general direction of Graves and the rest of the men of *Santa Maria* and *Charles Rex.* "These men are with us now," he said. He said it again in Spanish. Graves waited for more, but that, apparently, was it.

Like I figured, this is your lucky day, you Moorish bastards, Graves thought.

"The rest of you," Maja said, indicating the filibusteros who were still sitting with hands bound, "will help sway the cargo out. And you'll work with a will, if you know what's best."

Graves looked at the pirates' sullen faces. He knew one of them would say something. One always did.

That little wiry fellow, I reckon, Graves predicted, and sure enough it was the wiry one who straightened and opened his mouth to offer some protest or some act of defiance.

"We'll help, will we? That so?" the man asked. Maja stopped in mid-stride, turned and stared down at the man, and the pirate stared back, back into Maja's dark and expressionless face.

I wouldn't, if I were you, Graves thought.

The pirate seemed to come to the same conclusion, and his mouth froze just as the next word was forming. Graves saw the defiance melt away under Maja's utterly merciless, animal gaze

"What?" Maja asked softly, but the filibustero just shut his mouth, shook his head and looked away.

Ten minutes later the pirates' hands were free and they were hard at it. A half dozen of them were down in the hold, securing the cargo to the stay tackle, while others were heaving away, hoisting Maja's booty, formerly their booty, up into the daylight. From there it was swayed over to *Santa Rosa* where it disappeared again down into that ship's waiting hold.

By the time the second load had come up, Graves understood what Maja meant by "it's good". This was not the sort of booty the filibusteros generally scored. This was not some purloined cargo of rough woolen cloth and crates of shoes and the sort of wine served in taverns that catered to sailors and ignorant laborers. These filibusteros had been lucky indeed in their hunting.

Bolts of silk and the finest linen and brocade rose up from below. There was glassware from the Low Countries and perfume and bags of spices. There were fine leather saddles and bridles all tricked out with silver, and communion plates and chalices and candlestick which, to judge from the amount of silver and gold and jewels that had gone into their crafting, were bound for a cathedral of some prominence. Whatever ship these rogues had plundered, it was a ship carrying the goods of some merchant who was very wealthy indeed.

Graves suspected there was gold and silver as well, coins and ingots and jewelry. He did not doubt that Maja had found it already and was keeping it secret. That sort of thing could put unhealthy ideas into the heads of even the most loyal of crews.

Maja was standing at the filibusteros's larboard rail. His eyes were everywhere: on the cargo coming up, the men working the tackle, the men down in the hold. Graves stepped casually up to him, as if he just happened to see him on a street corner.

"Good haul," he said.

Maja nodded.

"What of this ship? We taking this?" Graves asked, pointing at the filibusteros's deck.

"No," Maja said.

"Really?" Graves asked. "I'd think Señor Corregidor would thank us for bringing him a ship."

"Not this rotten bucket," Maja said. "Don't have enough men to sail three ships anyway." He looked over at Graves. "Were you going to suggest you take command of one of them?"

"No, no," Graves said, and as he spoke he thought, *Well, I didn't get too far with that one.*

They stood for a moment in silence, watching the cargo come up from below and swing from one ship to another. Then Graves tried another tack.

"Sure is a rich cargo, ain't it?" he said, a casual observation. "A rich cargo to bring to a man like Señor Corregidor. Who's pretty damned rich already."

Maja, who could be quite inscrutable, looked at Graves with an expression that was uncharacteristically easy to read. It said that Maja knew where Graves was going with this. It said that the Englishman was standing into danger.

"I'm only saying, Señor Corregidor'll be damned pleased by what you brought in," Graves protested. "What *we* brought in. I'd be obligated if you saw to it he knows about my part in all this." Graves gestured at the crates of what he guessed were fine tableware coming up from below.

Maja nodded. "I'll see to it Señor Corregidor hears all about you," he said.

They worked late into the afternoon getting the wealth of plunder up from the belly of the pirate ship and down into *Santa Rosa*. When that was done they hoisted the six-pounder cannons off the pirates' deck and sent those into *Santa Rosa*'s hold as well, along with the gun carriages and the rammers, sponges and the like. They rolled the barrels of gunpowder out of the pirates' magazine and took those as well. The examined the stores of food and drink that the filibusteros had aboard, but decided it was not worth the taking.

It was getting near dark when Maja gave a few words of instruction to Ortiz, who then led a handful of men over to *Charles Rex*. They set the fore and main sails and cast off the ropes holding the ship alongside the filibustero. The sails filled in the evening breeze and *Charles Rex* ghosted away from the pirates' side until there was a few hundred yards of water between the two.

Maja made the filibusteros sit once again and ordered their hands tied. That done, he led the rest of his men, and Graves's former men, back aboard *Santa Rosa*. He called to two of the Black men, the filibusteros whom he had just recruited, and when they approached he spoke to them in a language that Graves did not entirely recognize. He guessed it was the pidgin spoken on the West African coast. He had heard it before. After they exchanged a few words Maja turned to Graves.

"I have business aboard the filibustero. These fellows," he nodded toward the former pirates who were now flanking Graves, "will see you don't get up to any mischief. Don't do anything to make them suspicious. They don't speak English. You won't be able to explain yourself."

With that Maja climbed over *Santa Rosa*'s bulwark and back aboard the filibusteros. The bound men glared at him as he disappeared below, and then all was quiet, the only sound the lap of water on the hull and the occasional flap of sailcloth and the creaking of the two ships as they rolled against each other. After a while Maja reappeared on deck and climbed back aboard *Santa Rosa*.

"Set the foresail! Set the mainsail!" he called and hands moved to cast off lines to let the sails fall from where they had been hauled up to the yards. "Cast us off, there!"

With sails set *Santa Rosa* began to draw away from the filibusteros's ship, which wallowed in the swells like some wounded and helpless creature. They had left the filibusteros bound by the hands and tied to pinrails and various deck furniture so they could not assist one another in getting free. It did not mean they could not free themselves, just that it would take some time. Time enough for *Santa Rosa* and *Charles Rex* to get clear, not that the de-fanged pirate posed much of a threat to them now.

Santa Rosa was barely making way in the light breeze and Maja sent men to set the topsails. Graves stood aft, watching the filibustero in their wake, his mind wallowing like the ship. He thought about the cargo they would bring to Señor Corregidor and what good, if any, it might do him. He thought about the greedy bastard pirates who could not be content with the haul they had made. He thought about how Maja had left them tied in place, but still alive.

Lucky bastards, Graves thought. *More mercy than I would have expected from a savage like Maja.*

Just as that thought was moving through his head he saw the thin column of smoke rising up from the filibusteros's main hatch, rising up and bending slightly in the breeze. The filibusteros seemed to notice it just then as well. Across the quarter mile of water Graves could hear the shouts of alarm and what he guessed were curses hurled their way. He could hear the sound of the voices but he could not make out the words.

Dear God...their hands are tied, Graves thought. He had precious little concern for filibusteros but the thought of any man, even them, being burned alive was a little hard to stomach. He wondered if they would get free in time to help themselves. Perhaps. Perhaps not.

A moment later the smoke had doubled in volume and then doubled again, and in the fading light Graves was certain he could see flames licking up from the hatch. Whatever Maja had touched off in that trip aboard was fully engulfed now. Even if they did manage to get free of their bonds in time, the pirates would not be extinguishing that blaze. They would have to abandon the ship, though they had no boat. The best they could do would be to float away on debris or some makeshift raft, give themselves up as prey to the sharks and barracudas and the merciless sun.

Graves caught a figure in the corner of his eye and turned. Maja had come aft as well where he could get the clearest view of his work. He stood silent watching the distant fire like an ancient spirit from the underworld rising up from the filibusteros's hold.

"Vermin," he said. "Nothing but damned vermin. A plague."

"Filibusteros?" Graves asked.

"The lot of you," Maja replied.

Chapter Twenty-Three

LeBoeuf remained on the beach long enough to drink two cups of rumbullian, long enough to be certain there would be no more brawling over the plunder, and then he and Henriette returned to the ship. They left the canoe on the beach and took one of the smaller periaguas, a boat that was bigger, more stable, and much more to LeBoeuf's liking.

Le Rongeur, sitting on the ship's main hatch, a wine bottle in hand, made some comment as LeBoeuf came up through the gangway. LeBoeuf did not hear the words, only the sound of Le Rongeur's voice, like a buzzing insect, and he ignored it. LeBoeuf was suddenly aware of how very weary he was, how heavy his arms and legs felt. How ready he was to lay down on the bunk in the master's cabin — his cabin — and be gone from the conscious world, at least until the sun came up again.

He took the lantern down from where it hung on the main shrouds and moved aft. He ducked under the quarterdeck and found the door to the great cabin and stepped inside. He breathed in deep through his nose. Le Rongeur had not been there. If he had been, his scent would still linger in the air.

LeBoeuf crossed the small space. He set the lantern on the table and was about to sit on the edge of the bunk when Henriette spoke.

"Hold a moment. I'm going to change my smock. Go somewhere else and close your eyes."

LeBoeuf grunted. He did not know if by 'somewhere else' Henriette meant for him to leave the great cabin, but he had no intention of doing that. Instead he took a few steps aft and sat on the settee, larboard side. He ignored Henriette's instructions to close his eyes but he did do her the courtesy of keeping his eyes averted.

I've never sat in this particular place, he thought, *never seen the cabin from here.* Tired as he was it was the most insightful thought he could muster. He heard the rustle of Henriette's clothing as she stripped off petticoat and overbody.

"I hope your eyes are closed, you great beast," she said.

LeBoeuf grunted again, an ambiguous response.

Women...dear Lord... he thought.

Henriette did not want him to see her naked, but he also had the strong impression, bordering on certainty, that she was annoyed that he had not made love to her. Or maybe she was only annoyed that he had not tried. Maybe she was eager for the chance to refuse him. After climbing into his bed every night.

He shook his head. Such circular thinking was more than he could grapple with just then. Instead he ran his eyes over the settee on the starboard side, the cupboard built against the side of the cabin, the clean deck underfoot. The rug that had once been there, which had been soaked through with salt-water, had begun to stink intolerably, so LeBoeuf had thrown it out the stern windows along with the rest of the debris which the hurricano had scattered about the cabin. Now there was only the smooth, white-painted deck planks by way of a floor.

The low angle of the lantern's light cast long, strange shadows over the space, giving it an odd, almost mysterious quality. The trim on the cupboard and the settee stood out in bold relief, and each tiny imperfection in the deck seemed to be marked by shadow.

And then LeBoeuf's eyes stopped on a section of the deck, a single plank, that caught his eye. It seemed just the tiniest bit misaligned, so minor an imperfection that he could not even say for certain that it was one. Just something odd, something that would never have been visible at all were it not for the weak light coming from that unusual direction.

Now what have we here? LeBoeuf thought.

He stood slowly. He kept his eyes on the plank in question for fear that if he looked away he would never see it again.

"I did not give you leave to move!" Henriette said from behind him but he did not look at her or reply. He took two steps across the width of the cabin and sank slowly to his knees, then reached out and pressed his fingertips down on the deck. The deck plank felt solid under his hand, and yet again there was something off, something about the feel of the plank that made a bell ring in his head.

"What? What is it?" Henriette asked. He heard the soft padding of her bare feet and then she was kneeling next to him, wearing her fresh smock. She smelled of linen, washed and dried in the sun, and of the rough soap she used on her face and arms and hair.

"What do you see?" she asked. She spoke in a loud whisper, and there was a note of curiosity and wonder in her voice that he had not heard before.

"I don't know," LeBoeuf said. He was looking at the butt end of the deck plank, where it met with the next plank aft. He could see the round ends of the wooden pegs that fastened the plank down to the deck beam below. Forward, the plank ran off toward the front of the cabin; LeBoeuf imagined it was fifteen feet long at least, as such planks were.

He felt around the edge of the wood with his fingertips but it seemed as solidly fixed as any other in the deck. He wondered if maybe the lantern light was just playing tricks with his eyes, or if the beating the ship had taken in the storm had knocked something out of line.

"Well, I see nothing out of place," Henriette said, and LeBoeuf could hear the old disdain seeping back into her tone. He reached around and pulled his long hunting knife from its sheath and gently eased the tip down into the seam between the errant plank and the one beside it. The point met some resistance from the pitch in the seam but LeBoeuf forced it down and then gently pried sideways with the blade.

And the plank moved.

Just a bit, just a quarter of an inch, but it moved in a way that a plank made fast to deck beams below would not move. The pitch was like a glue holding the pine board in place, but LeBoeuf was able to use his long knife to lever it up, just a bit.

"So?" Henriette asked. "You're just prying up the deck."

"Decks don't generally pry up," LeBoeuf said. "Not that easy." He pulled the blade free and readjusted it and pushed down on the handle of the knife. The plank came up a bit more and LeBoeuf could see that it was not in fact fifteen feet long, it was only three feet long, but that had not been clear because the other end had been made to look as if it was part of a continuous piece. He pushed down on the knife again, lifting the plank enough that he could get his fingers under it now.

"Get that lantern," he said and for once Henriette obeyed, quickly and silently. She knelt beside him, holding the lantern a foot above the deck, but the weak light revealed nothing new. LeBoeuf grabbed the plank and lifted and felt the resistance of the pitch give way. And then the plank came free.

For a moment the two of them were silent, looking at the void where the deck plank had been, a long black rectangle of space. LeBoeuf set the piece of wood aside. "Hold that lantern close," he said and Henriette swung the lantern over the gap in the deck and they both leaned over and peered down.

They could see nothing. The light from the lantern was weak and it was coming from the sides of the tin cylinder. It cast no light downward. LeBoeuf considered lowering the lantern into the space but he could see it was too big to fit through the gap.

"Very well," LeBoeuf said. He reached forward to thrust his hand down into the opening and realized it was pointless to try. Like the lantern, LeBoeuf's arm would not fit through the deck. The planks were four inches wide; LeBoeuf knew he would not get more than his wrist through so narrow a gap.

"Here, reach down and see what's there," he said to Henriette.

"What? Me? Reach my hand in there?"

"Yes, do it. If there are snakes or crocodiles they're dead by now."

Henriette frowned, her curiosity wrestling with her apprehension. Then she set the lantern down and tentatively reached her hand, then her arm, down into the dark space below the deck. She moved it fore and aft, and then athwartships, as far as she could.

"Well?" LeBoeuf asked.

"There's something there," Henriette said. "I don't know what. Maybe just part of the ship."

"Hmm..." LeBoeuf said. "Can you move it?"

For a moment Henriette pushed against whatever it was her hand had lighted on. "No," she said.

"Hmm..." LeBoeuf said again. There had to be something. Someone had gone to a lot of trouble to install that removable, all but invisible section of deck planking. "Reach up under, see if there's some sort of mechanism or something."

Henriette frowned deeper, but she twisted around in such a way that she was able to feel up under the deck. Her arm moved back and forth, and then paused.

"There's something here..." she said and LeBoeuf heard the rattle of metal parts as she felt around. "I can't..." she said, then paused and felt around some more. "I think it's a bolt of some sort, like the kind used to bolt a door shut."

LeBoeuf forced himself to remain silent as Henriette continued to feel around under the deck, and then he heard the satisfying click of whatever she was fiddling with sliding free. He looked at Henriette and she was smiling and he wondered if he had ever seen that expression on her face before. She pulled her hand out of the gap in the deck.

"I think that was the bolt holding another part of the deck," she said, getting up on her knees and shuffling out of the way. LeBoeuf reached down and grabbed the edge of the deck where the single plank was gone. He lifted and felt another section coming free, this one four planks wide. Like the first plank it was held fast by the pitch that had been poured into the seams, but it too yielded to a strong tug.

Now there was a sizable gap in the deck, a hole three feet long and nearly two feet wide. LeBoeuf turned and set the section of planks in his hand on the settee. By the time he turned back Henriette had snatched up the lantern and was holding it over the hole and peering down below.

LeBoeuf leaned over and looked down as well, their heads just inches apart. In the dull light of the lantern he could see a dark shape wedged in the hole a few inches below the level of the deck. He reached down and touched it with his fingers. It was warm and slightly sticky and it yielded a bit to his touch.

"What is it?" Henriette asked, still speaking in a whisper.

"Something wrapped in tarred canvas," LeBoeuf said.

"I see that. But what is it?" Henriette demanded. Her tone suggested that LeBoeuf was a moron for not knowing.

LeBoeuf sighed. "Let's find out," he said. He reached down to the canvas-wrapped object and tried to get his fingers under it, but was not able to do so. He thought for a moment that it was fastened down somehow. He pushed against the side and it shifted just a bit and he realized that it was not fixed in place, it was just very heavy.

Hmm...that's encouraging... he thought.

"Here, move aside," he said to Henriette, and when she shuffled out of the way he repositioned himself so he could reach down on either side of the thing and grab it with both hands. He worked his fingertips under it. He could feel a hard, square edge and he guessed it was a chest of some sort.

More encouraging still.

He lifted straight up and heard the tarred canvas peel away from the boards. With both arms joined in the effort the chest did not feel so terribly heavy, but it was still heavy enough, much heavier than its size would suggest. LeBoeuf knew of only a few elements that carried so much weight in so small a size. One was lead, but he did not think anyone would go to such lengths to hide ingots of lead.

He stood with a grunt and set the chest on the table. Henriette grabbed the lantern and held it up. LeBoeuf could see her eyes shining in the light. He could see the hunger in her face. Such a look of raw desire, LeBoeuf imagined that Henriette was accustomed to seeing it on the faces of men looking at her. He grabbed the edges of the tarred canvas and began to unwrap.

It was indeed a chest, as he supposed, an iron chest about two feet long, a foot wide, and ten inches deep, bound with iron straps that were riveted in place. Not an elegant affair, but sturdy in the extreme.

Now, how the devil are we going to open this? LeBoeuf thought and then, to his surprise, he saw that there was no lock on the hasp. Whoever had placed it in its hole had apparently considered it secure enough in that hiding place.

"Let's see what Pandora has for us," LeBoeuf said and he flipped open the hasp and tilted back the lid. He could see in the weak light that the box was mostly crammed with soft leather bags bound with cords and packed so tight that there was no room for even the smallest thing more. But sitting on top of the bags was a parchment, a scroll of paper bound with a red ribbon, an impressive-looking document that took up the full length of the box. Beneath the scroll were two leather-bound books which looked to LeBoeuf very much like a ship's log and a manifest.

LeBoeuf picked up the scroll and had not lifted it two inches before Henriette's hand shot past his. She grabbed one of the leather bags and with some difficulty pulled it free from the rest. LeBoeuf set the scroll aside and picked up the first of the leather books and flipped it open. In the corner of his eye he could see Henriette eagerly untying the bag and spilling its contents out on the table. He heard the familiar clink of coins on coins, saw the dull yellow glint of gold. Escudos. He heard Henriette gasp.

She grabbed up another bag as LeBoeuf turned his attention back to the book. The pages were divided into five columns of differing width and covered over with writing in a neat, tight hand.

"What's that?" Henriette asked.

"Don't know," LeBoeuf said. "Looks like a ship's log, but I don't know letters. Do you?"

Henriette sighed as if her patience was all but worn out. "Of course I do," she said.

"What does that say?" LeBoeuf asked, pointing to the words, written large, at the top of the page. Henriette squinted at them for a moment.

"*Trois Frères*," she said. "And beneath it it says 'La Rochelle'. What does that mean?"

"Name of the ship and the port she hailed from," LeBoeuf said. He frowned as he looked at the words. They were not what had been painted on the stern of the ship. But of course, if this was the ship's log why would it be so well-hidden under the deck?

Someone was doing something he should not have been, LeBoeuf thought, but what exactly that was he did not know. He set the book down and picked up the scroll, slid the ribbon off and unrolled the parchment. He could see the tall, bold letters of some royal pronouncement, some official document of the court, and beneath it, in smaller script, some cramped writing, some dense legalese, he guessed. A letter patent, perhaps, an estate in the New World bequeathed to some fortunate soul by the king himself.

He heard more coins spill out on the table. He expected Henriette to grab the next bag, pointless as it would have been to do so, but she did not. She did not move, did not speak, stunned, apparently, into silence. LeBoeuf scanned the document in his hand, unrolling it a bit more.

"Here, can you read this?" LeBoeuf asked.

Henriette gave him her usual expression of exasperated condescension but she held out her hand and LeBoeuf passed her the parchment. She unrolled it further, squinted at it and angled it toward the feeble light from the lantern.

"Hmm…" she said.

"What does it say?" LeBoeuf asked.

"Hmm…" Henriette said again, and she brought the paper closer to her face. The body of the text might have been difficult to read in that dim light, but the first few lines were written in a large, ornate script, something befitting the apparent gravity of the document.

"Can you read it?" LeBoeuf asked.

"Hold a moment..." Henriette said, "This fancy writing's not so easy to read, you know."

LeBoeuf nodded and folded his arms and wondered if Henriette was really so adept at reading as she implied. Finally she cleared her throat and spoke.

"It's a letter patent," she said. "It's a grant of some land or a plantation or some such. It says...Tort...?" She held the paper closer to her face.

"Tortuga?"

"Yes, that might be it," Henriette said. She put the parchment down on the table and let it roll itself back up. "But sod the damned letter patent," she continued. "These bags are full of gold. A fortune. What shall we do with it?"

"I don't know," LeBoeuf said. "Should we find the rightful owner and return it?"

"Don't be an ass."

LeBoeuf knew what she was asking, of course. His bargain with the other buccaneers had been a simple one — the ship in exchange for his portion of everything that was aboard her. That would have included this gold, had they known it was there. But now?

What shall we do with it? That was what Henriette asked, a question that raised other questions. Neither she nor any of the women had shared in the ship's cargo. LeBoeuf wondered why she thought she had any claim to a portion of the gold, regardless of what he chose to do.

"I truly don't know," LeBoeuf said. "And I'm too weary now to think on it. We'll put this back where it was. It was safe enough there. There's no need to make any decision now."

Henriette frowned and her eyebrows came together in their now-familiar way, but she did not argue. They put the gold back in the chest, shut the lid, and wrapped it in the tarred canvas once again. LeBoeuf carried it back to the secret hiding place and set it down where it had been and replaced the planks in the deck.

With the pitch having been dislodged as the planks were pried up, the hiding place was no longer terribly secret, but LeBoeuf was not concerned. No one but LeBoeuf or Henriette ever went into the master's cabin. Of those two, LeBoeuf trusted one of them completely, and the other had no way of getting off the ship even if she did hope to abscond with the plunder.

LeBoeuf rolled up the letter patent again, slipped the ribbon back on, and thrust it, along with the leather-bound books, into a cubby in the cupboard on the starboard side where various other scrolls — LeBoeuf assumed they were charts — were already stored.

"In the morning, when you have some light, you can read more of that," he said, nodding toward the document.

"Why do you care?"

LeBoeuf shrugged. "Don't know. Maybe just curious." And it was true. He did not know. But something about the letter intrigued him, something about it suggested possibilities. New beginnings, perhaps. He had no real notion of what the patent granted, or what use he could possibly make of it, but still it intrigued him.

He moved around the table, stopped by the edge of the bunk, unbuckled his belt and set it and the knives down. He shuffled out of his trousers and let them drop to the deck and then climbed onto the straw-filled mattress. He stretched out as much as he could, and as the excitement of their late discovery drained away he felt the exhaustion wash over him again.

Henriette blew out the candle in the lantern and climbed into the bunk with him. He breathed in the smell of her hair and skin, anticipated the feel of her back pressed against his chest. But she did not press her back against him this time. Instead, she draped her arm over his shoulder and eased her slight frame half on top of him, her leg over his thigh, her breasts, which he could feel through his linen shirt and her thin smock, pressed against him. Her fingers ran along his cheek. They pushed his long hair aside and she buried her face in his beard until her lips were on his neck.

"You are a very attractive man, have I told you that?" she said, her voice muffled by hair and beard.

"Hmm..." LeBoeuf said as he pondered the uncanny way that a chest of gold could so improve a man's looks. He reached around and put his big hand on her waist and ran it up her back and under her hair and ran his fingers over the back of her neck. She made a soft guttural noise in her throat and ran her lips up his neck and behind his ear. He breathed deep and let himself be carried off by the luxurious sensations. Then he felt the exhaustion come over him once more, not like the wash of an incoming tide but like a breaker crashing down on him.

And then he was asleep.

With the moonlight coming in through the stern windows, Le Rongeur could see a tolerable amount, even after Henriette blew out the lantern. He could make out her dark outline as she climbed into the bunk where LeBoeuf was already stretched out. He was fairly certain he saw her throw a leg over LeBoeuf's legs — the pale skin of her thigh appeared ghostly in the dark — and pull herself halfway on top of him.

He scrutinized every move, dissected every moving shadow. He listened keenly to the rustle of the two of them in the bunk, the soft sounds that came from their throats. But his mind was elsewhere.

This, of course, was what he had hoped to see. It was clear that he himself would not be rutting with the whore Henriette, not as long as LeBoeuf remained alive, and LeBoeuf seemed to have an unfortunate ability to do so. So, Le Rongeur figured, if he could not hump her he could at least watch LeBoeuf hump her. It would be nearly as good as doing it himself. Better in some ways. Easier.

But even that had eluded him. He took what few opportunities he had to examine the bulkhead that made up the front wall of the master's cabin but he was never able to find even the smallest crack that would allow him to see into the cabin itself. At night, after LeBoeuf and the whore retired, Le Rongeur would stand silently outside the cabin, listening for any hint of what was going on within and looking for places where the lantern light might reveal gaps in the planking, but there were none that he could see.

Son of a bitch, son of a bitch, he thought as he searched the face of the painted wood. *The damned ship lives through a hurricano and there's not even a crack?* It was frustrating in the extreme.

Then, just that night, for the first time since they had returned from the cave and taken the periagua out to the wrecked ship, Le Rongeur found himself onboard and alone. Once LeBoeuf's boat had disappeared into the dark he went to work. He found a chisel and mallet in the tool box on deck and with those in hand approached the bulkhead in the same stealthy way he once had stalked the wild pigs on Hispaniola.

He examined the wall with care, searching for the best place to make his cut. He unlatched the door to the cabin, slowly pushed it open and leaned in, checking the bulkhead from the inside to make sure his efforts would cause no visible damage. He did not dare enter; if he did, LeBoeuf would know. Le Rongeur was not sure how, but he was certain LeBoeuf would know. He shut the door again, took a deep breath, and set the chisel to the wood.

It took Le Rongeur ten minutes to widen out the joint between two of the planks, leaving a long, narrow gash that was invisible to anything but the most minute inspection. He pressed his face against the warm wood and peered through and was rewarded with a nearly unlimited view of the cabin within. He smiled and felt his excitement grow.

That done he replaced the tools and found a bottle of wine and sat on the hatch and waited. It was another hour at least before he heard the sound of a paddle dipping in the water and the soft thump of a boat alongside. LeBoeuf came up through the gangway. He was moving slowly, the weariness evident as he took the lantern down from the main shrouds.

"Did you convince them to make you king of Hispaniola?" Le Rongeur called out. "Looks like being king has done you in."

LeBoeuf glanced at Le Rongeur as he headed aft toward the cabin but he did not reply. The whore Henriette came up behind him and she did not so much as honor Le Rongeur with a glance as she followed LeBoeuf aft.

Bitch... Le Rongeur thought.

He waited a minute or so after the door had clicked shut before standing and moving silently across the deck. With the lantern glowing inside the cabin the gap in the planks stood out clearly, a dull streak of light against the black surface, obvious from the outside, invisible from within.

He put his eye to the crack and almost gasped. LeBoeuf was sitting aft on the settee, eyes looking down, and not three feet in front of where Le Rongeur stood, Henriette was pulling her smock up over her head. She pulled her arms free and tossed the garment aside and for a moment she just stood there, the feeble light playing off her naked body, her extraordinary naked body.

Le Rongeur could feel himself getting erect and he reached down and touched himself through his canvas slops. He tried to keep his breathing quiet and regular as he watched her shuffle into a clean smock, her lovely skin and fine curves now hidden away, but the memory of her nakedness there for Le Rongeur to enjoy over and over.

He continued to watch, expecting LeBoeuf to climb into the bunk and Henriette to climb in after and for their second act to begin. But it did not play out the way he had expected.

Instead, he saw LeBoeuf kneel down on the deck and he heard Henriette say, "I did not give you leave to move!" When LeBoeuf did not reply Henriette picked up the lantern and knelt down beside him. They continued to speak in low and secretive tones. Le Rongeur could not make out the words, and he could no longer see them as they were hidden behind the table.

Now, what the devil? Le Rongeur wondered. This was odd indeed, so odd that the memory of the naked Henriette fled from his mind. He stood motionless, watching, but he could see nothing. He pressed his ear to the crack and could hear sounds — voices, and creaking and grunting noises — but he could not guess what they might mean. And just as he felt his frustration starting to boil, LeBoeuf stood and set something on the table. Something not so big, but apparently heavy.

What the devil? Le Rongeur thought again, and this time his question was answered, and answered quickly. He watched LeBoeuf unwrap the thing, which turned out to be an iron chest, and he watched him open it. He watched LeBoeuf pull some sort of scroll out of the chest and he watched Henriette pull out a small pouch and untie it and spill gold coins across the top of the table.

The excitement Le Rongeur felt on seeing the gold spill from the bag eclipsed even the excitement of seeing Henriette disrobing, and the thrill was doubled when Henriette did the same with a second bag. Incredibly, LeBoeuf seemed to not even notice the coins lying in a heap beside him, but rather was examining some book that had also been in the chest.

He is a great dumb ox, ain't he? Le Rongeur thought as he watched them. LeBoeuf set the book down and he and Henriette tried to read what was on the scroll, but they did not spend much time at it. A moment later they put the gold back in the chest and put the chest back wherever they had found it. Under the deck planks, most likely.

Le Rongeur continued to watch as LeBoeuf climbed into his bunk and Henriette climbed in after him, and even though he was all but certain they were going to make the beast with two backs his mind was somewhere else completely.

It's a fortune, it's a damned fortune, Le Rongeur thought. Even if those two bags of coins were the only two in the chest, which he doubted, it would still be more money than he could ever hope to gain in his miserable life. And it was right there, ten feet away, with only two frail lives standing between him and it.

But maybe not so frail. LeBoeuf would not be so easily killed. It would have to be done with stealth, but how, exactly? Le Rongeur could stab the man in his sleep, but did he dare try? He would have to kill him with the first stroke: if he left even a bit of life in the great beast, LeBoeuf would tear him apart.

I'll shoot him… Le Rongeur thought next. *Go in and shoot him in the head. Take two guns, shoot the bitch, too. Or not. Keep her alive, maybe.*

And then he remembered that LeBoeuf had secured all the firearms and powder and ball in the master's cabin. Le Rongeur had objected at the time, accused LeBoeuf of having no trust in him, his partner in matelotage.

Stupid bastard, LeBoeuf… Le Rongeur thought. *Very well.*

He could not stab LeBoeuf and he could not shoot him, at least not immediately. Wait for a chance to sneak into the cabin and steal a pistol? Yes, that might be the answer. But then how to get clear of Hispaniola with the plunder? Some of the bigger periaguas could take to the sea, but could he sail one by himself?

In his frustration Le Rongeur nearly cursed out loud and only caught himself at the last moment.

Think, think… He despised this sort of thing, having to devise a plan, having to consider all the obstacles in his way. It felt like running through knee-high mud. But he was willing to do it. Willing to do it now. Because he understood that the greatest opportunity of his life had just been laid at his feet.

Chapter Twenty-Four

Santa Rosa sat motionless in the water. Her yards were squared, her sails furled, but Maja could still hear a soft liquid murmur of water passing down her sides, larboard and starboard. It was like an echo of the six days they had spent plowing through the sea on their passage from St. Christopher, as if that sound was all that remained of their brief voyage. But this time the sound was not made by the ship moving through the water: rather it was the water moving past the ship, the current of the Rio Ozama as it flowed down the barque's sides on its way to the sea.

Off the larboard side, Santo Domingo loomed like a dark threat in the night. With only the stars for light Maja could see little, but he could feel the weight of the city walls, the towering Fortaleza Ozama, the cathedral, Nuestra Señora de la Encarnación, which sat like a great stone outcropping just back from the edge of the cliffs. Lanterns made pinpoints of light in the dark, some stationary, some moving. The odd shout or scream or raucous laugh drifted across the river, loud enough to reach the ship anchored one hundred yards from shore.

Maja turned and looked over the starboard side where *Charles Rex* rode at anchor. A pool of light spilled from a lantern hanging from her mizzen forestay and made a yellow circle on her deck. He could see the silhouette of the man on anchor watch, but who it was he could not tell. Like *Santa Rosa*, *Charles Rex*'s bow was pointing unwaveringly upstream, her anchor cable rising taut out of the water. But their anchors were sunk deep in the river mud below and they were safe where they lay.

"Maja..." a voice came from the dark, just the one word, just his name, but Maja knew what it meant. He made a grunting noise to let the lookout know he had heard then turned his attention back to the city to the west.

It took him a moment to see it, one light among the dozens along the low-lying waterfront of warehouses and merchants catering to the maritime trade, and taverns and brothels of the lowest sort. A single light moving away from the shore, moving in their direction. It glimmered for a few seconds more and then went out. Light enough for the men to get in the boat and get underway; they did not need or want any more than that.

Maja looked down at the narrow steps bolted to the ship's side. He considered ordering a more substantial ladder put down, or a boatswain's chair rigged from the yardarm. Señor Corregidor was not the most nimble of men.

Damn his eyes, Maja thought. If Señor Corregidor wanted a ladder or a boatswain's chair he could ask for one.

The boat was swallowed up by the dark of the river, but soon Maja could hear the soft creak of the oars in the tholes and the splash of the blades as they dipped into the water.

"Kusi," he said, then called out a few words in the *lingua franca* of the West Coast of Africa. A moment later Kusi, who a week before had been languishing in chains in *Charles Rex*'s hold, appeared, lantern in hand. He held the lantern over the ship's side just as the boat came gliding out of the night.

Señor Corregidor was sitting in the sternsheets, a big man wrapped in a rough wool cape, the hood pulled up over his head. A man sat beside him, hand on the tiller. There were four others pulling oars; big men, ugly, quiet and dangerous.

Maja knew them all, at least by sight. They worked together. They worked for Señor Corregidor at times, for Carlos Hernández at other times, or for some of the others on the waterfront of Santo Domingo. They worked for men who required muscle and discretion and they were not much concerned about the disposition of their immortal souls. They were known as El Cinco. The Five. They were feared, or so Maja understood. He had no firsthand knowledge of that. Maja had not experienced fear in many years, not since his childhood, not since Spanish raiders had delivered such a surfeit of fear to his village that the flame had been quenched for good. He could remember fear, a bit, but he could not understand it.

The four on the thwarts laid their oars down as the boat bumped against *Santa Rosa*'s side. Señor Corregidor flipped back the hood of his cape, revealing a head of gray hair, dark eyes, pale skin and a thick moustache that curled at the tips and looked like the roof of a house sitting atop his pointed goatee.

He stood with a grunt and moved awkwardly forward until he could get his hands on the steps. He was a fat man, and not young, but Maja guessed he would not risk his pride by asking for a boatswain's chair, and indeed he did not. Instead he climbed slowly, laboriously up the side and stepped through the gangway as Maja and Kusi made room.

Señor Corregidor did not greet Maja and Maja did not greet him. Instead the older man walked part-way across the deck then stopped, looking carefully fore and aft.

"There's damage," Señor Corregidor said.

"Filibusteros," Maja said. Señor Corregidor did not reply, just made a skeptical grunting sound in his throat. He ran his eyes over the rig and then looked at Maja.

"You have his ship," Señor Corregidor said, nodding toward *Charles Rex*. "You have him?"

Maja nodded. "In the cabin," he said.

Señor Corregidor looked over at Kusi, still holding the lantern, looked him up and down and then looked back at Maja.

"Why does that blackbird have a knife on him?" Señor Corregidor asked.

"He's a sailor," Maja said.

Señor Corregidor made a snorting noise. "Sailor... Well, if he cuts *your* throat it's none of my worry. Now, show me that sorry whore's son."

Maja turned to Kusi and said "Cabin," in the African tongue and the man nodded and led the way, holding the lantern high. They walked aft and then down a steep ladder and aft again to the bulkhead that separated the master's quarters from the 'tween decks. Kusi opened the door and stepped in. He hung the lantern from a deck beam and moved quickly out of the way as Maja and Señor Corregidor came in behind him.

It was a small cabin, but big enough to have a separate walled off space for sleeping and a wide settee all the way aft below the stern windows. Benjamin Graves was sitting on that settee, a gag in his mouth, his hands and feet bound. His eyes were wide. Maja wondered if Señor Corregidor would kill him then and there. He was certain that Graves was wondering the same thing.

The Spaniard crossed the cabin and stopped a few feet in front of Graves, folded his arms and looked down at the bound man. He did not speak and Maja did not speak. Graves, gagged as he was, could not speak, though Maja had no doubt he would be spouting like a whale otherwise. Finally Señor Corregidor nodded his head.

"Good," he said, and then without warning, and faster than Maja would have guessed him able, he twisted halfway around and swung backhand at Graves's face. He hit with a loud smacking sound, hard enough to jerk Graves's head sideways and tumble him over onto the settee. A trickle of blood ran from under the gag. Graves did not try to right himself, but rather stayed as he was, looking up at Señor Corregidor, waiting for what would come next.

But Señor Corregidor was apparently done with him. He turned to Maja. "I don't have time for this maggot just now. I have another issue that's come up, a more immediate problem. So I must be patient. Since I intend to take my time with Señor Graves."

Maja nodded.

"He'll stay aboard here," the Spaniard continued. "Safer. He might have friends on shore who'd be tempted to help. But he has no friends here. Does he, Maja?"

"Don't think so," Maja said. "Didn't reckon he had any friends anywhere." But even as he said that, Maja wondered if it was true. He could not imagine anyone feeling anything but contempt for Benjamin Graves. A maggot, like Señor Corregidor said. But Maja did not always read people right, these white people in particular, and he knew it. Men from the east, from across the sea, their minds did not work the way his did.

Señor Corregidor stared down at Graves for a minute, as if debating whether or not to hit him again. Then he turned back to Maja.

"My cargo still on board the maggot's ship?"

Maja shook his head. "He off-loaded it. At St. Christopher. And then the hurricano came and took it all."

Señor Corregidor's mouth turned down and his eyes half closed and even in the deep shadow of the single lantern Maja could see the fury building there. "Took it all?" Señor Corregidor said. "You're saying the cargo is gone? Destroyed?"

Maja nodded. Señor Corregidor's fury made no impression on him: it was as if he was watching a storm from far off, as if he had no part in this business. His expressionless face reflected that disinterest, and he knew it made Señor Corregidor even more angry. Maja was not afraid of Señor Corregidor and he did not care about the man's anger, and Señor Corregidor was not accustomed to that.

"You saw this?" the Spaniard demanded, his voice going lower, which most men would take as a warning. "You went ashore and saw that the warehouse was blown away?"

"No," Maja said. "The Spanish fleet arrived just then. There was no time."

Señor Corregidor was silent, staring into Maja's eyes as Maja stared back. Then, when the silence had hung in the air long enough, Maja said, "We have the cargo from the filibusteros."

"Filibusteros?"

"The ones that attacked us. We took them. Took their cargo."

"*Cargo…*" the Spaniard said derisively. "As if the pathetic rubbish from a filibustero could make up for my loss."

"It was a good haul," Maja said. "Valuable. Graves played his part in the fight."

"Graves? You let that maggot have a weapon? Are you a fool?"

Maja did not reply. He had advocated for Graves, fulfilled what minor obligation he had to the man for the part Graves had played in taking the pirate. He did not feel the need to say anything more in Graves's defense.

"Very well, let's see this cargo," Señor Corregidor said. "See what you call a 'good haul.'"

Once again Kusi took the lantern and led the way, forward and down into *Santa Maria*'s hold. The air was stuffy and warm and heavy with the odor of mud dried on the cables and bilge water and tar and, incongruously, the smell of the perfume and spice they had liberated from the filibustero.

It was a tight space, even tighter than the master's cabin, so Kusi scrambled up the great stack of cable coiled down amidships and squatted there like a gargoyle, holding the lantern out in front of him. Señor Corregidor came next down the ladder. He had shed his cape on the 'tween deck and now the light made a dull reflection on the silk of his doublet and glinted off the silver buttons down the front. He wore silk stockings which had been ruined somewhere in the night's travels. Maja doubted Señor Corregidor would be much concerned about their loss, though the stockings alone were worth half a year's wages for a common sailor.

The fat Spaniard was already poking through the cargo stacked and lashed in place by the time Maja stepped down into the hold. Señor Corregidor's face was red, and sweat was standing out on his forehead and running down his cheeks. He was making grunting noises as he rummaged through the various things. He grabbed a handful of cloth and pulled it from the bolt for closer inspection. Red silk, as fine as any Maja had ever seen. He grunted again.

"What's in those crates?" Señor Corregidor demanded, pointing to a stack of wooden crates against the larboard side.

"Venetian glass," Maja said. Señor Corregidor nodded.

"And those others?" he asked.

"Silver, the sort they use in churches," Maja said. "There are sacks of cochineal as well. Spices. Perfume. You can smell it. And there's specie. And ingots."

"Hmm..." Señor Corregidor said, looking around. "Not bad. Not worth half of what the maggot Graves stole from me, but it will help make up the loss."

Maja nodded and he thought, *You're a fat liar, you whore's son. What Graves stole wasn't worth a quarter of this, I'll wager.*

"Very well," the Spaniard said next. "Let us get back on deck before I die for want of air."

Kusi climbed down from the cables and led the way up to the 'tween decks and then topside. The air was cool and fresh after the stifling hold. Maja drew a deep and welcome breath as Señor Corregidor came up through the scuttle behind him, his breathing labored from the climb.

Once the Spaniard was able to speak he said, "So, you took those pirates' cargo. What of their ship?"

"Burned it," Maja said.

"What? You burned a perfectly good ship?"

"No, I burned a rotten washtub," Maja said.

"And the filibusteros, what of them?"

"Burned them, too," Maja said.

"Huh," Señor Corregidor said. "I hope none of those bastards were blackbirds. They'd have been worth a damn bit of money. Probably could have sold the white men to the mines as well. Still, what you brought back, it's worth something, as I said. We'll get it ashore once I make some arrangements."

Maja nodded. "A ship master makes a prize like this, it's usual practice he gets his share. Him and his men," he said. "As you know."

Señor Corregidor's eyebrows came together again and his pointed and curled moustache twitched. "You're saying you should have a share of this?" he demanded.

"Yes. Me and my men."

"Well, damn my eyes. That's a damned bit of impertinence, and from a savage, no less. You...have a share? You didn't do half of what I told you to do. You brought the maggot back, to be sure, but you lost everything he stole from me. And you managed to half destroy my ship in the bargain. You just be glad if I decide to give you your wages, which I ain't yet decided to do. A share? Damned ridiculous."

"I see," Maja said. He could feel his patience with Señor Corregidor running out like water through imperfectly cupped hands.

"And another thing," the Spaniard said, pointing to Kusi who was now standing a discreet distance away. "You might think you're clever calling that one a sailor, but you don't fool me. He was part of my cargo, him and the others. He's my property and he'll stay my property. So when I send word for this cargo to be brought ashore, him and those other blackbirds had best be with it."

With that Señor Corregidor turned and climbed awkwardly down the steps and into the waiting boat. When he was settled Maja tossed his wool cape down to him without a word.

Good, Maja thought. He had been uncertain as to what loyalty he owed Señor Corregidor, but he was uncertain no longer.

Chapter Twenty-Five

Ave Maria, gratia plena, Dominus tecum..." Father Pedro intoned, the familiar words soft and rhythmic. Don Alonso, kneeling beside his wife, fingered the appropriate beads and spoke the prayer with a reflex as thoughtless as breathing. His mind, as usual, was moving like a swallow, whipping here and there, alighting on one thing or another.

They were in the small chapel just off the main room in the apartments Don Alonso shared with Francisca. The chapel was smaller even than their bed-chamber, but it had enjoyed quite a bit of Francisca's attention in the six weeks they had been ensconced in Las Casas Reales in the heart of Santo Domingo.

The very day Francisca was well enough to rise from her sick bed she had ordered the chapel stripped of all its contents, then scrubbed and whitewashed. The alter and tabernacle she had replaced with much more elaborate and expensive installations. Rich carpet was laid down the center aisle. The confessional Francisca had deemed worthy of keeping, but only after it had been stripped down to bare wood, a rich mahogany, and refinished with so many coats of varnish it looked as if it was encased in ice. Gold candlesticks, gold monstrance, gold platters, gold incensors all took their place in the refurbished chapel. When it was finally done to her satisfaction, Francisca had the space consecrated to Nuestra Señora de Atocha.

The cost had been considerable but Alonso made no protest. Even he could see the hand of God in their miraculous salvation. Giving thanks by creating such a beautiful place of worship seemed reasonable enough, and far simpler than any of the many other forms of penance that Francisca might have come up with.

Nor was it gratitude alone that drove Alonso's generosity. The hurricano, the shipwreck, the injuries which had nearly killed her, all seemed to have worked some great confusion on Francisca's mind. She launched herself into the chapel's rejuvenation with an enthusiasm that bordered on manic, and Alonso did not care to disturb her further with talk of money. He did not dare. And, to be sure, Francisca had brought to their marriage most of the wealth they now enjoyed.

That will not be true much longer, Alonso thought. He had several plans already unfolding, schemes long in the works, now coming to fruition. Soon he would have such wealth pouring in that it would make his father-in-law look like a fish monger.

If I could get off my damned knees...

Francisca never left the apartments at first, spending the bulk of each day in the chapel, praying and confessing and attending Mass and praying some more. But as the weeks passed she grew more willing to venture out. Like some timid, frightened creature — a rabbit or squirrel or some such — coming tentatively from its burrow, she had slowly emerged from the safety of the Casas, walking out into the courtyard, clinging to Alonso's arm, willing to wander farther from her new home and for longer periods with each passing day.

But still the chapel was the center of her life, which kept it near the center of Alonso's life as well and the lives of all the people who swirled around them. And on that day in particular, with Francisca having committed to her first real social engagement since arriving at Santo Domingo, a dinner that would require her to be her old lively, gracious self, it was a given that Alonso and the others would spend a significant amount of time beforehand on their knees.

And so they were, Alonso kneeling beside Francisca, rosary in hand, head bowed. Gabriella was kneeling somewhere behind him. Every now and then he caught a whiff of her perfume through the smell of the incense and he found it supremely distracting.

The new girl, Lucia, was kneeling beside Gabriella. She was young, sixteen perhaps, gangly with big teeth. She might grow into her looks eventually but Alonso did not think it likely. She seemed more the sort who would give up her maidenhead to some stable-hand or a boy who worked in the kitchen, but she was not for him.

He hoped Francisca would decide to hire yet another girl, in which case he would make more of an effort to influence her decision. But Francisca's days were mostly taken up with prayer, and he did not think she was giving much consideration to the help.

The thought of Francisca's spiritual life led to thoughts of Father Pedro and the considerable amount of time he and Francisca spent together. It was only to be expected, of course. He was her priest, her advisor in matters of the faith. He was duty-bound to be as attentive as she wished. Still, Alonso had to wonder just how attentive Francisca expected him to be.

The bastard knows better than to piss away this plum situation, Alonso thought. *I'm sure he wouldn't care to end up ministering to the sick and dying in some shit-caked slum or some filthy village in the mountains of Andalusia...*

He was a good-looking young man, Alonso could admit that. Some women might even find his vow of chastity alluring, he imagined. A challenge. For that matter, he did not doubt that Father Pedro, eloquent and smooth, could convince Francisca to do whatever he wished.

Don't be an idiot! Alonso chastised himself. It was hardly the first time his mind had wandered down that road, and every time it did he had to curse himself for a fool. Francisca was genuine. Pure. Guileless.

Not everyone is so loathsome as you, you know…

The whole issue created a turmoil in Alonso's mind. On the one hand he was sickened by the thought of another man touching his wife, and the humiliation of being made a cuckold would be more than he could bear. On the other hand, catching Francisca in an infidelity would give him almost limitless power over her. He would never again have to worry about what she might say to her father.

To drive those unpleasant considerations from his mind he thought instead of Carlos Hernández, the merchant in the lower town. They had met again, six days before, and the memory of that meeting made Alonso so angry that any thoughts of Francisca's possible affair were put clear out of his head.

Don Alonso, I assure you I am as eager as you to see your goods off to market on the Main, but there are so few ships to be found now, since the hurricano. We can expect more soon, I'm sure, but as for now…

Hernández was the very picture of obsequies humility and he never once uttered an objectionable word or contradicted anything Alonso had to say. He met every one of Alonso's queries and demands with replies that were optimistic and reassuring.

Señor, it would be a fine thing if this brigantine Captain Nuñez spoke of turned out to be yours, saved by the Lord our God from the storm, but sure it is too much to hope for? Of course I can send someone to find out, but I wonder…

Don Alonso, I know a man who would be just the one to send after your brigantine. He has not yet returned to Santo Domingo, though I look for him every day…

It was only later that Alonso realized the man had said nothing, promised nothing, assured him of nothing. Demands that the goods in Hernández's warehouse be sent to market, Alonso's insistence that Hernández find a ship to hunt the brigantine seen on the northwest coast to see if it was the *Trois Frères* of La Rochelle, all of those things Hernández brushed aside with the skill of a fencing master parrying one thrust after another.

I was a fool to tell the man everything… Alonso thought next, but he pushed that uncomfortable notion aside. He was not so naïve as to believe Hernández felt any loyalty toward him. But he did know that men such as Hernández would bend the knee to whoever had the most wealth and power in Santo Domingo. And right now that was Don Alonso Menéndez de Aviles, Knight of the Order of Santiago, lieutenant governor of Hispaniola, son-in-law to Don Cristóbal de Seville.

Out of the corner of his eye Alonso saw Francisca making the Sign of the Cross and he realized that the rosary was over, so he made the sign himself, then stood and helped his wife to her feet.

"Now my dear, you must make yourself ready for the mayor's dinner," he said, holding both her hands in his. He could see the hint of worry on his wife's face.

"If we must, my dear Alonso, of course," Francisca said.

"We must, I fear," Alonso said, tender and reassuring. "It will be fine, my darling, and I promise we'll not stay long."

Francisca gave him a weak smile, an attempt to show a brave face, then she turned and headed for the bed-chamber with Gabriella and Lucia trailing behind.

Alonso retired to his own dressing room where his manservant helped him out of the suit he had worn to the chapel and into the finer clothes he had laid out for the mayor's dinner. It was all a great bother. Alonso felt the irritation creeping over him as his servant hooked his trousers to his tunic and fussed over the folds of the cloth. He cursed the man, by way of venting his frustration, and meant to follow that with a solid kick in the next minute or so.

The servant moved quickly, sensing from long experience that the kick was on its way, and he stepped back just moments before Alonso's anger boiled over. Alonso stepped over to the tall mirror, looked himself up and down, nodded his approval. He left the manservant to tidy his dressing room and stepped back into the main room to wait for his wife.

Francisca, left to her own devises, would take the better part of an hour to dress, and Alonso would have a hard time hiding his irritation. But he knew that Gabriella was taking charge of the effort, and she would see to it that Francisca was ready when her husband's business required that she be.

Gabriella...

She was well worth the reals he slipped to her now and then. Her service to Francisca alone made her worth it. Her service to him was a welcome addition, though he reckoned that the pleasure he gave her in return was worth more than the gold in her hand.

At last Francisca came sailing out of their bedchamber, her hair done up in an elegant style and laced through with sprigs festooned with tiny white flowers. Her gown was black velvet, elaborately embroidered with red and gold and silver thread. Vast sleeves hung down from her elbows, and around her neck she wore a large silver cross, studded with rubies and emeralds and diamonds, suspended from a necklace of rectangular sapphire beads.

"My darling, you look beautiful," Alonso said, taking her hands in his and kissing her softly on the cheek. She smiled at him, a smile of genuine gratitude.

"Thank you, my dear Alonso. The lieutenant governor or Hispaniola cannot have a wife who looks like a dairy maid."

"Even dressed as a dairy maid you would be the most beautiful woman in the West Indies. Or the East Indies. Or in between."

"Oh, you are such a flatterer, Don Alonso!" Francisca said, reddening a bit but not looking displeased. And, flattering as Alonso's words might be, there was no denying the fact that Francisca was a beautiful woman.

The servants opened the doors for them and they swept out of the apartments and down the long hall with its whitewashed walls and polished red tile floor, then out into the wide courtyard where the stone walkway was interrupted here and there with bursts of green native flora and brilliant flowers. The heat was like a physical presence after the cool of the interior, but heat such as that had been part of their lives from birth and it did not even warrant a comment. Instead, Francisca surveyed the courtyard and the balconies above as they crossed the way, her arm in his.

"I tell you, husband," she said, "I had no notion of what to expect from Santo Domingo. I'll confess I feared it would be some dirty little fishing village, peopled with savages and filibusteros. One hears such tales of the New World. I had no notion it would be so like Old Spain."

"It is like," Alonso agreed. "In good ways and bad. Las Casas Reales, this is as fine a place as any in Madrid, sure. And the government people as well, the governor, the mayor, they are the same fat old fools one meets in Old Spain. Just as lazy and incompetent."

"Oh, Alonso!" Francisca said, scandalized by the words. "You must not speak like that. And about our host, the mayor."

"You are too good, my dear. You see only the good in people." Alonso said. "But you'll see the truth of what I say."

They entered the building again at the far side of the courtyard and made their way up the steps to the apartments of Don Nicolás Pérez de Maldonaldo, mayor of Santo Domingo. Two servants in matching livery stood outside the tall, elaborately carved doors, and they swung them open on well-oiled hinges as Don Alonso and Francisca approached, revealing the apartment within and the cumulative sound of numerous and simultaneous conversations.

"Ah, Don Alonso!" The mayor's voice, weighty as the man himself, came booming through the noise. He seemed to materialize as they stepped through the door, his ample belly, his wide smile splitting moustache from goatee. "An honor, an honor, sir!" He held out a hand and Alonso took it and the mayor grasped Alonso's hand in both of his and shook.

He looked at Francisca and his face lit up as if he was seeing a vision of the Blessed Virgin herself. "My dear Lady Francisca! How very delightful it is to see you here, and seemingly on the mend." He dropped Alonso's hands and scooped up one of Francisca's and pressed it gently to his lips. "How do you fare, my dear lady?" he asked.

"God bless you, Don Nicolás," Francisca said, a little flustered by the enthusiasm of the mayor's greeting. "I'm better by the day. My dear husband is ever so solicitous."

"As well he should be!" Don Nicolás declared. "Here, please, come in, let me escort you to your seat. You will sit by me, of course. If I could find some business to send Don Alonso off on I would do it, so that I might have you to myself!"

"Oh, Don Nicolás, you are too much!" Francisca said, but not in a way that might discourage further flattery.

The mayor led them to the head of a long table and seated them side by side, facing the comptroller-general and his wife.

"The governor was not able to attend today," Don Nicolás said. "Which is just as well. He's an old man and he prattles on, as you know." The mayor's infectious smile never left his face as he spoke.

You are birds of a feather, you and the governor, Alonso thought as he smiled up at Don Nicolás.

"The governor does well, I think, given how little help he gets from Madrid," Alonso said. The truth, he had discovered, was that Madrid did not care to have any colonial officials do much of anything on their own. Madrid wanted them to follow orders sent from Madrid, which Madrid rarely sent, and as a result very little was ever accomplished.

Which was fine with Don Alonso Menéndez. It left little to distract him, and almost nothing standing in his way.

"Ah, Madrid!" the mayor exclaimed. "They have no idea of our problems here, and they care even less. But forgive me, Don Alonso, Lady Francisca, I see more guest arriving and I must greet them, so they do not think I am wanting as a host."

"No one could find you wanting in any way, Don Nicolás," Francisca assured him, and she was rewarded by a vast smile as the mayor bowed and stepped away. They could hear his bellowing voice calling out to the newest arrivals as he made for the door.

A servant appeared at Don Alonso's side and filled his wineglass and then filled Francisca's as he made his way from the head of the table to the foot. Alonso glanced up at the comptroller-general, a dour, humorless bureaucrat with whom he had interacted just a few times during the course of his official business. Those interactions had not been particularly enjoyable and he doubted that their pending social intercourse would be much better.

By way of avoiding conversation with the man Alonso reached for his wine and thought, *Let's see what sort of thing the old man serves at table.* He lifted the delicate glass to his lips, braced himself for what he guessed would be a decidedly inferior vintage, and took a sip.

The first taste confused him. Not what he had anticipated. He took another, concentrating on the sensation. Not inferior, not at all. A wonderful, fruity taste, with hints of oak. As good as anything he, Don Alonso, would serve at table. Better, in fact, than he would serve to most.

"Hmm…" Alonso said.

"What is it, my dear?" Francisca asked.

"The wine," Alonso said. "It's excellent."

"And why shouldn't it be, husband? Don Nicolás is obviously a man of fine taste." The mayor's flattery was still working on her.

Soon after, just as Alonso was bringing himself to introduce Francisca to the dreary comptroller-general, Don Nicolás returned to his place at the head of the table. He called for quiet, and when at last the conversation faded away he lifted his glass up high.

"Join me, my dear guests, in toasting those many people who are so deserving of our recognition!" He waited while the two dozen others stood and raised their glasses, and then he led them in a toast to King Philip and his queen, Elisabeth, to the royal governor Gabriel de Chávez y Osorio, and to Don Fadrique Álvarez de Toledo y Mendoza, who was just then subduing the foreign scum on St. Christopher and Nevis and who soon would bless Santo Domingo with his presence.

Last of all he led a toast to Don Alonso Menéndez de Aviles, Knight of the Order of Santiago, and his beautiful wife Francisca, both of whom God had seen fit to shelter from the deadly hurricano so that they might take their rightful place on Hispaniola.

"Thank you, my dear mayor," Alonso said, raising his glass and sipping again. They sat and the bishop led them in the blessing and then the servants descended, bearing platters that were running over with food.

"Don Nicolás," Alonso said when he was finally able to get the mayor's attention. "I compliment you on your wine, Señor. I have not tasted its like since…well, since leaving Spain, I should think."

"Thank you, my dear lieutenant governor!" Don Nicolás said. "For my guests, I want nothing but the best! And, to be honest, I want the best for myself as well. This particular wine is from La Rioja. Very hard to get in the West Indies."

"Indeed," Alonso said, smiling the contented smile of a man who knows a secret. *Hard for some,* he thought. He had barrels of it hidden in Carlos Hernández's warehouse, just waiting to reach an eager market.

Perhaps I'll sell some to you, old man, Alonso thought. To his left a servant presented a plate of broiled fish and Alonso served himself a piece, and then asparagus in a cream sauce. A small bowl of olives and peppers in oil was set down in front of him.

"Here, you must try some of those," the mayor said, gesturing toward the bowl. "Manzanilla olives in the most delicate oil you have ever tasted. Please, try!"

Alonso nodded and speared an olive with his fork and put it in his mouth. He chewed the meat off the pit and savored the taste. It was indeed a marvelous thing.

I'll make my fortune off the mayor alone, Alonso thought. Like the wine, he had barrels of such olives secured in Hernández's hidden room.

Alonso turned to the mayor. "You are a man of great taste, Don Nicolás," he said. "Your table is..."

He stopped, his mouth still open. The mayor's clothing: an elegant doublet, a rich brocade of red and gold, and trousers of the same luxurious material. Alonso had noticed it but had not really looked at it, not closely. But he was looking at it now, and he recognized it. He recognized the fabric. He had examined it in Hernández's warehouse weeks before.

He turned away. The servants fussing over various guests along the table were dressed in jerkins of blue velvet. Blue velvet. That cloth was also part of the inventory he had imported from Spain. He felt his mouth go dry, his stomach convulse.

"Please, Don Alonso, you were in the midst of complimenting me!" the mayor said with his wide smile. "Go on, go on!"

"Well..." Alonso stammered. "I was just saying, your table is...wonderfully laid...." He looked up and searched around the room and realized there was something else different, some addition since the last time he had visited the mayor's apartments. Mounted on the walls were various coats of arms, and above each was a pair of crossed rapiers. Fine Toledo steel.

"My dear..." Francisca said, her voice a loud whisper, thick with concern. "Are you well? The color has quite gone from your face."

"Yes, Don Alonso, have your found something amiss?" the mayor asked, and his gracious tone and jovial good humor seemed to have drained completely away.

Chapter Twenty-Six

It was well past dawn, with the sunlight coming brilliant through the stern windows, when LeBoeuf finally shook off sleep. He was alone in the bunk.

He lay stretched out, eyes closed, as the odd twists of the previous night began to reform in his mind, like a letter torn to shreds and then reassembled piece by piece. He recalled the fight on the beach and the iron chest under the deck planks. He remembered crawling weary into bed and Henriette climbing in with him, rolling on top of him, taking the initiative in a way that LeBoeuf had thus far failed to do.

He realized he must have fallen asleep at some point, before things had progressed much beyond the opening salvo. He remembered reflecting on the correlation between a man's attractiveness and the amount of gold in his possession, but nothing much after that.

He felt a sudden stab of panic and his eyes flew open, though the rest of him did not move. To his relief, and a bit to his surprise, he saw that Henriette was still there. She was sitting on the settee aft, her knees drawn up under her chin. She seemed to be looking absently at the deck, but LeBoeuf knew that was not the case. She was looking at a particular section of deck. The section that held beneath it that great fortune.

What did you think she was going to do? LeBoeuf asked himself. She could convince Le Rongeur to kill him in his sleep. That would be easy enough. And then she could kill Le Rongeur. But that would not leave her in a good place. He doubted she could even lift the iron box on her own.

So she would have to convince Le Rongeur to take her ashore, promise him half the gold with the intention of killing him before she had to make good on that. But once ashore she would still be stuck on the godless coast of Hispaniola. What's more, the buccaneers would certainly discover the fortune and demand the gold be divided up among them, and they would be within their rights to do so.

No, Henriette was stuck, just like all the buccaneers and their women. To get off that desolate beach they were all dependent on Jean-Baptiste LeBoeuf, owner and master of the only ship around. What's more, Henriette had ambitions beyond just getting to Tortuga. She was looking to get her hands on some or all of the gold as well, and this charade of affection for LeBoeuf was her best chance at that, or so she seemed to have concluded.

And she would understand, as he did, that it was essential that no one else know about the fortune under the deck. If word got out, blood would most certainly spill.

LeBoeuf propped himself up on his elbow and Henriette swiveled her head in his direction. She did not look particularly happy, but then she never did.

"Well rested, I hope," she said dryly.

"Very," LeBoeuf said.

They sat in silence for a moment, then Henriette said, "Have you decided…what you'll do?" She nodded toward the hiding place in the deck.

"Mmm," LeBoeuf said. "My first task is to keep you from stealing it all."

Henriette scowled. LeBoeuf smiled. She could not suppress her irritability, even while feigning desire for him. She opened her mouth to make some biting retort but was interrupted by the sound of voices, outside the cabin and far off. LeBoeuf turned and looked toward the bulkhead. He could guess who it was: the buccaneers, now sufficiently sober and rowing out to begin the work that would get them off Hispaniola.

He looked back at Henriette and he could see the genuine anxiety on her face. He did not know what part of the gold she thought was her due, or why she thought any of it was, but he could see it was no trivial concern. To Henriette, the fortune under the deck represented the best, perhaps only chance she had to get herself away from the nightmare of the West Indies and back to France. Or so LeBoeuf imagined.

And what is so great about France? LeBoeuf wondered. *What would you do there, Henriette? Sell yourself on the streets of Paris?* Maybe she thought her part of the gold would be wealth enough to set herself up as a lady of quality, but he did not think her situation would be much improved if she returned to France.

How about you, *Monsieur LeBoeuf?* he thought next. *Would* you *like to return to France? This gold could get you there in fine style.*

He shook his head as if to physically drive the thought from his mind. It was not a thing he was prepared to consider, not just then. Perhaps not ever.

He looked Henriette in the eyes. His expression was serious and when he spoke his tone was sincere.

"This will be our secret for now," he said, and he could see the flush of relief on Henriette's face.

He sat up and swung his legs over the edge of the bunk then stood carefully so as not to slam his head into the deck beams above. There would be plenty of things to annoy him that day, he was sure, and he did not need them to start before he was even dressed.

"Come now, we had best go greet our guests," he said.

"*Our* guests?" Henriette said. "Are we lord and lady of the manor now?"

LeBoeuf shrugged. "Didn't you tell me you used to be the queen of France?"

"I told you I was a lady in waiting to Anne d'Autriche, you dumb ox."

"Oh…of course." LeBoeuf said. "That's what you told me."

He pulled his shirt on over his head and buckled his belt around his waist and stepped out onto the deck just as Van Loudersong was stepping up through the gangway. The night before he had been dressed for celebration, with a fine linen doublet and a velvet hat, complete with peacock feather, but now he was dressed for work in the same rough canvas clothing he wore when hunting pigs. Like LeBoeuf, like most of the men, he wore a wide belt around his waist with a couple of knives hanging off it.

"LeBoeuf, good morrow!" the Dutchman said, smiling. "We have come to get your *yatch* fit to take us away from this godforsaken place."

"Good," LeBoeuf said. "Good." The two men stepped aside as the rest filed up through the gangway: Pierre le Chasseur, Boylan, D'Anton, the taciturn former slave, all the men who a few weeks ago had made their living through the bloody business of killing feral swine and smoking their meat on the native boucans.

There had been little for them to do since returning from Van Loudersong's cave, and plenty of drink had been liberated from the *Santiago*'s hold, and LeBoeuf could see that situation had done the men no good. Van Loudersong seemed largely intact, but most of the others looked sallow and pained with dark circles under their eyes. Some wore torn clothing and sported various bruises and bandaged lacerations. No one was moving with much gusto. Idle time and copious drink was a bad combination for men such as sailors and buccaneers.

In normal circumstances, financial limitations would have saved such men from their own debauchery. Coming ashore with pay or plunder, they would spend it all in a wild spree, raining silver and gold down on the heads of tavern keepers and whores until it was exhausted, which was generally not long. Then it was off to sea again, and something close to sobriety, until their purses were filled once more.

But there on Hispaniola the natural rhythm had been interrupted. It was not a matter of running out of specie: the drink and the women were already theirs. They could debauch themselves until the drink was gone, but it would take quite some time to exhaust all that they had. It should have been the buccaneers' idea of paradise, but LeBoeuf wondered if in reality they'd had enough. He wondered how many of these men had come out to rig *Santiago* because they could no longer endure the unrestrained revelry. Half a dozen of the former hunters had already managed to drink themselves to death. He wondered if the rest were eager to get to sea before they did the same.

He looked over the ship's side. The men had come out in five boats; three periaguas and two canoes. Now the last of the buccaneers was coming up the ladder and the boats had been left to drift at the ends of their painters. He turned to the men assembled on deck.

"Prithee, see, we've already got some of the work done…" he started in but Van Loudersong cut him off.

"Lots more to do, my friend," he said, stepping past LeBoeuf and looking down at the main topsail yard lying on the deck, broken nearly in two and stripped of its gear. "Not sure why you took everything off the yard here, it's still serviceable. We'll fish it where it's sprung, sort of like a splint, you see, and put the gear back on. No need to make a new one."

He turned to the others. "Levasseur, Boylan, Lessard, find some wood we can cut up to fish this yard, and some rope to bind it up. We'll need — "

"No," LeBoeuf said. He said it just loud enough to be heard, and just emphatically enough to make it clear he meant it. "We're not fishing the yard. We'll make a new one."

Van Loudersong smiled. "My dear LeBoeuf, it's a waste of time. When I fish this yard it will be as if it was new."

LeBoeuf shook his head. He had given Van Loudersong free rein before, but it was time for that to stop.

"No," he said again. "We make a new one."

For a moment he and Van Loudersong stood fixed in their spots, ten feet between them, eyes meeting eyes. LeBoeuf watched the emotions play on the Dutchman's face, as subtle as a soft breeze but unmistakable. Van Loudersong gave off an aura of command such that the rest were inclined to follow him, which they generally did. He considered himself in charge now and did not expect to be challenged, certainly not from the hulking, silent, dim-witted LeBoeuf.

LeBoeuf could all but hear the debate in Van Loudersong's head, whether it was worth it or not to try to exert command on a ship that was not his to command.

Then Van Loudersong smiled and shrugged. "As you wish, LeBoeuf," he said. "You know something about the rigging of ships, do you?"

"Something," LeBoeuf said.

"Then I am ready to take my orders," Van Loudersong said, giving a shallow bow, but he did not sound like a man willing to take orders. He sounded like a man who considered himself slighted and who would not forget the slight, just as he would not forget LeBoeuf's interference on the beach the night before or his inviting the rest of the buccaneers to shelter in his cave. None of which concerned LeBoeuf in the least. He turned to the others.

"We need two new topsail yards and a main topmast," he said. "It will be no great amount of work, making those up. I'll need a dozen of you to go ashore and find the trees we need. Limb them, cut them to length, tow them back out here."

At first no one moved, but then they began to nod and shuffle around and a dozen sorted themselves out and gathered at the gangway, Van Loudersong among them.

"Hold there, Van Loudersong," LeBoeuf said. "We can leave limbing trees to these others. A skilled man like you, who knows his way around a ship, I need him aboard here with me."

Van Loudersong considered that, nodded, stepped away from the gangway. It was true, what LeBoeuf said. It was a waste of talent to send an experienced mariner to cut wood. But mostly LeBoeuf did not want Van Loudersong to be left alone with the shore party. He did not want the Dutchman spreading whatever poison he was inclined to spread. Van Loudersong would understand that as well.

And for all his less desirable qualities, the Dutchman did indeed know his way around a ship, so LeBoeuf gave him the jobs that only a skilled rigger might be expected to do: long-splicing frayed lines, passing rose lashings around the mast, turning Flemish eyes that were wormed, parceled and served. The others he set to tasks commensurate with their skill and sobriety, and soon there were men aloft and men working on the deck and even men down in the hold undertaking the unenviable job of overhauling the spare anchor cables that had been turned into a jumbled heap by the violence of the hurricano.

Henriette positioned herself on top of a water barrel under the break of the quarterdeck, out of the unrelenting sun and out of the way of the laboring men. She appeared to be doing nothing in particular, but LeBoeuf was perfectly aware of the job she had set for herself: making certain that no one other than she or LeBoeuf set foot in the master's cabin.

It was nearing noon when LeBoeuf was finally able to leave his work long enough to speak with her. He ducked under the quarterdeck, into the delicious shade. He opened his mouth to speak but she cut him off before he could say a word.

"We should put a rug or some such on the floor of the cabin," she said in a hiss, "to cover where the boards are pulled up."

"We should," LeBoeuf agreed. "But I don't reckon there's a rug aboard. Maybe find a blanket to put down."

Henriette nodded.

"But see here," LeBoeuf went on. "There's another thing I'd thank you to do. That letter patent we found…the scroll? I'd be pleased was you to read it and tell me all that it says."

Henriette frowned and looked at him suspiciously. "Why? Of what import is it?"

LeBoeuf shrugged. "I don't know," he said. "I don't know what it says. Maybe if you can tell me, then I'll know if it's of any import at all."

She continued to regard him with suspicion and more than a little skepticism, but she nodded her head at last. LeBoeuf did not know if her facility with the written word was everything she suggested it was, but he knew she would be happy spending the day as close to the gold under the deck planks as she could get.

She hopped down from the barrel. "I'll lock the door," she said. "Knock three times if you wish me to open it."

"Thank you, I will," LeBoeuf said. He wondered if she would find a way to pilfer some of the gold, maybe hide it on her person.

She might, he thought. *It might be well to strip her down and search her.* The idea was not at all unpleasant. His interest in women, like his interest in life itself, seemed to have been rekindled by whatever magic *Santiago* held in her fabric of wood, iron and rope.

A short time later the men sent to fetch the felled trees returned. In their periagua they brought a side of cold roast pig and a barrel of beer, and towing astern were three straight, clear logs. The logs were allowed to float alongside while the pork and beer were hoisted aboard and dinner made from them. Once each man had eaten and drunk his fill he found some patch of shade on the deck and stretched out for a nap.

LeBoeuf found this profoundly annoying, like hitting his head on the deck beams, but he was not entirely sure what to do about it. At another time, aboard another ship, he would have kicked a few of the sleeping men into the scuppers and that would have served as a hint to the others that it was time to get back to work. But he could not drive the buccaneers the way he drove other crews because the buccaneers could still abandon him *en masse*. They needed each other, LeBoeuf and his fellow pig hunters, but LeBoeuf was not certain that the others entirely understood that. So he let them sleep.

At least for a while. An hour or so. Then he stood and said in a loud voice, more like a bellow, calculated to cut though the deepest slumber, "Very well, now, time to be back at it!"

Slowly, with groans and soft curses, the men pushed themselves up off the warm deck and returned to their work. The yard tackle was swung out over the water and lines were made fast to the small trees floating alongside and they were hoisted aboard. LeBoeuf asked who among them were the most skilled with axes and adzes and when those men were found they were set to work shaping the trunks into tapered spars, filling the deck with heaps of wood chips and trimmings.

They worked until the sun began to set and then by mutual and unspoken agreement they laid down their tools and filled cups and pipes and found places on the ship's deck to sit. They were mostly quiet as they enjoyed the warmth of the evening and the pleasure to be had in the work they had accomplished.

There was still quite a bit to do, no one had any illusions about that, least of all LeBoeuf, but they had made a good start that day. It gave LeBoeuf a sense of satisfaction. Contemplating what they would do next, and then after that, and all the work beyond did not fill him with despair but rather gave him a sense of hope.

Both those things, satisfaction and hope, had an odd and foreign quality about them. He had not felt either in a very long time. But now he recalled why they were things men sought after, like women and food and drink.

Le Rongeur half remembered certain stories, Bible stories, which he had heard as a child. There were people in those stories who saw things and had their lives changed in unimaginable ways. When he considered the moment he had peeked through the crack in the cabin bulkhead, he thought of those stories. Like those long-dead worthies, the entire trajectory of his life had changed in an instant.

He had done quite a bit of thinking since then, not something he was much accustomed to doing, having spent most of his life acting on impulse. He realized that nearly every conscious decision he had ever made had been a mistake to one degree or another. True, those mistakes were rarely his fault: it was always someone else or some circumstance that thwarted his plans. Still, things generally did not work out the way he hoped.

But this time it would be different.

The image of the gold coins spread over the top of the table and glinting in the lantern light seemed burned into his mind. On occasion he would also remember the sight of Henriette standing naked just a few feet in front of him and that memory would amuse him briefly, but then the coins would reassert themselves. More wealth than he could ever have dreamed of, just twenty feet away, and only two lives standing between it and him. He could not recall having ever been so utterly consumed by anything.

So for nearly every waking moment since, and even a few times while he slept, he worked through all the possible plays he could make for that gold. The whole process was utterly maddening. He was not very good at thinking things through, seeing what might happen if he did one thing, what might happen if he did another. It reminded him of that game, chess, that he had watched people play. So many complicated moves that would lead to this outcome or that. Le Rongeur had never even been able to learn the rules, never mind play the game.

Thus, for all his thinking, he could not come up with a way to claim the treasure for himself. Even if he could kill LeBoeuf and Henriette he had no way of getting off the beach without the help of the others, and he could not hide the gold from them forever. At some point he would have to retrieve it from under the deck planks, and he doubted he could do that in secret. He would need to carry it off the ship, lower it down into a boat, row it ashore, and that would not go unnoticed.

Finally he reached a conclusion, frustrating yet unavoidable — he had no way of keeping the gold all to himself. The best he could do would be to share it with as few others as possible. He and LeBoeuf would have to remain partners. Their matelotage would have to still stand.

Now, decision made, and with the sun going down on their first full day of work on the ship, their first day with all hands at it, Le Rongeur knew that he had to act. As terrified as he was of confronting LeBoeuf — and he was shitting-in-his-breeches frightened by the thought — the call of the gold was louder than the shrieking of his fear. It was time to make his move.

He stood aft, near the stern of the ship, leaning on the bulwark and looking forward. The others were lounging at various places in the waist or bow, smoking pipes, drinking, enjoying the evening. At first, Le Rongeur planned on waiting until they had all gone back ashore so that he could talk to LeBoeuf in private, no suspicions raised. But then he realized that with the others gone there was nothing preventing LeBoeuf from just killing him then and there, squeezing the life out of him with those monstrous hands.

If anyone asked why he did it LeBoeuf could simply claim Le Rongeur had attacked Henriette. Again. And that would be an end to it. But Le Rongeur knew that if LeBoeuf killed him no one would care enough to even bother asking why.

No, he had to talk to LeBoeuf in private, but while the others were still aboard. Regardless of how despised Le Rongeur might be, LeBoeuf could not so easily murder him with forty fellow buccaneers just twenty feet away. Questions would be asked. Le Rongeur was proud of himself for having so cleverly worked that out.

Very well then, damn your eyes, now's the time, he thought, and with that thought he felt his stomach convulse with fear.

None of that, none of that… he told himself. *Bastard can't do nothing to you with them others aboard.* The thought mollified him a bit. He swallowed hard and pushed himself off the bulwark and walked forward. He stopped at the break of the quarterdeck and looked down at the waist.

LeBoeuf was leaning on the rail, a pipe between his lips, but Le Rongeur did not want to call out to him. He wanted their discussion to go unnoticed if possible, so he waited until LeBoeuf looked up and then jerked his head toward the stern to indicate that LeBoeuf should follow him there.

LeBoeuf did not move. In the fading light Le Rongeur could see him scowl. He jerked his head again, and again LeBoeuf did not move.

He'll come, Le Rongeur thought. *He'll be too curious not to.* He headed aft alone. When he reached the stern he turned and had the satisfaction of seeing LeBoeuf mount the stairs and come rolling after him. LeBoeuf stopped five feet away and pulled the pipe from his lips.

"Yes?" LeBoeuf asked, putting a surprising degree of threat into that one syllable.

Le Rongeur swallowed hard. He had played this scene out in his head a dozen times, crafted and recrafted the words he would speak, and now it all flew out of his head as if his thoughts were a startled pheasant. He cleared his throat, looked side to side and then back at LeBoeuf, and to his great relief the words returned.

"You know, when you made the deal with them others...the ship for your share of what was aboard...that meant everything that was aboard. You know that, right?" He waited for LeBoeuf to start arguing, to make some protest or feign ignorance, but LeBoeuf just put the pipe back in his mouth and stared at him. Le Rongeur found it unnerving. He waited a few seconds more and then went on.

"So, the thing is this...I know there's a fortune in gold in the master's cabin. A fortune you didn't tell them others about." LeBoeuf scowled and took another step closer but this, too, Le Rongeur had anticipated. He held his hands up, palms out, as if to ward the big man off.

"No you don't, LeBoeuf!" he said in a harsh whisper. "One more step and I'll shout it out, and won't them others be curious about that gold? Think you can kill me before I yell?"

LeBoeuf stopped. He folded his arms and for a moment the two of them stared at one another. Finally LeBoeuf spoke.

"Well?" he asked.

"Well, I can keep a secret, too, if I reckon it's worth it," Le Rongeur said. "You split that fortune with me, and you do it before we sail to Tortuga, and I don't say nothing. If you don't agree, then I'll tell them others. They'll kill you and I'll still get a share, even if it ain't as much as half."

He stopped and folded his arms as well. He tried to look calm, a man who knew he had the upper hand, but in truth he was bracing for some reply he had not considered, some move on LeBoeuf's part that he had not been smart enough to anticipate.

Then, to his surprise, LeBoeuf nodded. Le Rongeur waited for what would come after — the cursing, the bargaining, the threatening — but beyond nodding LeBoeuf seemed to have nothing more to add.

"So…a deal then?" Le Rongeur said. "Half for me, half for you? And you share it out before we sail for Tortuga, hear? You do that and all's well. You try to raise the anchor without I have my share, then I tell the rest and God help you then."

Again he waited for LeBoeuf to reply, and again LeBoeuf only stared at him. Le Rongeur realized he was fidgeting and he made himself stop. He extended a hand out toward LeBoeuf.

"Matelotage, yes?" he said, forcing a smile on his face. LeBoeuf looked down at the hand and up at Le Rongeur again. He pulled the pipe from his lips, blew a cloud of gray smoke and then replaced the pipe without saying a word.

"Very well, be like that, if that's what you want," Le Rongeur said, his frustration getting the better of his fear. "I'm doing you a favor, truth be told. Not that I expect no thanks." He pushed past LeBoeuf and headed forward. Dark had settled on the deck and he and LeBoeuf were all but lost from sight of the others and that realization made Le Rongeur nervous.

Still, as he walked forward, he felt an odd sense of pride glowing deep inside. He had done it. He had made a plan, thought it through, carried it out. He had summoned the courage to stand up to the great ox LeBoeuf and LeBoeuf had not even had the presence of mind to say one word in reply.

The others considered LeBoeuf to be a dull-witted beast. Le Rongeur had always agreed with that, though sometimes he seemed to catch a hint that perhaps the man was more clever than he was letting on. Now, at last, he could see that LeBoeuf was not so clever at all.

Chapter Twenty-Seven

It was late, but not so late that the streets of Santo Domingo were deserted. The narrow, cobbled ways were still crowded with people: people carousing, drinking, fighting, laughing. The working people, who were finished with that day's work. It was just the tavern keepers who were still at their labors, and their servant girls, and the boys who fetched bottles and rolled barrels from store rooms, and the whores who frequented the taverns or patrolled the streets.

Don Alonso knew the streets would be crowded, though not with the sort with whom he associated. Still, the danger of his being recognized remained. He was, after all, the lieutenant governor, the second most powerful official on Hispaniola. He was a man who made his presence known, riding through the streets on regular inspections, his mounted patrol following behind. Alonso understood that he could not take charge of the people if the people did not know he was there, in charge.

But that night was different. That night he did not wish to be recognized, so he took his usual precautions. Plain doublet and trousers, the dress of a working man of some moderate means, a wide hat pulled down low over his face, a rapier hanging from a shoulder belt, a pistol thrust into a pocket in his cape. He followed behind another man who wore canvas slop trousers and a cassock and thrum cap, clothing that marked him as a sailor. An intermediary. A man Carlos Hernández had put in place to arrange communication between him and Alonso, in case they needed to speak. Which Alonso felt they did, and without delay. In fact, he was growing increasingly frantic on that point.

The very moment he had returned from the mayor's dinner he sent Juan Cardero off to contact the sailor by whatever means the two of them had arranged. Word came back at last, a meeting with Carlos Hernández arranged for the following night. He made his excuses to Francisca, told her there was business that needed attending to, apologized for working at such a late hour.

Francisca had nodded, had stroked his face, and said comforting things. She had not been blind to Alonso's unsettled state of mind, though she had not asked him about it. Another woman, a less trusting woman, indeed almost any other woman, would have found Alonso's behavior suspicious at the very least, but Francisca was nothing except sympathy.

Now Alonso hurried to keep up with the sailor who led the way through the crowded streets, through the gate and down the narrow stone steps to the lower town. He moved with a confidence born of familiarity through that rough section, a thing Alonso certainly could not do. Alonso had walked that way only twice before, and he suspected that even if he walked them another dozen times he would not be able to find his way through that tangle of slums and warehouses and dubious businesses, each looking the same as the last. Even during his regular inspections of the city, even with an armed escort, he did not venture down to the lower town. Better not to know what was taking place there.

But the sailor seemed to have no such problems and he held his lantern high as he led Alonso on a winding course through the streets and alleys. It was not until they reached the nondescript door of Hernandez's warehouse that Alonso recognized anything at all.

The sailor knocked, soft and rapid. The door opened a crack and the lantern light revealed Carlos Hernández's worried face. His eyes went from the sailor to Alonso and he nodded and stepped back, opening the door a bit wider for them. The sailor stepped aside to let Alonso pass, then spun around and hurried off in another direction as Alonso stepped through the door.

"Don Alonso…" Hernández said.

"Show me my goods, damn your eyes," Alonso snapped, "and for your sake they had better be here, every last thing that was on the manifest."

"Yes, señor …" Hernández said, but he did not move immediately, and his hesitation made Alonso angrier still. Then, before Alonso could curse him again, Hernández turned and said, "Please, come this way."

He led Alonso through the maze of barrels and crates and stacks of sundry goods. They came to the spot where the empty barrels had been stacked to hide the small door behind, but now the barrels were gone, the door fully visible in the light of the lantern.

Hernández stopped and gestured for Alonso to go first. Alonso ducked and lifted the latch of the door and pulled it open. He stepped through into a room he did not recognize.

The last time he was there the space had been jammed full, but now it was nearly empty. A few barrels were pushed up against the far wall, some crates of something or other off to the right. A lantern hung from a hook near the middle of the room. A rope hung from a beam on the ceiling, its bitter end tied in a noose, and just below the noose, a chair.

Alonso took three steps into the room and stopped, his thoughts writhing. He was already furious, and the sight of the empty room, which he had half expected, redoubled that fury. But the rope was a surprise, and though he was too angry to consider what it meant, it did summon up feelings of menace and confusion. And then, pushing through those other amorphous feelings, he felt the first inklings of fear.

"Damn you, Hernández!" he shouted. He was starting to turn when he felt hands clamp onto his arms, left and right. He thought at first that Hernández had grabbed him, then realized there were two men holding him, strong men, stronger than Hernández was likely to be. Their hands felt like iron bands bound around his arms. He twisted side to side but he could not move at all, as if he was lashed to stone pillars.

"You bastards!" Alonso shouted. His body was held fast but he craned his neck to see who it was holding him. Big men, each several inches taller than he was, with thick beards and the rough clothing of working men, or sailors.

"I command you to..." Alonso began, anger reasserting itself, but the two men seemed not in the least interested in Alonso's commands. They dragged him farther into the room, toward the chair and the noose, and once again fear eclipsed the outrage.

"Damn you, you wouldn't dare, I'm the lieutenant governor, damn your eyes!" he protested. He could hear the edge of terror in his voice, could feel his guts convulsing. His knees buckled but the men on either side of him were supporting his full weight with ease and he did not fall. They stopped with the noose hanging just above Alonso's head.

"See here, see here, I have money you know, more than you can imagine..." Alonso said, aware that his voice was rising to a feminine pitch. The men holding him jerked his arms straight up. He felt the coarse rope around his wrists as the noose was cinched tight. The men released his arms and he dropped half a foot, his terror-weakened legs refusing to support him, and then he jerked to a stop at the end of the rope.

He gave a cry of pain as the rough hemp dug into his flesh and he forced his legs to take his weight. He stood, and felt the rope come taut as someone hauled on the other end, lifting him off the floor until he had to support himself with his toes to keep from dangling by his wrists.

He craned his head to look over his shoulder, trying to see how many were in the room. There were the two men who had dragged him to the rope, and a third who had hoisted him up. He thought he could see a fourth as well, back in the shadows.

Then he heard movement in front of him and he turned back. Carlos Hernández was moving the chair back five feet from where Alonso all but hung from his wrists. Their eyes met.

"I tried to tell you, señor," Hernandez said. He set the chair down, and from somewhere near the door Don Nicolás Pérez de Maldonaldo, mayor of Santo Domingo, approached and sat. Hernandez nodded to him and without a word disappeared in the direction of the door.

For a long moment they looked at one another, Don Alonso and Don Nicolás. The man in front of him was the man Alonso knew, certainly: the familiar sweep of hair, the moustache with its proud curls, belly that spoke of good living. But at the same time the man was almost unrecognizable. There was no trace of the perpetual smile, the aura of jolly graciousness. In its place was menace. Simply menace. There was nothing else.

Frightening and strange as the man looked, Alonso took some odd comfort in his presence. This was not some stranger, not someone who failed to understand Alonso's status, rank and connections. The two of them, him and Don Nicolás, were familiar with one another. Each knew where the other stood in the hierarchy of things. Alonso felt a certain boldness come over him.

"Don Nicolás," he said with a forced calm in his voice, "this cannot end well. I am the lieutenant governor…"

Don Nicolás nodded to someone Alonso could not see and one of the men in the room stepped up beside him. He had a club in his hand, three feet of some polished tropical hardwood. He swung it in a wide backhand stroke and hit Alonso square in the stomach. The blow knocked the breath out of him and he gasped and kicked and thrashed at the end of the rope. He sucked at the air in a frenzy and then finally his breath caught and he pulled in a lungful, and then another.

"I talk," Don Nicolás said quietly. "You don't talk. I talk."

Alonso nodded.

"So, Señor Lieutenant Governor…apparently you had big dreams of the riches you would make in the West Indies," the mayor began.

"I meant only to…" Alonso started. The man with the club swung it again, this time hitting Alonso on the back of his thighs. His legs folded and he fell. His full weight came onto his wrists and he felt the rope dig deeper and he shouted with the pain.

"You are very forgetful," Don Nicolás said. "I talk. You don't talk. Do you need another reminder?"

Alonso shook his head.

Don Nicolás nodded and for a moment he said nothing, just looked at Alonso as if collecting his thoughts. When he did speak his voice was low and gravelly in a way Alonso had never heard it before.

"Now listen, little boy, you pathetic little shit," Don Nicolás said. "You have no idea what you have gotten yourself into. *Lieutenant governor…*" He spit the words out as if they left a foul taste in his mouth, then stood and paced back and forth for a moment, silent, looking at the floor.

"I imagine," he said, turning back to Alonso, "you are wondering if I mean to kill you here and now. I could, of course. You could simply vanish. Poof! But that would raise a lot of questions. And it might upset your wife. That is, if she stopped humping that handsome priest long enough to care."

He paced some more. Alonso got his feet under him and tried to raise himself up on his toes but he did not have the strength. He watched Don Nicolás walk back and forth and tried to summon some courage, or even think of something he might say to improve his situation. He actually opened his mouth to speak and then remembered that he was not to do so, so he closed it again.

Don Nicolás stopped pacing, turned, looked at Alonso and gave a tiny nod of his head. The man at Alonso's side stepped around and slammed a fist into Alonso's stomach and Alonso doubled up as much as he could. He coughed up bile and spit it out and felt it run down his face.

"So here we are," the mayor said. "I have that sorry little cargo that you thought would be the seed of your great fortune, which I will keep and enjoy. You will never do anything of the sort again. You will do your duty as a good lieutenant governor and nothing more. Nothing. You will never again try to swim in waters too dangerous for the likes of you. Is that clear?"

Despite the pain, despite the fear, Alonso looked the mayor in the eye and held his gaze. But defiance, at least at that moment, was clearly pointless. His only option was to promise what he needed to promise to get out of the warehouse alive. And then he would reassess.

He nodded his head.

"Good," Don Nicolás said. "So, let us discuss a few other things. Your father-in-law, Don Cristóbal de Seville, to start. It's no secret that you owe your current position to him. Did you know he wrote to me, asking that I welcome you and your dear wife? He did. We are old friends. Now, if he was *your* father, that would be one thing. I would expect nothing to come between you. But he is not your father, he is your father-in-law. You understand? His love is for his daughter, not for you."

Alonso continued to stare at the man, even as he tensed for another blow, but it did not come. Don Nicolás pulled a folded paper from his belt, unfolded it and held it up to Alonso's face. The writing that covered the sheet was crude, not the work of a well-educated individual, but tolerably neat and legible.

"This is a letter written by that little whore Gabriella. Do you recognize the hand?"

Alonso stared at the words. He could barely make them out, but he did indeed recognize the hand. It was a rarity among servants, but Gabriella could read and write, and that letter had been written by her.

Don Nicolás folded the letter again. "I don't have time to wait while you try to read that scrawl. Suffice to say it is a confession to your dear wife concerning the many times you rutted with that little tart. Poor Gabriella pleads forgiveness from Francisca and from God for her sins. This letter would find its way to your wife soon after Gabriella disappeared. Or was found dead in your bed. Either way, I suspect it would taint your marriage, and thus the affections of Don Cristóbal. What do you think?"

Alonso glared at Don Nicolás but he did not respond. He did not tell Don Nicolás what he thought because he did not know what he thought. Fear, rage, pain, they were all making rational thought impossible.

Don Nicolás looked off to his left and nodded again and another man, one Alonso had not seen, a fifth man, stepped up and slammed a fist into his lower back. Alonso nearly screamed as the pain shot through him and he twisted against the rope.

The mayor took a step closer. "Forgive me...I give you leave to speak, Don Alonso. Now tell me, what do you think?"

Again Alonso glared at Don Nicolás for a moment before he replied. "You have the best of me, Señor Mayor," he said, his voice reduced to a growl by the pain and the anger. "I will do as you wish."

Don Nicolás nodded. "Good, good," he said. "But here's the thing of it. I see the defiance that's still in you. I see it in your eyes, your hateful eyes. You are not a broken man, and that's a problem, because I dare not have you beaten any more. If your injuries are too visible, it will raise questions, just as your disappearance would. So my five fellows here will see to it that before you leave this place you are indeed a broken man. They will give you something to recall whenever you feel the wish to defy me. But as to me, I shall leave now. Because, honestly, what's about to happen to you, I can't bear to watch."

He reached up and patted Alonso on the cheek and gave him the briefest of smiles, a momentary glimpse of the man Alonso had thought Don Nicolás to be. Then the mayor nodded to the others, turned and left the room, closing the door behind him with a decisive thump.

Alonso looked around. He fear was back now, in full force. He could not think what Don Nicolás had in mind that would be worse than the beatings, but he knew he would find out directly, and he knew now to take the man's threats seriously. He felt his stomach convulse in terror.

He heard a grating sound to his left. One of Nicolás's men had tilted a barrel on its side. He rolled it over to Alonso, positioned it right in front of him so that it was touching his shins. Alonso frowned and looked up at the man and then he felt hands behind him, reaching under his doublet. He felt fingers grip the top of his trousers, and with a jerk his trousers were ripped from the hooks that held them up and fell in a heap around his ankles.

"Oh, no..." Alonso said, realizing now what Don Nicolás had ordered these men to do. "Oh, no..."

Suddenly the rope that held him aloft went slack and he felt himself falling, felt hands on his arms directing his fall so that he went stomach-down over the barrel. He heard the shuffle of men moving around behind him and he braced for the feel of hands on his naked flesh. He thought he might vomit.

"No, no, no…" he said. His voice rang with desperation but he did not care. "Look here, look here, I have money, I'm an important man, more important than the mayor…" He could hear rustling behind him, the sound, he feared, of one or more of the men loosening their own breeches. The panic was overwhelming him. He started to push himself up off the barrel and someone pushed him down again so he was sprawled out and helpless. He heard someone behind him chuckle.

"Keep begging," one of the men said, a voice that was harsh and cracked. "Go on. We like it when you beg."

He felt hands like rough stone on his buttocks. He gritted his teeth and made a screaming sound in his throat, a cry of fear and humiliation. And then he heard the door to the warehouse swing open and hit hard against the wall. The hands on his skin disappeared. He heard feet moving by the door, feet behind him as the men in the room reacted to this new presence.

No one spoke. Alonso rolled himself back so that he was sitting on the floor, the stone cool against his bare ass. He looked over toward the door. A man was standing there, a sailor by the look of him, but no one Alonso recognized. He wore faded canvas slop trousers and a faded shirt with a leather jerkin, a red cloth bound around his head. His complexion was dark but his race was not clear — African, Arawak? Some Spanish blood? Alonso could not tell. The man had two pistols in his belt, a cutlass at his side, and in his hand was a club of some sort, square-sided and covered with intricate carvings.

Behind him, lined up against the wall, were six other men, all African by the looks of them. They, too, wore sailor's clothes, though some of them wore silk scarves and gold chains and bright-colored sashes. One man was wearing what must have once been a fine silk tunic but was now ripped and stained. They were big men, bigger than the first man was, and like him they were well armed. Their eyes met the eyes of Don Nicolás's men. There was no expression on any of their faces.

The silence was broken by one of Don Nicolás's men. "This has naught to do with you, Maja."

The man with the club, the one named Maja, apparently, nodded but did not speak.

"Be gone, then," another of the mayor's men said. "This ain't your business."

"I guess I'll decide, is it my business or no," Maja said at last. His voice was calm. Conversational. His accent, like his race, seemed an odd mix. "And it seems I decided it is."

There was quiet again as the two parties looked at one another across the ten feet that separated them. *Filibusteros?* Alonso wondered. They were dressed like pirates, some of them, and certainly armed like pirates. He had heard that escaped slaves sometimes joined in with those people. His fear and horror were gone now, and in their place, just confusion.

Maja spoke again. "I don't reckon you five want to die for Señor Corregidor," he said. "You go now, and Señor Corregidor hears nothing of this." He stepped aside, leaving a clear path to the open door.

Again there was silence. No one moved. The Black men stared at Don Nicolás's five, and the five stared back, and Alonso wondered who would yield. The filibusteros were frightening to behold, but Don Nicolás's men did not seem the sort to be frightened by anyone.

And then Alonso realized that Don Nicolás's men were not armed, as far as he could tell, save for sheath knives on their belts, and the one man with a club. Even as that thought came to him, one of the Black men to Maja's left drew a pistol from his belt and pushed the hammer back with his palm until it made a loud click in the near-empty room. And then another, and then two more did the same.

There was a moment still of silence, then one of the mayor's men grunted and stepped forward, cinching his belt up as he walked. He made for the door and the rest followed behind. The Black men did not move or react in any way, they just watched as the lumbering Spaniards filed out the door.

With that moment passed, Don Alonso recalled his humiliating situation, his bare arse on the floor, the noose still binding his wrists, trousers around his ankles. He looked up at Maja, wondering if the man was going to lend him a hand. But Maja remained motionless, staring at Alonso the way he had stared at Don Nicolás's men.

Seeing that he would get no help, Alonso twisted his hands to loosen the rope, and when it was loose enough he slipped it off. He stood and grabbed his trousers, pulled them up, and managed to find two hooks that had not been torn free, enough to keep the trousers in place, more or less.

Finally he looked up at Maja. "I don't know who you are," he said, "but I thank you." Maja gave a small nod but said nothing.

"So...may I go?" Alonso asked, gesturing toward the door. Maja shook his head, but still he did not speak.

Alonso frowned. *Say something, you damned savage,* he thought. There had to be a reason this Maja had done what he had done. Alonso did not think it was an act of charity or kindness. Indeed, what Maja had in mind might be even worse than what the mayor's men had intended.

He was trapped still, at the mercy of barbarians still. He felt the fear starting to boil once again.

"Why did you...why are you here? What do you want of me?" Alonso asked, trying to keep a vestige of authority in his voice.

Maja took a few steps in his direction, his eyes never leaving Alonso's. "Our friend Señor Carlos Hernández told me you would be here," he said. "He told me you are no friend of the mayor's. I am not a friend of the mayor either."

"I am not a friend of the mayor," Alonso agreed. "You saw what the mayor meant to do to me. To have his men do to me." He felt his stomach turn even as he said those words.

Maja nodded.

"Is that why you helped me? Because you hate the mayor as I do?" Alonso asked, but once again Maja shook his head.

"Señor Hernández told me something else," Maja said. "He told me about a brigantine. It was seen on the northwest coast. He said you think it might be yours, and you were willing to pay gold to see it returned."

Hernández... Alonso thought. *The bastard moves men around like chess pieces.*

Alonso had asked him to find a ship and a master to go after the brigantine, not to tell the world about it. But now, with Hernández having tossed the secret around like chicken feed, it was clear to Alonso that he had lost control. He might as well abandon the entire enterprise.

But...

That ship, the *Nostra Sennora de Santiago*...the *Trois Frères*...was still the best chance he had to build his empire. The only chance. To build it far from the knowing eyes of Don Nicolás Pérez de Maldonaldo. He was not ready to give it up. He was not broken.

"Whatever Señor Hernández told you, it was not..." Alonso began, but Maja cut him off.

"Those men, the ones we told to leave?" he said. "They are known as El Cinco. A tavern on the next block...that's where they are now, I'll warrant. I can send for them, if you like. And they will come, believe me. What they were about to do to you, it was not just because Señor Corregidor told them to. They wanted to do it."

Alonso pressed his lips together and he tried to think through this thing, but his mind was far too twisted up now to form any coherent thought. He had only impressions, fleeting emotions of which he was barely aware. Foremost, terror at the thought of those five men returning.

"Yes," Alonso said, finally. "There was a brigantine, called *Nostra Sennora de Santiago*. It sailed with me from Spain. Had a rich cargo in its hold. It was bound for Tortuga, on my orders, where the master was instructed to sell the cargo for a good profit. I would pay to have that ship and cargo returned."

Maja cocked his head a bit and looked at Alonso as if he was some odd species of animal, something vaguely curious. "You had two ships. One you instructed to come here. That is what Señor Hernández said. But this other you send off to Tortuga? Into the arms of the filibusteros?"

Alonso did not reply. He could feel his resolve melting away. He did not have the strength to continue these games. He might not be broken, but he was played out. He wanted only to be free of the warehouse, clear of the lower town. Away from this savage who currently had complete control over his life, as if he, Alonso, was a slave and this man his master.

"There was more than cargo aboard the ship, señor," Alonso said. "There was gold, hidden under the deck in the master's cabin. Not a fortune, but near to it. And there was something else. More valuable, I think. To me, anyway. Something I worked very hard to acquire. A letter patent. From the king of France. For an estate on Tortuga. A plantation." He wondered if this man would know what a letter patent was.

Maja cocked his head again. After a moment's consideration he spoke. "What good is that?" he asked. "A letter patent from the king of France? Spain lays claim to Tortuga. They lay claim to all this land."

"Tortuga's in French hands now, and I do not think my country has the strength or the will to take it back," Alonso said. "And I should know. I'm a government official, after all. Now, if a man had a legal estate on a French island he would have a place to operate from. Smuggling. Pirating. A place to keep goods without relying on a bastard like Hernández. Maybe even grow tobacco."

"You're a Spanish government official. And you reckoned you could be a French smuggler as well," Maja said. "And more."

Alonso shrugged. "That was the idea, but it is gone now."

Maja was silent, his eyes still on Alonso, but his thoughts apparently far off. Finally he said, "This estate, it could not be yours. No one could know it is. You are a Spaniard. You meant to have another man claim it. Run it for you. Your agent. Overseer."

Alonso nodded. "That's right," he said. "The master of the ship, he was supposed to be the owner in my stead. Where he is now, I do not know. Dead, I should think."

For a long moment they just stood there: Alonso, Maja, the other men. No one spoke. Alonso ached to leave, to ask Maja if he could leave, but he did not dare.

Finally, when he could bear the silence no longer, when his desire to leave that place outweighed any other, he spoke.

"There, I have told you the truth," he said. "I had word that a brigantine was seen on the coast, the northwest coast of Hispaniola. It might be *Sennora de Santiago*. It might not. I don't know, nor do I care. She is yours to hunt down if you wish, and *vía con Dios*."

Still Maja did not speak, and in the silence, the unbearable silence, Alonso thought he might scream. He was about to say something else, anything else, when at last Maja spoke.

"If the brigantine is yours, and she is still there," he said, and his tone was thoughtful, "then a man could still use the letter patent. Still claim the estate."

"Yes," Alonso said. "Be my guest. I am done with it."

"No, no," Maja said, and he seemed to be warming to the idea. To some idea. "It still needs you. Your money, your influence. Just as you have planned."

"Yes..." Alonso said. "Yes, but..." He stopped, afraid to state the obvious.

"But it could not be me who claims it," Maja said. "A savage. Is that what you were to say?"

"No, of course not," Alonso protested but Maja ignored him.

"But an Englishman could," Maja said. He seemed to be speaking as much to himself as to Alonso.

"An Englishman could," Alonso agreed. "It's a French patent, sure, but that could be explained away."

Maja looked off toward the far end of the room and once again fell silent, and once again he remained silent until Alonso was ready to scream. Finally he looked back at Alonso. "We must act quickly," he said.

His face still betrayed no expression at all.

Chapter Twenty-Eight

LeBoeuf watched Le Rongeur walk forward toward the break of the quarterdeck and he could not help but see the hint of jauntiness in his step. The little turd was clearly proud of himself, and that alone made LeBoeuf want to stomp the man into the deck until no identifiable part of him remained.

*Give him his due…*LeBoeuf thought. *He managed to work that through, and it's more clever than you would have reckoned possible of him.*

For some time LeBoeuf remained in the stern, staring forward, drawing on his pipe until the tobacco was gone, allowing his thoughts to go where they would. It was dark now, and he could see only what was visible in the pools of light spilling out from the lanterns hanging in the rigging or sitting on the main hatch.

Damn the little bastard, LeBoeuf thought. His first question: how had Le Rongeur discovered the gold? He must have been peeking into the master's cabin when they hauled the chest out, but how he managed to do that LeBoeuf did not know. There was no place where one could see through the bulkhead.

LeBoeuf knew that for certain. He had checked it personally, knowing Le Rongeur would try to indulge his voyeuristic tendencies. On a dark night LeBoeuf had set a lantern inside the cabin and examined the bulkhead from the outside to see if any light was leaking through. He had found nothing.

So, the little shit must have cut a hole when we were ashore, he thought. He pushed those considerations aside. It did not matter. Le Rongeur knew about the treasure now, and that was the reality with which LeBoeuf had to contend.

There was only one thing he knew for certain, and he knew it before he even considered any of his options — Le Rongeur would not get a single escudo. Not one. Just on principle alone he would dump the lot of it into the sea before he let that little bastard enrich himself in any way.

He let his thoughts wander until he hit on a realization that surprised him, surprised him enough to make him stand more upright and frown at the darkness: he was not actually angry about this. He would kill Le Rongeur for this outrage, certainly. But he would do it because Le Rongeur had earned that fate, not because he, LeBoeuf, had to vent his own personal fury.

The truth, the startling truth, was that he did not really care about the gold. Dumping it in the sea would not be so great a tragedy. Less of a tragedy than letting Le Rongeur get his hands on any of it. He would hate to see Henriette lose her share, but beyond that he did not really care.

He tilted his head back and looked up. The lower masts and what rigging they had managed to put in place were outlined against the great field of stars. It was the ship he cared about, the freedom it offered. The potential. He could toss a fortune away. If he had a ship under his feet, he could earn another.

"Sod the little bastard," LeBoeuf said out loud. There was no rush. He had until they were ready to weigh anchor before he needed to deal with Le Rongeur. Plenty of time to arrange some accident or other.

Forward, LeBoeuf heard Van Loudersong say, "I, for one, am ready to rest weary bones." With that the buccaneers rose to their feet, many groaning as they did. LeBoeuf crossed the quarterdeck and stepped down into the waist as the others began to shuffle over to the gangway and climb down into the boats alongside. Le Rongeur was among them, trying to be inconspicuous, his gear rolled up in a blanket slung over his shoulder.

Guess you're not so stupid as to stay aboard with me, LeBoeuf thought. That was a shame. He could have solved the problem that very night.

"We'll see you gentlemen on the morrow," he said, taking care to keep the tenor of the words somewhere between a request, an order, and an observation. Some of the men nodded or waved, some called out their acknowledgement, some seemed not to hear. Soon they were all back in the boats, pushing off for the short trip back to the beach, back to their food and drink and women and whatever makeshift shelters they had cobbled together.

LeBoeuf turned and walked aft. He paused at the cabin door and knocked three times, smiling at the absurdity of it. He heard movement inside and then Henriette's voice, "LeBoeuf?"

"Yes," LeBoeuf said. "I'm sorry, we should have arranged some secret code word."

He heard the latch move and the door swung open and Henriette was frowning at him. "You think it's a joke, protecting…what we found?" she asked. "You're such a funny man, it's no wonder you don't have a pot to piss in."

"Don't be ridiculous," LeBoeuf said, stepping into the cabin. "I'm a rich man. I have this ship. And a fortune under the deck. And you as my wife…or something. My servant?"

Henriette made a sound of disgust but LeBoeuf was thinking about what she had said. *You're such a funny man*… She clearly did not mean it as a compliment, but still, it had been long time since anyone had accused him of such a thing.

LeBoeuf dropped his belt and knives on the table. The lantern was sitting there, throwing its weak light over the polished wood. The scroll was there as well, loosely rolled, the red ribbon lying beside it.

"Did you read that? The letter patent?" LeBoeuf asked, sitting on the edge of the bunk.

"I did," Henriette said.

"And?"

Henriette shrugged. "It's what I thought, more or less. It's a grant of an estate to someone named…" She picked up the scroll and partially unrolled it and angled it toward the lantern. "Chevalier Philippe Guillemeau de Beaune. Signed by the king, though certainly written by another. That lazy pig Louis would not have the patience to write such a tedious thing."

"Methinks the king has others to do that sort of work," LeBoeuf said.

"The estate is on Tortuga. A good part of the letter is about where it's found, the boundaries and such. And there's some nonsense about taxes and obligations. And other things."

"I see," LeBoeuf said. He wondered how much of Henriette's report was based on close reading of the document, how much on a cursory look and how much on guessing. Either way, he suspected she had the gist of it. A grant of land from the king of France to someone who managed to find favor with the old buggerer.

"Well…what of it?" Henriette asked.

"I don't know," LeBoeuf said. "A mystery, still. I don't see as the king of France has any business giving away land on Tortuga."

"Why not?" Henriette asked. "He's the king. He can give things away as he pleases."

"I don't think Tortuga belongs to France," LeBoeuf said. "And I'd wager the Don Diegos in Santo Domingo don't think so, either. They'd consider it a Spanish island. They reckon everything here is Spanish."

"Maybe France has claimed it. Or taken it."

"Maybe," LeBoeuf said. "Who knows? Certainly not me. I know little about what's acting in the world. Just what I can see from the quarterdeck above us."

"And it's no business of yours anyway," Henriette said. "Makes no difference. You have all you need."

LeBoeuf nodded but his mind was still working over the letter patent and what it could mean. *Chevalier Philippe Guillemeau de Beaune…* He wondered if the man had been the master of *Santiago*, or a passenger, or even if he had been aboard at all. In any case, it was an odd thing for a French Chevalier to be sailing on a ship called *Nostra Sennora de Santiago*.

Though that, of course, was not the name of the ship written in the log books he had found. In the log book she was the thoroughly French *Trois Frères*.

LeBoeuf shook his head. Intrigue upon intrigue, it seemed, and him too ignorant and too tired to pry it apart. He pulled his shirt over his head and tossed it aside, then laid down on the bunk and stretched out as much as he could. He groaned with the pleasure of it and closed his eyes.

A moment later he felt Henriette climb into the bunk with him. He wondered if she would put a leg over him, wondered if she was still driven with a desire sparked by the riches under the deck. But she did not. Instead she pressed her back against him, the linen of her smock soft against his chest, and lay still. But this time LeBoeuf felt a stirring deep in his gut, such as he had not felt in some time.

He put his big hand down on her hip and pulled her a little closer to him, so that she was pressed tighter to his chest. She made a little guttural sound in her throat but said nothing. LeBoeuf slid his hand up along her side, following the curve of her waist, running it up to her small shoulders, softly pushing aside her thick dark hair, with its lighter streaks from sun and saltwater. Henriette made another sound, louder and more deliberate, and pressed herself back against him.

LeBoeuf raised himself up on his elbow and leaned over and pressed his thick beard into Henriette's neck until his lips touched skin. He kissed her gently then ran his lips up toward her jaw.

"Hmm…" Henriette said, softly. "I wondered if maybe you preferred Le Rongeur to me."

"He has his charms…but no," LeBoeuf said, running his hand back down her side. He felt the linen of her smock catching in the rough skin of his calloused and leathery fingers and palm, more fit for hauling a line or skinning a boar than stroking so lovely a creature as Henriette.

"You might want to take off those filthy trousers," Henriette whispered, "before they make me puke."

LeBoeuf's trousers were stiff with dried sea water and sweat and tar and blood. He reached down and tugged the cord binding the waist until it came loose then kicked them off.

"You are such a sweet and demure thing, it's no wonder the king couldn't resist you," he said as he pressed his lips to her neck once again.

"Hmm…" she said, and her tone was half irritation, half arousal. She rolled over toward him and he eased himself up over her, straddling her small frame with his elbows.

"Oof, you're a great ox," she said but the sharp edge was gone from her voice. LeBoeuf kissed the smooth skin at the neck of her smock. He had learned how to compensate for his great size in situations such as this, how to hold himself prone against a woman without crushing her underneath.

He eased himself forward until his face was over hers and he pressed his lips against hers and she reached up and ran her fingers into his thick, tangled hair.

He shifted so that more of his body was over hers. She felt frail and insubstantial under him, as women generally did. He ran his hand down along her neck, over her breast, down over her stomach and thighs, barely able to feel the thin fabric of her smock with his battered hands. He found the hem and eased it up a bit, a signal more than an attempt to get the garment off.

Henriette reached down and grabbed handfuls of cloth. LeBoeuf rolled back a bit and Henriette half sat up and pulled the smock up over her head and tossed it aside. She was every bit of what LeBoeuf thought she would be naked: lithe and smooth, taut, her skin pale in the moonlight coming in through the stern windows. If she had indeed been the lover of His Most Christian Majesty Louis XIII it would be no surprise. Such beauty as hers would be right at home in the Tuileries; so fine a creature worthy of the attention of a king.

Neither of them it seemed felt any need to rush things along, and so they didn't. Rather, they took their time and relished the luxurious pleasure, a rare commodity in the brutal world of the Spanish West Indies. Henriette seemed to have tossed away her bitterness and cynicism along with her smock, and in their place she showed skills commensurate with a royal courtesan.

When they were done at last they lay quiet in the bunk, LeBoeuf on his back, Henriette pressed up against him, since his bulk made it impossible for her to lay across his chest.

"That was nice," LeBoeuf said, his voice just a whisper. He felt like he was casting the lead, feeling for the bottom, trying to determine how deep or shallow Henriette's feelings ran.

"Mmm…" she said at last, a soft, noncommittal, half-asleep sound.

In the dark LeBoeuf smiled to himself. *There's no danger of this one falling in love, methinks.* And then he too was asleep.

He woke before Henriette did, the first time he could remember that happening. It was early morning, the first light just coming in through the stern windows as he opened his eyes. There on the table, just a few feet away, lay the letter patent, right where they had left it the night before. He stared at it blankly for a moment, and then suddenly all the questions and the intrigue and the sense of possibility it raised came flooding back. He wanted very much to climb out of the bunk and look at it once more, though he was not even sure why. But Henriette was pressed against him and sleeping still and since he did not want to wake her he remained as he was.

He felt her shift a few moments later, then she propped herself up and looked at him, then over at the letter patent and then back at him. She gave a snort of disgust.

"Well, you got what you wanted from me," she said. "Now I suppose you can sell me to Le Rongeur or one of the others."

LeBoeuf smiled. *Incredible.* He wondered if she said such things by reflex or if she genuinely believed it was a possibility. "I would just as soon sell my right arm," he said.

"Or your cock?"

"Or that, too. But look, there's no selling you, not anymore. You're a rich woman."

That observation had the effect he hoped it would. For a second, no more, he saw the pinched and angry look on Henriette's face soften, her lips part just a bit, her eyes open a little wider. Then she rolled onto her back.

"Humph," she said, all the doubt and suspicion back again.

In truth, LeBoeuf could not cast her off even if he wanted to. She had him in the same bind that Le Rongeur did. If he tried to keep her half of the gold she would tell the others about it and they would kill him for trying to cheat them out of it.

I wonder if that's occurred to her, LeBoeuf thought, and then realized, *Of course it has.*

Henriette was far too wily a creature for it not to have occurred to her. She just knew better than to wield that threat until it was needed. As far as she knew, LeBoeuf's response might be to strangle her in her sleep.

That was the difference between her and Le Rongeur. LeBoeuf was more than willing, eager even, to kill Le Rongeur. He was not willing to kill Henriette, nor did he object to sharing the treasure with her. He was not entirely sure why that was. Beyond fornicating and occasionally washing his shirt she had never been particularly pleasant to him.

LeBoeuf's eyes wandered back to the letter patent, and the sight of it gave him a strange mix of feelings. Curiosity. Desire. A sense that, elusive as it was, there was something much deeper, something more profound going on. This was not something ephemeral or fleeting. This was his fate.

Chapter Twenty-Nine

Benjamin Graves, perched on the settee in the master's cabin of *Santa Rosa*, stared at the leg iron around his ankle. He knew both very well by now — cabin and leg iron. It had been two days since they dropped anchor in the Rio Ozama and he had been sequestered in that cabin the whole time, and held fast by the leg iron for nearly as long.

He had been bound hand and foot at first, in preparation for that unpleasant visit from Señor Corregidor, trussed up like some animal off to the slaughter. It was a similarity that had not eluded Graves. Slaughter was pretty much what he had counted on when the old man came barging into the cabin, Maja behind him like a faithful dog.

Of all the times in his life that Benjamin Graves had been in the neighborhood of death, and he had wandered that way often, he had never been more sure that he had finally arrived. But in the end he had suffered only a blow, and by no means the worst blow he had ever endured.

The visit had ended. Graves heard Señor Corregidor's boat pull away. Then Kusi appeared in the cabin. He untied Graves's hands and feet and removed the gag from his mouth, then made a leg iron fast to his ankle. The iron was fixed with a pin, bent over with blows from a heavy maul, such that it would not come off without considerable effort. A length of chain was made fast to the other end of the iron and the chain in turn was bolted to the deck. It gave Graves a bit of a range of movement, a bit of comfort. A big improvement over the bindings.

Now what the devil… Graves thought. Kusi could only be acting on Maja's orders, but why Maja would do anything to make Graves less miserable he could not imagine. He had expected to be trussed up and dumped in the wettest, darkest part of the hold until Señor Corregidor called for him. Nor could he ask Kusi, who spoke no English or Spanish, which would make him, in Maja's mind, the ideal jailor.

Later, when Kusi brought food, real food — cold meat and fresh bread and ale — Graves was more confused still. He thought briefly that Maja might be displaying some tiny spark of humanity, but that did not seem right. Finally he concluded that Maja wanted him to be as comfortable as possible so that he might more easily ponder his coming fate and all the horrors that would entail. It was the only explanation he could imagine.

And Graves did indeed ponder his coming fate. In the quiet of the master's cabin, on a ship that was all but deserted, it was hard to think on anything else. He had been distracted for a while with the sound of the cargo being off-loaded and the thought of that great fortune, won through his own cunning, being dumped in Señor Corregidor's lap with not the slightest benefit to himself. But it had not taken above half a day to empty the hold and then there was only silence, save for the sound of the water running past the hull and the occasional noise from the waterfront or Kusi's appearance with food.

Now Graves contemplated the leg iron once again. Just the sight of it made his fingers throb with pain. He had worked at that bent pin with all his strength, from every angle and with every makeshift tool he could devise and he had not been able to straighten it even the tiniest bit. He had worked at the chain, worked at the bolt, tried to slip his foot through the leg iron and had met with no success at any of those endeavors.

He sighed and looked out the stern window. The sun was going down and the water and the land were lit up golden in that light. *Santa Rosa*'s bow was pointing downriver, which meant the tide was on the flood and Graves was looking north at the jungles of Hispaniola off the larboard side with glimpses of Santo Domingo to starboard.

If he could get free of the leg irons he could slip out the window and climb down the rudder to the water below. He could find something in the cabin that would float and he could ease into the river and let it sweep him upstream. He could lose himself in the forest until such time as he could find a canoe or periagua in which to make his escape.

He had it all planned out. In his mind he had seen the whole thing unfold. But he could not get free of the irons.

Graves looked away from the river and its siren song of freedom and turned forward. The cabin was in deep shadows now with the evening coming on but he could still make out the rack of bottles on the bulkhead. Wine and brandy mostly, and not the sort of miserable rot-gut he was usually condemned to drink. This was quality stuff, the sort of spirits that Señor Corregidor would reserve for himself.

But it was only because of the fineness of the bottles that Graves knew that. He had never actually tasted any of it. If he stretched the chain as far as it would go, and his arms and legs as well, then the liquor was still about a foot out of reach. He had tried to get his hands on a bottle almost as often as he had tried to bend the pin in the leg iron, and with as much success. This, too, he guessed, was part of Maja's not-so-subtle torment.

He sighed again and closed his eyes. He knew he would be asleep soon. He slept quite a lot. It was about all he had to do to pass the time, and with the wine and brandy out of reach the only means he had of silencing the panicked voices in his head.

When he woke again it was full dark, with the light from the moon and stars coming in through the stern windows and offering the most insubstantial of illumination. Graves had been upright when sleep came over him but when he opened his eyes again he found he was lying on his side, his arm under him, and now there was no feeling at all in that limb. He cursed and pushed himself up with his other arm and shook the numb one, trying to restore it to life.

He heard something bump against the hull and he sat more upright and forgot entirely about his arm. To most men the sound and the slight vibration would have meant nothing, but Benjamin Graves, who had spent the bulk of his life at sea, knew instantly that there was a boat alongside. It was probably what woke him in the first place, the sound of one of the men in the boat grabbing the chains with a boathook.

He felt his insides convulse and felt a wave of panic wash over him, leaving behind a film of perspiration. If a boat was coming at that hour it was probably coming for him, and that meant Señor Corregidor was done with his other business and ready to give Graves his full attention.

"Oh, damn, damn damn..." Graves muttered. He grabbed the chain and pulled as if he could yank the bolt from the deck now after having failed a dozen times before, but it was just as unyielding as ever.

He could hear feet on the deck above, bare feet on the planks, only just audible. That had to mean that Señor Corregidor was not one of those who had come aboard.

"Good, good, that's good..." Graves said as he looked around the dark cabin for...something. Anything. He did not know what he was looking for. Inspiration, perhaps.

He heard the sound of the bare feet moving overhead, followed the sound as the men made their way down the ladder to the 'tween decks. Around the edge of the cabin door he could see a thin line of light, the illumination cast off by the lantern someone was holding. He heard the sound of the door latch lifting and the door swung open. In the light from the lantern Graves could see the dark shapes of men behind, but he could see nothing beyond that.

Graves turned his head a bit and held a hand up to shield his eyes from the light, weak though it was. "Maja, is that you?" he said. "Good. Thank God above you're here."

He was just talking now, letting words spill from his mouth, hoping they would form themselves into some reason that Maja should not do whatever he had come to do. "I been thinking quite a bit, you know, and it seems to me..."

"Shut your mouth," Maja said. Graves still could not see him behind the light of the lantern, but that voice, like two rough stones grinding together, could not be mistaken.

"You might think you don't want to hear this, but..." Graves continued. Maja lifted the lantern and took a step forward.

"I said shut your mouth," he said again, and this time the demand came with an unstated promise that bad things would happen if Graves did not comply. Graves shut his mouth.

There were four men with Maja: Kusi, two of the Black filibusteros and another of the former slaves Maja had liberated at St. Christopher. They were all heavily armed now, the former pirates still wearing the bits of jewelry and fine clothing that their sort so enjoyed.

Maja set the lantern down on the deck and Kusi knelt down at Graves's feet. He had a maul in his hand and with a few deft blows he straightened the pin in the leg iron and pulled it free.

You couldn't have done that five hours ago, before this bastard Maja got here? Graves thought, but he knew, or at least felt certain, that Kusi's loyalty was entirely with Maja. As was that of the filibusteros. Saving a man from an ugly death tended to have that effect. Graves wondered if Maja might save him for the same reason, and dismissed the idea immediately.

He knows you have no loyalty to anyone but yourself, you stupid whore's son, he admonished himself.

Kusi stood and held the lantern up. Graves remained seated. He did not intend to cooperate in any way.

Maja took a step closer. "Which is the better ship, this, or the one I took from you at St. Christopher?" he asked.

Graves frowned. The question was so unexpected he was not certain he had heard it right. "What?" he asked.

"Which ship is better? This one, *Santa Rosa*, or the one you had at St. Christopher?"

"The one I had...*Charles Rex*?"

"Whatever damned thing you called her," Maja said.

"Well..." Graves said, considering the answer. As one who genuinely appreciated the finer points of sailing vessels, their hull forms, sail plans, deck lay-outs, armament, he could pontificate at some length on that subject, but he suspected Maja was not so terribly interested.

"*Santa Rosa*'s a bit bigger, more tonnage for cargo," Graves said. "But she's slower, too. Not as quick in stays. Seems to me she carries too much weather helm, but that could be fixed. She's a bit better armed than *Charles Rex*, but that ain't saying much. *Charles Rex*'s handier, for certain, and she could bear the weight of bigger guns. Guess it depends what you want. You want to carry cargo, and don't much care how fast you go, it's *Santa Rosa*. You want privateering or such, it would be *Charles Rex*."

Maja nodded. "Get up," he said.

Graves had been distracted by this consideration of the ships' relative merits, but Maja's words brought him back to the ugly present. "Now, see here, Maja, I do believe…" he began as he got to his feet, still hoping to talk his way into inspiration.

"Shut your mouth," Maja said and again Graves deemed it advisable to shut his mouth.

Kusi, holding the lantern, led the way back out of the cabin and Maja followed behind. One of the other men gave Graves a bit of a shove to get him moving and the rest flanked him as they made their way topside. At the gangway, Kusi led the way down the ship's boarding steps and into the boat alongside.

Graves took the steps quickly, then stepped over onto a thwart and down. It was a big boat, bigger than he would have expected, twenty-five feet long with places for ten rowers, though Maja had only four.

"You want me to take an oar?" Graves asked, looking up at Maja who was still aboard.

"Sit in the stern sheets," Maja said. "And shut your mouth."

Graves made his way aft and sat. Maja climbed down and sat beside him and grabbed the tiller. The man in the bow shoved off with the boat hook; the others lowered their oars and pulled and the boat gathered way, leaving *Santa Rosa* astern.

He didn't tie my hands, Graves thought. He fought to urge to look down at them lest Maja guess what he was thinking and bind him up. He looked down at the water instead. The tide had turned. It was ebbing now, the bows of *Santa Rosa* and *Charles Rex* pointing upstream.

I could jump, just go right overboard, Graves thought. *Might be able to stay afloat long enough to reach the shore.* He could not swim, and he was actually pretty certain he could not stay afloat that long, but his options were quickly growing scarce.

Just jump and drown your sorry arse, he thought next. *Just let the water take you. The sea will get you in the end anyway, if Señor Corregidor doesn't.*

And there it was. The choice, the horrible choice. His only choice, now. Die by his own hand or by that of Señor Corregidor. How terrible would it be to drown? He had no idea. He had known plenty of men who drowned, but none had come back to describe the experience.

The death that Señor Corregidor would give him was less of an unknown. That would certainly be hellish, as terrible as one could imagine. The Spanish, Graves knew, had a special talent for such things.

Do it, you damned coward, do it…jump… Graves thought. He looked over at Maja but Maja was paying no attention to him.

Bastard doesn't think I'll jump, Graves thought. *All the more reason to do it. Wouldn't Maja like to explain to Señor Corregidor how he lost the chance to kill me? He'd probably take my place at the slaughter.*

It was tempting, after a fashion: the thought of slipping under the water, depriving them all of the satisfaction of killing him, but still he knew he would not do it. As long as he could talk there was the chance he could talk his way out of whatever trouble he had worked his way into. Right up until the moment he was screaming out his life, probably at Maja's hands.

He looked forward again, surprised to see *Charles Rex* looming over them, her tall masts and squared yards like trees in winter moonlight. Maja made a soft grunting noise and the men lifted the oars straight up and the man nearest the bow set his oar down and grabbed up the boathook and grabbed onto the fore chains. Kusi scrambled up the side of the ship with the boat's painter in hand, and two of the filibusteros followed behind.

"Go," Maja said, looking at Graves and jerking his head toward the ship.

Graves swallowed down the dozen questions which were all wanting to come out at one. He stood, stepped over the thwarts and climbed up to the deck. He took three steps toward the main hatch. He breathed deep, sucking in the rich scent of tar and linseed oil and pitch, and for a short moment he forgot the questions and the fear.

Benjamin Graves had been master of a number of vessels, several of which he had also owned, and of those a few he had owned legally. *Charles Rex* was not his absolute favorite, but she was near to top of the list. Quick and weatherly, able to move in light air but also a ship that could take a beating in foul weather and come out the other side, she was a ship to make any mariner proud, and he could not help but feel delight at standing on her deck once more.

They brought me here to kill me, he thought next, and the fine feeling melted away. No reason for Señor Corregidor to risk being caught on shore. He could just kill Graves aboard his own ship, toss his mangled corpse overboard on the ebb tide. An added dose of cruelty to kill him aboard the ship he loved. He heard Maja stepping through the gangway behind him and he turned to face the man.

"Well?" Graves demanded. No reason to be obsequious now. Maja was going to do whatever he was going to do, and there was nothing Graves could say or do that would have any bearing on it.

Maja paused for a moment, looked fore and aft, looked up at the rig and then over the side. "I'm going to slip the cable," he said. "Let the ship drift out to sea on the ebb. Set sail once we've been pushed clear of the river." It was a statement, but there was the edge of a question in Maja's tone, as if he was asking Graves, without actually asking, if that plan would work.

Graves's first impulse was to ask *Why in hell would you do that?* but something told him that was not the right response. Instead he nodded his head thoughtfully and looked over toward the western bank of the river, where the city of Santo Domingo was visible in the few lights burning at that time of night. They were anchored toward the southern end of the city, not too far from the mouth of the river. Graves knew the river bottom and the currents and eddies well. There was no reason that the ship would not be swept clear out of the river mouth.

"That should work. Don't see why not," Graves said. "Nothing to hit, really, betwixt here and open water. Should have a land breeze filling in soon. Likely by the time the ship's well clear of the land."

"Good," Maja said, and as if on some unspoken signal more men emerged from the scuttle, a few more of the Black filibusteros and some of the men Graves recognized from *Santa Rosa*: Sánchez, Díez, Ortiz, and some others he did not know. Thirty men or there-abouts, three times more than were actually need to sail a ship such as *Charles Rex*. Like Maja and the men who had come for Graves aboard *Santa Rosa*, they were well-armed. Unlike those men, many of them were armed with muskets as well as pistols and blades.

"Let the cable go," Maja said to Sánchez, and Sánchez waved to a couple of the others and hurried forward. Maja jerked his head toward the side of the ship and the other men spread out, crouching behind the bulwarks, weapons in hand, peering out over the top of the rail. Ready for an enemy who, as far as Graves could tell, was not there.

And suddenly Graves and Maja were alone near the main hatch. Graves watched Sánchez and the others wrestling the heavy anchor cable off the bitts. He turned to Maja and opened his mouth to ask what in all hell was going on, but he took one look at Maja's face and closed it again. He ran his eyes over the masts and rigging and along the deck. All seemed in order. He turned to Maja once again.

"Want me to cast off that boat, let it drift away?" he asked. *Charles Rex* already had a boat sitting on the main hatch: the big one alongside seemed unnecessary.

"No," Maja said.

"You sure?" Graves asked. "It can slow us down some, pulling that along."

"No," Maja said again. "We'll need it."

Need it for what, damn your eyes? Graves thought. He had very little tolerance for Maja's taciturn nonsense, but there was not one damned thing he could do about it. Which made it even more intolerable.

He heard a thump forward. Sánchez and his men had worked the cable off the bitts and dropped it to the deck. The current took *Charles Rex* in hand and pushed her downstream as the cable snaked across the deck and disappeared out the hawse pipe.

Bloody waste... Graves thought. They were going to leave a perfectly good anchor and forty fathoms of two-inch anchor cable on the bottom of the river. But Maja apparently had some reason to want to be underway fast and silently, even if he was unwilling to explain what that reason was.

Graves looked off to the west. He could see the outline of Santo Domingo against the starry sky, could see it sweeping past as the river carried the ship out to sea. They were still well enough off shore that he was not worried about going aground. He looked to the east. *Santa Rosa*, still riding at anchor, was nearly lost from sight in the darkness.

A moment later he felt the motion of the ship underfoot change from its subtle rocking motion in the river's current to a deeper roll as the Rio Ozama emptied out into the Caribbean and the *Charles Rex* met the first of the incoming ocean swells. Maja looked at Graves, eyebrows slightly raised.

"Let the river take us another mile or so," Graves said. "Current's still strong enough to do us some good." He looked to the east. There was no sign of dawn yet, which should bring with it a tolerable off-shore breeze, but he could feel on his cheek that there was wind enough already to drive *Charles Rex* along.

Maja nodded, which encouraged Graves to continue. "In the turn of a glass we can send men aloft to loosen off all plain sail," he said. "There's breeze enough for us to use." He waited for Maja's rebuke, his assurance that if he tried to give orders again he, Maja, would beat him to death. But Maja only nodded once again.

For some time they stood in silence, glancing ashore every now and then. With the ship drifting on the tide there was nothing much for anyone to do: no steering or navigating or sail handling to be done. As the dark shore of Hispaniola become more distant the men at the bulwarks straightened and became less vigilant in proportion to the growing distance.

Maja, who had been looking over the rail, turned inboard and shouted a few words down the deck, the loudest words that had been spoken since they had come aboard the ship, and Graves jumped in surprise. He did not understand the Spanish, but as the men fore and aft laid weapons down and climbed up into the shrouds and headed aloft, he guessed they were orders to loosen sail.

Grave watched them climb, then turned to Maja once again. "So," he said. "Are you going to tell me what the hell is happening?"

Maja looked back at him with his expressionless hawk face. For a moment he said nothing, as if weighing how to respond. "You're alive, still," he said at last. "Be happy with that."

Graves nodded. Maja had a point. Wherever they were bound, it had to be better than the place Señor Corregidor meant to send him.

Chapter Thirty

Smoke was rising in a sticky black column from the fire on the beach a couple cable-lengths away. A dozen men were moving around it. Occasionally, a quirk in the breeze brought the familiar scent to LeBoeuf's nose: pig, drying on a boucan, its bones and fat kindling the flames. It was a good smell, but it was a smell from his past. He liked it. And he would be perfectly happy if he never smelled it again.

The ship, which by universal decree they had renamed *Navire Chanceux*, *Lucky Ship*, was riding at her anchor, bow-on to the shore. LeBoeuf pulled his eyes from the boucan and turned around, facing aft, where gangs of men were still hard at work, getting the ship ready for sea.

At first there had been jobs enough for all. There had been work finding fallen trees of the proper size, cutting them to length, hauling them out to the ship, shaping them into spars. Work turning sections of tree trunks into boards. There had been work using those boards to repair the places in the bulwark and deck and the hatches and bitts and rails which had not been so *chanceux* during the hurricano and had been crushed by gear falling from aloft.

There had been work aplenty straightening out the wreckage of the hold and the 'tween decks, since everything that had been stored there, lashed tight or no, had been tumbled and flung about like dry leaves in a gale. The buccaneers had taken everything of value when they claimed the cargo as their own, but there was still enough left behind to turn the lower decks into a chaos of debris. Cordage and spare sails and boatswain's stores and cables and a hundred other things had to be gathered up, stored and secured once more before the ship met the first of the Caribbean rollers.

For more than a week they were at it — aloft, on deck, down below. There were about forty men who still had enough life in them to work after the ravages of the hurricano and the debauchery and fighting on the beach, and they were eager to get at it. They were eager to be gone from that ruined coast, eager to get to Tortuga and the nascent pleasures the island had to offer.

LeBoeuf labored alongside them, getting his hands into every part of the effort, making certain it was done to his satisfaction, making sure the momentum did not stall. He was pleased with the progress, to a point. Had this been a real crew, men he could call his own, men who could not just throw down their tools and walk away if they wished, then he would have been considerably less polite. He would have been less willing to let them take their leisure when the sun grew hot and their throats grew dry for want of brandy and their eyes grew heavy for want of a nap.

But as it was he had to endure those things, because, eager as the men were to be gone, they still felt no real sense of urgency. That philosophy — doing only what needed to be done and not doing it with any great hurry or concern — was a chief tenet of the lives of the pig hunters, the buccaneers. LeBoeuf understood that, and he knew he could only coax so much work out of them, and if he tried to browbeat them into more then he would get no work from them at all.

It took a week of suggesting and cajoling and humoring to finish those jobs that required more muscle than brain. The 'tween decks and hold were in decent order, the loose gear stowed and secured, the rough carpentry on deck and below finished in satisfactory fashion.

The work that remained: rebuilding the rig and setting it up again, and the finer carpentry that could not be done with just a strong arm and an ax and a hammer. It was work that required a degree of skill and experience that not all of the buccaneers possessed. Suddenly LeBoeuf had more hands than he needed.

"I been thinking," LeBoeuf said one afternoon as the men were taking their dinner, before they sprawled out on the deck for their nap.

"This is something new, LeBoeuf," Van Loudersong said and the men laughed and LeBoeuf laughed because that was what big, dumb men such as himself did.

"Been thinking, maybe we don't need everyone on board now," LeBoeuf continued. "Lot of the work's been done. And I reckon by now the pigs have come out of hiding. Might make sense for some folk to go a'hunting. Set up a boucan before we leave. It'll give us something to eat on board and something more to sell at Tortuga."

Some men nodded at the suggestion and some did not but LeBoeuf was sure that even the dimmest of them would see that his words made sense. They ate in silence for a bit more, then D'Anton said in his African-tinged French, "I'm no sailor. This..." he waved his hand to indicate the yards sitting on the deck, the rigging, the sails, "is all a mystery. I'm a hunter. I'll go hunt pigs."

"I'll go too," Le Rongeur said quickly. "I ain't no sailor, there's naught for me to do here."

Damn my eyes, LeBoeuf thought. That was a problem he had not anticipated. Since their *tête-à-tête* on the quarterdeck Le Rongeur had been careful to keep his distance, working as far from LeBoeuf as he could and going ashore whenever possible. Whether through reason or instinct he had apparently come to understand that LeBoeuf might be looking to engineer some fatal accident and he was taking care to keep out of the way of such a thing.

Well, you can't keep clear of me forever, you vermin...

More nodding followed Le Rongeur's words. Boylan spoke next. "I'm with them two," he said. "Rather hunt pig than play with rope and such. Besides, LeBoeuf, he drives us like slaves and this was his plantation."

There were more chuckles, since the idea of LeBoeuf driving them hard was almost as ludicrous as the idea of LeBoeuf thinking.

Pierre le Chasseur turned toward Boylan. "LeBoeuf?" he said. "That's Captain LeBoeuf to you, *cochon.*"

"Admiral LeBoeuf," Van Loudersong said to more chuckles, more laughter.

"It's no joke," Le Chasseur said. "LeBoeuf's just the sort would make admiral. I never did meet an officer of the navy had the brains of a tunny fish."

"No, no, LeBoeuf wouldn't make an officer," Levesque argued. "He ain't noble blood. This navy Richelieu's building, you don't have to be any smarter than LeBoeuf, but you got to born to the right family."

"See, LeBoeuf," Van Loudersong said. "If you'd been smarter you'd have seen to it you were born to the right family."

LeBoeuf nodded. "Wish I'd thought of that before it was too late," he said.

The others smiled as they continued to dig into their bread and cheese and cold roast meat.

"Hey, LeBoeuf," Levesque asked a moment later, "did you ever serve aboard a man-of-war?"

LeBoeuf shook his head.

"Well, you know your way around ships, I'll give you that," Levesque said. "How'd you learn that trade?"

LeBoeuf shrugged. "Been to sea most of my life. Fishing at first. Merchantmen. Sailed out of La Rochelle, mostly. Gunner on a privateer. That was a good berth." It was a common enough life story for a man raised on the coast of France.

"Seems to me," Pierre le Chasseur said, "I heard of a naval officer not too different from LeBoeuf here. So don't say it ain't possible."

"What naval officer like LeBoeuf?" Van Loudersong asked.

"Old shipmate of mine told me about him," Le Chasseur said. "I remember now. An officer he served under. Big bastard, like LeBoeuf. Not so old, but tough as iron. I don't recall anything else."

"Was he named Le Duc de LeBoeuf?" Levesque asked. "Might be our man here."

"You men are funny," LeBoeuf said. "That's why I love you all. But I reckon it's time we got back to work."

"Sod that," Billy Solent offered. "I reckon it's time we get to what them Don Diegos call a *siesta*."

"See, not everything them sheep-biting Spaniards come up with is stupid," Pierre le Chasseur said, and one by one the men wandered off and found bits of shaded deck to stretch out on and sleep off the meat and bread and ale they had consumed for dinner.

LeBoeuf said nothing. There really was nothing for him to say. So he let them have their siesta and even laid down himself in the shade of the windlass near the bow, his mind working through how the topmasts would be swayed aloft, how the yards would be crossed and the running rigging rove off.

Later, when he judged that sufficient time had been devoted to napping, LeBoeuf rose and nudged the others back to work. Those who had volunteered to take up their muskets again and go in search of the wild pigs climbed back into the boats and pulled ashore. The rest of them picked up their tools, the tools of craftsmen — serving mallets and marlinspikes and sailmaker's palms, chisels and saws and block planes — and set back to work.

And so it went for a week following. Ashore, gangs of men headed out into the fields which were just now recovering from the destruction of the hurricano, and hunted the wild pigs that had first brought them to that coast. The work was harder now, with no dogs, all of which had been run off or killed. Without the dogs the swine would scatter before the hunters could shoot more than a few of them. But that was no hardship, since anything they shot they had to carry back to camp themselves, and there was only so much they were able or willing to carry.

LeBoeuf paid little attention to those men. He did not care how many pigs they killed and smoked. His only concern was keeping them occupied with hunting so they would not get drunk and cause trouble. He did not want the men he needed working on the ship to see the others taking their leisure.

He could see the day approaching when he would sail from that wretched coast, when he would feel the ship alive under him and feel his soul lift with each wave that passed under her bow. Like a point of land seen from far off, and growing more distinct with each mile covered, he was making way toward the start of that new life and he would let nothing alter his course.

Things moved faster on board after that, with LeBoeuf able to give his full attention to the finer points of fitting out the rig. The topmasts were shaped and finished off, the yards built and sails and gear bent on. One by one they were sent aloft and the standing rigging was looped over the mastheads and set up taut, and then yards, sails and running gear sent up soon after. From a half-sunk wreck, driven onto a sandbar, heeled over so she looked as if she might sink with the next tide, this ship, this *Navire Chanceux*, was born again as a lovely and seaworthy vessel.

Twenty-one days after LeBoeuf had stopped Van Loudersong and Le Chasseur from killing one another on the beach they crossed the lateen yard on the mizzen mast, the final task before LeBoeuf would declare the ship's refit complete. A few of the men took a periagua ashore and returned with the others and the women and with a barrel of wine, good wine, part of the ship's original cargo. They stove the barrel in and dipped their cups and drank deep and relished the thing they had done, how they had raised this wood and iron and rope Lazarus from the dead. It might have been LeBoeuf's ship, but they all felt a sense of ownership and accomplishment.

They drank long into the night, drank until there was no more wine to be had, not even when they lifted the barrel and tilted it upside down over their cups. Disappointing, but they were too drunk by then and too exhausted and content to care overmuch. Some of them loaded into the boats and pulled back for shore, and some just collapsed where they were, taking the odd coil of rope for a pillow and falling into immediate sleep.

LeBoeuf and Henriette retired to the master's cabin. It was what they did every night. Once there they would climb into the bunk and they would make love. Or they would climb into the bunk and fall asleep. The routine did not differ much beyond that.

Henriette, naked and in bed with him, seemed to have a sincerity, a fragility, that was otherwise entirely absent. Fully dressed and on her feet she was her old self, the familiar Henriette, Henriette of the caustic tongue and biting wit and general disgust and disdain for LeBoeuf and for everyone else.

Which of the two was the real Henriette de Labonté LeBoeuf did not know. Both, perhaps. Which was fine. If she had suddenly become pleasant and agreeable at all times LeBoeuf would have known it to be an act. Instead, she remained mostly unbearable, which had the advantage of sincerity, and made LeBoeuf think that the sex was something other than purely transactional.

On the night of the mizzen yard crossing LeBoeuf did not climb into bed, however. Despite the day's work in the hot sun, the wine and the late hour, he knew he could not sleep. His mind was like a ship caught by wind and tide, driven along beyond human control.

He set the lantern down on the table and stood, staring at the black glass of the stern windows as Henriette shed her petticoats and overbody and climbed into the bunk. There was something tugging at him, something he wanted to do, but he could not quite place what it was.

"Are you lost in the fog?" Henriette asked. "Just follow my voice if you can't find the bed."

With those words LeBoeuf realized what it was. He crossed the cabin with two steps and pulled the letter patent from the cubby, then sat down on the chair at the table. He shifted the lantern closer and unrolled the document and stared at the now-familiar flow of words on the page. His eyes were sharp, and despite the poor light he could make out the writing, small and precise. Henriette had done a tolerable job of translating the legalese, dense though it was. He wondered how long she had struggled with it.

"Oh, *mon Dieu*," Henriette said in disgust. She had kept her exasperation in check for the length of time it took LeBoeuf to retrieve the document and sit, which was longer than he had expected she would. LeBoeuf was impressed.

"I thought you didn't know letters," Henriette said, the old edge in her voice.

"I don't," LeBoeuf said. "But this…this is a thing of beauty. I like looking on it. The way I like looking on you."

Henriette gave a snort. "There is no magic in that, you know," she continued. "Staring at it will not bring you good luck."

"I know," LeBoeuf said. "Still…" The official language, a gift from a king, the signature of the king himself, the description of an estate, the seed of an empire, maybe. LeBoeuf loved to look on it.

Henriette gave a long, dramatic sigh but LeBoeuf ignored her. A moment later she set in again.

"And speaking of luck," she continued, still trying to get a reaction from LeBoeuf, a thing she had been trying and failing at since he had first purchased her on the beach. "*Navire Chanceux* is a stupid name for a ship. What could be more unlucky than to name a ship *Lucky Ship*?"

"I don't know about luck," LeBoeuf said.

"That's obvious. Just look at you. I would not say luck has been your friend."

"I've no need for your opinion," LeBoeuf said. "Sailors have enough superstitions already without you making up more." And then, since she had finally managed to touch a nerve, he added, "The name is fine and it's the name and that's an end to it. You know nothing about these things."

Just as you know nothing about the Tuileries, you silly tart, he thought, *since you've never been there, have you?*

In the cave she had entertained him with a lovingly detailed description of the royal palace, its grounds and its interior. LeBoeuf knew her description for what it was: an impressive work of imagination.

He had never said as much to her, had rarely even thought about it. But he did now because he was annoyed, even more annoyed than when

Henriette was at her most biting, and he knew why: that name, *Navire Chanceux*, bothered him as well. The others had hit upon and liked it. None of them seemed to think it unlucky, and he had no other name in mind, so he agreed, just to maintain the *esprite de corps*. He meant to change it as soon as he could. But he did not care to have Henriette remind him of his concerns.

He continued to stare at the fine text on the velum scroll and said no more.

"Humph," Henriette said. She rolled on her back and folded her arms. That noncommittal sound was her way of getting the last word when she judged that one more actual word would be one word too many, even when talking to the dull-witted LeBoeuf.

Tortuga… he thought. He had never actually been there, only heard tales of the place. It was only a few years before that the French established something that might be considered a town on that mountainous, jungle-covered island. The Spanish considered it their own, of course, as they did all of the West Indies, but they did not seem to have the resources or the motivation to drive the interlopers out. For Paris it was a foothold…a toehold…like St. Christopher and Nevis. It was French now, and that claim was only going to grow stronger as Spain grew weaker.

It was that very uncertainty that made Tortuga so damned attractive. Beyond the edge of government and law, a blank slate, a wild country. The sort of people who wished to live and do business beyond the reach of government and laws were already swarming to the place.

LeBoeuf did not know what this fellow, this Chevalier Philippe Guillemeau de Beaune, to whom the letter patent had been issued, had in mind, but he could well imagine. Set up a plantation to which he had an unshakable legal right, regardless of what Paris ended up doing with the island. Grow tobacco, import goods from the continent, fit out privateers. It was as if the fog was lifting to reveal an extraordinary vista LeBoeuf did not even know was there.

And here he was, standing on the edge.

Hendrick Harmansz Van Lauwersoog, known to the community of buccaneers as Van Loudersong, was a patient man, an observant man. He watched, he took note, he studied the interplay of those around him, the friendships and the jealousies and the petty hostilities. He found it endlessly fascinating, and often profitable.

For that reason he had not missed it when, a week or so earlier, the little rat Le Rongeur had surreptitiously called LeBoeuf to the stern of the ship for a private word.

As he watched it play out, Van Loudersong could not quite imagine what was going on there. Le Rongeur was terrified of LeBoeuf. That was obvious. And well he might be. Matelotage notwithstanding, LeBoeuf despised Le Rongeur. The only reason LeBoeuf had not yet killed the little bastard, or so Van Loudersong reckoned, was that he did not think it worth the effort. LeBoeuf probably figured someone else would kill Le Rongeur soon enough, and that was not an unreasonable assumption.

LeBoeuf ignored Le Rongeur's summons at first, but then he relented, mounting the steps to the quarterdeck and following Le Rongeur aft. Van Loudersong stood and drifted toward the bow, where he could see over the break of the deck to where the two men stood at the ship's stern. He watched them from there, but there was nothing much to see. At one point LeBoeuf seemed to advance of Le Rongeur as if he had finally decided to kill him, and then stopped, but it was not entirely clear what had happened.

Eventually Le Rongeur came back down to the waist, leaving LeBoeuf alone, smoking and apparently lost in thought. As much thought as a great, dull ox like LeBoeuf could summon, which was not much. Or so Van Loudersong had long assumed. But he was starting to wonder.

*Very strange…*Van Loudersong thought as he drifted back among the others. Something was going on there. He would have to discover what it was. Hendrick Harmansz Van Lauwersoog was on the lookout for opportunity. He was looking to make his fortune. Again.

Van Loudersong — Hendrick Harmansz Van Lauwersoog — considered life to be much like an ocean voyage, the result of having spent a majority of his years at sea. One encountered many things in life, a great spectrum, just as one did at sea. Some of those things were good, some bad. Some could make you rich, some could make you dead. Calms, storms, great wealth, desperate poverty, hope, despair — his voyage had seen it all.

He had not been born into the sort of desperate squalor from whence most of the miserable buccaneers had sprung. Born in The Hague, the second son of a successful merchant father, a man with connections who was able to secure a berth for young Hendrick as midshipman in the ever-expanding navy of the Netherlands. He entered the service at twelve years old, a boy raised in relative luxury, terrified of the rolling, stinking, brutal new world into which he had been thrust.

The fear did not last long. He advanced quickly, being smart and driven and as ruthless as he needed be to achieve his ambitions. From a midshipman's berth to a lieutenant's commission Van Lauwersoog grew from boy to man, not a terribly tall man, but strong and athletic, and his knowledge, his insight, his ambitions grew as well. He sailed with old men-of-war's men, tough as boiled leather, who had been part of the notorious Sea Beggars in younger years. He learned from them that rules and authority stood as impediments to dreams of wealth and power.

It was an easy step from the naval service to privateering, and not long before privateering brought him to the West Indies, where real fortunes were to be made. He had his hands in a variety of endeavors, some of which paid off big, some of which swept that wealth away like the hurricano had done to their camp.

It was his last bad decision, joining up with a Frenchman in a poorly planned raid on Santa Marta in the Audiencia of Santa Fé that left him penniless on the buccaneer coast. But he had spent the past year rebuilding his wealth and he was penniless no longer. But neither was he rich, and now he was looking for the next big chance.

He wondered if perhaps he had caught a glimpse of it, in this secretive discussion between LeBoeuf and Le Rongeur.

It would be a good thing, to slaughter that great ox LeBoeuf, Van Loudersong thought.

He had not given LeBoeuf much thought in the ten months or so that they had been fellow hunters and boucaniers. LeBoeuf seemed pretty much like the others, some miserable creature who had always been a miserable creature and would continue to be so for the remainder of his short life. Bigger, stronger, quieter, dumber than most, but generally not too different from the rest of the breed.

The incident with the cave had changed that. How LeBoeuf knew about the cave Van Loudersong did not know, but it made him furious that he did, and his revealing it made Van Loudersong more furious still.

LeBoeuf had not been the only one to see the hurricano coming. It had been the Dutchman's intention to steal off to the cave on his own just before the storm rolled over them, secure himself there, let the others fend for themselves. When the devastation was over, Van Loudersong would glean whatever was left behind.

The great ox had ruined that plan. Worse, he had forced Van Loudersong to find a new place to hide his loot, lest one of the thieving bastards on the beach make his way back to the cave and clean it out.

His fury with LeBoeuf was mollified a bit when the idiot agreed to give up his share of the loot in the hold of the wrecked ship in exchange for the ship itself. A fool's bargain that helped Van Loudersong further enrich himself and demonstrated that LeBoeuf was indeed as stupid as he seemed. But even there things had not worked out as Van Loudersong had envisioned.

The barque had been more seaworthy that Van Loudersong thought, and with the dearth of shipping in the wake of the hurricano it gave LeBoeuf quite a bit of leverage. LeBoeuf was lucky, if nothing else, and he had effectively fended off Van Loudersong's attempts to wrest control of the vessel from him.

Dumb bastard...I've had enough of him... Van Loudersong thought as he strolled aft again and rejoined the others. He drank his wine, smoked his pipe, made jokes, but he kept his lookout sharp. LeBoeuf remained aft on the quarterdeck. Le Rongeur had disappeared below, and when he emerged on deck once more he had a blanket rolled around what Van Loudersong guessed were his pathetic belongings.

Going ashore, are you? he thought. That was an interesting development. Le Rongeur had always stuck close to LeBoeuf, hoping to win him over, Van Loudersong imagined. A ridiculous notion. But now the man seemed intent on not remaining alone in LeBoeuf's company.

Interesting.

And just as Van Loudersong suspected, when it came time for the men to return to their camp on the beach, to bed down on shore after a long day of work, Le Rongeur joined them. And that meant that there was something going on between Le Rongeur and LeBoeuf, and Van Loudersong would have to know what it was.

How will we do this? Van Loudersong thought as he watched Le Rongeur shuffling up the beach, looking for a place to unroll his blanket.

There were two obvious approaches. He could hold a knife to Le Rongeur's throat and insist that the nasty vermin tell him everything he and LeBoeuf had discussed. Or he could cultivate a friendship with the miserable bastard and gather the information that way.

The first approach had much to recommend it. It was quick and did not involve the distasteful act of befriending Le Rongeur. But it was also less reliable. A man with a knife to his throat would not necessarily say what was true but rather what he thought would keep him alive. If Van Loudersong then cut his throat there would be no more information to be had. If he didn't cut his throat then there was no telling what mischief Le Rongeur might get up to.

So, it was friendship.

"Holloa, there, Le Rongeur," Van Loudersong called as he approached the man. Le Rongeur turned and looked at him. There was moonlight enough for Van Loudersong to see the wariness on the man's rat face.

"Van Loudersong..." he said, a noncommittal reply.

"Come, bed down near me," Van Loudersong said. "I have some wine. Let's have a glass."

Le Rongeur did not reply, nor did he move, which did not surprise Van Loudersong. The man was not used to finding a welcome anywhere, so naturally he would be suspicious when one came his way.

"See here, my man," Van Loudersong said. "I'll be honest. I've felt sorry for you. I see how that ox LeBoeuf treats you. And you so loyal to him. Matelotage means nothing to the man, I can see that."

Le Rongeur grunted. "Don't mean nothing to him," he agreed.

"Well, come, have a cup of wine with me," Van Loudersong said. "Soon enough we sail away from this damnable beach and we'll be done with him. You get your part of *Navire Chanceux*'s cargo. Plus the share that LeBoeuf stupidly gave up. That's a respectable amount of money you'll make. Not so bad, with what you've had to suffer from that ox."

Le Rongeur nodded and followed Van Loudersong up the beach to where the Dutchman had set up a small lean-to and made his temporary camp. He poured two cups of wine and handed one to Le Rongeur. They took their seats.

"LeBoeuf must be a miserable bastard to share a camp with," Van Loudersong said. He took a sip of wine and steeled himself for what he knew would come next: a seemingly endless and utterly tedious diatribe about the horrors that LeBoeuf had unleashed on Le Rongeur and the rest of the known world.

Van Loudersong knew Le Rongeur's sort. All that discontent and fury bottled up, he was like a loaded cannon with its muzzle plugged tight — put a spark to the powder charge and the whole thing blows to hell.

This is the work I must do, Van Loudersong reminded himself as Le Rongeur went on and on like a lover spurned. Every task had its unpleasant aspects, every worthwhile effort involved doing some miserable thing or other. In this instance it meant hearing Le Rongeur's raving.

Not listening, of course. Just hearing. Van Loudersong had no idea what the man was saying because he was paying not the least bit of attention. Still, he had no choice but to endure the buzzing of Le Rongeur's voice, and that was unpleasant enough.

It took several evenings of that. Le Rongeur did not return to the ship, but rather joined the men going out into the field to hunt pigs. That was too bad. Van Loudersong would have liked to watch him and LeBoeuf together. He might have gleaned more information from observing that interaction. But Le Rongeur's decision to go hunting also told Van Loudersong quite a bit.

While Le Rongeur hunted pigs, Van Loudersong did his part in hauling the cargo out to *Navire Chanceux* and storing it down in the hold for the short voyage to Tortuga. It was a tedious process with only a smattering of small boats to move the goods and the need to keep everything separated into each man's particular hoard. At night he and Le Rongeur would meet again at camp and Van Loudersong would feed Le Rongeur his cheapest wine and nod patiently as the little shit went on and on. Occasionally Van Loudersong would ask a question, stoke the outrage and resentment, watch as Le Rongeur sunk deeper into the embrace of the wine.

Until, finally, Van Loudersong judged that Le Rongeur's trust and intoxication had reached their proper levels.

"I sympathize, my friend," Van Loudersong said, when LeBoeuf had paused long enough to take a drink. "Still, I see LeBoeuf confides in you."

"He does?" Le Rongeur asked, confused.

"Well, certainly," Van Loudersong said. "When was it...the day we finished work on the ship. Five days ago? I saw you call to him, ask him to join you in the stern, and he did. Seemed to me you two had a friendly talk."

Le Rongeur smirked, a coy and knowing look. "Yes, he talked to me all right," he said. "Didn't have much choice."

"No?" Van Loudersong said, taking care to sound only vaguely curious. "Why not? I guess he could have ignored you, if he wished."

"No," Le Rongeur said. "Not when I know something that's so important to him."

"Indeed? Very mysterious." Van Loudersong did not ask what that thing was. He knew he did not need to. Le Rongeur would not be able to hold a secret any longer than he could hold his urine after drinking so much wine.

"See, here's the thing of it..." Le Rongeur began a moment later, leaning closer and speaking in a soft voice.

"Yes?" Van Loudersong said. He, too, leaned in closer, and relished the fact that the brutal work of listening to Le Rongeur for all those hours was about to pay off.

Chapter Thirty-One

Mayor Nicolás Pérez de Maldonaldo was sitting on a wooden chair, elaborately carved and upholstered in rich fabric, a small table to his left on which sat two cups of tea on two saucers. Sitting on the far side of the table in an identical chair was Carlos Hernández, the ubiquitous Carlos Hernández.

Don Nicolás had expected to be a happy man of late, but he was not, and he meant to find out why that was. He suspected that Hernández, of all men, could explain the reasons for his discontent.

Greetings made, tea served, servants dismissed, the two men sat opposite one another. Neither man spoke or even moved. Music was playing somewhere out in the courtyard of Las Casas Reales. It came drifting softly into the mayor's office but neither man made mention of it. Like fencers, each waiting for the other to take the first thrust, to make a move that could be exploited.

"I thank you, Señor, for coming so promptly," Nicolás said at last, leaning over and taking up his teacup. He had only so much patience for such games, nor did he really need to play them, not when the power he wielded in Santo Domingo was so vastly greater than that of the villain sitting across from him.

Hernández shrugged. "It is my pleasure to do the bidding of my mayor," he said.

It is, and it had better stay that way, Nicolás thought. That sorry little turd Alonso Menéndez de Aviles might go slinking down to the lower town seeking an audience with Carlos Hernández, but Nicolás de Maldonaldo did not. If Don Nicolás wished to speak to Carlos Hernández then Carlos Hernández would come to him, and he would come quickly when summoned.

Alonso Menéndez, the mayor suspected, found it exciting to walk is disguise through those rough streets. He probably fancied himself a dangerous individual, the head of some great, illicit enterprise. A man to be feared.

Pathetic shit, Nicolás thought.

Still, thinking of Menéndez made him uneasy, and stoked the smoldering fury that had led him to summoning Hernández to Las Casas Reales. After the beating, and, more to the point, after what El Cinco had inflicted on him, all five of them, Don Nicolás expected Alonso Menéndez to be a visibly broken man. He had expected him to be unable to meet the eyes of other men. He had expected him to sequester himself in his apartments, to shun public events. He had expected the shame and humiliation of being used in the way the five had used him to put an end to the silly upstart's pretensions. But as far as he could tell, it had not.

"Tell me," Don Nicolás said, pronouncing the words slow and precise to convey all the threat that he meant to convey. "What happened with our friend the lieutenant-governor?"

Carlos Hernández frowned. "You know all that I know, Señor. We were there together for the...the first act. I left with you. You know that. I did not have the stomach for what would come next."

Don Nicolás stared at him. Hernández was always so cool, so unflappable. He betrayed nothing. It was one of the qualities that made him so good at his business. And his business, Don Nicolás understood, was to further himself by playing every man against another, with genuine loyalty toward none save Carlos Hernández.

But for all his singular self-interest, Carlos Hernández was still a partner worth cultivating. His cunning was legendary and his contacts in the West Indies and beyond were unmatched. When those things were harnessed the man could be a valuable ally. The only way to render him trustworthy, however, was to be the one who could do him the most good, as well as the most harm. That man was Don Nicolás, on both counts. He thought Carlos Hernández understood that.

"I returned here," Don Nicolás said, indicating his office with a sweep of his hand. "You remained in your warehouse. You must have some notion of what took place."

"I do not. I did not remain in my warehouse. I did not want to hear, any more than I wanted to see."

Don Nicolás stared at him. Hernández stared back, unflinching. "You saw no one come or go?" the mayor said. "El Cinco? You did not see the little turd, Alonso, when he crawled out of there?"

Hernández shook his head. "There are some things I like to be witness to," he said. "Some things I do not. When it was over I went back and locked the door. By then they were gone."

"This morning the little turd joined the governor and me for an inspection of the city," Don Nicolás said. He could hear the calm slipping from his voice and he forced it back again. "It has been what? Five days? I did not expect him to be able to sit a horse yet, never mind show his face in public. Yet there he was, as if nothing had happened. Did nothing happen?"

Hernández shrugged. "As I said, I know nothing more than you. Less, probably."

They fell silent again, the fencers, weapons *en guarde*. "Tell me of the cargo that Maja brought in," Don Nicolás said at last.

At the mention of that agreeable subject Hernández nodded. "It was what Maja said. Excellent. Worth...a great deal. The filibusteros, the ones Maja took the cargo from, they must have been very lucky. Very lucky. Until they met Maja of course. When men meet Maja, that's generally the end of their luck."

"It's ashore?" the mayor asked. "The cargo? It's in your warehouse?"

"Yes, Don Nicolás," Hernández said. "Safe in the side room. I'm waiting word from a man I know in Veracruz. I think that will be the best market for you."

"What of the blackbirds? Did Maja send the slaves ashore, too?"

"I don't deal in slaves," Hernández said. "You know that. Maja knows that. He might have sent them to someone else, but he did not send them to me. I would have thought he told you where he sent them."

Don Nicolás nodded thoughtfully. Maja had not told him what he had done with the slaves. In fact, he'd had no word from Maja for days. Nor had any of his people seen any sign of the savage during that time. A picture was beginning to form in Don Nicolás's mind, and it was one of the sources of his unhappiness.

"And my ship?" he asked softly.

"*Santa Rosa*? She's fine. She still rides at anchor in the river."

Don Nicolás nodded again, his face as calm as Hernández's, so calm that Hernández could not see that his smug and slightly obsequious tone, his willful ignorance, had finally pushed Nicolás over the edge of the abyss.

There were few who really understood Don Nicolás Pérez de Maldonaldo. The mayor. Fat and jovial and not terribly clever: Nicolás presented that façade because it was much advantage to do so, but those things were not who he was.

Even those who knew him by his other title, Señor Corregidor, did not always understand his true nature and what he was capable of doing. Hernández knew Señor Corregidor, but he seemed to have forgotten just who Señor Corregidor was. Time for another lesson.

Don Nicolás shot to his feet, a motion so fast and unexpected that Carlos Hernández could only open his mouth and eyes wide in surprise. The mayor took two steps and drove a beautifully polished boot into Hernández's chest, sending him sprawling back, his arms and legs flying in a most satisfying way, the delicate wooden chair shattering under him.

Nicolás leapt forward, kicking the debris of the chair out of his way, pulling the dagger from the sheath on his belt. It was an ornamental thing, worn as an accessory to his clothing, but it was good steel nonetheless, and sharp as a razor. He knelt, as if to say prayers, one knee on Hernández's chest. Here was something else that few understood about Don Nicolás: he was much quicker and much more powerful than one would think him to be.

Hernández was just trying to push himself to his elbows when Nicolás's knee drove him back down to the floor. His arms were reaching up to grab Nicolás's doublet or his throat or hair, anything to give him purchase enough to get the big man off him. But before he could get hold, Nicolás's knife was at his throat, edge pressed into the skin, a little trickle of blood already running down the man's neck.

The cool edge of the dagger took the fight out of Hernández. He stopped, arms still up, motionless, his eyes wide and looking up at Don Nicolás. Slowly he lowered his arms back to the floor.

"We have...several ventures together now, don't we?" Nicolás asked and Hernández nodded, as much as the dagger allowed him to nod.

"And if I kill you, I stand to lose money, don't I?"

Hernández nodded again.

"But I don't care," Nicolás explained. "I would rather spill your filthy blood all over my lovely carpet then suffer a second more of your disrespect. Do you believe that?" He moved the knife away a fraction of an inch to allow Hernández to speak.

"I would never disrespect you, Don Nicolás ..." he began. Nicolás pressed the knife against his throat once more and Hernández gasped and shut his mouth.

"Words..." Don Nicolás said. "They mean nothing. Particularly coming from a man like you, you understand? You show respect by telling me the truth. Because I could kill you here and my people would roll you up in this carpet and carry you away and that would be an end to it. You believe that?"

Once again Hernández gave his stunted nod. Nicolás paused and looked into Hernández's eyes. There was fear there, to be certain. But he could see the calculation as well: Hernández weighing the odds of Señor Corregidor's actually carrying through with the threat. Would he throw away the small fortune in fiscal entanglements that would surely be lost if Carlos Hernández were to disappear, just to punish a lack of respect?

In truth, Don Nicolás did not know himself, and he would not know until he had either released the man or cut his throat.

"Now," Nicolás continued, once again easing the pressure on the knife. "When I said let's talk about my ship, I did not mean the *Santa Rosa*. You know I did not mean the *Santa Rosa*. I meant the other one. The one that belonged to the whore's son Graves, before Maja took it. That ship is not, in fact, at anchor in the river." He had noticed that during the inspection that morning. How long it had been gone he did not know. He had not left

Las Casas Reales in days, eager as he was to observe the results of his handiwork on the lieutenant governor.

For a moment Hernández did not answer, and again Nicolás could see the calculation in his eyes. Whatever Hernández had to say, he knew that the mayor would not like it. But he also knew that the mayor would like falsehoods and equivocating even less. Nicolás could practically hear the merchant sifting through the truth and lies as he tried to assemble the story that was least likely to get his throat cut.

"Maja took the ship, Don Nicolás," Hernández said, all but gasping the words.

"And Graves? And the blackbirds? He took them with him?"

"Yes, Don Nicolás." There was real fear in his eyes now, as well there should be. The loss of the slaves and the ship would make Don Nicolás furious, Hernández understood that, but he understood as well that it was nothing compared to the loss of Graves and Maja's betrayal. Hernández had known about it for days, and he had said nothing.

For a long moment Nicolás did not speak or move, he just looked into Hernández's eyes and let the man suffer with the question of what he would get: life, or immediate death, or something in between. In truth Don Nicolás's fury had gone to a place even he did not recognize, a fury so profound that he was paralyzed by it, an outrage so complete he was unable to act or even move. It took him some time before he could speak again.

"Where did they go?" he asked softly.

"They went after a ship, Don Nicolás. I knew nothing of this at the time, I have only heard of it from others, I swear to all that is holy," Hernández said. During the moment of silence he had clearly figured out what he would say.

"A ship?"

"A ship that Alonso told them of. I don't know how true this is, I hear it from others, but Alonso told them of a ship that had come out with the convoy that brought him from Spain," Hernández said. "A brigantine that seemed to have survived the hurricano. It had something aboard of great value. I don't know what. Treasure? Some cargo of great value? Something that made it worth the trouble to go after."

Don Nicolás frowned. *A brigantine?* He would expect a galleon or a big merchantman to carry something of great value, but not so insubstantial a vessel as a brigantine.

"Where are they looking for this brigantine?" Don Nicolás asked.

"Hispaniola. The northwest coast. A league or so east of Tortuga. What they call *la costa bucanero.*"

La costa bucanero...the buccaneer coast... That added another layer of difficulty. If those rogues had not been wiped out by the hurricano, and if they had taken hold of the brigantine first, then it might be no easy matter to wrest it from them. He looked back at Hernández.

"And this is the first you've heard of this? This brigantine?"

"Yes, Don Nicolás," Hernández said, a bit too emphatically. "That turd Alonso came to me about his cargo, the one aboard *León de Bilbao*, and I came to you right away. I would have done the same if I had known about the brigantine."

Don Nicolás stared at him for a moment. He suspected the man was lying, that he had known about this brigantine all along and for whatever reason he had been holding out. Hoping to cultivate the new lieutenant governor, no doubt, thinking that the man was a new potential source of wealth.

Whatever this little weasel intended, it does not matter, Don Nicolás thought. He knew about the brigantine now, and how valuable it was, and that was what mattered. And the men who had gone after it, the mixed-blood mongrel Maja and that thieving bastard Graves, they had betrayed him and he knew that too. That was what mattered.

He looked down at Carlos Hernández, still pinned to the floor under his knee. "You find a master who isn't a drunken fool, someone who can be trusted," he said. "You get a crew together and you send them after the dog Maja in *Santa Rosa*. You understand? I want Maja, I want Graves, and I want the cargo of that brigantine. You see that *Santa Rosa* is off to sea on tomorrow's ebb tide or by God you'll regret it."

Hernández nodded and suddenly Don Nicolás felt the fury boiling up again. This man had betrayed him as much as Maja had. He could not go unpunished. Don Nicolás might have further need of him, but still he could not go unpunished. There had to be consequences. There had to be a lesson taught.

He reached out and grabbed the top of Hernández's left ear and with a quick swipe of his dagger cut the upper part of the ear clean off. Blood poured from the wound like wine from a cup knocked over.

"Ahh! Bastard!" Hernández shouted and clapped his left hand over his ear, thrashing under the mayor's knee. "Bastard!"

Don Nicolás leaned closer and held the severed section of ear up in front of Hernández's face. "You see this?" he asked, but Hernández's eyes were closed and his teeth clenched. Nicolás pushed his knee harder into Hernández's chest and Hernández opened his eyes and looked at the ear and looked at Nicolás.

"You see this?" Nicolás asked again and this time Hernández nodded. "You take it. Go on, take it." He waited a moment for Hernández to understand the command. Slowly the man reached out with his right hand and Don Nicolás placed the bloody ear in his palm.

"You keep this," Nicolás said. "You keep it with you. Every time I see you, you will show me this ear. Do you understand? That way I'll know that you remember what happens when you try to cheat me. Do you understand?"

It took Hernández a moment, but then he nodded his head.

"Good," Nicolás said, and with a groan he lifted his knee from Hernández's chest and pushed himself to his feet. Hernández remained on the floor for a moment, until the mayor had taken a step back, and then he stood as well, hand still clapped over his ear, blood running through his fingers.

"Go now," Nicolás said. He turned his back and walked away, Carlos Hernández already forgotten, his mind working on what riches this alleged brigantine could possibly contain.

Chapter Thirty-Two

Jean-Baptiste LeBoeuf was not surprised to hear Van Loudersong hail from aloft. He had been waiting for it: the summons, the private *tête-à-tête* in some corner of the ship.

"Holloa there, LeBoeuf," the Dutchman called down.

LeBoeuf looked up at the maintop, forty feet above. He squinted against the glare of the mid-afternoon sun. "Yes?"

"There's a crack here at the base of the topmast," Van Loudersong called back down. "Could bring the mast down if it goes. Reckon you better come have a look."

LeBoeuf sighed. As a reason to call him up to the maintop it was as good as any, though he knew perfectly well that the topmast was as sound as a spar could be. Everything aloft was as sound as it could be. He had personally made certain that it was.

"I'll be up directly," LeBoeuf called back. He looked around the deck. The sight was all too familiar. Forty or more buccaneers sprawled out in the shade, sleeping, smoking pipes, chewing on dried meat, drinking ale or rumbullian. Familiar, mostly, but different as well.

The women, for one thing. It was not just the buccaneers crowding the decks now but also the dozen women who had been part of the hunting camp. And there were no tools, no gear, no half-made spars or rigging hauled out on a stretch. The work was done, the ship was complete, the cargo stowed down. They were waiting now for those things that sailors had waited for since the dawn of seafaring: wind and tide.

The final bits of cargo had come aboard an hour before the last of the ebb. An hour after that, when they finished stowing it in the hold and battening the hatches down, the wind was light and the tide was coming in and the current was pushing *Navire Chanceux* toward the beach. If they had weighed anchor then, the ship would have been hard on the sand and heeling over mere minutes after the hook had broken free.

So they would have to wait. Wait until the end of the flood tide and the beginning of the ebb when the current would sweep the ship out to sea, with plenty of water under the keel. But that would not happen until well after dark, at which point they would not be able to feel their way through the tricky new sandbars laid down by the hurricano. So they would wait through the next tide as well, and hope to be underway at the beginning of the ebb on the following day.

It was maddening. It was part of the mariner's life. It was something LeBoeuf had encountered hundreds of times during his years at sea. But it was maddening nonetheless.

It was also maddening to see men laying idle on deck, smoking and drinking and sleeping. But there was genuinely nothing that needed doing, and the buccaneers were not about to do anything that LeBoeuf might order them to do just to keep them busy.

And the only reason he was even thinking about any of that, he knew, was to put off having to deal with whatever unwelcome shit Van Loudersong was about to shovel at his feet.

He sighed again, then stepped onto a pinrail and swung himself up into the shrouds and started to climb. He checked each ratline as he made his way up, inspected each hitch and seizing without even being aware that he was doing it. He reached the futtock shrouds and scrambled up and over the edge of the round maintop.

Van Loudersong was sitting on the far side, arms folded, a smug look on his face. LeBoeuf wondered if he could take two quick steps across the top and shove the Dutchman over the edge, but he guessed Van Loudersong would be too nimble to be caught that way.

This is your own damnable fault, you know, LeBoeuf chastised himself, which it was, but not entirely. He had meant to kill Le Rongeur long before this, but the little bastard had been surprisingly adept at staying out of reach. He had at least hoped Le Rongeur would keep their secret to himself, but that was a ridiculous thing to hope for.

He wondered how hard it had been for Van Loudersong to get it out of him. Not hard, he imagined.

"Don't bother looking for a split in the mast, there is none," Van Loudersong said, though LeBoeuf had made no move to inspect the mast. Instead he stepped down into the top and looked at Van Loudersong and said nothing.

"I've been talking with that tedious little rat Le Rongeur," Van Loudersong said. He paused, hoping apparently for some reaction from LeBoeuf, but in that he was disappointed, so he went on. "He tells me there was more aboard this ship than we knew. Something you've failed to mention to the others."

LeBoeuf had no patience for Van Loudersong's coy games. "There was," he said. "I failed to mention it. And you won't mention it either."

"No," Van Loudersong said. "No, I won't. I'm not the sort who is much given to sharing."

"You better kill Le Rongeur, then," LeBoeuf said.

"In due time. Right now it serves me to have him alive. Because, as it stands, you'd have to kill us both if you want to keep the riches to yourself."

"I could do that," LeBoeuf said.

"Ah, but before one of us is able to tell the others? I think not."

LeBoeuf nodded. He had wondered why Van Loudersong was bothering to tell him any of this, and there it was. As long as both Le Rongeur and Van Loudersong knew about the gold, LeBoeuf could not kill either one without the other revealing the secret to the company of buccaneers. Not checkmate, but a clever check, and it made LeBoeuf furious.

"Le Rongeur expects me to share out the gold with him before we weigh anchor," LeBoeuf said, but Van Loudersong gave a dismissive wave of his hand.

"Le Rongeur expects nothing save for what I tell him to expect," Van Loudersong said.

Well, that's one problem solved, LeBoeuf thought. With sailing imminent, he had been wondering how he would get around Le Rongeur's demand.

"We'll share out this gold when we reach Tortuga," Van Loudersong continued. "Share it out two ways. You and me."

LeBoeuf nodded. The Dutchman, of course, had no intention of sharing anything. He would find some means to kill LeBoeuf and then dispose of Le Rongeur at his leisure.

Sod him and sod the gold, LeBoeuf thought. As soon as they sailed he would announce to the ship's company that he had discovered the hidden wealth under the deck. He'd tell them he had found it just that moment. Tell them that it, like the cargo, was to be shared by all.

The buccaneers would be so delighted by the windfall that they would not question how long LeBoeuf had known about it. Henriette would be disappointed, certainly, but Van Loudersong and Le Rongeur would be furious, and that alone would make the loss of a fortune worthwhile. Stalemate. Still, it was better than letting the Dutchman win.

"Very well," LeBoeuf said. "When we reach Tortuga, we split it, you and me." He turned away, unable to bear Van Loudersong's half-smile of triumph. As he turned he scanned the horizon to the north and then stopped as something caught his eye. He frowned and squinted and concentrated on the anomaly far off over the light blue water.

"What is it?" Van Loudersong asked.

"Sail," LeBoeuf said.

"Sail? A ship?" Behind him LeBoeuf heard Van Loudersong stand and he felt the maintop shake as the Dutchman stepped across.

"No," LeBoeuf said. "Boat, it looks like." It was far off, a mile and a half at least, but LeBoeuf could make out the distinctive shape of a lug sail, the dark slash on the water that was the boat's hull. Not a small boat, to be visible over that distance: twenty or twenty-five feet long, LeBoeuf guessed.

Van Loudersong made a grunting sound. "Turtle hunters," he said, as if that was the definitive explanation. He turned and stepped up onto the rail of the maintop, swung outboard of the shrouds and climbed down without speaking another word. The Dutchman was not one for endless talk. It was one of the very few things that LeBoeuf appreciated about the man.

LeBoeuf kept his eyes on the boat, moving slowly east to west. It was the first bit of humanity he had seen in weeks outside the company of buccaneers, the first since that one ship had poked its nose into the bay and then sailed off again. With his mind and body concentrated on bringing his own ship back to life, it had not really occurred to LeBoeuf how odd it was, in so well-traveled a part of the world, to so rarely see anything moving out on the water.

He continued to watch the boat as it made its slow transit along the horizon, a boat like many thousands such boats in the West Indies. He could not fathom why the sight of it gave him such an uneasy feeling in his gut.

Idiot... he thought. *You're too twisted up in your own daydreams, you're seeing monsters under the bed, like a child.* He watched the shape of the distant sail change, the dark line of its hull foreshorten as the boat tacked around, turning one hundred and eighty degrees and settling on its new course, west to east.

LeBoeuf frowned and slowly scratched his chin through his thick beard. *They came about,* he thought. *That's all they did. They came about. Is there anything strange in that? It's what boats do.*

There was nothing strange in that. But still it added to that uneasy feeling.

He looked off to the east. The countryside inland from the long, sweeping arc of beach was mostly flat, but the eastern end of the bay terminated in an odd hump of a headland that blocked the view of the sea beyond. If there was a ship anchored behind that headland, or two, or the entire plate fleet, he would not be able to see it.

Turtle hunters, LeBoeuf thought as he grabbed hold of the topmast shrouds and began climbing back to deck. He did not often agree with Van Loudersong, and in his heart he did not agree with him now, but he forced himself to believe that the man was right.

Henriette was waiting by the main shrouds as he swung himself back onto the deck. "What did that Dutch bastard want?" she asked, her voice soft enough to not be heard by anyone who was listening, though no one was.

"Showed me a crack in the topmast. It won't be a problem. Don't fear."

She glared at him, arms folded. "That was it?"

"Yes. Why?"

Henriette shook her head. "I don't know. That little turd Le Rongeur. He's been acting...I don't know. He's been acting. That's all I can say. And Van Loudersong. Like something's going on and he's pretending it isn't. I can smell his lies even through the stink of all you pig hunters."

LeBoeuf nodded. He was impressed. She had seen through Van Loudersong's charade and insulted every one of the buccaneers, all in one sentence.

How long until she sees through my *lies?* he wondered. *She'll know soon enough that I was lying about Van Loudersong. I wonder if she'll see deeper than that.*

"Don't worry about Van Loudersong or Le Rongeur," he said. "We'll be free of them soon."

"Humph," Henriette said. "How soon? Why aren't we sailing?"

"I told you, the tide is coming in now. If we try to sail we'll end up on the beach."

"That was hours ago," Henriette said. "The tide is still coming in?"

"Yes. It will be hours before it turns, and by then it will be dark and we dare not sail in the dark," LeBoeuf explained, not for the first time.

Henriette made a sound that conveyed her exasperation and disgust. "Do you know anything of sailing ships?" she asked, then answered the question herself. "I think not."

LeBoeuf opened his mouth, ready to offer her command, but she turned and marched off before he could land even that weak riposte.

The sun was starting to drop low and the women were cooking stew over a makeshift brick fireplace that had been built up on the deck. LeBoeuf stayed in the waist long enough to eat and drink several cups of ale and smoke his pipe. He spoke a few words with the others, but mostly he listened, as was his wont.

Van Loudersong held court, as was *his* wont, loud and jocular, droll and clever. Le Rongeur stayed clear, hanging at the edge of the crowd, as far from LeBoeuf as he could get and still be part of the company.

It was full dark when LeBoeuf bid the others good night, leaving them with the assurance that the next day would bring the right combination of daylight and tide for them to weigh the anchor and stand out to sea, even if they had to tow the ship with the boats. He walked aft, forcing himself to move at his usual lumbering pace, despite the energy shooting through him like St. Elmo's fire.

All of it — the hidden gold, the letter patent, Henriette, Van Loudersong, Le Rongeur, Tortuga, the ship, the strange boat — it was all whirling around in his head, so many considerations, so many variables, ingredients in a great stew of anxiety, a foreign and unwelcome feeling. The appeal of hunting pigs on the buccaneer coast was the absolute simplicity of the life, but the hurricano had wiped that away just as it had so much else.

He opened the door to the master's cabin and ducked his head and stepped inside. A lantern was hanging from a hook over the table. Henriette was sitting on the settee aft, her legs drawn up and her arms around her knees. She was looking out the stern windows but seeing only her reflection in the dark glass.

LeBoeuf paused where he stood. He waited for her to say something but she did not even look over at him. He let his eyes move around the cabin, which was mostly lost in deep shadow. He could feel in his gut a desire to do something, a great urgency to do it, but what it was he could not fathom.

His eyes settled on a sleeve of oiled canvas leaning against the cabin side, the sword he claimed to have liberated from a dead Spanish officer, and he realized what it was that he felt called to do. He made his way around the table and lifted the sword, holding it carefully as if it was a delicate object, which is most certainly was not. He untied the cord that was holding the sleeve closed and pulled the weapon out of the stiff cloth.

The grip was bound in silver wire and the pommel was oval shaped and fluted like some sort of exotic fruit. The guard was made up of elegantly curved, brightly-polished bends of steel that wove around in an almost mysterious pattern, creating a deceptively complete protection for the hand.

He took hold of the grip and drew the sword part-way out of the lacquered wood scabbard. Below the guard the blade was straight and long. The weapon seemed oversized, like a normal sword that had grown too large, but it fit LeBoeuf's massive hand perfectly. A sword that would have felt awkward and heavy to another man felt to LeBoeuf like an extension of his arm.

He sheathed the sword and set it down on the table, then bent over and pulled a wooden chest out from under the settee. This he set on the table as well and opened the lid. Inside rested two braces of wheellock pistols, nice weapons, a gentleman's weapons, but still more functional than ornate.

Along with the pistols, the box contained powder and balls, a spanner for cocking the weapons and sundry supplies for cleaning. LeBoeuf had found the guns and accoutrements in the master's cabin, well-hidden, missed by the others, and he decided to consider them his, a part of the ship's inventory, and not cargo.

He took up each of the pistols in turn, cocked the wheels, set the dogs in the firing position, then pulled the triggers. In the dim light of the cabin he could easily see the shower of sparks coming off the iron pyrite held in the jaws of the dog and spilling into the unprimed pans. Satisfied, he began loading each pistol.

"Why are you doing that?" Henriette asked. LeBoeuf shrugged without looking up. He did not answer because he did not really know the answer.

"Do you think Van Loudersong will try to kill you in your sleep?" Henriette persisted. "Kill us?"

LeBoeuf rammed a ball down the barrel of one of the pistols and looked up. Henriette had not moved, save to turn her head toward him.

"I don't think anything," he said. "Sometimes my gut tells me to do a thing and I do it. Oft times my gut works better than my brain."

"I don't doubt it," Henriette said. She turned back to her reflection and LeBoeuf turned back to loading his guns. He considered going back on deck, telling the others to load their weapons as well, to post a look-out, to stand ready.

Stand ready for what?

That would be the obvious question, and he would have no answer, and they would ignore him. Here, again, the flaw in the undisciplined world of the buccaneers. Had this been his ship and crew, truly his ship and crew, he would have simply told them to stand ready and suffered no questions. They would have grumbled, quietly. They would have speculated, once he had gone below. Still, they would have obeyed. But that was not the world of the buccaneer coast.

"I'll want to go back to France," Henriette said, her voice soft and surprisingly vulnerable.

"What?"

"When I have my share of the gold, I'll want to go back to France."

LeBoeuf nodded. "You'll be able to return in high style," he said.

"Come with me," she said.

LeBoeuf paused, taken a bit aback by that suggestion. If it was a suggestion. A demand, perhaps?

"Do you want me with you in France, or do you just want my protection getting there?"

"I won't leave you after we arrive. So it doesn't really matter, does it?"

"I suppose not," LeBoeuf said. "But there's nothing for me in France. And there's an estate on Tortuga." His eyes moved involuntarily toward the rolled letter patent in its cubby against the side of the cabin.

"Oh I forgot. Pray forgive me," Henriette said. "You mean to set yourself up as the Grand Duke of Tortuga."

"Or some such," LeBoeuf said. "King of Tortuga, perhaps."

"Humph," Henriette said. LeBoeuf finished loading one of the guns and set it down on the table. He looked up. Henriette was staring at her reflection again, ignoring him.

"I'll help you find passage back to France, don't worry about that," he said. "I can promise you that much." Henriette smiled. LeBoeuf could see it both in her profile and in her reflection. There was no humor in the expression.

"Men's promises," she said. "I've heard a few of those."

LeBoeuf finished loading the last of the guns and set it down. He found two lengths of twine and tied the butts of each brace together, leaving long loops so that the guns could be draped around his neck. He looked around the cabin and could think of nothing more to do, but his nerves were firing too fast for sleep so he went back out on deck, into the cool of the night.

He stepped out from under the break of the quarterdeck, straightened and looked around. A single lantern still burned and it cast a bit of light over the waist of the ship, and the moon and stars added to its illumination. LeBoeuf could see nothing amiss, nothing even moving, the ship all but motionless on the still water.

Normally, on such a calm night, LeBoeuf would have heard the sound of the water lapping the beach, the buzz of insects on the shore and the noise of whatever odd creatures haunted the jungle at night. But as it was he could hear only the snoring of the forty or so buccaneers sprawled out on deck. It was like some beastly chorus and it made him uneasy. The darkness left him mostly blind and now the noisy slumber of the men left him mostly deaf, but there was nothing for it.

He climbed up onto the quarterdeck and walked aft, looking out over the stern at the dark ocean to the north. He could make out the odd hump of land to the east where it stood pressed against the star-filled sky, but other than that he could not discern the horizon, and he could see nothing he did not expect to see.

I'll be happy to be away from this damnable coast, he thought. It was making him paranoid, afraid of ghosts and shadows.

For another few minutes he stood on the quarterdeck and looked out over the water and still there was nothing to see but the pinprick of stars, the quarter moon, hints of the shoreline and blackness. With a sigh he turned and made his way back down into the master's cabin.

Henriette was in the bunk, her body forming a small hump under the single white linen sheet. LeBoeuf paused, waiting for her to say something, but she did not, so he supposed she was either asleep or not speaking to him just then. He considered climbing into the bunk with her. He tried to fathom what he felt like doing — sleeping, making love, holding her in his arms — but in the end decided he wanted to do none of those things.

Instead, he stepped aft and sat on the settee. He leaned back against the stern windows and folded his arms and stared blankly into the dim cabin. No conscious thoughts moved through his head. It was the sort of night which he just had to get through, no more, a featureless road he needed to travel to reach the place he actually wanted to be.

He fell asleep at some point, the transition so seamless that he was not aware he had slept until he was awake again. His eyes flew open and his chin came up from his chest and he was staring into the dark cabin, alert and slightly confused. The lantern was still lit and giving off its feeble light and the ship was as motionless as ever. Through the bulkhead he could still hear the ugly snores of the sleeping men.

What in all hell... he thought. Something had woken him, he was all but certain, but what it was he had no idea. He frowned and concentrated on the sounds coming from out on deck.

Snoring. That was it. And then what might have been a footfall, but soft, stealthy. LeBoeuf sat more upright. He heard a rustling, a thumping. And then, coming sharp and loud through the bulkhead, a single short scream, a woman in panicked terror, and LeBoeuf was on his feet and bolting forward, crouched low under the deck beams above.

Chapter Thirty-Three

LeBoeuf moved with urgency, but not with panic. He had experienced panic often enough in the younger days, but that spirit had not possessed him in many years.

He snatched up the two braces of pistols and draped them around his neck so they hung by the twine. He grabbed the wire-bound grip of his sword and with a flick of his wrist tossed the scabbard aside. Two steps and he was at the door and his hand found the latch and swung it open. He heard Henriette behind him call out "What…?" as he plunged through the door and under the quarterdeck above.

He burst out into the waist, straightened and looked out over the scene before him. Not ten seconds had passed since he had heard the woman's scream but already it was chaos there. Men were coming over the sides, larboard and starboard, and sweeping over the deck. The buccaneers were still sprawled out, caught in drunken sleep and struggling to get to their feet, get to their weapons.

Twenty feet forward, standing on the main hatch, LeBoeuf could see a man in a leather jerkin, a dark cloth bound around his head. He had a cutlass in one hand, but it was the club in the other that he was wielding with deadly energy. At his feet, a man fighting to kick off his blanket. The one in the jerkin swung the club backhand into the half-sitting man's head, snapping him back and down, the club's momentum never slowing as it came up again.

LeBoeuf grabbed up one of the pistols hanging around his neck and leveled it at the man with the club. His finger pressed against the trigger but his eye caught movement to his left. He swung around as another of the boarders vaulted over the bulwark, pistol in hand. The boarder hit the deck, stumbled, recovered. He was just starting to level the weapon at LeBoeuf when the ball from LeBoeuf's pistol blew the left side of his head apart.

LeBoeuf dropped the pistol and let it hang and grabbed up another. He took two steps forward. The deck was alive with moving shadows and blasts of brilliant light from the muzzles of guns, the clash of steel, shouts of surprise and rage and agony and terror. A man struggling to stand ten feet from LeBoeuf, one of the boarders looming over him, a cutlass held high and slashing down.

The gun in LeBoeuf's hand was coming up when another of the buccaneers — Levasseur, he thought — fired his long hunting gun into the cutlass-wielding man from three feet away. The punch of the musket ball knocked the man back into the bulwark and dropped him to the deck.

The one with the club was still flailing right and left. He looked like a man possessed, like some demon whirling in a hellish dance. He seemed like the key to this surprise attack, the leader, the pole star, and though LeBoeuf had no reason to think he was in command, somehow he knew that he was. Which meant he had to die.

Once again LeBoeuf leveled his pistol and found the man over the top of the long steel barrel. He pressed his finger against the trigger, and a hair's breadth before the trigger tripped the wheel Pierre le Chasseur came stumbling in front of him, cursing and swinging his cutlass. LeBoeuf eased off the trigger and raised the gun an instant before he would have put the ball through Chasseur's chest.

"Merde!" LeBoeuf shouted. He swung the pistol right and found a man just coming over the rail, a Black man, his face obscured, the steel of his cutlass blade glinting, and LeBoeuf shot him.

Smoke gutted from the muzzle of the pistol and from the pan, and in the second it took the smoke to clear the Black man was gone, tossed back into the sea. LeBoeuf dropped that pistol, grabbed the third, still looking for the madman with the club.

It seemed as if they had been fighting for some time now, though experience told LeBoeuf it had been no more than a minute, two at most. Most of the buccaneers had managed to get to their feet: those still stretched out on the deck would probably never stand again. LeBoeuf advanced another four steps, his eyes moving left and right.

Damn this bastard, they're boarding both sides... he thought. Whoever planned this attack had the good sense to send at least two boats and to board from both sides at once, creating the maximum of confusion. And they were still coming.

A tangle of fighting men stood between LeBoeuf and the man with the club, leaving no shot, so LeBoeuf swung his pistol to starboard. D'Anton was fighting there, a short sword in his left hand, his right arm hanging limp. He was hurt, a stab wound or a bullet, and LeBoeuf fired his pistol into the man who was just about to separate D'Anton's head from his lower parts.

As the gun recoiled in his hand and LeBoeuf looked out at the men fighting for their lives and the men coming over the bulwarks and spreading across the decks, his decks, he felt an immense rage come over him. They were snatching his ship away, his beautiful ship that had been laid at his feet, the ship that had raised him like Lazarus from the grave, and he was suddenly engulfed by fury and outrage.

Another man in front of him, no one LeBoeuf recognized and coming on with raised cutlass — the next who would die at LeBoeuf's hand. LeBoeuf stood motionless. The man stopped an arm's length away and slashed, an awkward but powerful stroke, the blade coming around at LeBoeuf's unprotected head. It was half-way there when LeBoeuf raised his sword to the vertical and the man's wrist hit the fine honed edge. The sword was an immovable object in LeBoeuf's powerful grip and the momentum of the man's swing all but severed his own hand.

The cutlass fell with a thump to the deck and the man screamed and grabbed his wrist and looked up at LeBoeuf with wide, pain-filled, panicked eyes.

Spaniard... LeBoeuf thought as he hefted the last of his loaded guns and pressed the muzzle to the man's head. He saw the man's mouth drop open and he squeezed the trigger.

For a fraction of a second the muzzle flash illuminated the hole in the man's forehead and the spray of brains and shards of skull that spewed out from the back of his head as he was flung to the deck. It was the faintest taste of vengeance, but the man's death did nothing to temper LeBoeuf's rage.

He snatched the pistols from around his neck and flung them across the deck. He shifted his sword from his left hand to his right and felt the anger ripple through him. LeBoeuf, stolid, a mountain, was in truth a volcano, the eruptions of rage exceedingly rare but excessively violent.

A bellow grew in his gut and came rushing like a wave up his throat and he opened his mouth and roared like a mindless, savage beast. And indeed he was at that moment nothing more or less.

His roar rolled down the deck and blotted out the shouting and the clash of weapons. He saw men turn and look, he saw wide eyes and faces streaked with blood and weapons sweeping through the dark. He roared again and leapt forward, his sword in motion, ready to cut down anyone — everyone — who stood in his path.

Le Rongeur was up in the bow when they came, pressed against the base of the bowsprit, wanting to put as many feet of deck between him and LeBoeuf as he could on that small ship. And it was a good thing he did so, he reckoned. A damned good thing. He had been well out of the way and well-hidden when the pirates...or Spaniards...or whoever in all hell they were, had come swarming up over the side.

He was not asleep when they appeared. His mind was turning over and over too fast for him to sleep. It had been that way for days, ever since he had told Van Loudersong about the gold under the deck, despite vowing to himself that he would tell no one.

He had considered the situation from every angle he could image and he was all but certain he had LeBoeuf in a corner. The bastard would have to share the gold with him. If not, then he, Le Rongeur, would inform the others, and LeBoeuf would be forced to share it all around. And the others would likely kill him in the bargain.

So why did I tell that sheep-biting Dutchman? Le Rongeur wondered. Sitting there in Van Loudersong's camp the words just seemed to come spilling out of him, as if he was vomiting them up, as if he had no control. And ever since that moment he had been trying to figure if telling Van Loudersong had been a stupid thing to do, or a smart one.

According to Van Loudersong it was a smart thing to do. He had pointed out that it kept Le Rongeur safe — LeBoeuf could easily kill one man who knew the secret, but not two. And he was right. That made sense. But somehow Le Rongeur felt there was more to it than that. He just could not puzzle out what it was.

All those questions he had pondered a hundred times, and he was pondering them again when the first of the boarders came up over the rail. Le Rongeur had not heard them coming. He could not hear anything over the beastly snoring of the buccaneers. But he had seen the man come, seen him move silently over the top of the bulwark and drop to the deck like a cat, and he was confused. He did not know who this son of a bitch was.

Le Rongeur thought at first that he was one of the buccaneers who had climbed down the ship's side for some reason and was now climbing back. He continued to think that right up until the man raised some sort of club and slammed it down on the head of some poor bastard sleeping on the main hatch. The weapon moved so fast Le Rongeur could not see it in motion, but he heard the man on the hatch grunt as it hit and heard the soft crunching sound as it shattered his skull.

"Oh, damn my eyes!" Le Rongeur gasped. He sat more upright but did not feel compelled to stand or to move at all from that dark and well-hidden spot, nor was he inclined to shout a warning and thus give himself away. Instead he just watched as more and more boarders came up over the side, starboard and larboard, hacking at the sleeping men with cutlasses.

A woman screamed, the sound startling in the still night, and suddenly the deck was swept up in chaos as the buccaneers came awake and grabbed up weapons and struggled to stand and fight before they were killed where they lay.

"Oh damn, oh damn…" Le Rongeur said, over and over, but that was the only action he took. This fight did not seem to be going well for the buccaneers, and it was not something he had any intention of joining.

Now think, now think, now think... he told himself. The canoes and periaguas were still tied alongside. He could easily slip over the rail and down into one of the boats. He could row it ashore, get clear of all the butchery. In this madness he would never be seen.

But what if the pig hunters win? he thought next. How would that be, if he had to row back out to the ship after having fled the fight?

They'd kill me for a coward, he thought.

"So, I'll wait..." he said out loud, and the sound of his own voice calmed him a bit. He could stay there, unseen, well clear of the fighting. He was safe for the moment. Another few minutes would tell him which side was likely to win, and if it was not the pig hunters then there would still be time for him to get into a boat and get away.

Pistols were firing now, and on occasion the deeper sound of a musket as the hunters found their weapons and discharged them into the enemy. The night was full of shouting and cursing and screaming, steel clashing on steel, the thud of feet and men hitting the deck.

Le Rongeur had seen his share of fights, brawls in taverns and gangs of men going at each other for some reason or other, but he had never seen anything like this. He wanted to shriek in terror but he was afraid to give himself away, so he kept his mouth shut tight.

Suddenly a new sound cut through the fighting, louder, deeper, more savage than anything yet. Le Rongeur looked aft and he saw LeBoeuf charging forward, sword in hand. He loomed over all the others and he slashed left and right and his size and his fury made him seem less like a man and more like something from an ancient legend.

A pistol fired into LeBoeuf from ten feet away. Le Rongeur did not see how it could have missed, but it seemed to have no effect on LeBoeuf as he raged forward, his sword cutting like a scythe through the press of men. Two of the boarders were on him, cutlasses flailing, but LeBoeuf stopped one blade with the edge of his sword as if the man had hacked into a tree trunk. He grabbed the other man's wrist with his left hand, pulling him down and stomping on his knee in one fluid motion, snapping the man's leg and dropping him screaming to the deck.

Le Rongeur's eyes shifted aft. Under the break of the quarterdeck he could just see the outline of the door to the master's cabin. There must have been a lantern lit inside, its weak light spilling out the entrance way. Then, in that light, he saw the outline of Henriette as she stood there motionless as if unsure what to do. She remained fixed in that place for a moment, then slipped out onto the deck, moving carefully off to the larboard side, clear of the fighting.

Once again Le Rongeur's eyes moved to the master's cabin door, open and inviting, unprotected and unobserved. An idea began to form in his head, a vision of opportunity so ripe, so perfect, that he did not even consider the potential danger.

"Fortune calls," he said to himself. He was actually smiling as he stood and climbed over the windlass and headed aft.

Henriette de Labonté, pulled from slumber, had no idea why LeBoeuf was racing across the small cabin, but she guessed it could not be good. And when he paused to sling his pistols around his neck and flick the scabbard off his sword before charging out the door she was quite certain of it.

Mon Dieu, what the hell is happening? she thought as she swung her legs over the side of the bunk, staring at the open door, just visible on the starboard side of the bulkhead. Then she heard it: the muffled cries, the thumping and grunting and cursing. And then the shouting, the screaming, the pistol shots.

"Oh, what in hell?" she said out loud as her feet found the deck and she stood. "Are these stupid bastards at it again?"

It was the only thing she could imagine, Van Loudersong and Pierre le Chasseur resuming their foolishness, or some other combination of the filthy beasts coming to blows and dragging the rest of them into their fight, just as they were nearly free of that damned coast.

She hurried across the cabin to the door and looked out at the waist. There was moonlight and a single lantern, light enough for her to see was happening, mostly, but she still did not understand. There were more men than just the buccaneers, she was sure of that. The deck seemed to be filled with struggling men, with cutlasses and pistols and one man who seemed to be wielding a club.

LeBoeuf was ten feet in front of her, his bulk blocking much of her view of the deck. She saw his arm come up and the pistol in his hand fire and the muzzle flash all but blinded her. She cursed, rubbed her eyes, opened them again and tried to imagine what was going on.

They're attacking us, she realized. Men were coming over the side of the ship, coming over both sides and joining in the fight, but who they were she had no idea. She stood frozen in the doorway, watching the madness, knowing she should do something, but with no idea what that might be.

The sons of bitches, they're coming for my gold, she thought next. She knew that was irrational — no one knew about the gold save for her and LeBoeuf — but still she could not shake that idea. She looked on that gold as her salvation. Any threat to it was a threat to her very existence, and with that realization came an understanding of what she had to do.

Kill them, she thought. *Kill them.* That was what she had to do. Whoever they were, they were no friends of hers. As much as she despised the buccaneers she imagined these whores' sons would be worse. And even if they never found the gold, it would still be lost to her if they took the ship.

She turned and raced back into the cabin. LeBoeuf had stored his hunting gear in the far corner. His long musket was leaning against the cabinet, the belt and cartridge box hanging from a hook on the starboard side, and various knives and machetes were laid out on the settee.

She considered the musket. It was a flintlock and she knew how to load and fire such a weapon, and she knew how deadly the punch of that heavy ball would be. But loading it would take too long, and she would get just a single shot for the effort. Nor was she certain she could even lift the thing high enough to aim.

Instead she grabbed the machete, three feet of a wide steel blade that she knew was honed to razor sharpness. Whether she could actually slash a man or not she did not know and she did not waste time wondering. She turned and fled back across the cabin and out the open door.

Henriette had seen many things in her short life but she had never seen anything like what was happening on deck. There were men lying sprawled out in dark pools, or thrashing and clawing at wounds. There were men hacking at one another with swords and firing pistols into other men just feet away, and the sound, the screaming, the cursing, the clashing, was just what she might have expected to hear in Hell itself.

She shifted the machete to her left hand and with her trembling right hand she made the Sign of the Cross, something she had not done in a long time. Then she shifted the weapon back and stepped carefully off toward the larboard side.

She had her eyes on the fighting, looking for someone to attack, or someone who might attack her, when her foot caught something and she stumbled.

"Merde!" she said aloud and looked down at the face of a dead man on the deck. Or half his face at least. The right half. The left seemed to have been torn away. Henriette felt her stomach convulse and she looked up before she vomited, then stumbled on, coming to a stop with her hand on top of the bulwark.

She turned and surveyed the fighting amidships. Of all the men on deck LeBoeuf was the only one she recognized, and him only by his size. She might have thought him a dumb ox before, but he was more the raging bull now, roaring and slashing with his sword, marching through the pack of men, thrusting and cutting, kicking and punching.

Henriette pressed her lips together and renewed her grip on the machete and steeled herself to jump into the fight, to pick one of these men and slash him with the blade.

Which one...which one? she thought. In the dark she could not tell the pig hunters from the men who were coming aboard. Forward she could see a man in a leather jerkin, a slight man, dark-skinned, and like LeBoeuf fighting like a thing possessed. He was not one of the buccaneer crew, of that she was sure, but she did not think she could get to him, and even if she could he seemed far too frightening to approach.

There... she thought. Van Loudersong was exchanging blows with another man, cutlass against cutlass, and since Van Loudersong was one of the pig hunters she assumed the other man was not, and was therefore a man to be killed.

She took a tentative step toward him, then felt a hand clamp over her mouth and pull her back. She screamed into the calloused palm, clawed at the hand, but the arm was powerful and unyielding, an attacker who seemed to have materialized out of the night.

Up the side... she thought as she kicked and screamed. The bastard had not appeared out of thin air, he had been coming up the side of the ship when he grabbed her from behind.

The villain was pulling her back, the panic just starting to overwhelm her when she remembered the machete in her hand. She hacked at the man, an awkward move, then hacked again. She grabbed the back of the blade with her left hand and with both hands drove it deep into the bare flesh of the arm, then sawed it back and forth.

Behind her, right in her ear, she heard the scream, and the grip of the hand on her mouth slipped. She pushed off and broke free and spun around. The man had black hair bound in a rag, a dark pointed beard, one leg over the rail, his eyes wide with surprise and pain. He had been holding a dagger in his right hand but he had dropped it to clap that hand over his bleeding arm.

Henriette raised the machete straight up and hacked down at the man's head. He jerked to one side and the blade took off his ear and continued down, cutting deep into his shoulder. The man screamed louder still and grabbed the blade as he began to fall back. Henriette tightened her grip but she could not hold on and the machete was dragged from her hands as the man plunged backward into the sea.

"Merde!" Henriette shouted again. She whirled around to face the fighting on deck but she could not tell what was happening or who, if anyone, was winning. She wondered if they would kill to the last man. She had a sudden image of herself, when it was done, standing alone among the bodies of dozens of dead men.

She looked left and right. She saw someone moving through the press of men, not fighting but moving with purpose, moving aft. He was lost from sight behind the main mast for a moment, then reemerged, ducking under the break of the quarterdeck. She saw him silhouetted against the dim light of the open cabin door, and then the light was gone as the door was shut.

"Oh, you son of a bitch!" Henriette shouted, as she realized who it was, or most likely was. She had thought the hidden gold was known only to her and LeBoeuf, but if anyone else knew about it, it would be Le Rongeur, who had stayed with them aboard the ship and was always watching with his rat eyes.

She hurried aft, oblivious to the fighting now, intent only on protecting the fortune under the deck. It was as precious to her as life, because without it her life would be nothing beyond nightmarish and short.

She stepped under the quarterdeck and unlike LeBoeuf and the others she did not have to duck. The bulkhead was lost in shadow now with the meager light from the open door gone and she moved with hands held in front of her until her palms came up against the painted wood. She felt her way toward the starboard side. Her fingers brushed over the frame of the door and found the iron latch.

She grabbed hold of the handle and lifted but it would not move. Whoever had gone in had the presence of mind to secure the latch from the inside. She jerked and tugged and cursed but the latch would not give. She pounded on the door with her fists, shouting "Open this door! Open this door now, you son of a bitch!" though she understood that the shouting and pounding were as pointless as pulling on the latch.

Furious, she stepped back and kicked at the door, a gesture of frustration and not an actual attempt to kick it in. She stepped back and stared at the bulkhead, its white paint just barely discernible. And she remembered that just behind her was a tool chest lashed to ringbolts in the deck, and in the tool box was, among other things, an ax.

She turned and reached out and found the side of the ship, then moved forward until her feet found the chest. She dropped to her knees and felt for the hasp and then pushed the lid up. The contents of the box were completely lost in the dark so she reached in and felt around, running her fingers over cool iron until they fell on what she guessed was a wooden handle. She pulled it out and held it up but the tool seemed to be some sort of massive chisel so she tossed it aside and started digging around again.

She felt another handle, half-buried. She got her fingers around it and worked it free and was rewarded with the sight of an ax in her hand, a heavy, sharp iron head at the end of a three-foot shaft of ash. She leapt to her feet and moved back toward the door, taking a proper grip on the handle as she approached. She was not well-versed in wielding an ax — her life in Paris had involved no such thing — but since being thrown in with the buccaneers she had split enough firewood that her once-flawless hands were now as calloused as a fishwife's, to her disgust.

Three feet from the door she stopped. The fight was still raging behind her but it might as well have been aboard another ship for all she cared about it now. She clenched her teeth and lifted the ax as high as she could under the quarterdeck, then drove it down toward the door.

It was an ineffectual blow. The corner of the ax head just barely embedded itself in the door, and the feebleness of her effort infuriated her. But in addition to giving her skill with an ax, Henriette's time with the buccaneers had given her a strength of arm she had never enjoyed before. She jerked the ax free and raised it again, shouting in anger now as she swung it at the door a second time, putting that new-found muscle behind the blow.

This time the ax hit with enough force to shatter the thin wood of the door. Henriette saw the boards splinter and the weak light from the lantern inside come spilling out of the crack. And for some reason the sight of the door half torn apart but still standing made her more furious still. She worked the ax free and brought it back over her head and with another cry of anger drove it down once again.

The third blow was the *coup de grâce*. The ax hit the door and kept on going, tearing through the vertical boards and the horizontal frame and smashing the latch clean away, leaving the door to swing on its hinges. Henriette pulled the ax head free. She held the tool — now a weapon — in both hands, kicked the door open and burst into the master's cabin.

The lantern was hanging from a hook in an overhead beam, and beyond it Le Rongeur was standing on the far side of the table. If he had found the gold or not she did not know: the table blocked Henriette's view of the deck at Le Rongeur's feet, and she was more concerned about LeBoeuf's musket, which Le Rongeur was aiming right at her chest.

"Put the ax down, you bitch," Le Rongeur said.

Henriette glared at him, breathing hard, and for once she was too furious to speak.

"Put the ax down. Whore."

Henriette glanced over at the starboard side of the cabin. The belt and cartridge box were still hanging where they had been earlier. She knew for certain that LeBoeuf had not loaded the long musket. Had Le Rongeur had time to load it? Probably. The pig hunters were all very fast at loading their guns. But would he have then hung the cartridge box back where it had been?

She took a step toward him, moving around the table, and rather than setting the ax down she adjusted her grip on the handle.

"Put the ax down or by God I promise I'll blow your slut head off!" Le Rongeur said, his voice rising in pitch, the muzzle of the gun following Henriette as she moved. Henriette said nothing, she just held his eyes with hers because she knew that Le Rongeur would find it unnerving.

She could see the growing panic on his face. He raised the musket higher and shifted his aim from her chest to her head and she knew for certain then that the gun was not loaded. Had it been, he would have killed her already. There was nothing stopping him. She continued to move around the table, circling closer in, and her eyes flicked down to the deck at Le Rongeur's feet.

The boards were torn up, revealing the secret place beneath. It would have been easy enough to find. The space had been well hidden at first, but once LeBoeuf pulled the deck up the loose planks became obvious. But there was no sign of the iron box. Le Rongeur, apparently, had not managed to get that far.

It the fraction of a second that Henriette was looking down, Le Rongeur made his move. By the time she looked up he had flipped the musket around and was swinging it like a club, her head well within the arc of the long weapon. She gasped and ducked and felt the wind of the butt passing inches above her, heard the clang of the musket hitting the lantern hanging from the hook.

The cabin was filled with tumbling shadows as the lantern flew toward the larboard side. Henriette straightened, bringing the ax up as she did. The momentum of the gun had twisted Le Rongeur around and now he was half turned away from her, so Henriette took a step forward and swung the ax sideways as if she was felling a tree.

The blade bit into his back and he arched and screamed and dropped the musket to the deck. Le Rongeur twisted away and the ax came free and Henriette wound up and struck him again. She slashed him across the belly this time, opening up a deep wound that was gushing blood even while the ax was still in motion.

The ax came back over Henriette's shoulder and stopped, cocked like a flintlock. Henriette swung it again, a backhand blow that struck Le Rongeur in the head with the butt end and sent him flying across the cabin.

He fell across the settee and rolled onto the deck and Henriette leapt after him, bringing the ax up as high as the low overhead would permit. Le Rongeur was not moving and she knew he was likely dead but she did not care. Her rage was a demon trapped inside, and it seemed that swinging the ax was the only way to shake it free. She swung again and felt the blade bite into Le Rongeur's body, jerked it loose and chopped down again.

She stopped then, heaving for breath, one hand resting on the handle, the head of the ax embedded in Le Rongeur's torso. He was lying face-down on the deck, his arm still flung over the settee and his legs at odd angles. Blood was seeping out from under him in a spreading pool.

Henriette stared at the body at her feet as she gulped air. She had never killed anyone before, and now that she had she felt no remorse at all, and that surprised her a bit.

Filthy rat, he deserved it, she thought. She wondered if she would be so sanguine if he was lying face-up and she could see the vicious wounds she had doled out. But even face-down she could see a lot. The cabin, she realized, seemed much brighter lit than it had before.

It was a puzzle, a mystery. Henriette frowned as she tried to work it out. And then she gasped and spun around. The lantern Le Rongeur had struck with the musket was lying shattered in the bunk she shared with LeBoeuf, and the flames that had spilled free had already engulfed the bedding and the mattress and were working their way up the cabin's side.

Chapter Thirty-Four

Jean-Baptiste LeBoeuf cut his way from the break of the quarterdeck to the aft end of the main hatch. His beautiful sword whirled and danced in his right hand. He held a cutlass in his left, though he did not recall picking it up. He did not recall much at all. It was emotion alone that was driving him now. One single emotion. Rage.

Men loomed in front of him, weapons seemed to come at him out of the dark, and his arms and legs in turn seemed to move of their own accord. He parried blades, lunged and felt steel meet steel or steel meet flesh and drive on through with little resistance. His head was filled with the sounds of the shouting and screaming and gunshots, his nose with the smell of blood and smoke. His hands felt sticky on the grips of his weapons.

For all the hurt that LeBoeuf was doling out, he was receiving plenty in return. He was wounded and he knew it. He could feel warm blood running down his skin under his shirt and he was pretty certain he had taken a bullet in the side. But there was no pain. He knew it would come, later, if he lived through the night. But in that blind moment he was simply aware of being hurt. He could not feel it.

Ten feet, he was ten feet from the bastard with the leather jerkin and the club, and there was little between them now. The battle was only minutes old, but that was a long time for such things, and men were falling away, exhausted, wounded, dead, done with fighting. But not LeBoeuf and not the man with the club, whose energy and enthusiasm seemed not to have waned in the least.

LeBoeuf took two steps forward and another of the boarders was in front of him, a tall man, wiry and quick, but his sword-work was crude, a man who had learned his trade in exactly that sort of mindless hacking brawl. He swung at LeBoeuf's head as if he was wielding an ax at a tree, not a blade at a swordsman. LeBoeuf stopped the blade with the cutlass in his left hand, stepped in and thrust with the sword in his right.

The wiry man saw it coming and leapt back fast — not fast enough to stop the point of LeBoeuf's blade from sinking deep, but fast enough to avoid a fatal thrust. The cutlass fell from his hand and he doubled over and grabbed at the wound. He would have died there if LeBoeuf had bothered to follow up with another stroke, but he did not: instead he kicked the man aside and moved on.

There was nothing but space now between LeBoeuf and the man with the club. Between the two of them they had cleared away all the others within reach of their weapons. Now they stood alone on the forward end of the main hatch, looking at one another. LeBoeuf had an odd sense that he had achieved something, accomplished some goal, cutting his way to this man. He was not sure why he felt that way, save that the man with the club seemed to be the one most responsible for this outrage, this attack, and thus was the one who most needed to die.

But he would not die easily, that was clear. LeBoeuf had caught glimpses of him through the dark and the press of bodies and he could see that the man fought like the devil himself. They were close enough now that LeBoeuf could see he was not European, not a Spaniard or Frenchman or English. A native of the West Indies. Carib. Taino, most likely. That explained the odd, square club which LeBoeuf understood was a weapon favored by the native people.

In the dim light he could see little of the man's face, but what he could see looked as if it was made of oiled wood. There was no fear or anger or rage or sympathy there. There was nothing.

Then the man moved, so fast and sudden that it took LeBoeuf nearly by surprise. One second he was motionless and the next he was in flight, it seemed, coming at LeBoeuf with weapons whirling. He bound across the few feet separating them, slashing with the cutlass in his left hand, making a great display of the attack, but LeBoeuf knew it was the club in his right hand he had to watch for.

He raised his sword high, pommel up, blade down, to catch the clumsy swing of the cutlass but his eyes were down and left, watching the club coming up from the man's side. LeBoeuf extended his cutlass, catching the club before it took him in the side of the head, then lifted a foot and slammed it into the Taino's belly, sending him hurtling back.

The dark man stumbled, arms out as he tried to catch himself and LeBoeuf leapt forward, hoping to drive his sword into the man before he recovered. He lunged full out with his powerful arm and massive reach and would have put the point of his sword right through the man's chest if the club had not come around and swatted the blade aside, so fast that LeBoeuf saw only a blur.

Damn your eyes… LeBoeuf thought as he stepped back, clear of the man's counterstroke with the cutlass. The blade whipped past his face and LeBoeuf could hear the sound if it cutting the air. He saw his chance then, the man's left side exposed as he twisted sideways. LeBoeuf brought his sword up, but before he could even begin to lunge the club came around and hit him in the ribs with staggering force.

"Ahhhhh!" He shouted in agony and hunched over, but he clamped his left arm down, trapping the club between his arm and his side. The pain tore through him as he squeezed arm and club against what he was sure were broken ribs, but he knew he could not let the man get the weapon free.

LeBoeuf straightened and twisted, club pinned to his side, trying to drag it from the man's grip, but the Taino, the warrior, would not let go. They were too close to one another now for their long blades, but as LeBoeuf looked up he saw the Taino's fist, encased in the hand guard of his cutlass, swinging for his face. The man was striking with his left hand, not as nimble and strong as the right. LeBoeuf whipped the hilt of his sword around and knocked the cutlass grip out of line, the metal ringing on metal and making a sound like a bell.

Then LeBoeuf straightened his arm, driving his hand guard into the Taino's face, a solid punch with his right hand that sent the man staggering back. LeBoeuf was still struggling to hold the club trapped against his side but he felt it slipping as the man maintained his powerful grip. LeBoeuf slashed down and to the left with his sword, hoping to catch the man's hand, but too late. The club came free and the man stumbled back and the sword found only air.

But that presented another chance, the man off-balance, maybe disoriented by the blow to his head. LeBoeuf stepped forward and raised the cutlass in his left hand high and gave a mighty swipe down and across. It was not a pretty stroke, but it was not meant to be. It was meant to distract, to clear the way for the sword in his right hand that would do the real work.

The Taino was still fighting to keep on his feet as the cutlass came down at him. He twisted and made a feeble attempt to parry the blade with his own cutlass and the two weapons rang against one another. Then LeBoeuf brought the sword around, holding it horizontal, the point driving for the man's belly.

The dark man saw it coming a heartbeat too late. He twisted sideways. The dagger-sharp blade caught his leather jerkin, tore right through and sliced him across the stomach. It was a deep slash, LeBoeuf knew, though he felt little resistance as the fine-honed edge passed through leather and flesh. Deep, but not deep enough to kill. At least not immediately.

The Taino shouted, a cry of pain, certainly, but even more of fury, LeBoeuf thought, fury that someone had managed to get a blade on him and do real hurt. He brought the club around and knocked LeBoeuf's sword clear, but the damage was done, the wound that might end the fight delivered.

The dark man backed away, three feet, four feet, stepping down off the main hatch and onto the deck. LeBoeuf could see the tear in his jerkin and the blood running down the leather and onto his slop trousers. If the sword stroke had sliced deep into muscle then the man would be crippled and LeBoeuf would put an end to him in the next moment or so, though as it was the fight was clearly not out of him yet.

The man readjusted his grip on the weapons, cutlass and club, and held them low and extended, ready. His eyes were on LeBoeuf's. The brief moment of fury was over, and in its place was the nothingness of before.

LeBoeuf adjusted his grip on his own weapons, his teeth clenched against the pain in his ribs. But something was different now, he could sense it. The sound of the shouting had changed, the noise of battle had shifted to something else. His eyes were on the man in front of him but his ears were picking apart the din from behind. He saw the dark man's eyes shift right and left, and then the man took another step back.

What in all hell? LeBoeuf wondered. He took a step toward the other man, his cutlass to one side, his sword in the *en garde* stance, waiting for his moment. The shouting behind him was getting louder and more urgent. There seemed to be no clashing of weapons now or sound of fighting. He saw the man's eyes move left and right again, and then glance up overhead.

And then there was a new sound, a crackling, and a low, dull roar. LeBoeuf was suddenly engulfed in the smell of burning wood and burning paint and burning flesh, and without thinking he turned and looked.

The after end of the ship was on fire, fully involved. The bulkhead to the master's cabin had collapsed, revealing nothing but a wall of flame where an hour before LeBoeuf's home had been. The flames had reached up to the quarterdeck above and wrapped themselves around the rails and the hatch and they were working their way up the rigging toward the dry canvas sails.

LeBoeuf stared at the scene for a second or two, no more, and then he heard in his head the shriek of alarm, the warning cry of danger. He whirled back around, raising sword and cutlass to defend against the inevitable attack.

He whirled too late. The club was already in motion, moving in an upward arc toward his head. LeBoeuf nearly caught the dark man's arm with the cutlass. He was just a few inches shy of the parry when the club connected with the side of his head. He saw a burst of light, brighter even than the flames consuming his beloved ship, and then all was dark and silent.

It remained silent. For quite a long time. The silence and the dark seemed to stretch on and on. And it was nice.

And then LeBoeuf was being dragged from the silence, violently, but he did not want to go. He fought back, trying to stay in that place. He knew there would be pain if he let the dark and the silence go. Terrific pain. His head, his ribs, his legs.

And that would not be the worst of it. If he left the darkness behind, he would discover that some vital part of him had been ripped away. There was something — he did not know what — something that had given him cause to continue, and that thing was no more. In the silence he could not recall what that thing was, or why it was no longer there, or why he cared. But once the silence was gone he knew he would remember, and he did not want to remember.

As hard as he struggled against it, he still felt the darkness slipping away. He caught the first hints of pain in his ribs and in his head, and he knew this was just the *apéritif*, the prelude of what was to come. He knew that if he could just get back to the darkness and the silence then soon he would be able to stay there forever.

But it wasn't silent anymore, and it wasn't still. He was being shoved side to side. Not violently, no more than a ship at anchor in a low swell, but he was definitely being shoved. He made some low noise in his throat, or at least he thought he did. He was not sure. And then the shoving stopped and he tried to claw his way back to the silence.

For a moment he remained in that place, unmolested, half ensconced in the dark and the quiet. And then suddenly he felt a great wash of liquid, warm as blood, rushing over his head and face and shoulders.

He opened his eyes. Henriette was standing over him, a bucket in her hands. She was brilliantly illuminated with yellow dancing light and LeBoeuf had a notion that they were near some great bonfire. He could feel the heat on his back and that only reinforced the idea. Then Henriette dropped to her knees and shook him as hard as she could, which was not hard, and shouted into his ear.

"LeBoeuf! Come on, you great dumb ox! Get up! The damned ship is on fire!"

LeBoeuf frowned and looked up at her but he did not move. She shook harder and yelled again. "Come on, damn your eyes, or I'll leave you here, you worthless beast!"

Then LeBoeuf began to remember. All those things he had not wanted to remember started coming back. The boarders. The man with the club. The fire.

He pushed himself up on his elbow and roared with the agony of it. Henriette grabbed him under the arm and lifted, providing not the least bit of help for her efforts. He sat upright and swiveled around. The entire after end of the ship was fully engulfed in flame. He could see nothing but fire from the break of the quarterdeck aft.

Overhead, the main mast was also burning: the sail along the main yard and the top above that seemed like some massive torch. Bits of burning rope and canvas were fluttering down to the deck. Then some of the rigging gave way and the starboard end of main yard dropped, swinging down ten feet before it came to a stop. A minute more and the entire thing would plummet to the deck.

Bit by bit LeBoeuf began to understand. He thought he had been in the silence for hours, even days, but he could see now it had been minutes at the most. In the brilliant light of the flames he could see dead men scattered around the deck, some with their clothing already on fire. He could see no one else alive.

"They've left us!" Henriette shouted, answering LeBoeuf's question even before he asked it. "They're all gone, they left us!"

LeBoeuf shook his head, but he did not mean to convey anything with the gesture. He continued to stare dumbly around, trying to puzzle things out.

"Get up, you great idiot! Stand up!" Henriette shouted. She got to her feet as if to demonstrate what he must do. She bent over and once again grabbed him under the arms and lifted, which once again had no effect whatsoever. But LeBoeuf had recovered enough of his wits to see that standing made some sort of sense so he clenched his teeth and put his hand down on the warm deck and forced himself up.

He swayed a bit as he stood. He felt a great rushing sensation in his head, and a pounding like the man with the club was striking him again and again. He half turned, looking behind him, to make certain that was not the case, but the man with the club was gone, as were apparently everyone else who had not been cut down or shot in the fighting.

LeBoeuf looked back toward the master's cabin and he felt the loss and the desperation spreading like blood from a wound. He took a step in that direction and when he did not fall he took another and another.

"No, you dumb ox!" Henriette shouted. "It's gone, do you hear? The gold, everything, it's all gone! We have to get off this damned ship!"

He turned again and looked at her. Her overbody was torn and her face was streaked with soot and blood. Her eyes were wide and he could see the terror in them.

"Please!" she shouted over the roaring of the flames. "Please!" Her tone was plaintive and vulnerable and it took him by surprise. Had she not been there, he knew, he would have plunged headlong into the burning cabin. It would be like rushing in through the gates of Hell. But that was something he'd reckoned on doing some day in any event. It might as well be then. He was quite ready.

"How?" LeBoeuf asked, the first word he had spoken since returning from the dark. His voice sounded odd and strained.

"There's a boat, I think," Henriette said. She grabbed his hand and tugged in the direction of the larboard side. "I think they left a boat."

LeBoeuf nodded and took a few uncertain steps, yielding to the pressure of her pulling on his arm. Then he stopped and looked around the deck at his feet. "Sword," he said.

Henriette stared at him, uncertain, then nodded her head and ran off, just a few steps. And then she was back with his fine sword in her hand. "Here," she said. "Here it is. Now, come on!"

She did not hand him the sword, but rather grabbed his arm again and continued tugging him to the rail. He put his hands on the bulwark and looked down. Most of the boats were gone, but there was still a canoe and a small periagua tied alongside.

"What should I do?" Henriette pleaded. "Tell me what to do!"

LeBoeuf shook his head. His mind was clearing now, the sense of unreality dissipating. He body was a torment and his head was like an anvil under a smith's blows, but he could think, and he knew he could act. He took a few steps forward and found the painter that led to the periagua's bow. He untied it and pulled the boat over until it bumped against the side of the ship at the bottom of the boarding steps.

"Go," he said, nodding down at the boat. Henriette turned and found the top step with her bare foot, stepping down backward step by step, LeBoeuf's fine sword still in her hand. Her foot found the bottom of the boat and she stepped in and sat on a thwart forward.

LeBoeuf turned as well and began to make his way down the steps after her, his eyes running over the deck as he did, and he paused. That amorphous sense of loss, of something vital being ripped away, suddenly took form and substance. His ship. The thing that had raised him from the grave into which he had fallen. It was being consumed by flame. Once again he felt the strength seeping from his body. Once again he wanted to fling himself into the fire as well.

"LeBoeuf!" Henriette shouted, and in the same instant the last of the rigging holding the main yard parted and the massive spar, forty feet long, plunged to the deck. It smashed into the bulwark just fifteen feet aft of where LeBoeuf stood and hit the main hatch with a great burst of flame, the impact sending a death rattle through the fabric of the ship.

"LeBoeuf, damn you!" Henriette shouted again. LeBoeuf reached down with his foot and found the next step and the next. He came to the bottom and stepped gingerly into the periagua, his body moving quite on its own, his mind as blank as it had been when he lay unconscious on the deck.

He sat on the thwart aft and found one of the oars and pushed the boat away from the ship's side. He took up another and set the two of them in the tholes. He took a long stroke and felt the oars bite and the periagua began to gather way.

Another stroke and the narrow boat moved faster. Facing aft, LeBoeuf saw nothing but the burning ship, his beloved ship, in its death agony. He closed his eyes and pulled again. He could not watch. But neither could he block out the horrible choking smell of burning wood and canvas and flesh, or the roar and groan as the ship was consumed by flame.

Chapter Thirty-Five

Nearly three miles separated *Charles Rex*, anchored behind the high headland that formed the eastern end of the wide half-moon bay, and the ship which they had been sent to find and take. The ship owned by Alonso Menendez, which was thought lost, but perhaps not.

The long pull in had seemed to take an ungodly amount of time, with the boats rowed as silently as they could be and a bloody fight most likely waiting for them on their arrival. But the return trip seemed many, many times longer. It was like some sort of purgatory or an outer circle of Hell.

Benjamin Graves had given no order to abandon the fight. Nor had Maja. They did not have to. Once the after bulkhead collapsed, revealing the great sheet of flame, it was obvious to every man aboard, both the buccaneers and the men of *Charles Rex*, that it was over, the ship lost.

One moment the lot of them, the buccaneers and his and Maja's men, were in the middle of a brutal melee, and then the next, by some sort of unspoken agreement, the fight was done. Weapons were sheathed or tossed aside, men raced for the bulwarks and grabbed up the painters for the boats and clambered over the rails. It was one of the strangest things Graves had ever seen, and he had seen many very strange things.

Graves still had no idea what the ship carried that was so damned valuable — if Maja knew he had never told him — but whatever it was, it was gone.

The hard part had not been getting the men off the burning ship, but rather preventing Maja's rogues from just leaping into their boats and rowing away, leaving the slow and the wounded behind. Maja had been little help in stopping them. He had taken a terrible slash across the gut that seemed to leave him weak and dumb for want of blood.

That bastard'd be lying dead on the deck if it weren't for me, Graves thought as he steered the longboat around the hump of island that hid *Charles Rex* from the beach. *And will he thank me? Ha!*

Maja was the last to quit fighting. He had been locked in it with some great beast of a man, a looming mountain of hair and muscle. Graves, turning to watch the fight, had guessed it would be brutal and short. In size, the buccaneer was two of Maja, but that had to mean he would be slow and clumsy, a brute used to getting by on strength alone.

But Graves, to his surprise, was wrong. Fast as Maja was, the big man was just as fast, and he used his sword like a sword, not like a bludgeon with an edge. He fought like a man with formal training, not like one who had learned his craft in tavern fights and plundering hapless merchant ships.

Sword and cutlass against Maja's cutlass and boutou, the fighting was vicious and precise. Until the big man, stupidly, turned his back on Maja. A second or two, no more, but that was all it took.

Once the big man went down Graves had crossed over to where Maja stood gasping and pressing his hand against his midriff. He walked with a limp, having taken a nasty wound to the thigh, and his left arm hung at his side. He could raise it if need be, but thanks to a cutlass point in the shoulder it was less painful to just let it hang.

"It's over, our men are giving up the ship!" Graves shouted over the yelling and the flames. He expected Maja to react in some way, to curse or give orders or kill someone. But Maja just nodded, his eyes glassy, his face slack in a way Graves had never seen. It was then that Graves noticed the blood seeping out around the man's fingers.

"Very well, I'll see the bastards don't leave us all behind," Graves said, then began grabbing men as they headed for the rails and shoving them back across the deck, ordering them to collect up their wounded and get them into the boats, threatening to run them through if they did not.

And they obeyed, after a fashion, helping those who were not beyond help down over the side, though he suspected they had been overly quick to declare some of their shipmates dead or near enough as to not be worth saving.

They were eager, after all, to get off that floating inferno. There was danger enough from the burning decks and flaming rigging dropping all around them, but worse, under their feet there was doubtless some quantity of gunpowder which would not react well when the fire reached it.

Happily for them, the buccaneers were more eager still to get clear. By the time the two boats from *Charles Rex* were loaded, all of the others who could still get off the ship had done so. Graves took the tiller of the bigger boat, Maja stretched out on a thwart just ahead of him, his eyes closed, his body still, such that Graves wondered if he was dead until he rolled his head and gave a soft moan.

Why didn't I leave that bastard behind? Graves wondered, looking at Maja lying on the thwart, his body rocking gently side to side with the motion of the boat. He seemed much smaller now, and not particularly frightening. Graves realized that this was the first time he had ever seen the man when he did not seem to radiate violence.

Could have done it... Graves thought. Maja had all but passed out by the time they got him into the boat. Graves could easily have left him aboard the burning ship. For that matter he could have slit the man's throat and no one would have been the wiser. Take *Charles Rex* back, find some new means to make his fortune.

But he had not. And, oddly, it had not even occurred to him until they were in the boat and half a mile away from the burning ship.

So why didn't I? he wondered. *Because the bastard saved me from Señor Corregidor's kindly ministrations?*

Maybe, though he understood that Maja had saved him because he needed his seamanship, and because he knew it would send Señor Corregidor into a fury, and not out of any love for Benjamin Graves.

Still, the result was the same: Maja had saved him from a protracted and ugly death. But in truth Graves had no idea why he had saved the man, just as he had no idea why he did most of the stupid things he did. And he was too tired and hurt to think on it.

They rounded the headland and far off they could see the single lantern burning aboard *Charles Rex.* All of the men still fit to pull an oar were doing so, but there were not so many now, not enough to man every oar. The progress was slow and it seemed quite a while before they were alongside and the men left aboard began helping the wounded up, then passing Maja hand over hand to the deck.

Kusi, who had not joined them in the attack, was there, a worried look on his face, and with gestures and words no one understood he had Maja laid out on the canvas of the main hatch. He pulled a knife from his belt and looked all the world as if he meant to sacrifice Maja then and there to some pagan god. Instead he carefully cut Maja's jerkin and shirt away, peeling the blood-soaked cloth back to reveal the long, wicked gash.

Graves staggered up through the gangway. He looked longingly at the deck, eager to just fall to the smooth planking and let sleep wash over him. But there was something he wanted even more than that, something he wanted so badly he was willing to keep on his feet and keep moving for a few moments more.

He made his way to the scuttle that led below. He clambered down the ladder and stumbled aft until he found his sea chest, lashed down to the deck. He opened the lid and fished around inside and pulled out a mostly full bottle of rumbullian, then, gripping the bottle like a holy relic, he made his way back on deck.

He found a spot where he could see Kusi at work because he did not want to miss something as entertaining as Maja possibly bleeding to death. He sat on the deck and leaned back against one of the cannons. He pulled the cork from the bottle and took a long drink. He felt the burn of the liquor running down his throat and he relished the sensation.

All around the deck, men were sprawled out or tending to their wounds or tending to their shipmates' wounds. Graves could feel the cloth of his shirt and breeches sticking to the dried blood that coated his skin, but his need to drink seemed greater than his need to tend his wounds, so the rumbullian took precedence.

Kusi had rigged several lanterns so they cast their light over Maja, who still lay flat out and motionless on the hatch. A bucket of water and a small wooden chest sat beside him. Kusi pulled a cloth from the bucket and wrung it out, then cleaned Maja's wound as best he could. From the chest he pulled some sort of ointment and spread it over the wound, and then a long needle and a ball of thread.

This should be good, Graves thought, and for the next twenty minutes or so he remained where he was, drinking his rumbullian and watching Kusi carefully stitch Maja back together. Kusi was still at it when Graves's eyes finally rolled back in his head and he slumped over onto the deck, passed out cold.

He woke to someone nudging him, prodding him on the shoulder. He was lying on his side, pressed into the deck. He grumbled without opening is eyes and swatted the hand or foot away. But then it was back, nudging harder. Graves opened his eyes, carefully.

Maja's feet were ten inches from his face. He could see them clearly, which meant the sun was up, which meant he had been sleeping for a few hours at least. Slowly Graves rolled onto his back. His wounds were tight and they ached and most of the rest of him ached as well. He shielded his eyes as he looked up. Maja was looking down at him. He was wearing a new shirt, a clean shirt. He looked rested.

"Are you still alive?" Graves asked. "How are you still alive?"

"Get up," Maja said. "There's a ship."

Graves closed his eyes again and let his head fall back against the deck. "Why should I give a damn if there's a ship?" he asked. The very thought of standing made him feel sick and weak.

"You'll give a damn," Maja said. "Now stand up."

There would be no peace until he stood, Graves knew that, and he guessed that any more resistance would earn him a kick in the ribs, so he rolled back onto his side and pushed himself up to a sitting position. With both hands on the gun carriage he hoisted himself to his feet. His head was swimming and he took a minute to let it settle. He tried to straighten, to stand fully upright, but he could not, and he knew it would be a few minutes at least before he could.

"What ship?" Graves asked at last.

"Can't see it from deck," Maja said. "Man aloft saw it."

Graves nodded. *You made me stand for a ship I can't even bloody see?* he thought. He wondered how Maja could possibly look so hale. He knew that he himself looked considerably worse than Maja did, and his wounds were not nearly as bad as the laceration Maja had taken.

Maybe it's the blood he lost, Graves thought. *Like having a doctor bleed you to make you well.*

"This ship," Maja went on. "It's *Santa Rosa,* methinks."

"*Santa Rosa?* That son of a bitch Señor Corregidor's *Santa Rosa?*"

Maja nodded. "The señor was bound to find out what we were about. And when he did he was bound to send *Santa Rosa* to stop us, take Don Alonso's ship for himself. Best I could hope for was a head start. Which we got."

For all the damned good it did us, Graves thought.

"We got to go," Maja said.

"Go?" Graves said. His mind was not working as well as it might just then, and he knew it.

Maja took his eyes from Graves and looked around the deck, and Graves followed his glance. Most of the men were still sprawled out, most with wounds bound in bloody cloth. Some, judging from their posture and skin color, or lack of it, had not lived through the night.

"Reckon we're not in a condition to fight," Graves said.

"Reckon not," Maja said. "Be lucky if we can sail. I might have to send your fat arse up aloft again."

But in the end that was not necessary, to Graves's great relief. He stumbled aft to the tiller, which was effort enough. He called for hands to man the capstan and others to head aloft to cast off the gaskets on the topsails, and happily there were enough men who had not gone on the raid, and enough who had not been too badly wounded, to see all those tasks done.

By the time *Charles Rex* was underway with her anchor hanging from the cathead and fore and mainsails set and drawing, the ship astern was visible from deck, with her sails above the horizon and her hull showing now and again as she rose on the swells. Graves could not tell if it was *Santa Rosa* or not, and he had no interest in hanging back and finding out. There was nothing keeping them there, not with the lieutenant governor's ship a charred wreck, and every reason to keep clear of Señor Corregidor's grasp.

"That bastard you were fighting, the big one," Graves said as *Charles Rex* settled on her course directly away from the approaching ship. He was talking to Maja, who was leaning on the weather bulwark a few feet away. "You kill the son of a bitch?"

"Don't know," Maja said. "The blow I give him with my boutou, it would have killed most men. That one, I don't know."

Graves nodded. He looked off to larboard. The half-moon bay was opening up as they left the headland astern. He could just make out the blackened remains of the burned ship peaking up above the water a little over a mile away. They were marked by a thin column of smoke still rising from the hulk. Graves stared at it wistfully for a moment, then looked forward, past the bow.

"That ship there," he said, jerking his head sideways toward the beach. "What was on it that was worth so damned much?" He wondered if Maja would bother to answer, and to his surprise he did.

"Gold, mostly," Maja said. "Hidden in the master's cabin. And a letter patent. Title to an estate. Don Alonso, lieutenant governor, he had plans."

Graves nodded but he did not reply. He looked out to sea, looked astern, looked up at the rigging overhead. He called for the men to set the topsails, and then the mizzen. Soon *Charles Rex* was plowing along with the wind betwixt two sheets, leaving the buccaneer coast and *Santa Rosa* at the far end of her wake.

"If there was gold aboard that ship," Graves said some time later, "then it's still there. Might be melted into one big ugly pile, but it's still gold."

"Yes?" Maja said.

"I'm just saying it," Graves said, and said no more. If Maja wanted to play the dullard Graves would not interfere.

They stood on like that for some time longer, with the headland and the half-moon bay sinking behind them. The ship in their wake, *Santa Rosa* or whatever ship it was, rounded the headland and stood in toward the beach. It seemed to have no interest in *Charles Rex*. If it had been sent by Señor Corregidor then it had been sent to go after Menendez's ship first. Vengeance was always high on Señor Corregidor's list of priorities, but not as high as gold.

"So," Graves said as the bell rang out, four bells in the afternoon watch. "Where are we bound? Reckon we could just keep sailing, but we might want to sail to some place."

"Might," Maja said.

Graves had been thinking about this for some time. "I guess we ain't going back to Santo Domingo," he said.

"Guess not," Maja said. They would do well to avoid Señor Corregidor, at least for the rest of their lives. And even if Don Alonso, the lieutenant governor, could shield them from the mayor's wrath, which Graves doubted he could, he did not think the man would do so. Not after they had made such a hash of getting his ship back to him.

"So?" Graves said, though he had an idea what the answer would be. They were without a home port now, and powerful men wanted their heads. They were not the citizens of any particular country. They were English and Spanish, a few French and Taino and Africans, and for such as them there was only one place in the West Indies where they could safely go.

"Tortuga," Maja said.

"Tortuga," Graves agreed.

Chapter Thirty-Six

The bow of the periagua ground up on the beach. LeBoeuf unshipped the oars and laid them down. He picked up his sword and stepped into the knee-high water and began to walk. He walked up the sloping sand toward the men and women huddled there, though he did not intend to join them. He intended to join the darkness beyond.

The flames from the burning ship threw a surprising amount of light over the shoreline, as if a great bonfire was lit at the water's edge. It illuminated the people in yellow and orange and deep shadows where the light would not reach. Some of the men were standing, some lying on the beach. Some of those lying were twisting with the agony of their wounds and some were lying very still. There were not nearly as many of them as there had been: the funeral pyre that was their ship was consuming the rest.

Eyes shifted toward LeBoeuf as he approached. He could see angry stares, accusatory looks, as if his failure had cost them all the ship and the cargo they had dreamed would bring them wealth. But mostly they looked at him with blank faces, because they did not know what to think or feel. They were caught broadside by fate, rolled on their beam ends, and they did not know which was up and which was down.

LeBoeuf ignored them all. He ignored the burning ship behind him, did not even turn to look. He ignored Henriette, who called his name once and then fell silent. He walked past the far edge of the people on the beach and kept on walking, across the sand, inland, toward the jungle, without the least thought as to where he was going or why. He was done. He was simply done.

For my sins… he thought.

He did not, as a rule, think much about God, despite the care his mother took to see he was well catechized as a boy. He rarely saw the hand of God in the affairs of men — things always seemed to him too random and capricious to be the work of an omniscient deity. But it was pretty hard to ignore this. Brought low by his own sins, God had laid this ship at his feet, offered this temptation. For a miserable pig hunter such as him, it was akin to God showing him all the kingdoms of the world in their magnificence and saying, "All these I shall give to you…"

LeBoeuf had accepted the gift. And for his hubris it had been snatched away. God, he could see, would not smite him with a bolt of lightning. God would not allow him so easy an end.

He was limping, he realized, his various wounds starting to announce themselves, but the torment in his body did not distract him at the least from the torment in his mind. The illumination from the burning ship began to fade as he walked inland and soon the only light came from the stars and the moon, which was enough for him to make out dark shapes: the few trees still standing at the tree line, the hills and mountains farther inland.

When he felt the sand yielding to undergrowth he stopped. His shoes, like everything else, save his sword and the clothes on his back, were gone, but that did not matter. The soles of his feet were like rawhide. He could have walked through the bracken as easily as if he was wearing boots. It was not for that reason he stopped, but rather because there was no point in going on. When you had nowhere to go, one place was as good as another.

He stood for a long time and looked inland at the dark shape of the hills pressed against the backdrop of stars, his back to the sea. *Turn around, you damned coward*, he chided himself. *Turn and look.*

It was the thing he least wanted to do. Like moving a wounded limb, he could anticipate the pain it would cause, so he made himself do it. He turned where he stood and looked north toward the half-moon bay. The ship was still burning: from that distance it looked like the flame of a candle, dancing and twisting, sometimes flaring up, sometimes settling back. The sight of it was every bit the agony LeBoeuf knew it would be, yet he kept looking.

You fool…you damned, damned fool… That ship had lifted him high from the depths of Hell, but only the greatest of fools would base their happiness, their very life, on something so impermanent. Only someone who'd had everything stripped away would do something so desperate as that. And here he could see what became of such fools.

He lifted the sword up in front of his face and twisted the blade until the light from the burning ship glinted off of it. *Fall on my sword?* he thought. It seemed both tragic and heroic, and he was not sure he deserved such an end.

He turned the blade some more until he could see his wrist and the cords of veins standing out under the sunburned skin.

Mayhaps that's the way of it, he thought. Run his wrists along that fine edge, feel the warm blood pulsing over his hands and legs. Bleeding out would give him ample time to look back over his life and his many, many failures.

Coward, he thought, though he was not certain what he meant by that. He reckoned himself a coward in so many ways. He could have let the lanceros finish him off and spared himself everything that had happened since, the ridiculous hope in which he had allowed himself to indulge, if he'd had the guts. Which he did not. That was cowardice.

And now, even as he contemplated taking up arms and making a final end to the turmoil, he was hesitating.

Here again…cowardice.

Or was it the suicide itself that was cowardice, the coward's way out? Was it shirking the great battle, running when he should stand and fight?

He lowered the sword and tilted his head back and looked up at the points of light overhead. He wished he had a bottle of brandy or rumbullian, but he did not, and there was nothing for it. All the men back on the beach, they, too, would be wishing the same thing, some desperately. But all the bottles and barrels they once owned were presently burning and shattering in the heat, the liquor inside steaming and evaporating as fast as it ran out.

After some time LeBoeuf lowered his head and sat down in the sand. He felt a weariness come over him, so profound that he felt as if he was drunk, or near death, both of which he so longed for. He had bled quite a bit from his wounds. His shirt and breeches were plastered to his skin with dried blood. He wondered if that was the cause of his exhaustion. He wondered if he had lost enough blood that he would die for want of it.

He laid down, rolling over on his side, his sword in front of him as if he was spooning it. *Mayhaps I'll sleep and not wake*, he thought. *Mayhaps I'll die of my wounds*. He felt a warm sort of comfort from that possibility.

Coward, he thought, and then he was asleep.

He dreamed of waves washing over him, small waves lapping over his face, wetting him, retreating, wetting him, retreating. It was nice at first, and then it was annoying. And then as sleep retreated he had the idea that it was something more than a dream.

He waved his hand in front of his face as if waving insects away. His fingers brushed over something soft, warm and wet. He opened his eyes and found himself looking at a red, lolling tongue, a row of wicked yellow teeth, a brown muzzle, two dark eyes. He pushed himself up on one arm.

"*Qu'est-ce que tu es?*" he said as he tried to bring mind and body back to the present. He had a sense that something profoundly bad had happened recently, and as soon as he remembered what it was he would be sick with despair, but that was all pushed aside by this surprise awakening. He looked at the creature sitting on its haunches and looking back at him.

"Other Dog?" he said. Other Dog panted as if in agreement.

"What are you…" LeBoeuf began, unsure what to say. He looked behind him, toward to undergrowth to see if the rest of the pack was there, but he saw only bracken and broken limbs. He turned back to Other Dog.

"Where in all hell have you been?" He waited for an answer but he received only further panting. "You've missed some excitement, I can tell you."

Still Other Dog did not respond and LeBoeuf began to suspect her motives. "You know, if you've come for my rumbullian, you are out of luck, *mon amie*. I have none. I have no luck, either, for that matter."

The two of them, partners in the pig hunt, looked at one another for a moment more, then LeBoeuf reached out and scratched Other Dog's neck, right under her jaw, right where she liked to be scratched.

"Seems you're the only one that lived. Or at least the only one that returned," he said. "It's good you're back. You were always the clever one, you know? I always suspected you were more clever than Big Dog, but I did not give you enough credit."

"That's very sweet, really," Henriette said. "Man and dog." The dripping tone registered even before the words, and even before LeBoeuf had a chance to be surprised at hearing her voice. He craned around. She was sitting in the sand about twenty feet away.

"How long have you been there?" he asked. Henriette shrugged in reply. For a moment they sat there in silence, the only sound the breeze rustling the undergrowth and the noise of the birds and insects and Other Dog panting in her heedless way.

"Well?" LeBoeuf asked at length.

"Well what?"

"Why are you here? What do you want?"

Henriette's eyebrows came together and LeBoeuf saw the flash of anger. "What do I want? Nothing that you can give me, you stupid ox. I thought you were going to kill yourself. I was hoping to watch."

LeBoeuf nodded. "Well, prithee, stay. I'm still deciding."

Henriette snorted in disgust. "You don't have the balls," she said.

"Does it take balls to kill yourself?" LeBoeuf asked. "Or does it take balls to not kill yourself?"

"How the devil should I know?"

LeBoeuf shrugged. "You never thought on it? You never considered those choices?"

Henriette scowled at him but did not reply. Then she bent over and lifted up the hem of her petticoat and reached her hand underneath.

"Here, you great beast, may you take your pleasure in it." She pulled the letter patent out from under her clothing and flung it at him. "God knows you lusted after it more than ever you lusted after me."

The scroll tumbled end over end in the air. Other Dog barked and LeBoeuf snatched the roll as it came at him. He held it in his hand and looked at it in the same sort of dumb way he had looked at Other Dog when he woke up. He looked up at Henriette and then back at the letter patent.

"You saved this?" he asked. "From the fire?"

Henriette rolled her eyes and made an even louder sound of disgust. "No, the Virgin Mary appeared and lifted it from the flames. Yes, of course I saved it, you idiot. It seemed the most important thing in all the world to you, great genius that you are, so I reckoned I'd grab it."

LeBoeuf nodded. He had a strange feeling in his gut, as if everything was turning over once again. Up and down, up and down, knocked sideways, rolled on his beam ends, it was like running under bare poles in a massive sea and there was nothing for it but to hang on and wait for fate to reveal itself.

The letter patent. He had seen so much possibility in its elaborate text, its great seal of the King of France. But that was when he had a ship, and a crew of well-armed, skilled fighting men that he could generally trick into doing his bidding. He had none of those things now. Now he had only a roll of vellum.

He stood slowly, forcing his way up through the stiffness and the pain and dried blood that cemented his clothing to his flesh. Other Dog barked again and pranced around his legs, excited, apparently, to see that LeBoeuf could still stand upright, after a fashion.

The sun was hanging over the high country to the east. LeBoeuf realized he had been asleep longer than he thought. He turned north, looking out over the beach and the sea beyond. The buccaneers and their women were still hunkered down near the water's edge. He could see people sitting and laying on the sand, or wandering about. He wondered if they were talking amongst themselves, making plans, trying to reckon what they would do next.

Do next? he thought. *There's little enough they can do next. Them or me.* They had no food and they had no tools or weapons with which to get food. They had no shelter. They had no alcohol. They could take their smattering of boats and try to reach someplace where they might find succor, or they could remain and die a slow death. That was pretty much the extent of their choices.

LeBoeuf wondered if Van Loudersong or Pierre le Chasseur had survived the fight. If they had both lived then most likely they were both trying to take charge. If so, the buccaneers would break into their old factions and kill each other with bare hands, right there on the beach.

And he, LeBoeuf, did not care. He had stopped that civil war once, when he had needed the men to crew his ship. But now his ship was just a mass of charred wood jutting up from the water, a trail of smoke lifting up from its remains and bending in the gentle breeze. LeBoeuf did not need his fellow hunters anymore. He did not need anyone anymore. As far as he was concerned they could all kill one another, or remain and die a slow death: himself, Henriette, Van Loudersong, all of them.

His eyes moved past the charred and smoking ruin of his ship, up toward the horizon, and they fell on the unmistakable sight of a ship under full sail, standing off to the west. The image gave him a little jolt of surprise, and he sucked in his breath.

"What?" Henriette asked. "What do you see?"

"Ship," LeBoeuf said, nodding toward the horizon. Henriette turned and shielded her eyes with her hand and looked.

"Some foeman? Someone who would do us harm?" she asked.

"No," LeBoeuf said. "They're quite done harming us now." It had come to him what ship it was; the ship from which the attack on his own vessel had been launched. They must have been at anchor on the far side of the high point of land at the eastern end of the bay, and now, with daylight here, they were sailing off. There was nothing left to keep them there.

"Are those the bastards who attacked us?" Henriette asked.

"Methinks they are," LeBoeuf said.

"Why?" Henriette asked. "Who are they?"

"I've no notion," LeBoeuf said. "I have no notion about either question."

Whether they had come hunting for his ship or just stumbled upon it LeBoeuf did not know and doubted he would ever know, and he did not feel much like thinking on it. But he did reckon he owed Henriette as much of an explanation as he could give. After all, her hope and her future had been snatched away just as his had been.

"Whoever sent that ship...our ship...he had some lofty plans, and what we found aboard was key to it all," LeBoeuf said. "There was a bounty in gold, and well hidden. And the letter patent. Securing such a gift from the king, that's no easy task. So, mayhaps they knew the ship had gone ashore here and sent those rogues to get all this back. How they knew the ship was here I don't know, but mayhaps they found out."

Henriette nodded. "I see," she said.

"Or mayhaps those rogues just came across us and decided we looked like an easy prize. Those bastards, they had the look of *flibustiers*. So, in the end no one gets anything because somehow the damned ship caught fire."

"Somehow," Henriette said.

LeBoeuf watched the ship sail off for a moment more. "*Les cochons*," he said. If ever there were pigs he wanted to shoot, they were aboard that distant vessel.

"That gold, you know, it's still there," Henriette said. She took a few steps closer to him and Other Dog gave an excited bark. She had always liked Henriette, despite the fact that Henriette could not stand her, or any dog.

James L. Nelson

"It might be all melted together," she went on, "but it did not burn up."

LeBoeuf nodded. That had occurred to him. He had imagined telling the others about it, and wondered if they would turn on him. He had imagined trying to salvage it from the burned wreck. They had no tools, save for some knives and cutlasses. He had pictured the effort to divide it up, beating the great melted heap with rocks and sticks like a bunch of savages to break it into equal parts. He envisioned the arguments that would follow, the violence that would follow that.

"It's there," LeBoeuf agreed. "But retrieving it? That would be the death of us all. In a hundred different ways."

LeBoeuf knew he was right about that. But that was only part of it. More to the point, he did not have the will to try salvaging the gold. He was still trying to muster the will to slit his wrists.

"Well," Henriette began, "if you aren't man enough to even make an effort I suppose Van Loudersong...what is it?" She could see that something else had caught LeBoeuf's eye.

"There's another ship," LeBoeuf said, nodding out to sea once again. Henriette fell silent for a moment and followed his gaze.

"Where?"

"Just coming around the headland," LeBoeuf said. He could see only the bowsprit and the foremast, but second by second the rest of the ship emerged from behind the jungle-covered point. A good-looking vessel as far as he could tell, barque-rigged and a bit bigger than the one that had proceeded it.

"What do they want?" Henriette asked. LeBoeuf wondered if she actually expected him to answer, if she thought he might somehow know. But he did not reply, he just kept his mouth shut and watched. Soon the second ship was well clear of the headland and standing to the west, sailing on pretty much the same heading as the first vessel.

Either sailing in company or sailing in pursuit, LeBoeuf thought. With so little shipping in the wake of the hurricano it seemed too much of a coincidence that two vessels would just happen to appear on that desolate coast.

And then to LeBoeuf's surprise the ship turned, her bow swinging around until it was pointed directly at the beach, directly, it seemed, at LeBoeuf himself. He watched the yards brace around as she came onto a beam reach, heeling a bit to starboard as she stood into the half-moon bay.

"Are they coming toward us?" Henriette asked.

"They are," LeBoeuf said.

"Well, we'll see what new horror these bastards bring down on our heads," Henriette said, and despite himself LeBoeuf smiled. She had the right of it.

"We shall see," he agreed.

The ship came straight on, her course unwavering, her sails set and drawing. The buccaneers were moving around now as they watched the oncoming ship. He could see them spreading out along the shore, making a more visible presence. He could imagine the debates flying around: flee inland or make a stand, send a welcome or a warning. They would be speculating as to whether these newcomers were more like to bring death or bring salvation.

He looked back at the ship which had changed neither her course nor the set of her sails.

Stupid, stupid…must be a Spaniard, he thought.

The half-moon bay might look like open water but it was not. It was littered with sandbars that shifted and rose and fell with the wind and seas. Even he, LeBoeuf, who knew the bay well, would not go charging in like that, just as he had not been willing to sail at night through that maze.

Lucky, so far, LeBoeuf thought. He was surprised that the Spaniard had not run aground, but even as he thought of it the Spaniard's luck ran out. The ship seemed to jerk and her masts whipped forward and she rolled a bit to one side as her forward momentum stopped in an instant.

"Humph," LeBoeuf said.

"What?" Henriette asked.

"She ran aground."

"Good." Henriette spat on the sand. "I hope they sink. I would fain hear them screaming in terror as they go down."

LeBoeuf did not take his eyes from the ship. He did not move, but he felt a twisting in his gut. It was the same sensation he had felt when he held the letter patent again, only more so. It was the same that had come over him when he first saw his ship hard on the sandbar after the hurricano. It was the spirit of chance, whispering in his ear.

But now he knew that whisper for what it was. God or the devil tempting him, toying with him, showing him all the riches that might be his. Showing him the way out of the dark place where he had gone, only to shove him back once he had nearly crawled free.

"I won't be played for a fool, not again," he said out loud.

"What?" Henriette asked but LeBoeuf ignored her. The Spaniard was taking in his sails, hauling up the courses, lowering the topsails. A little damned late, it seemed to LeBoeuf.

Am I such a fool as to be taken in by this, again? he asked himself, but he knew the answer, knew it perfectly well. He was most certainly such a fool, and he would most certainly be taken in again. And why not? Could he fall any further than he had already? He had nothing left to lose but his life, and he put little enough store in that.

"Here, Other Dog, should we go capture yon Spaniard? The fools stuck on the sandbar?" LeBoeuf asked. Other Dog's tongue was hanging out of her mouth and she was panting excitedly, and she barked at LeBoeuf's words.

"Capture the Spaniard?" Henriette asked. "You think you can talk the others into attacking that ship? They're as like to kill you as kill those Spaniards."

"I said nothing of the others," LeBoeuf said. "The others can help or not, as they wish, but Other Dog and me, we'll be fine on our own." He grabbed up his sword and ran the blade through his belt and started walking back across the beach, toward the small band of buccaneers and the boats pulled up on the shore.

There was a hint of a smile on his face and his steps felt light and easy, despite his wounds and the difficulty of walking on sand. He moved with the ease of a man who had made the right choice and knew it. Bugger cutting his wrists, bugger falling on his sword. If God wished to toy with him he would give the Almighty a most delicious opportunity.

Other Dog walked at his side and Henriette followed behind. LeBoeuf could not hear her footsteps in the sand but he could hear her slightly labored breath and he suspected that soon enough he would hear her shrill voice as well, and he was right.

"You stupid ox, what do you think you're about?" she demanded. "LeBoeuf! You think anyone is going to follow you?" LeBoeuf ignored her, knowing there were no words he could say that would shut her up.

He was fifty feet from the others before someone finally noticed him, so intent were they on watching the Spanish ship run up on the sand a mile off shore. LeBoeuf heard a murmur run through the men and women lined up on the beach. He saw heads turn.

Van Loudersong, having apparently not died in the fight, was the first to speak. "Here, LeBoeuf, we thought you'd gone off and died," he said.

"Should have done," someone else said. LeBoeuf could not tell who it was, and he did not reply and he did not look at any of the people there. His eyes were still on the Spanish ship. The crew was swaying a boat over the side: from that distance he could just see it rise off the deck and hang from the fore and main yardarms. Sending a party ashore, perhaps, or, more likely, going to see just how fast they were stuck.

LeBoeuf's eyes moved to the water's edge and the hard-packed wet sand which stretched another dozen feet before it disappeared under the small surf. The tide was a little past its midpoint and coming in. The Spaniard would be lifted off the sandbar in a couple of hours unless he had managed to jam himself on remarkably hard.

"Here, LeBoeuf, what ship is that stuck on the sand yonder?" Billy Solent called.

LeBoeuf shook his head, but the gesture was more to himself than the others. *Why do you think I know?* he wondered. It was akin to Henriette's asking him what the Spaniards wanted. Did she and the others think because he did not talk much that he was imbued with some sort of preternatural insight? Hadn't they always reckoned him stupid?

He did not in fact know who they were aboard that ship, nor was he in the mood for speculating or even speaking. He walked silently through the line of men and women, Other Dog at his side. He continued down toward the water's edge where the various boats were pulled up on shore.

Behind him he heard Levesque say, "Henriette, what in all hell is LeBoeuf about?" and he heard Henriette reply that she had no idea but he continued to ignore them. He stepped onto the cool, hard-packed sand and stopped. He looked over the boats resting in a ragged line and found the small periagua that would best suit his needs.

"Come along, Other Dog," he said. "Let's go die like the bold beasts we are."

He crossed the sand and grabbed the boat's bow and started to push it into the water. He looked back. The men and women had followed him down the beach and now stood looking on in silence, as if they had gathered to watch his execution.

LeBoeuf turned away and continued pushing the boat into the water.

"LeBoeuf, what the devil are you doing?" Van Loudersong said. There was amusement in his tone, and no small amount of irritation.

LeBoeuf stopped pushing the boat. He looked back at the buccaneers and their women, unsure whether or not he should answer. "I'm going to take that ship," he said at last, pointing with his thumb over his shoulder, in case there was some question as to what ship he meant.

"What? By yourself?" Van Loudersong asked.

"No," LeBoeuf said. "Me and Other Dog." That was met with a bit of laughter, a few snorts of disdain, but mostly silence.

"We won't join in this fool's errand, you know," Van Loudersong said.

LeBoeuf looked at him for a moment, long enough for the silence to become uncomfortable. "Didn't ask you to," he said at last.

He pushed the periagua into the water until it was floating free. "Other Dog, go," he said, and Other Dog bounded happily through the small surf and leapt into the boat, nearly upsetting it as she found her seat on the bottom. LeBoeuf pushed it farther out and waded alongside. He set the letter patent down on the forward-most thwart, taking care to wedge it in so it would not roll off into the bottom of the boat, and stepped carefully in. The periagua was not as tender as a canoe, but it was still not the most stable of craft, and LeBoeuf had to take care easing himself down onto the thwart.

He picked up the oars and set them in the tholes, positioning himself so he would be facing forward as he rowed. It was not as efficient, but that did not matter. It was more important that he be able to keep his eye on the enemy as he approached. He dipped the oars and stroked, pushing one oar, pulling the other, and the periagua spun around until LeBoeuf was back to the beach. He pushed both oars together and felt the boat move forward under the pressure of the blades.

"I was right, see, they are Spaniards," LeBoeuf said. He could make out the red and white quarters of the Habsburg flag waving at the masthead, lifting and falling in the light breeze. The Spaniards had their ship's boat in the water now. They had pulled around under the bow and were no doubt assessing how hard they were stuck on the sandbar. LeBoeuf could not tell if they had seen him approaching yet. If they had, they apparently did not much care.

"What say you, Other Dog?" he asked. "Will they come after us in their boat?"

That would be best, from his perspective. If he could fight them boat to boat he might have a chance. Other Dog could get aboard the Spaniard and do terrific damage in that confined space, while he, LeBoeuf, could go at them sword in hand. If he dispatched all the men in the boat then there would be that many fewer aboard the ship to kill.

"You're probably thinking I'm a fool, and you're right," LeBoeuf said, but Other Dog's mouth was half open and her tongue was lolling out and she seemed very excited. She had always been as eager for the hunt as Big Dog, and just as deadly. If she thought LeBoeuf a fool then she was keeping it to herself

They were halfway to the ship when the Spaniards abandoned their task at the bow and brought the boat back alongside. LeBoeuf could see men climbing out of the boat and back on deck, and that meant they would not be fighting boat to boat.

"Very well, I guess it's boarding up the side for us," LeBoeuf said, trying to picture how this might be done.

He and Other Dog could jump into the Spaniard's boat, which was still floating alongside the ship. LeBoeuf could hurl Other Dog up onto the deck, knock some of the bastards down, and let Other Dog have at them while he climbed up the side. With the big mastiff running mad through the close-packed defenders LeBoeuf might have time to reach the deck and start in with his sword.

That was, if the Spaniards did not have firelocks. Which they most certainly did, and which they most certainly would have loaded by then.

Very well... LeBoeuf thought. He never really expected to win in any event, just go out the way a man should go out. According to his family's lore, some ancestor of his, eight centuries back, had been tangled up with those wild Northmen known as Vikings. And the Vikings believed a man must die with sword in hand to make it to Heaven. Or whatever heaven those people believed in. Now it was time to discover the truth of that.

"Well, Other Dog, it's been a hell of a voyage, heh?" he said. "And I'm sorry to say it, but you missed the best parts."

He could see activity on the deck of the ship now, men up in the bow pointing in his direction, and others rushing here and there. Quite a lot of commotion. He watched the goings-on as he rowed, but his mind was going back over all the odd twists and turns of his life, the wild ride from highs to lows and back, like massive seas passing under the keel. He was all of twenty-six years old and he felt as if he was a hundred, as if he had already lived two or three lifetimes complete.

"I guess this run ashore ends now," he said. "Don't reckon we'll get another. If we do, maybe it will be you and me together a second time, heh? Would you like that?" Other Dog was looking at him now with that expression of eager anticipation.

"You would like that, I know. Because you're as big a fool as me."

He looked up at the ship again, closer now, and he could see the frenetic activity had not died down. Quite the opposite. There were men at the ship's side and as LeBoeuf watched they began to climb down and pile into the boat, a regular line of men coming down the side. LeBoeuf frowned.

Do they mean to fight us in the boat after all? he wondered. That made little sense. Surely they would see they were better off staying aboard the ship and just shooting him as he came alongside.

You idiot... he thought next. The Spaniards were not just manning the boat, they were crowding into it. Every thwart was filled and LeBoeuf thought he could see men sitting on the bottom as well. Even Spaniards would not get so worked up over an attack by one man and his dog. There had to be something else going on.

"Now what are these madmen about?" LeBoeuf asked. He watched as the boat shoved off from the ship's side. The oars came down and the rowers gave a pull, though the boat, heavy-laden as she was, seemed hardly to move. They pulled again and the boat rolled ahead, coming directly at LeBoeuf's periagua. They pulled again, and now the Spaniard's boat began to turn, the bow swinging away to the east and away from LeBoeuf's line of approach.

The Spaniards' strokes became steady as the boat turned more east. Rather than coming for LeBoeuf they seemed to be running away, heading off on a course as directly away from him as they could manage.

"What the devil?" LeBoeuf said out loud. And then another thought occurred to him. He lifted the oars and swiveled around on the thwart. A quarter-mile astern of him, spread out like a tiny fleet of ships sailing line abreast, were the rest of the boats, packed with the buccaneer host. Their oars rose and fell as they pulled for the stricken Spaniard.

There were thirty men at most. They had no firearms, only edged weapons, and not too many of those. Many of them were injured. They were not men primed and ready for battle.

But the Spaniards did not know that. They knew only that these were the desperate, bloody men of the north coast of Hispaniola. They were the half-savages who lived hunting wild pigs and cattle and smoking the meat, and hunting the Spanish when the opportunity arose. They were the buccaneers, and they were to be feared.

And fear them the Spanish did, at least the company of that one stranded ship. But they were the ship's company no more. They had abandoned their vessel in the face of the buccaneers' attack and now were rowing as hard as they could for the nearest point of land where they could make their escape on foot.

LeBoeuf smiled. "Do you see, Other Dog," he said. "People say the Spaniards are a wicked lot, but here they've given us their ship. I ask you, could anyone be more generous than that?"

Chapter Thirty-Seven

Don Alonso Menéndez de Aviles, Knight of the Order of Santiago, lieutenant governor of Hispaniola, stood pressed against the low wall that lined the eastern side of the plaza of Las Casas Reales. He could feel the rough, warm stone against his body, even through the thick silk of his embroidered doublet, his second-best suit of clothes.

His wife Francisca stood to his left, chattering like a squirrel, or like one of those birds that sang outside their bedchamber window at first light until Don Alonso dreamed of dispatching it with a full load of grape shot. He was paying no attention to Francisca's words, but happily she was not saying anything he needed to listen to, and he could placate her with an occasional nod or a "Yes, my sweet." At least half of her words were directed at Gabriella in any event, who stood beside her on the other side.

Francisca was excited, which Don Alonso appreciated and understood. Since the trauma of their arrival at Santo Domingo, half-drowned and tossed up on the beach by the hurricano, and suffering from various injuries, she had not been abroad much at all, even within the confines of the sprawling Las Casa Reales. But she was outside now, part of a great crowd, a crowd made up of nearly all the city, from the nobility at the height of government and the military down to the lowest of servants, and all watching an unprecedented sight unfolding below.

Incredible... Don Alonso thought as he looked down toward the Rio Ozama. After weeks of effort, crushing the English and French settlers on St. Christopher and Nevis, Fadrique Álvarez de Toledo y Mendoza, Captain General of King Philip IV's Ocean Sea Navy, had arrived with his fleet at Santo Domingo. Twenty great galleons, the *Armada de Sotavento*, were anchored in the river, their proud sterns rising high above the water, the elaborate gilt carvings glinting in the sun. The ships spoke of wealth and power at a level that was hard to imagine, even for Don Alonso, who was very adept at imagining wealth and power.

Several dozen smaller ships were also anchored there, troop transports and supply ships and small, quick dispatch vessels, like courtiers and servants among royalty. Don Alonso had never seen the river so packed with shipping. He had never seen, in the New World, such a display of the great military power that Spain could bring to bear where she chose. It was a good thing. It reminded him of the empire of which he was a part. It reminded anyone who might presume to stand up to Spain of the wrath and power Spain could still bring down on their heads.

"Husband, dear, tell me again, which is the flagship?" Francisca chirped, squeezing his arm.

"There," he said, pointing for what he was certain was the fifth time at least. "The great one with four masts, anchored closest to the city."

"Oh!" Francisca squealed. "She's magnificent, isn't she? See how her gold paint shines! And all the masts and things all done up so neatly. But Don Fadrique is like that, you know. Everything must be just so and the very best."

"I know, my dear," Alonso said, though he didn't really. He had met Fadrique Álvarez de Toledo y Mendoza on several occasions and thought there was a good chance the man might recognize him if and when he saw him again. But the bloody bastard was an old friend of Francisca's family and a frequent guest in their home.

To Francisca he was *Tío* Fadrique, Uncle Fadrique, and she referred to him that way until Alonso suggested that such an address was not appropriate in the setting of Las Casas Reales. And that was true, but more to the point it annoyed Don Alonso to distraction to hear her say it: an unsubtle and almost purposeful reminder of the enormous influence that Francisca's father wielded.

"He's such a fine man," Francisca said. "A great man."

He's a pompous fool, a puffed-up cock of the walk and a damned butcher, Alonso thought, but all he said was, "Yes, my sweet."

Fadrique Álvarez de Toledo was indeed a fool, a cock of the walk and a butcher, to Alonso's certain knowledge, but he was also a man who had earned power and respect through victories at sea and on land and in court. Now, as Don Alonso stood looking down on the great fleet of *galeones*, he felt a grudging respect, and an undeniable envy for the old villain. That was what real power looked like. That was the Promised Land, and Alonso meant to enter there.

He thought of his own ship, *Nostra Sennora de Santiago* somewhere off on the northwest coast of the island. Or perhaps sunk. Or perhaps in the hands of that savage, Maja. He had no idea. And he was embarrassed by the whole thing.

It all seemed so silly, so pathetic now, his grand plans, his dreams of building an empire. He had been so sure of himself. From the moment he had arrived at Santo Domingo he had believed himself to be winning at this complex game, moving the pieces on the board to his own advantage. Manipulating others with his clever plans. He had been so absurdly confident, right up to the point where the truth had been brutally and unambiguously revealed.

Don Nicolás Pérez de Maldonaldo, mayor of Santo Domingo, had opened his eyes. He, Don Alonso, had been a child playing a child's game while the adults looked on and laughed. Stupid, fat, lazy Don Nicolás was the clever one, the real power, the real brute. He was the one who had been moving the pieces all along.

No more... Alonso thought. Don Nicolás was standing just a dozen feet to his right, part of the entourage come to watch Fadrique Álvarez de Toledo's disembarkation. He could hear the fat mayor laughing his gluttonous laugh. Alonso had always found it irritating. But now, knowing the truth of the man, knowing how that laugh, that entire image of benign good humor, was a ruse, he found it an intolerable torment.

I'll shut you up yet, you fat pig, Alonso thought. He would not be played for a fool. He would never again trust anyone, never rely on anyone over whom he did not have powerful leverage. He would never again be impressed with his own cleverness.

Horns sounded from the ships on the river below, and a volley of muskets fired, and then a band started in as the tiny figure of Fadrique Álvarez de Toledo could be seen stepping through the companionway of his flagship and down the steps to the launch waiting alongside. Even from that distance Alonso could make out the launch's bright painted sides, the details in gold, the rich awning that hung over the sternsheets to shield the conqueror from the sun.

"Oh, see there, there's Tío Fadrique!" Francisca shouted, pointing. Alonso pressed his lips together and resisted correcting her. The boat was pulling away from the side of the ship; off to the south, at Fortaleza Ozama, cannons were firing out in salute as the crowd lining the waterfront cheered in waves of sound. Alonso felt sick with envy such as he never felt before.

A hand clapped him on the shoulder and he turned to see the governor, Gabriel de Chávez y Osorio, smiling at him through his thick moustache, but before Alonso could speak Don Gabriel turned his attention to Francisca. He snatched up her hand and bending as low as his belly would permit kissed it through her silk glove.

"My dear Francisca, I can't tell you how much it delights me to see you out of your chambers and enjoying this great triumph!" he said. "I know Don Fadrique is a great friend to you and your father."

"Thank you, dear governor," Francisca said with a small curtsey. "I feel ever so much better, and my dear husband has been like an angel in his attention to me. But I trust I have not kept him from his duties to you, and to government?"

"No, no," Don Gabriel said. "Your husband is a most active man. The Lord alone knows how I got along before you arrived." He turned toward

Alonso and added, "I do hope you're ready for more of these labors. Much more, I fear. Don Fadrique and his officers will all be descending on Las Casas Reales, and four thousand soldiers and sailors overrunning the taverns and whorehouses...beg your pardon my dear Lady Francisca."

"Of course, dear governor," Francisca said, her cheeks flushed red.

"I've alerted the city watch that they're to have twice the number of men on patrol at all hours," Alonso said, "and seen to it that the guard at Fortaleza Ozama is in constant readiness. To start."

"Excellent!" Don Gabriel said, slapping Alonso's shoulder again. "You see, my dear Francisca, I'd be lost without him!"

Alonso smiled and wondered what was under the mayor's veneer of jolly good humor. Not long ago he would have assumed there was nothing at all, he would have taken the man at face value, but he had learned better. It was an important lesson: if one was going to assume, then one should always assume the worst.

"It would help, Don Gabriel, if we knew how long the Armada de Sotavento will be gracing us with its presence here," Alonso said. News of Toledo's arrival at St. Christopher had come as a surprise, with only rumors of the fleet's destination reaching Santo Domingo. They had learned of Toledo's departure for Hispaniola the day he sailed from Nevis.

"I hear Don Fadrique means to spend a fortnight here," the governor said, "which will mean a month at least, if not more."

"And then he sails for the Main?"

The governor gave a sly smile and glanced to his right and left. He took a step closer to Alonso and Francisca. "I can tell you two, as I know you are the souls of discretion," he said in a low voice. "And anyway, you'll learn of it soon enough, in your office. I was informed just this morning. Before the fleet sails for the Main, Toledo will bring his ships to Tortuga and clean out that nest of vipers, like he did at St. Christopher and Nevis."

"Tortuga?" Alonso said. The name sparked a host of thoughts and conflicting emotions. That island had been so central to his plans.

"Yes," Don Gabriel said. "The damned French and even the English have settled there and they're becoming a great thorn in the side. Time to clear them away. We cannot allow that vermin to spread."

"Tortuga..." Alonso said again, his thoughts floating and twisting as if caught in the breeze. The estate he had planned would have been starting to prosper just as Toledo and his fleet arrived to burn it to the ground. It might even have come out that he was behind the whole illicit affair. Alonso had considered the loss of *Nostra Sennora de Santiago* and the gold and the letter patent a terrible blow, a disaster, but in the end it might have been his salvation.

"Whatever is the matter, my dear husband?" Francisca asked and Alonso looked up and smiled.

"Nothing, my sweet," he said, but in those few seconds of silence a very profound if amorphous idea had begun to solidify in his head.

There would be an attack on Tortuga by land and sea, and he, Don Alonso Menéndez de Aviles, was a military man. He had fought with distinction at Breda and at the Siege of Groenlo, and in many lesser skirmishes. He knew what opportunities could be found in the midst of a campaign. Opportunities that would not be available to the old and ponderous Don Gabriel or Don Nicolás Pérez.

Don Alonso could easily get himself attached to the campaign, serving at the highest level. The captain general, after all, was none other than Tío Fadrique.

He smiled at Francisca. "Forgive me, I was thinking, that's all," he said. He turned back to the governor. "Tortuga, yes, I agree. It cannot be ignored, Don Gabriel. The vermin there, they must be stamped out."

LeBoeuf approached the side of the Spanish ship cautiously, his eyes searching the length of the deck, as much as he could see from the thwart of the periagua. It seemed too much to hope for, far too much, that the crew had simply abandoned the ship to the buccaneers. Still, it did look as if that was what had happened.

Or perhaps not. It would be a good ruse if half the Spanish crew were hiding down below with loaded firelocks just waiting for the cocky flibustiers to come aboard, and LeBoeuf did not intend to let that happen. He was not really worried about losing his life, but he did not mean to lose it stupidly.

Other Dog was hunched low, silent, tongue housed, her body quivering with anticipation. This was the hunt, this was what she knew, and she was ready for it, even if she did not know what they were hunting for, or how. LeBoeuf gave one last pull and unshipped the oars and the periagua glided up to the ship's side. He reached out and grabbed a boarding step set into the side and brought the boat to a stop.

"*Allez! Allez!*" LeBoeuf shouted, and Other Dog was on her feet and leaping for the boarding steps. The steps ran up the near-vertical side of the ship, impossible for the dog to climb, but that did not slow her down in the least. She hit the third step with her front paws and pushed herself up as LeBoeuf stood and grabbed her under the haunches and shoved. The dog all but flew up the remainder of the steps and onto the deck, barking and snarling as if she was rabid, then disappeared from sight as she searched for something, anything, to attack.

LeBoeuf followed behind, but more cautiously. He had his sword in hand as his head came above the level of the deck and he paused and looked around. Nothing. Nothing living at all, save for Other Dog. LeBoeuf continued to climb and then stepped out into the ship's waist.

He would have found the scene unnerving if he had he not seen the crew leave. There were ropes left in heaps on the deck, and tools where the ship's carpenter had abandoned a job half finished. There was a powder charge and rammer and sponge lying beside a cannon that the men had apparently been loading. It was as if the men had simply vanished, right in the midst of an ordinary day.

But LeBoeuf was still not entirely convinced they were gone. He stepped over to the scuttle that led down to the lower deck, leaned cautiously over the edge and looked down. He could see nothing but a patch of deck lit up by the sun and around it only darkness.

"Other Dog!" he called and Other Dog abandoned her fruitless search and trotted over to him. LeBoeuf pointed down the scuttle. "*Allez! Allez!*" he said and Other Dog, with renewed enthusiasm, charged down the steep steps to the darkness of the lower deck.

LeBoeuf stepped closer and listened, but all he could hear was Other Dog's nails on the deck and the muffled sound of her barking as she raced around the 'tween decks. He let the animal hunt for a minute or two before deciding that the Spaniards had, indeed, abandoned the ship entirely rather than stand and fight the buccaneers.

Damned cowards, LeBoeuf said. He was disappointed, he realized. He had thought to end it all there, but now that would not happen. He found the disappointment surprising, and a bit unnerving.

Then he heard one of the big periaguas hit as it came alongside the ship, and felt the vibration from the impact underfoot.

Ah! he thought. *There may be the chance to end it all, yet!*

"Other Dog! To me!" LeBoeuf shouted and an instant later Other Dog came bounding up the steps and stood at his side. He turned toward the companionway as Van Loudersong stepped through, cutlass in hand, looking fore and aft.

"Welcome aboard, Van Loudersong," he said. Van Loudersong just nodded and stepped aside as D'Anton and then Levasseur and Billy Solent and the rest came on board. They spread out around the deck, looking with amazement at the ghost ship they had just boarded. The last vessel run up on those sands had been a near wreck, with dead men strew about. This one was intact and deserted.

LeBoeuf stepped up on the main hatch. As it was he loomed over every man there, but standing on the hatch made him more imposing still.

"Tide's flooding," he said in a loud voice. "In an hour or so I reckon we'll float free. Spritsail should swing our bow around, and we can stand straight out of this harbor if the wind holds."

The others stopped whatever they were doing and stared up at him. He saw no reaction of any kind, no looks of approval or disapproval, agreement or disagreement. He had caught them by surprise, but they would recover quick enough.

Van Loudersong spoke first, as LeBoeuf knew he would. "Prithee, now," he said. "There's much to discuss first. Questions to answer. Such as just who commands here."

"No," LeBoeuf said, and he said no more.

"No?" Van Loudersong said.

"No," LeBoeuf said again. He was done with discussion. Done with cajoling and placating and manipulating. This was his ship and he would have command of it or he would die fighting for command. Either way. But there could be no other option.

"I took the ship, I'm master of the ship," LeBoeuf continued. "Any man who'll sail with me, he'll sign articles and he'll be treated fair. An even share of all we take. But the ship is mine. Any man who wants to dispute the point, we'll do it here and now."

He held his sword in his massive right hand, held it low, the point nearly touching the deck. He did not brandish it or even raise it in the least, but he did not think he had to. He looked out over the faces looking up at him. He could see anger on some, curiosity on others, maybe even amusement. But there did not seem to be much passion or interest in resisting him.

"Or if the lot of you want to dispute it all at once, that would be fine as well," LeBoeuf said, wondering, even as the words left his mouth, why he felt the need to say such a thing. Would he prefer that they challenge him, kill him over possession of the ship? He could feel Other Dog stiffen and he knew without looking that the animal was barring his teeth. Other Dog had always been sensitive to the prevailing mood.

Then D'Anton spoke up in his oddly accented French. "I'm with you, LeBoeuf," he said.

"Me as well," said Levasseur. Heads were nodding now, and voices muttering agreement. Even Van Loudersong was nodding, all but imperceptibly.

"Good," LeBoeuf said. It had played out as he'd hoped, despite his efforts at self-sabotage. The fight had been drained from these men, for the time being, at least.

"We'll fetch the women off the beach," he continued, "and make ready to get underway."

"Where are we going?" Pierre le Chasseur asked.

"Tortuga," LeBoeuf said without hesitation. "Tortuga. I have business there."

Heads nodded again, and with more enthusiasm this time. The island had not been long settled, but it had been settled long enough for taverns and brothels to have sprouted like jungle foliage. In all the New World, Tortuga was the one place where men such as them — rootless men, brutal men, shunned men — might find a welcome. Because they were a cast apart. They were the buccaneers.

Visit our web site to sign up for our (occasional)
e-mail newsletter for information about new titles as
well as preview sample chapters and other good stuff
cheap (actually free):

www.jameslnelson.com

Other Fiction by
James L. Nelson:

The Norsemen Saga:
Novels of the Vikings in Ireland
Fin Gall
Dubh-linn
The Lord of Vík-ló
Glendalough Fair
Night Wolf
Raider's Wake
Loch Garman
A Vengeful Wind
Kings and Pawns
The Midgard Serpent

The Brethren of the Coast:
Piracy in Colonial America
The Guardship
The Blackbirder
The Pirate Round

The Only Life that Mattered:
The Story of Ann Bonny, Mary Read and Calico Jack Rackham

Glossary

Aft: toward the back end of a ship
After: behind, toward the stern or aft end
Amidships: around the middle of a ship
Astern: outside a ship and behind it
Barque: a three-masted vessel with square sails on the fore and main mast and fore and aft sails on the mizzen; generally refers to any small ship
Batten: long strips of wood secured to the edges of tarpaulins to keep the tarpaulins in place, often used to secure hatches
Beam ends: a vessel lying on her side is said to be on her beam ends, i.e. the ends of the deck beams are perpendicular to the water
Belaying pin: a club-shaped wooden pin, generally about eighteen inches in length, to which ropes are tied
Bend: to attach one thing to another; a sailor "bends" a sail to a **yard**
Binnacle: a cabinet just forward of the **helm** in which the compass is housed
Bitts: a heavy vertical structure near the bow to which the anchor cable is made fast
Block: nautical term for a pulley
Boatswain's chair: a seat attached to a rope sling by which a person can be hoisted up.
Bonaventure: in 16th and 17th century vessels, the fourth mast
Bow: the forward end of a ship's hull
Bowsprit: a sort of mast that extends up from the bow
Brace: a rope attached to the end of a yard and used to swing the yard on a horizontal plane to adjust the sail to the wind
Brace of pistols: a pair of pistols
Bulwark: the "walls," generally waist-high, that surround a ship's deck.
Burthen: the carrying capacity of a ship, expressed in tons
Butt: a large cask holding 126 gallons, roughly equal to two **hogsheads**
Cable length: two hundred yards
Capstan: a vertical wooden drum turned by means of men pushing on wooden bars that project horizontally from the top of the drum; used to lift anchors and other heavy weights

Capstan bar: wooden bars that are inserted into holes in the head of the capstan.

Chains: metalwork attaching the **deadeyes** to the sides of a ship; also used to mean the platform to which the deadeyes are attached, which is more correctly called the chain-wale, or channel

Combing: a raised frame surrounding a hatch or other opening in the deck.

Come about: to change a ship's heading by turning the bow through the wind; same meaning as to **tack**

Cunning: archaic word for conning, to oversee the direction of a ship by giving orders to the helmsman

Deadeye: a thick wooden disk with three holes attached to the end of a length of rigging; a rope passed through the holes is used to tighten the rigging

Fall: the rope from a block and tackle which is hauled upon

Fall off: to turn a ship's bow away from the direction of the wind

Fid: a wooden block that fits in a square hole in the base of an upper mast on which the upper mast rests

Fife rail: a horizontal rail at the base of a mast in which **belaying pins** are mounted

Firkin: a small cask, about a quarter of a barrel

Flemish eye: a type of eye splice, or fixed loop in the end of a rope

Flush-decked: a ship whose deck runs at one level from bow to stern, with no raised deck fore of aft

Fore: toward the front or bow of a ship.

Full and by: sailing with the bow pointed as close to the direction from which the wind is blowing as possible with the sails full

Gasket: a short rope used for tying a sail in place

Grapeshot: ordnance fired from a cannon consisting of a cluster of small iron balls; used as an anti-personnel weapon

Grating: a **hatch** cover made up of wooden slates arranged like a heavy wooden screen

Hatch: an opening in the deck to give access below

Headed: said of a ship when the wind shifts to come more directly over her bow

Hogshead: a cask holding approximately sixty-five gallons

Keel: a long timber that forms the very bottom of a ship and upon which the rest of a ship is built

Keelson: an internal keel that sits above the main keel

Larboard: the left side of a ship when looking forward; archaic term for *port*

Leeward: down-wind

Lift: a rope attached to the end of a yard to support the yard in a horizontal position

Line: any rope that serves a specific function on shipboard

Marline: a type of heavy-duty twine

Martnet: a series of ropes used to haul up the edges of a sail.

Mast: a vertical wooden pole used to support the **yards** and sails; on larger ships the masts were made in sections: the lower mast, topmast and topgallant mast

Mast rope: a rope used for lowering a topmast or topgallant mast down to the deck

Mizzen: the third mast back from the front of a ship.

Overbody: an article of women's clothing, similar to a bodice, generally made of wool or canvas and laced up the front

Painter: a rope attached to the bow of a boat, used for towing or tying the boat off

Parceling: old cloth wrapped around a rope to shield the rope from chafe or to keep water out

Periagua: a large canoe made up of the hollowed trunks of two trees; indigenous to the West Indies

Pinrail: a wooden rail mounted inside a ship's **bulwarks** in which **belaying pins** are inserted

Pounder: term used to describe the size of a cannon by the weight of the cannonball it fires; a four-pounder gun fires a ball that weighs four pounds, etc.

Ratline: pronounced *ratlin*; a rope tied horizontally across the **shrouds** to form a sort of rope ladder for climbing up a mast

Real Audiencia: the first court of the Spanish crown in America

Rigging: cumulative term for all the ropes and other gear used to control a ship's sails

Ringbolt: an iron rig mounted on the deck to which rigging or gun tackle is attached

Rose lashing: a type of knot used to fix a **block** to a **spar**

Round shot: a round iron ball; a cannon ball

Scuttle (noun): a small opening in the deck or side of a ship

Scuttle (verb): to deliberately make an opening in the hull of a ship to allow water in

Seizing: a lashing of small line used to bind two larger lines together

Sheet: a rope used to hold the corner or edge of a sail down so it can catch the wind

Shroud: heavy ropes leading from the side of a ship to the top of the mast; used to prevent the mast from falling

Spar: general term for any of the wooden poles that support a ship's sails

Spritsail: a square sail mounted under the **bowsprit**

Starboard: the right side of a ship when looking forward from the stern

Stay: a heavy rope used to prevent a mast from falling backward

Stay tackle: a block and tackle hanging from a ship's **stay**: mostly for lifting things in and out of the hold

Stern: the back end of a ship's hull

Stern sheets: the back end of a boat

Sweep (noun): a long oar

Sweep (verb): to propel a vessel with sweeps

Tack (noun): a rope attached to the corner of a lower square sail and used to pull the corner forward.

Tack (verb): to change the direction in which a ship is sailing by turning her bow through the wind

Tackle: any combination of ropes and **blocks** arranged to achieve mechanical advantage

Tarpaulin: canvas treated with tar or something similar to make it waterproof; used to cover hatches, boats, etc.

Thole: a wooden pin mounted vertically on the side of a boat to hold an oar in place

Thwart: the seat in a boat on which the rowers sit

Tiller: horizontal bar attached to a rudder by which a vessel is steered

Top: a platform located at the top of a lower mast, often erroneously called a "crow's nest"

Top hamper: general term for all the masts, spars, rigging and sails

Topmast: the mast mounted above the lower mast

Topmast stay: a rope that extends from the top of the topmast to some secure point lower down to prevent the topmast from falling backward

Tun: a very large cask, the equal of two **butts**

Waist: the middle section of a ship's upper deck

Weather (adj.): an object "to weather" is to windward

Weather (verb): to "weather" something such as a point of land is to pass to windward of it

Whipstaff: a vertical handle attached to a tiller and used to steer a ship; in use before the advent of the ship's wheel

Windlass: a machine for lifting heavy objects consisting of a horizontal barrel supported by vertical posts and rotated through the use of bars inserted into holes in the barrel

Windward: upwind

Worming: a rigging technique that involves laying small lines in the grooves between the strands of a rope

Yard: the horizontal **spars** from which square sails are hung

Yardarm: the very end of the yard, beyond the point where the sail is tied off

Yard tackle: a tackle hung from the end of a yard, used for hoisting boats and other heavy objects onboard

Printed in the USA
CPSIA information can be obtained
at www.ICGtesting.com
LVHW041800021023
759907LV00005B/137